D0406263

ONCE UPON TIME,
THERE WAS A WIZARD...

THEN IT ALL WENT TO HELL.

CURSE WORDS VOLUME #2: EXPLOSIONTOWN, FIRST PRINTING. JANUARY 2018. Copyright © 2018 SILENT E PRODUCTIONS, LLC. All rights reserved. Published by Image Comics, Inc. Office of publication: 2701 NW Vaughn St., Ste. 780, Portland, OR 97210. Contains material originally published in single magazine form as CURSE WORDS #6-10 and THE CURSE WORDS HOLIDAY SPECIAL. "CURSE WORDS" CURSE WORDS #6-10 and the likenesses of all characters herein are trademarks of SILENT E PRODUCTIONS, LLC, unless otherwise noted. "Image" and the Image Comics logos are registered trademarks of Image Comics, Inc. No part of this publication may be reproduced or transmitted, in any form or by any means (except for short excerpts for journalistic or review purposes), without the express written permission of SILENT E PRODUCTIONS, LLC or Image Comics, Inc. All names, characters, events, and locales in this publication are entirely fictional. Any resemblance to actual persons (living or dead), events, or places, without satiric intent, is coincidental. Printed in the USA. For information regarding the CPSIA on this printed material call: 203-595-3636 and provide reference #RICH–772932 . For international rights, contact:foreignlicensing@imagecomics.com. ISBN: 978-1-5343-0472-7

® IMAGE COMICS, INC.

Robert Kirkman—Chief Operating Officer
Erik Larsen—Chief Financial Officer
Todd McFarlane—President
Marc Silvestri—Chief Executive Officer
Jim Valentino—Vice President

Eric Stephenson—Publisher
Corey Hart—Director of Sales
Jeff Boison—Director of Publishing Planning
& Book Trade Sales
Chris Ross—Director of Digital Sales
Jeff Stang—Director of Specialty Sales
Kat Salazar—Director of PR & Marketing
Drew Gill—Art Director
Heather Doornink—Production Director
Bramwyn Bigglestone—Controller

image   IMAGECOMICS.COM

CURSE WORDS

VOLUME TWO: EXPLOSIONTOWN

CREATED BY
CHARLES SOULE & RYAN BROWNE

COLORS BY
**ADDISON DUKE &
RYAN BROWNE**

LETTERS BY
CHRIS CRANK

HOLIDAY SPECIAL DRAWN BY
MIKE NORTON

LOGO BY **SEAN DOVE**

BOOK DESIGN BY **RYAN BROWNE**

SIX

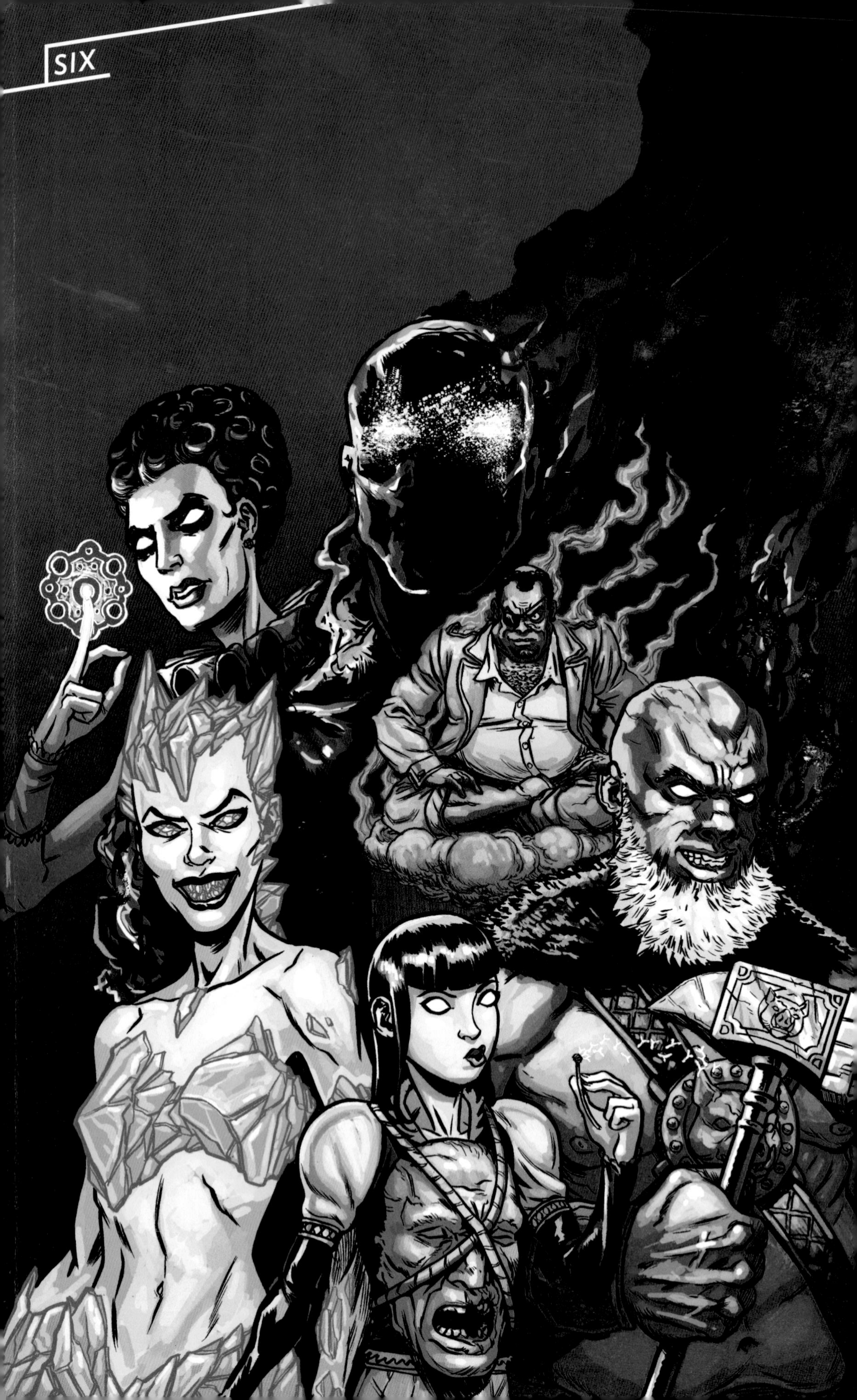

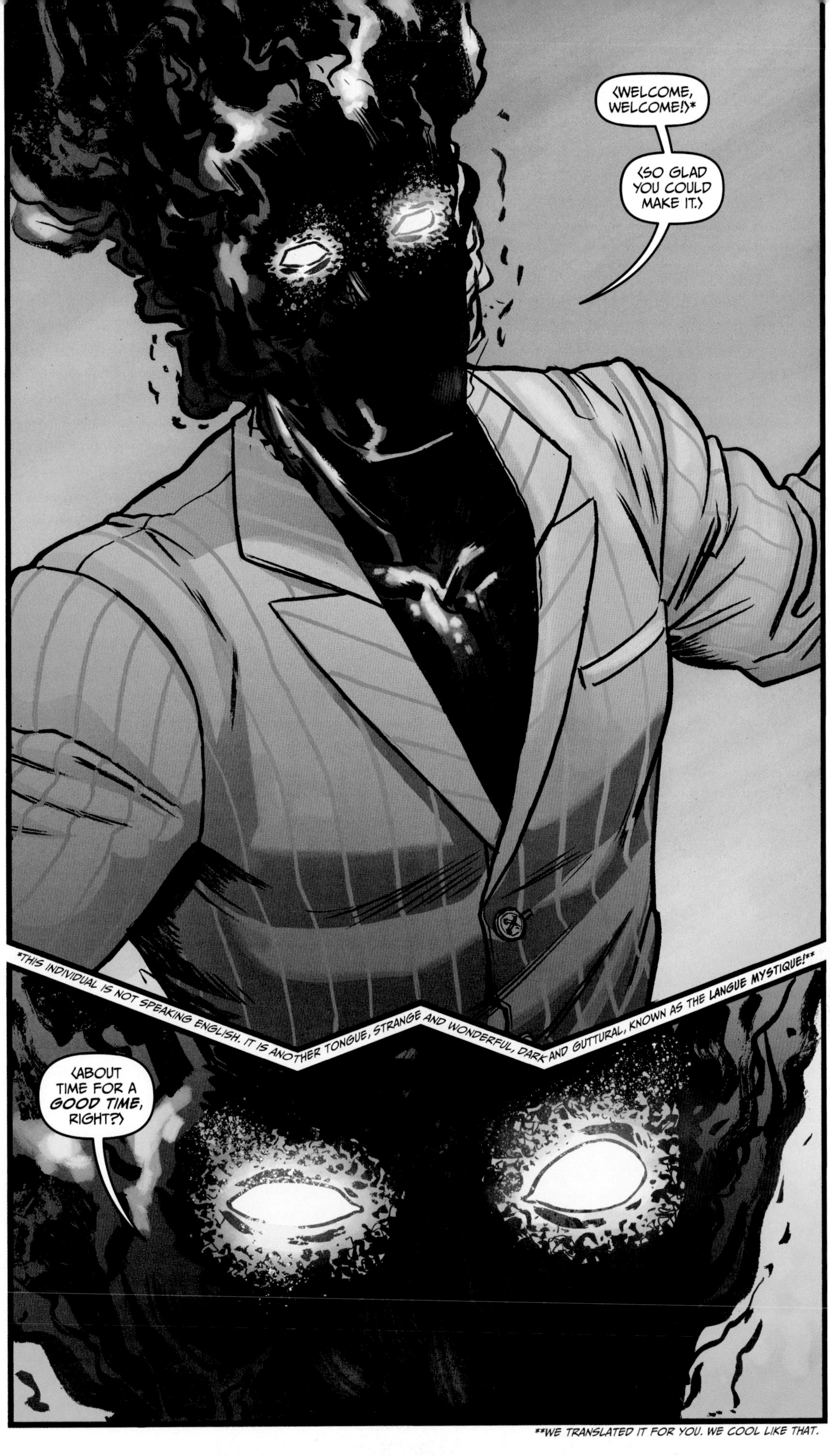
‹WELCOME, WELCOME!›*
‹SO GLAD YOU COULD MAKE IT.›
*THIS INDIVIDUAL IS NOT SPEAKING ENGLISH. IT IS ANOTHER TONGUE, STRANGE AND WONDERFUL, DARK AND GUTTURAL, KNOWN AS THE LANGUE MYSTIQUE!**
‹ABOUT TIME FOR A GOOD TIME, RIGHT?›

**WE TRANSLATED IT FOR YOU. WE COOL LIKE THAT.

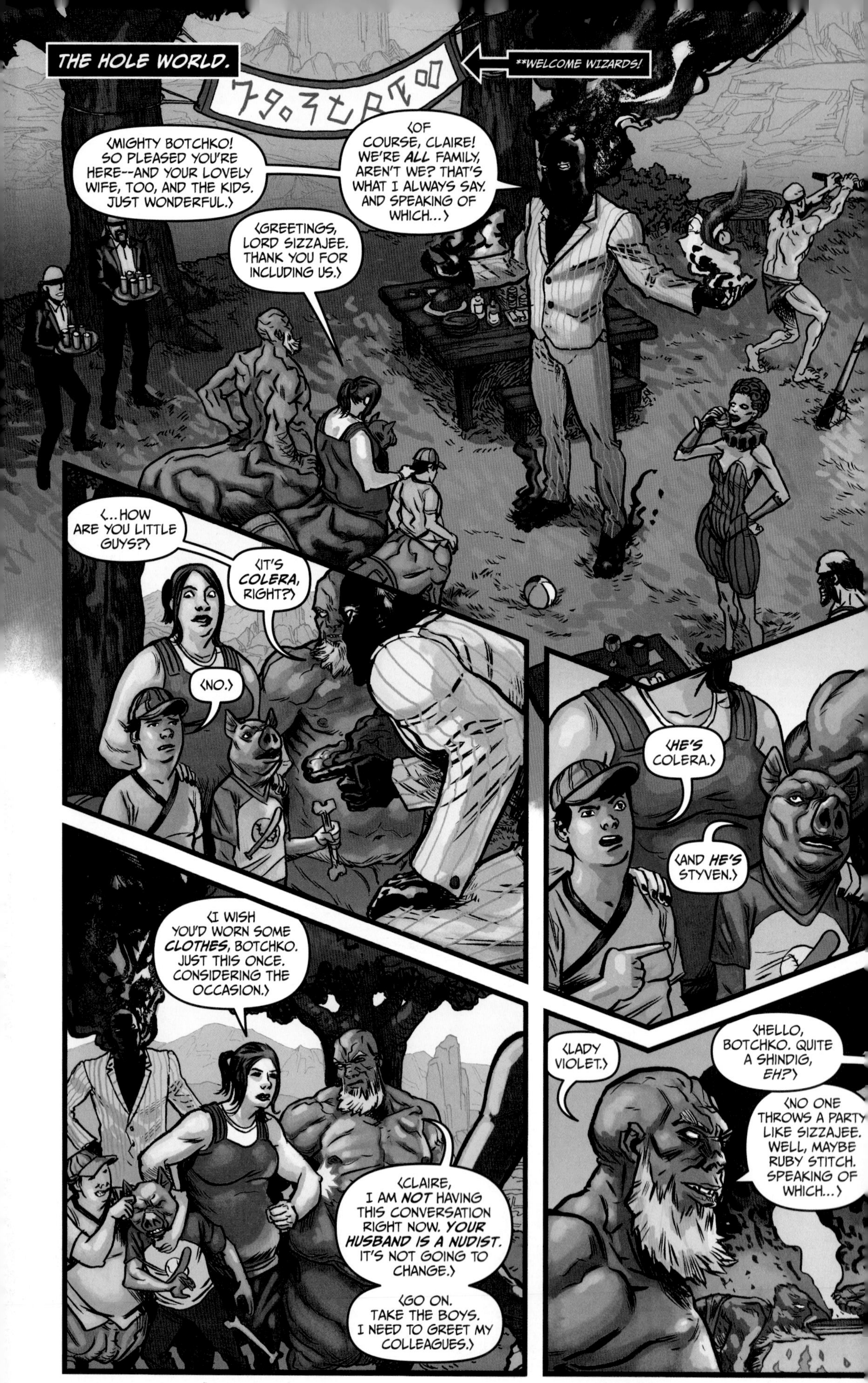
THE HOLE WORLD.
**WELCOME WIZARDS!
⟨MIGHTY BOTCHKO! SO PLEASED YOU'RE HERE--AND YOUR LOVELY WIFE, TOO, AND THE KIDS. JUST WONDERFUL.⟩
⟨OF COURSE, CLAIRE! WE'RE ALL FAMILY, AREN'T WE? THAT'S WHAT I ALWAYS SAY. AND SPEAKING OF WHICH...⟩
⟨GREETINGS, LORD SIZZAJEE. THANK YOU FOR INCLUDING US.⟩
⟨...HOW ARE YOU LITTLE GUYS?⟩
⟨IT'S COLERA, RIGHT?⟩
⟨NO.⟩
⟨HE'S COLERA.⟩
⟨AND HE'S STYVEN.⟩
⟨I WISH YOU'D WORN SOME CLOTHES, BOTCHKO. JUST THIS ONCE. CONSIDERING THE OCCASION.⟩
⟨CLAIRE, I AM NOT HAVING THIS CONVERSATION RIGHT NOW. YOUR HUSBAND IS A NUDIST. IT'S NOT GOING TO CHANGE.⟩
⟨GO ON. TAKE THE BOYS. I NEED TO GREET MY COLLEAGUES.⟩
⟨LADY VIOLET.⟩
⟨HELLO, BOTCHKO. QUITE A SHINDIG, EH?⟩
⟨NO ONE THROWS A PARTY LIKE SIZZAJEE. WELL, MAYBE RUBY STITCH. SPEAKING OF WHICH...⟩

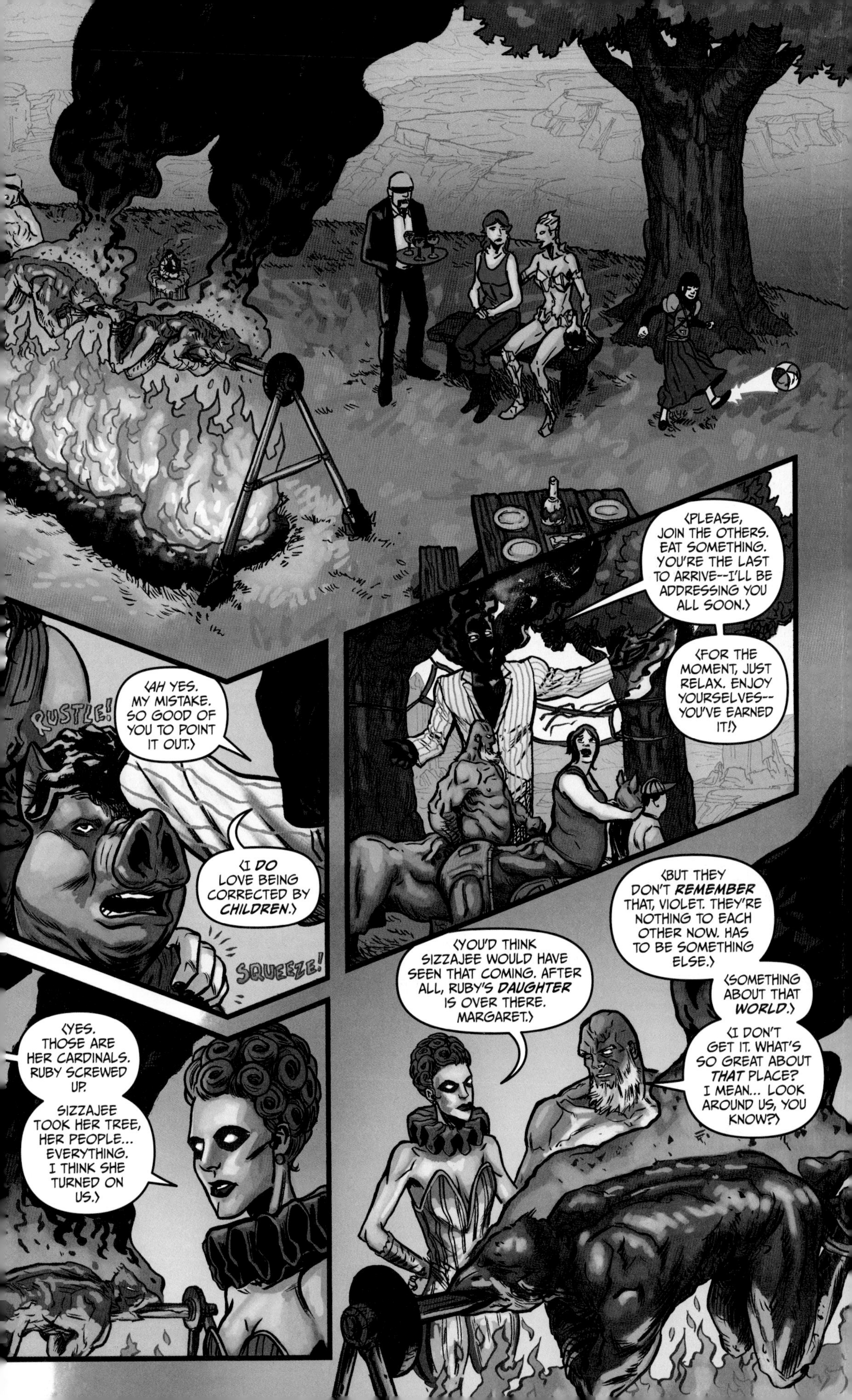

‹PLEASE, JOIN THE OTHERS. EAT SOMETHING. YOU'RE THE LAST TO ARRIVE--I'LL BE ADDRESSING YOU ALL SOON.›
‹FOR THE MOMENT, JUST RELAX. ENJOY YOURSELVES--YOU'VE EARNED IT!›
RUSTLE!
‹AH YES. MY MISTAKE. SO GOOD OF YOU TO POINT IT OUT.›
‹I DO LOVE BEING CORRECTED BY CHILDREN.›
SQUEEZE!
‹BUT THEY DON'T REMEMBER THAT, VIOLET. THEY'RE NOTHING TO EACH OTHER NOW. HAS TO BE SOMETHING ELSE.›
‹SOMETHING ABOUT THAT WORLD.›
‹YES. THOSE ARE HER CARDINALS. RUBY SCREWED UP.
SIZZAJEE TOOK HER TREE, HER PEOPLE... EVERYTHING. I THINK SHE TURNED ON US.›
‹YOU'D THINK SIZZAJEE WOULD HAVE SEEN THAT COMING. AFTER ALL, RUBY'S DAUGHTER IS OVER THERE. MARGARET.›
‹I DON'T GET IT. WHAT'S SO GREAT ABOUT THAT PLACE? I MEAN... LOOK AROUND US, YOU KNOW?›

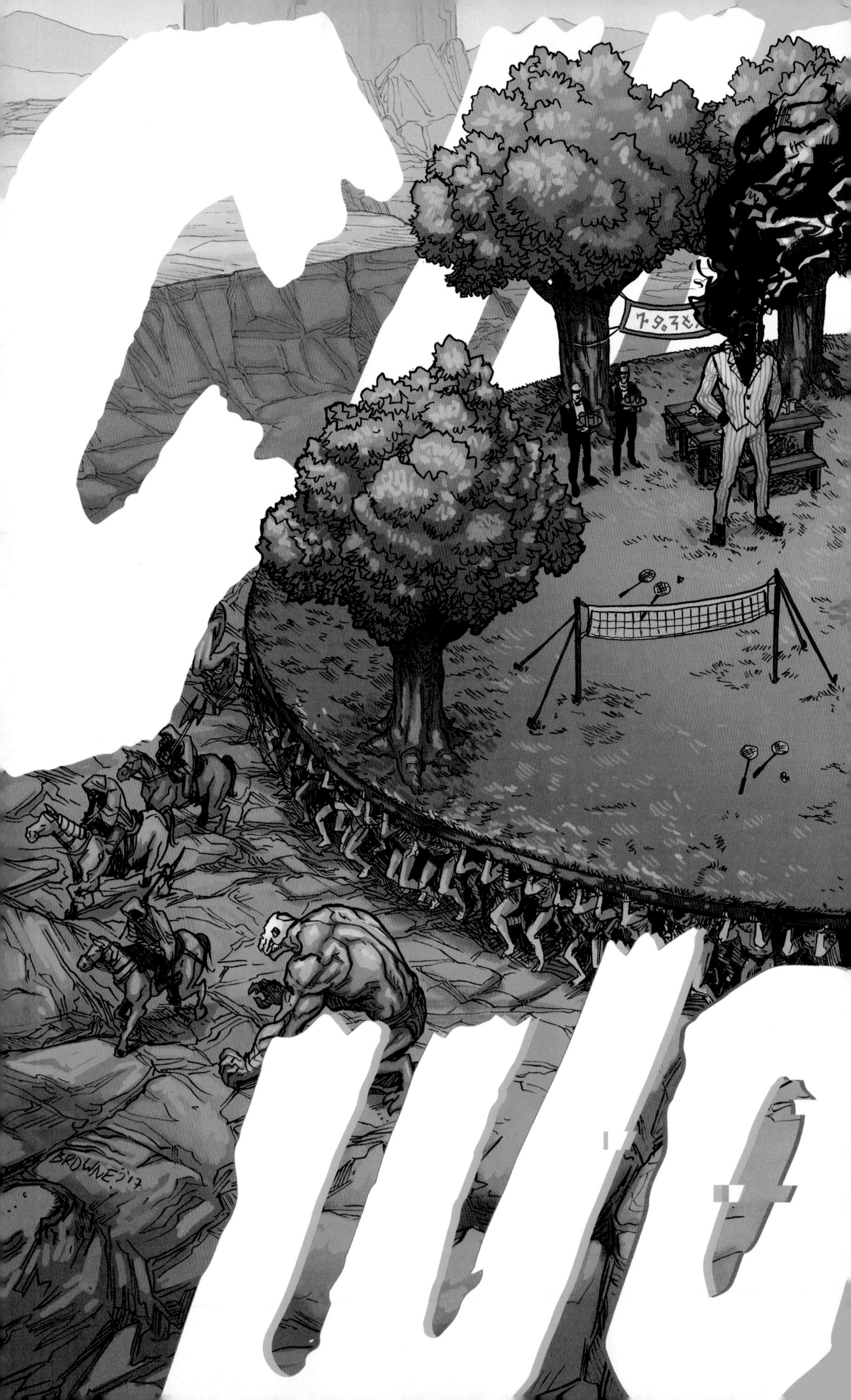
BROWNE'17

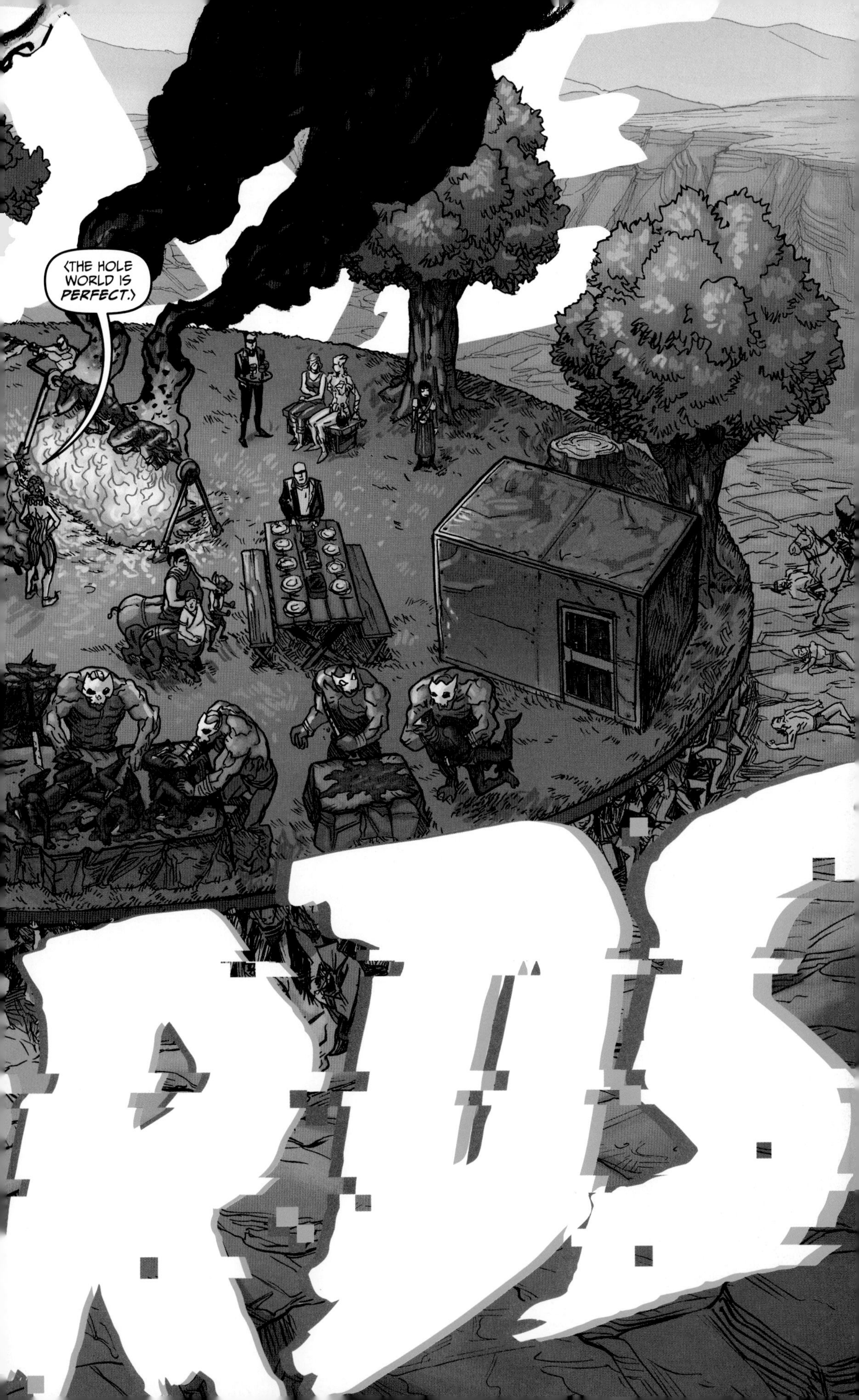

<THE HOLE WORLD IS PERFECT.>

NEW YORK CITY.

<YOU SAID YOU COULD GIVE ME BACK MY *POWER*, WIZORD.>

HUH. WEIRD. NORMALLY THERE ARE MORE PEOPLE AROUND HERE.

<I WILL, RUBY! I PROMISE. BUT FIRST, I'VE GOT A SURPRISE FOR YOU.>

<WHAT IS IT?>

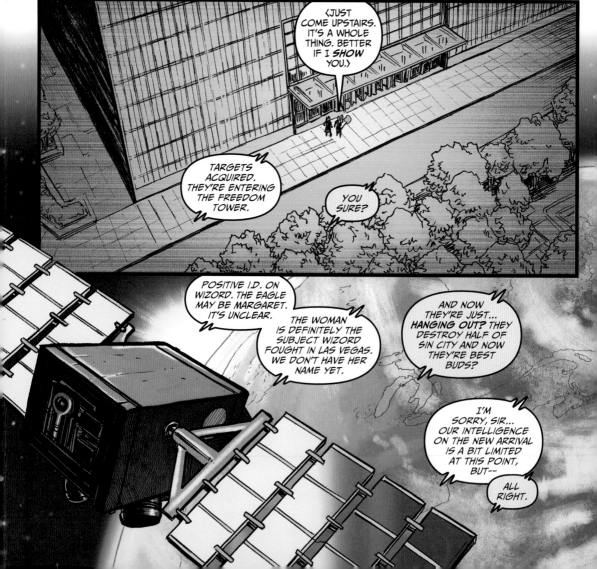

<JUST COME UPSTAIRS. IT'S A WHOLE THING. BETTER IF I *SHOW* YOU.>

TARGETS ACQUIRED. THEY'RE ENTERING THE FREEDOM TOWER.

YOU SURE?

POSITIVE I.D. ON WIZORD. THE EAGLE MAY BE MARGARET. IT'S UNCLEAR.

THE WOMAN IS DEFINITELY THE SUBJECT WIZORD FOUGHT IN LAS VEGAS. WE DON'T HAVE HER NAME YET.

AND NOW THEY'RE JUST... *HANGING OUT?* THEY DESTROY HALF OF SIN CITY AND NOW THEY'RE BEST BUDS?

I'M SORRY, SIR... OUR INTELLIGENCE ON THE NEW ARRIVAL IS A BIT LIMITED AT THIS POINT, BUT--

ALL RIGHT.

WHITE HOUSE SITUATION ROOM.

LET'S DO THIS. MISSION'S A GO.

OF COURSE, MR. PRESIDENT. RIGHT AWAY.

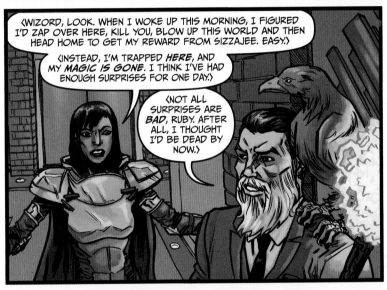

⟨WIZORD, LOOK. WHEN I WOKE UP THIS MORNING, I FIGURED I'D ZAP OVER HERE, KILL YOU, BLOW UP THIS WORLD AND THEN HEAD HOME TO GET MY REWARD FROM SIZZAJEE. EASY.⟩

⟨INSTEAD, I'M TRAPPED HERE, AND MY MAGIC IS GONE. I THINK I'VE HAD ENOUGH SURPRISES FOR ONE DAY.⟩

⟨NOT ALL SURPRISES ARE BAD, RUBY. AFTER ALL, I THOUGHT I'D BE DEAD BY NOW.⟩

⟨SURPRISE!⟩

⟨OKAY. THIS IS IT. CLOSE YOUR EYES.⟩

⟨NO.⟩

WIZORD
(WIZARD)

WIZORD
(WIZARD)

ZPOG.

WHATEVER.

ZISSSS

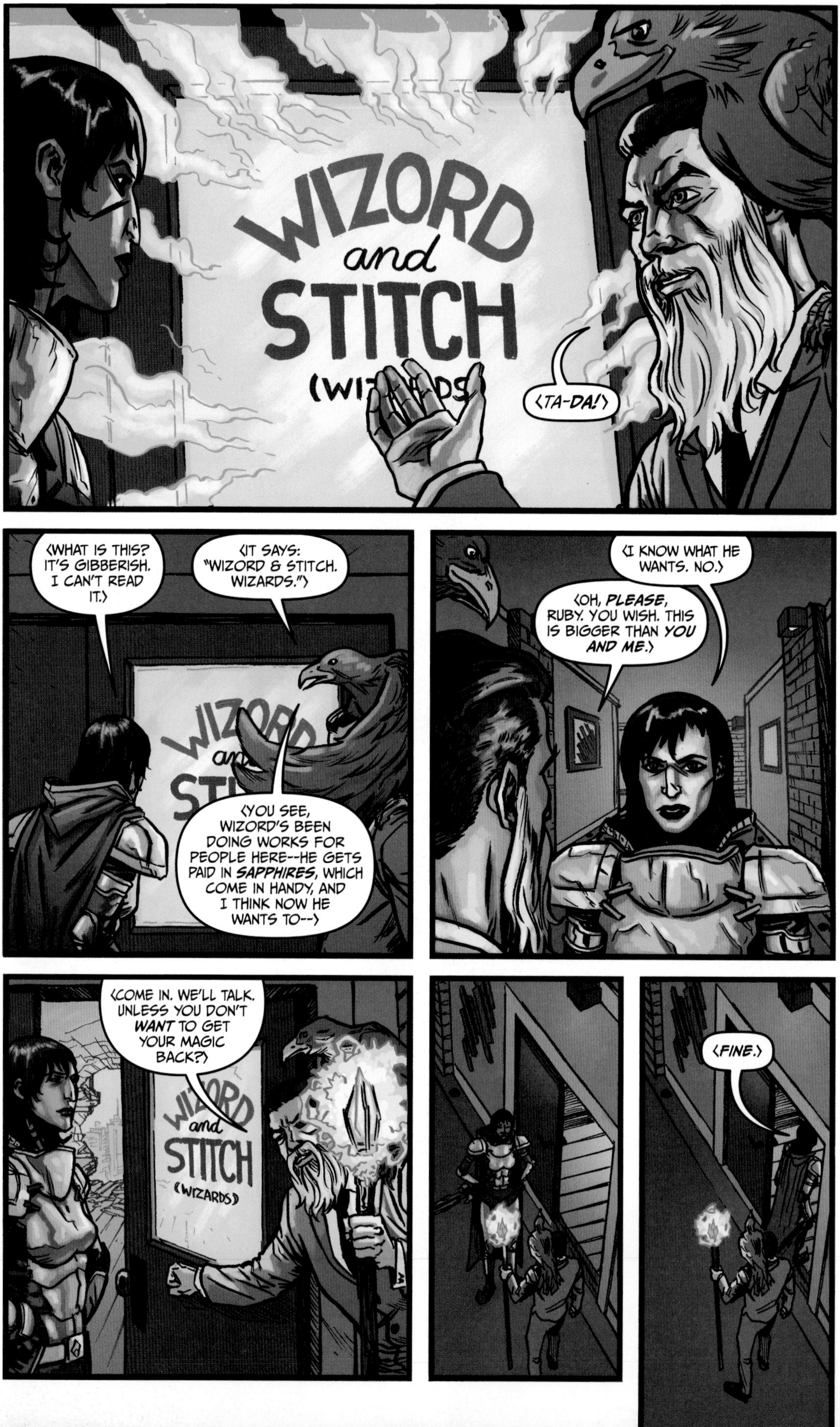
WIZORD and STITCH
⟨TA-DA!⟩
⟨WHAT IS THIS? IT'S GIBBERISH. I CAN'T READ IT.⟩
⟨IT SAYS: "WIZORD & STITCH. WIZARDS."⟩
⟨YOU SEE, WIZORD'S BEEN DOING WORKS FOR PEOPLE HERE--HE GETS PAID IN ***SAPPHIRES***, WHICH COME IN HANDY, AND I THINK NOW HE WANTS TO--⟩
⟨I KNOW WHAT HE WANTS. NO.⟩
⟨OH, ***PLEASE***, RUBY. YOU WISH. THIS IS BIGGER THAN ***YOU AND ME***.⟩
⟨COME IN. WE'LL TALK. UNLESS YOU DON'T ***WANT*** TO GET YOUR MAGIC BACK?⟩
WIZORD and STITCH (WIZARDS)
⟨***FINE***.⟩

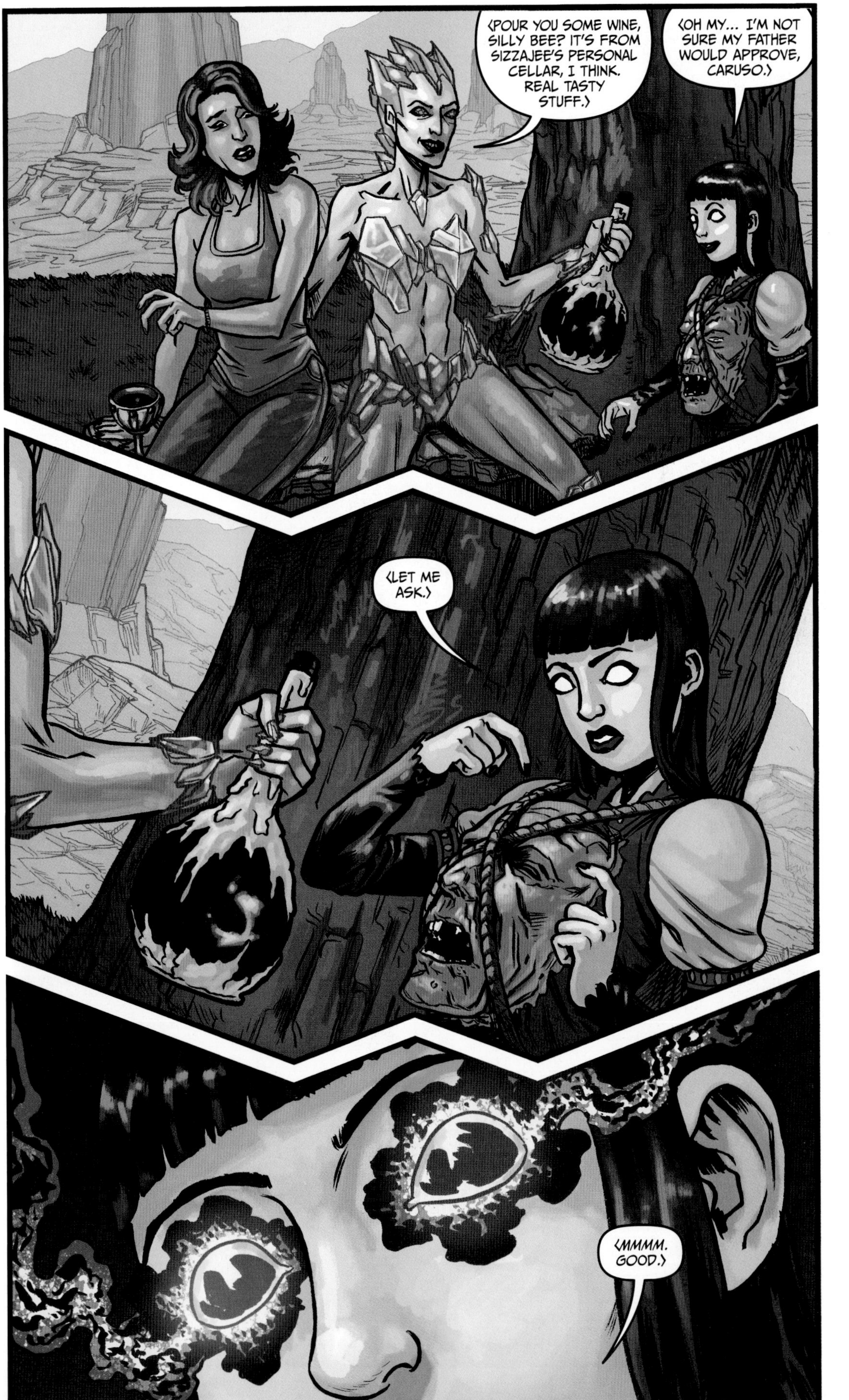
‹POUR YOU SOME WINE, SILLY BEE? IT'S FROM SIZZAJEE'S PERSONAL CELLAR, I THINK. REAL TASTY STUFF.›
‹OH MY... I'M NOT SURE MY FATHER WOULD APPROVE, CARUSO.›
‹LET ME ASK.›
‹MMMM. GOOD.›

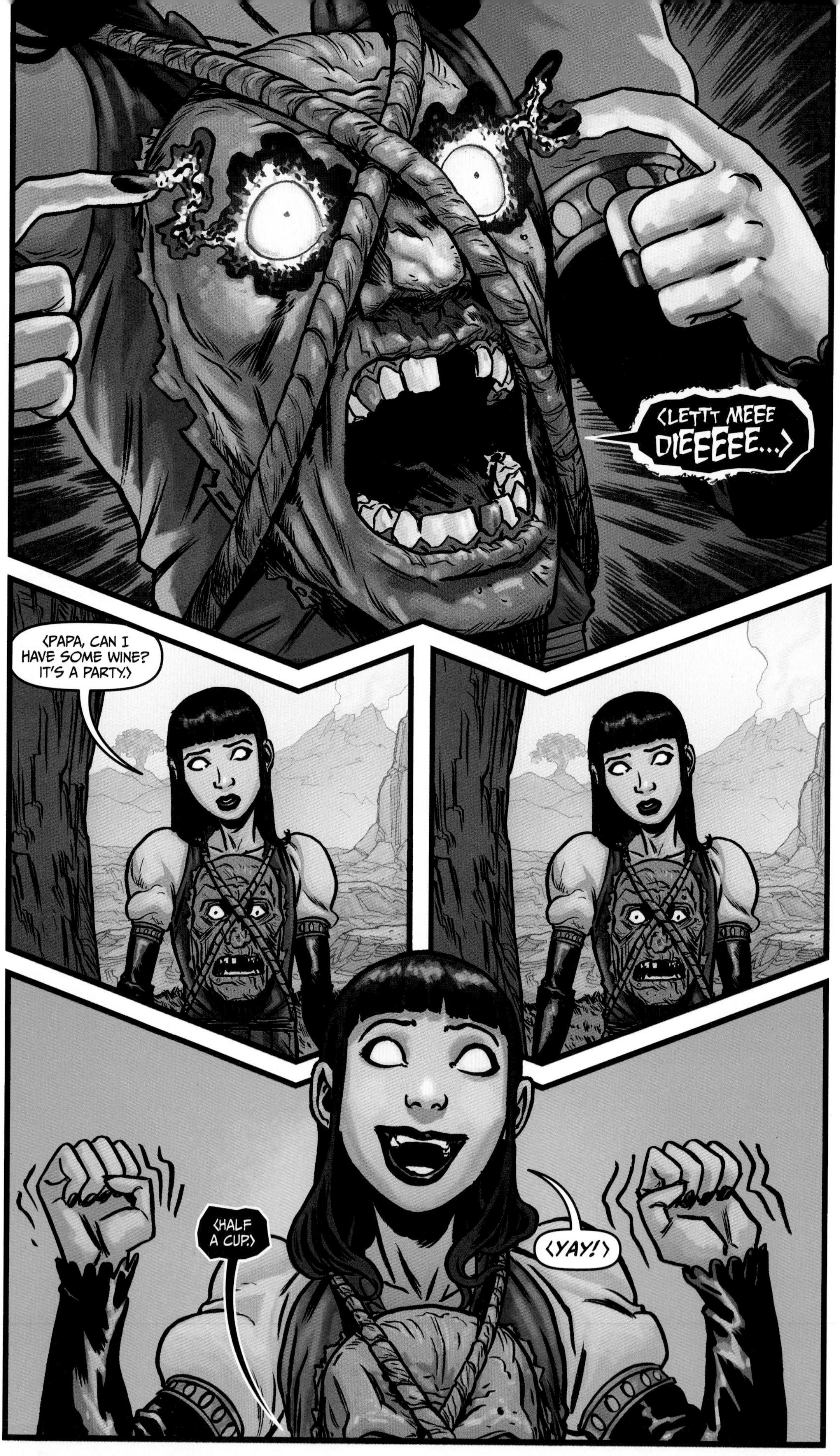
<LETTT MEEE DIEEEEE...>
<PAPA, CAN I HAVE SOME WINE? IT'S A PARTY.>
<YAY!>
<HALF A CUP.>

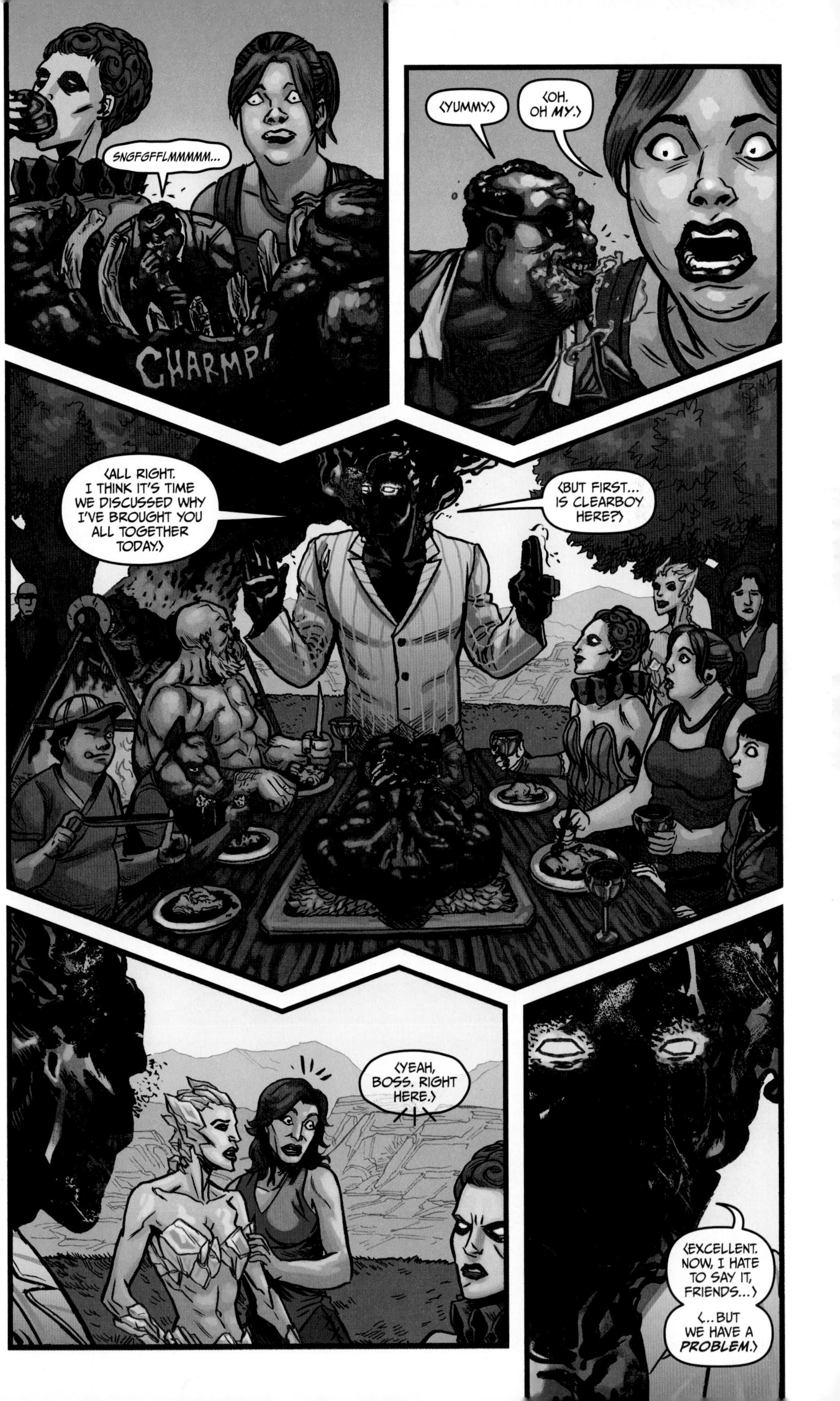
SNGFGFFLMMMMM...
CHARMP!
<YUMMY.>
<OH.
OH MY.>
<ALL RIGHT. I THINK IT'S TIME WE DISCUSSED WHY I'VE BROUGHT YOU ALL TOGETHER TODAY.>
<BUT FIRST... IS CLEARBOY HERE?>
<YEAH, BOSS. RIGHT HERE.>
<EXCELLENT. NOW, I HATE TO SAY IT, FRIENDS...>
<...BUT WE HAVE A PROBLEM.>

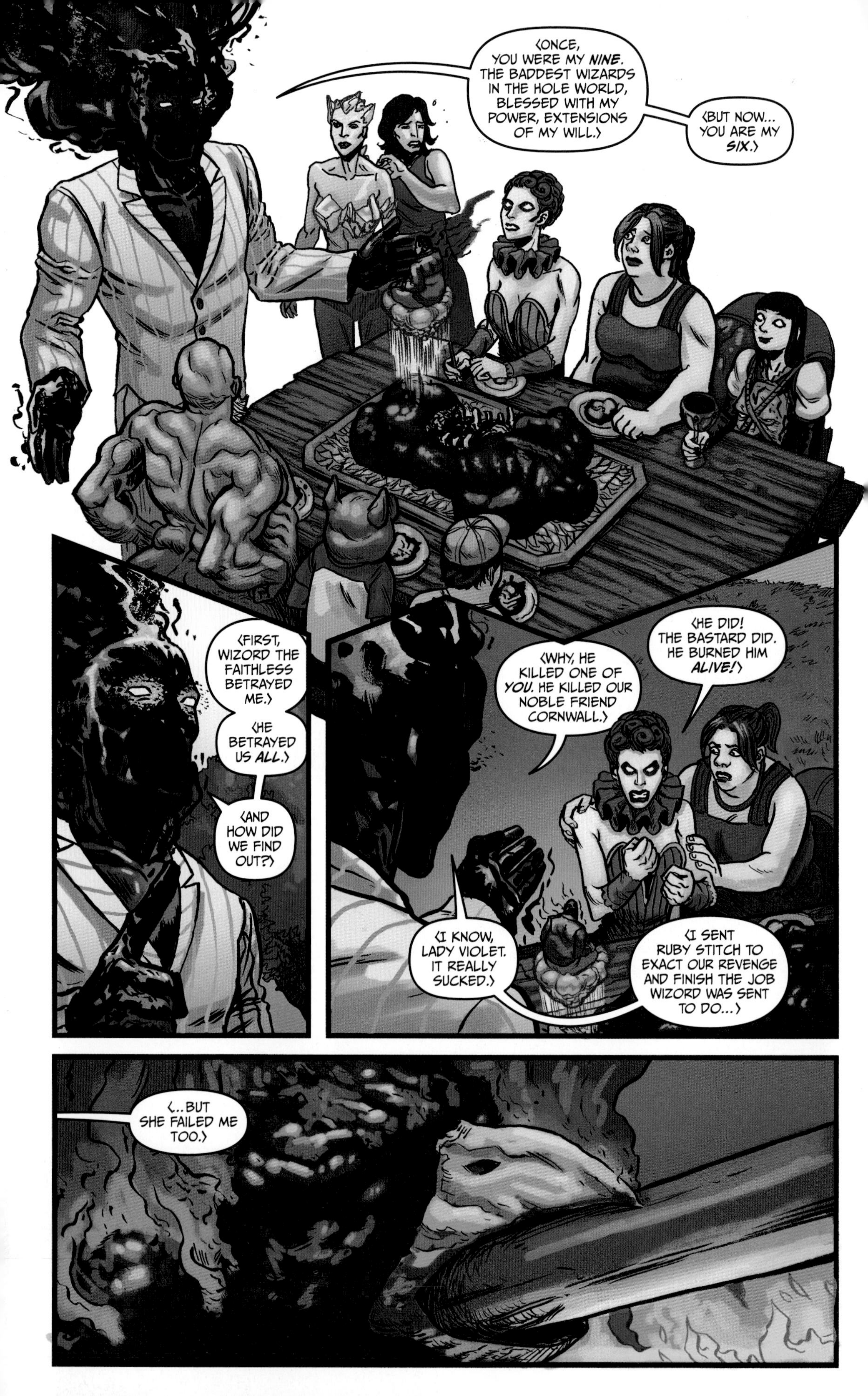
‹ONCE, YOU WERE MY *NINE*. THE BADDEST WIZARDS IN THE HOLE WORLD, BLESSED WITH MY POWER, EXTENSIONS OF MY WILL.›
‹BUT NOW... YOU ARE MY *SIX*.›
‹FIRST, WIZORD THE FAITHLESS BETRAYED ME.›
‹HE BETRAYED US *ALL*.›
‹AND HOW DID WE FIND OUT?›
‹WHY, HE KILLED ONE OF *YOU*. HE KILLED OUR NOBLE FRIEND CORNWALL.›
‹HE DID! THE BASTARD DID. HE BURNED HIM *ALIVE!*›
‹I KNOW, LADY VIOLET. IT REALLY SUCKED.›
‹I SENT RUBY STITCH TO EXACT OUR REVENGE AND FINISH THE JOB WIZORD WAS SENT TO DO...›
‹...BUT SHE FAILED ME TOO.›

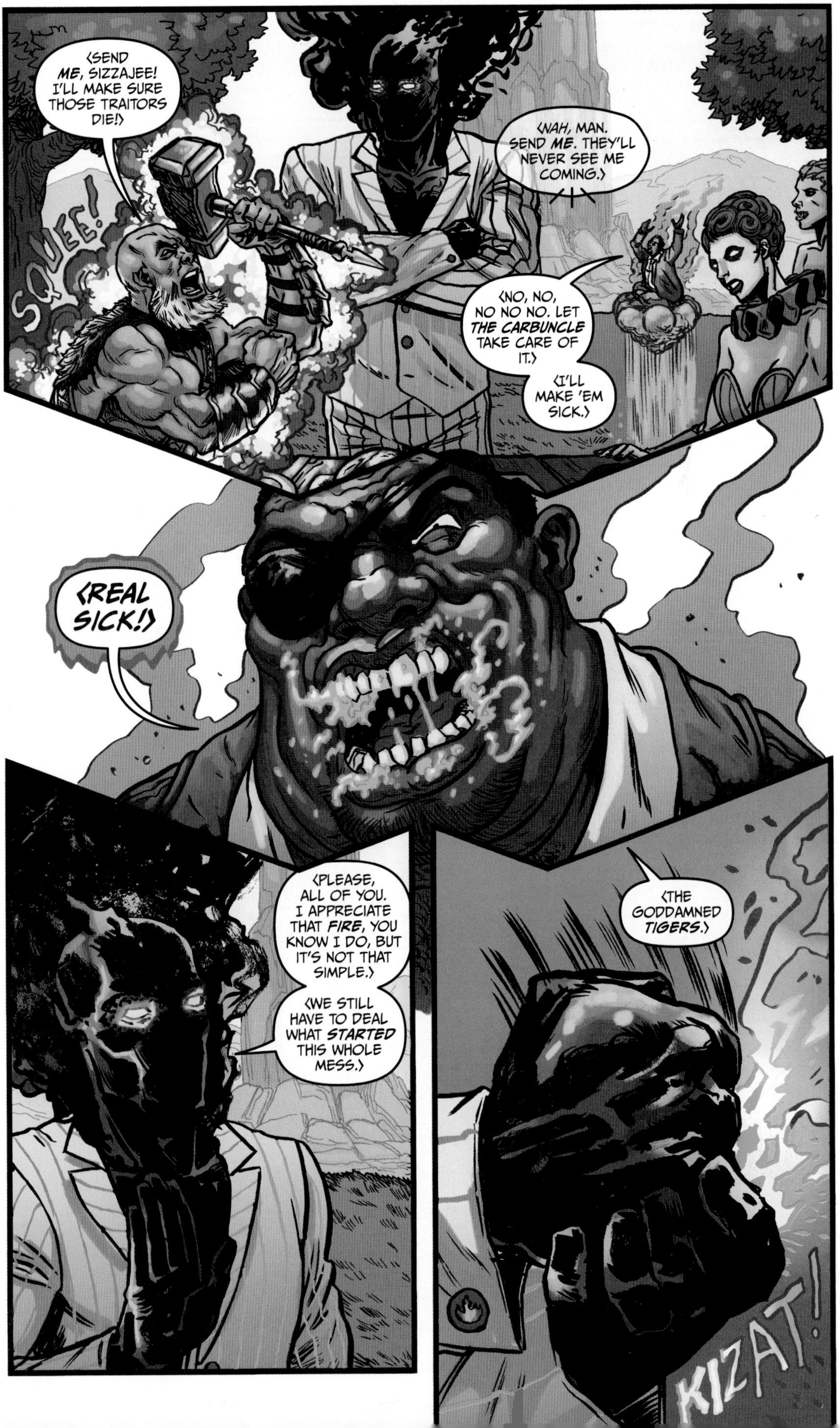

‹SEND ME, SIZZAJEE! I'LL MAKE SURE THOSE TRAITORS DIE!›
SQUEE!
‹NAH, MAN. SEND ME. THEY'LL NEVER SEE ME COMING.›
‹NO, NO, NO NO NO. LET THE CARBUNCLE TAKE CARE OF IT.›
‹I'LL MAKE 'EM SICK.›
‹REAL SICK!›
‹PLEASE, ALL OF YOU. I APPRECIATE THAT FIRE, YOU KNOW I DO, BUT IT'S NOT THAT SIMPLE.›
‹WE STILL HAVE TO DEAL WHAT STARTED THIS WHOLE MESS.›
‹THE GODDAMNED TIGERS.›
KIZAT!

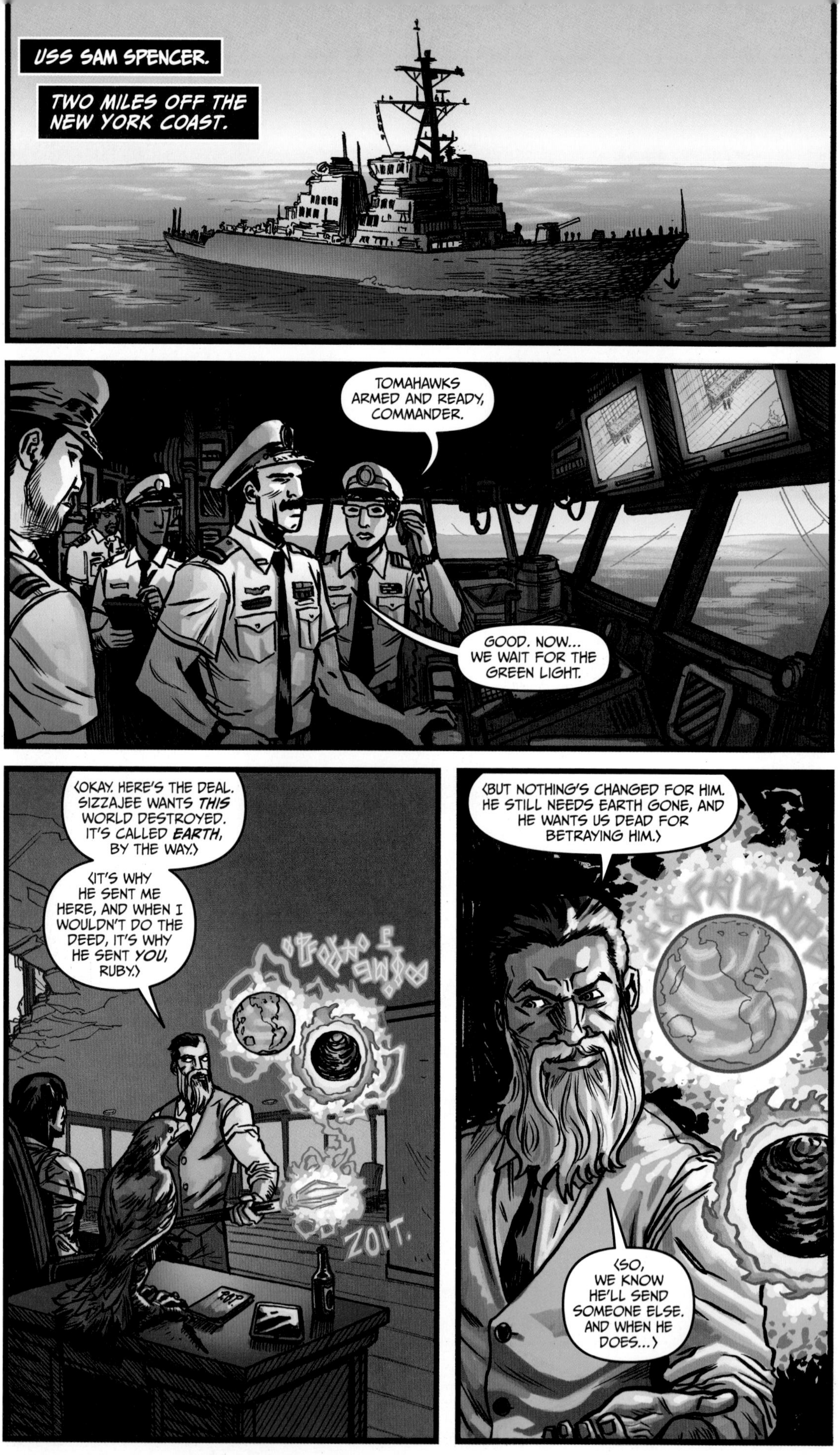
USS SAM SPENCER.
TWO MILES OFF THE NEW YORK COAST.
TOMAHAWKS ARMED AND READY, COMMANDER.
GOOD. NOW... WE WAIT FOR THE GREEN LIGHT.
‹OKAY. HERE'S THE DEAL. SIZZAJEE WANTS *THIS* WORLD DESTROYED. IT'S CALLED *EARTH*, BY THE WAY.›
‹IT'S WHY HE SENT ME HERE, AND WHEN I WOULDN'T DO THE DEED, IT'S WHY HE SENT *YOU*, RUBY.›
ZOIT.
‹BUT NOTHING'S CHANGED FOR HIM. HE STILL NEEDS EARTH GONE, AND HE WANTS US DEAD FOR BETRAYING HIM.›
‹SO, WE KNOW HE'LL SEND SOMEONE ELSE. AND WHEN HE DOES...›

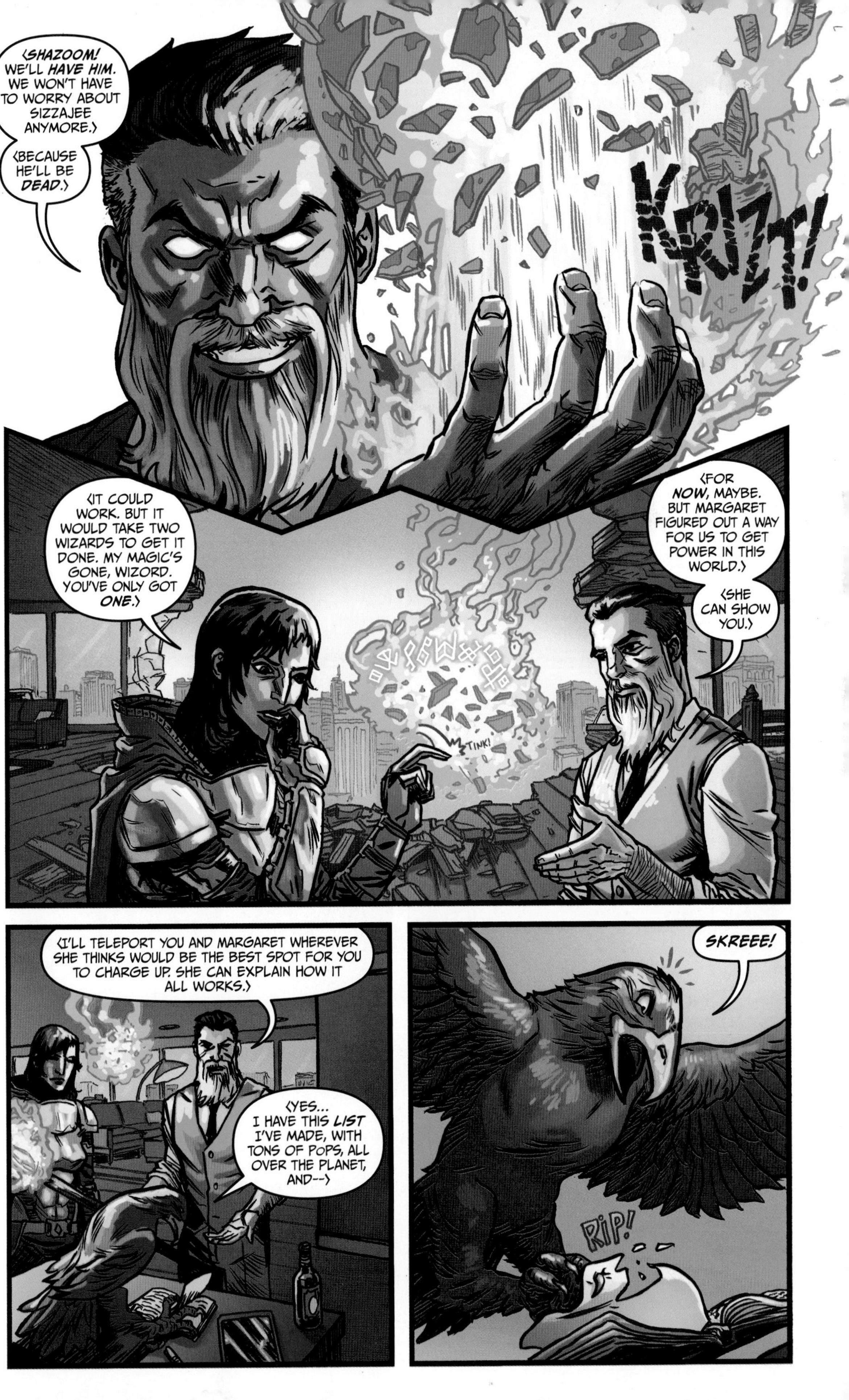
〈SHAZOOM! WE'LL HAVE HIM. WE WON'T HAVE TO WORRY ABOUT SIZZAJEE ANYMORE.〉
〈BECAUSE HE'LL BE DEAD.〉
KRIZT!
〈IT COULD WORK. BUT IT WOULD TAKE TWO WIZARDS TO GET IT DONE. MY MAGIC'S GONE, WIZORD. YOU'VE ONLY GOT ONE.〉
〈FOR NOW, MAYBE. BUT MARGARET FIGURED OUT A WAY FOR US TO GET POWER IN THIS WORLD.〉
〈SHE CAN SHOW YOU.〉
TINK!
〈I'LL TELEPORT YOU AND MARGARET WHEREVER SHE THINKS WOULD BE THE BEST SPOT FOR YOU TO CHARGE UP. SHE CAN EXPLAIN HOW IT ALL WORKS.〉
〈YES... I HAVE THIS LIST I'VE MADE, WITH TONS OF POPS, ALL OVER THE PLANET, AND--〉
SKREEE!
RIP!

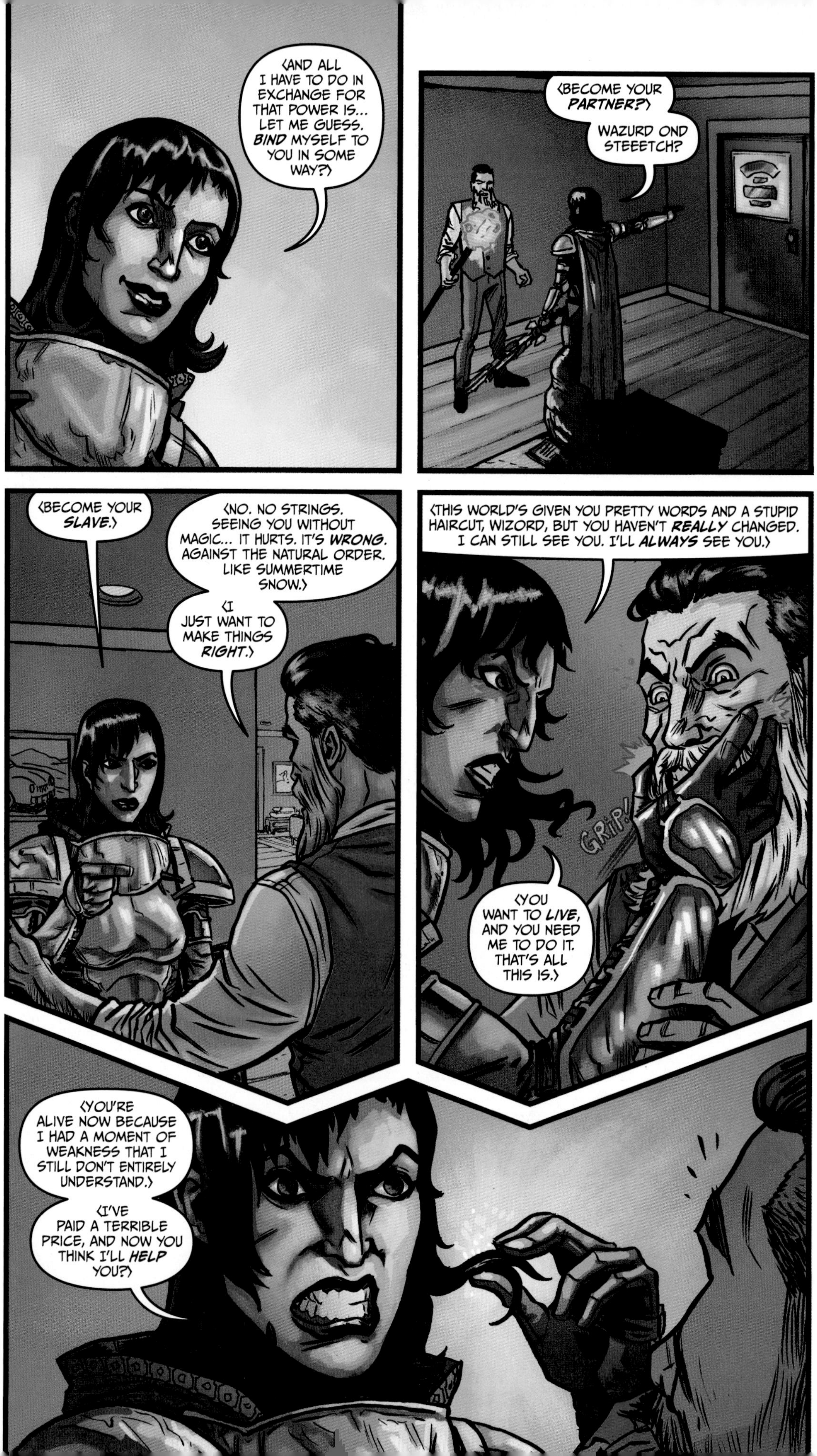

‹AND ALL I HAVE TO DO IN EXCHANGE FOR THAT POWER IS... LET ME GUESS. BIND MYSELF TO YOU IN SOME WAY?›
‹BECOME YOUR PARTNER?›
WAZURD OND STEEETCH?
‹BECOME YOUR SLAVE.›
‹NO. NO STRINGS. SEEING YOU WITHOUT MAGIC... IT HURTS. IT'S WRONG. AGAINST THE NATURAL ORDER. LIKE SUMMERTIME SNOW.›
‹I JUST WANT TO MAKE THINGS RIGHT.›
‹THIS WORLD'S GIVEN YOU PRETTY WORDS AND A STUPID HAIRCUT, WIZORD, BUT YOU HAVEN'T REALLY CHANGED. I CAN STILL SEE YOU. I'LL ALWAYS SEE YOU.›
GRIP!
‹YOU WANT TO LIVE, AND YOU NEED ME TO DO IT. THAT'S ALL THIS IS.›
‹YOU'RE ALIVE NOW BECAUSE I HAD A MOMENT OF WEAKNESS THAT I STILL DON'T ENTIRELY UNDERSTAND.›
‹I'VE PAID A TERRIBLE PRICE, AND NOW YOU THINK I'LL HELP YOU?›

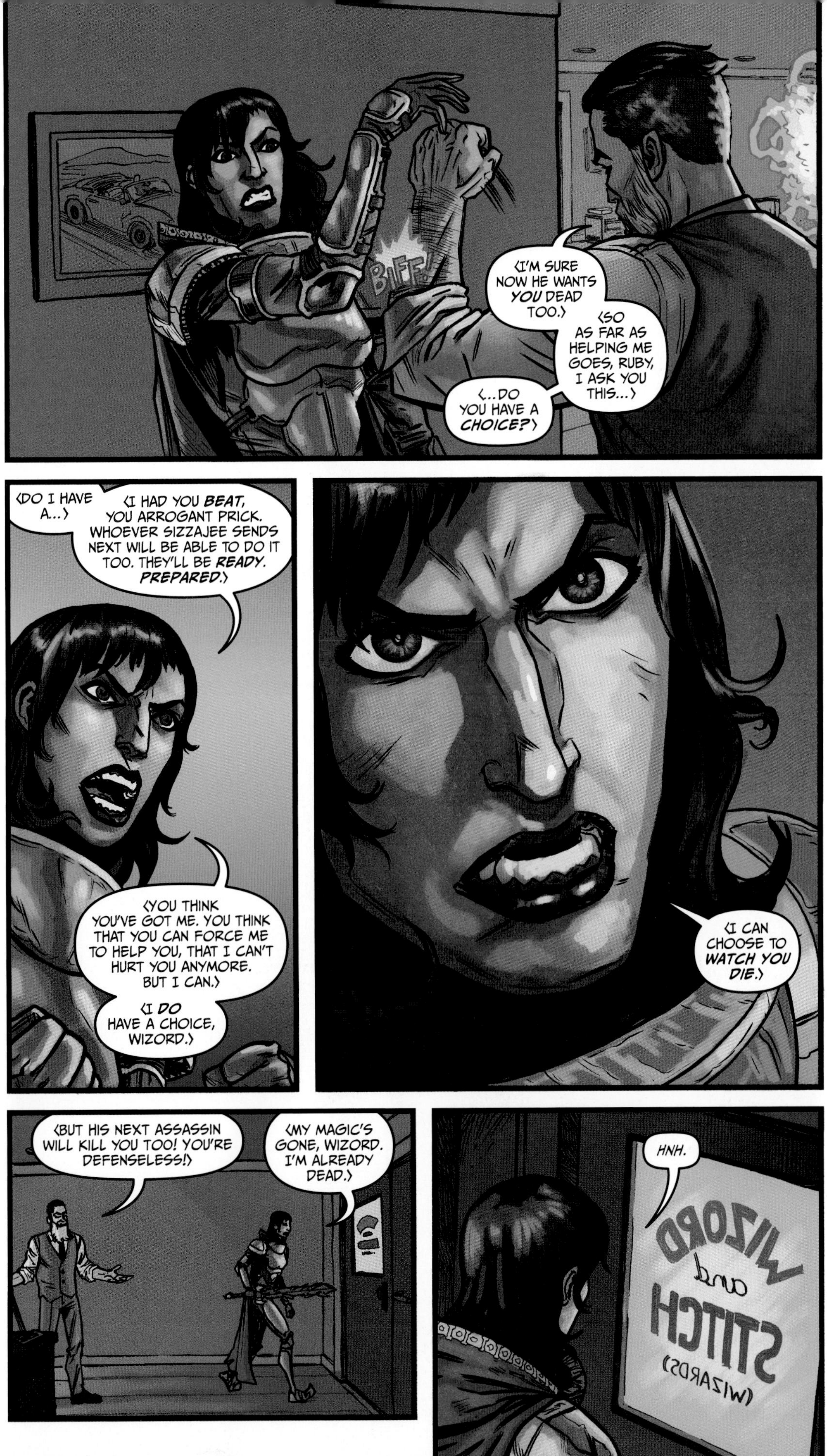
BIFF!
‹I'M SURE NOW HE WANTS *YOU* DEAD TOO.›
‹SO AS FAR AS HELPING ME GOES, RUBY, I ASK YOU THIS...›
‹...DO YOU HAVE A *CHOICE?*›
‹DO I HAVE A...›
‹I HAD YOU *BEAT*, YOU ARROGANT PRICK. WHOEVER SIZZAJEE SENDS NEXT WILL BE ABLE TO DO IT TOO. THEY'LL BE *READY*. *PREPARED*.›
‹YOU THINK YOU'VE GOT ME. YOU THINK THAT YOU CAN FORCE ME TO HELP YOU, THAT I CAN'T HURT YOU ANYMORE. BUT I CAN.›
‹I *DO* HAVE A CHOICE, WIZORD.›
‹I CAN CHOOSE TO *WATCH YOU DIE*.›
‹BUT HIS NEXT ASSASSIN WILL KILL YOU TOO! YOU'RE DEFENSELESS!›
‹MY MAGIC'S GONE, WIZORD. I'M ALREADY DEAD.›
HNH.
WIZORD and STITCH (WIZARDS)

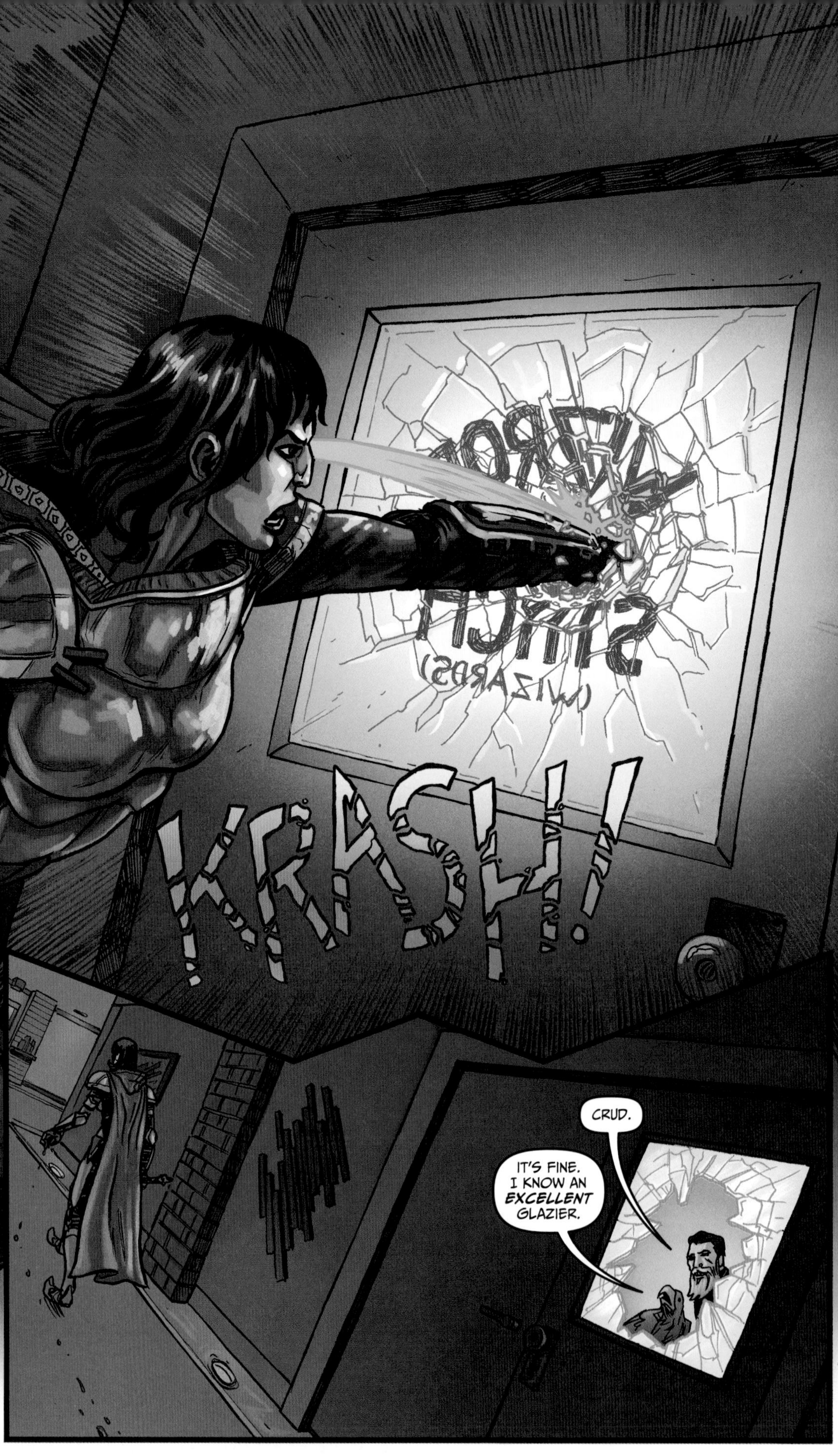
KRASH!!
CRUD.
IT'S FINE. I KNOW AN *EXCELLENT* GLAZIER.

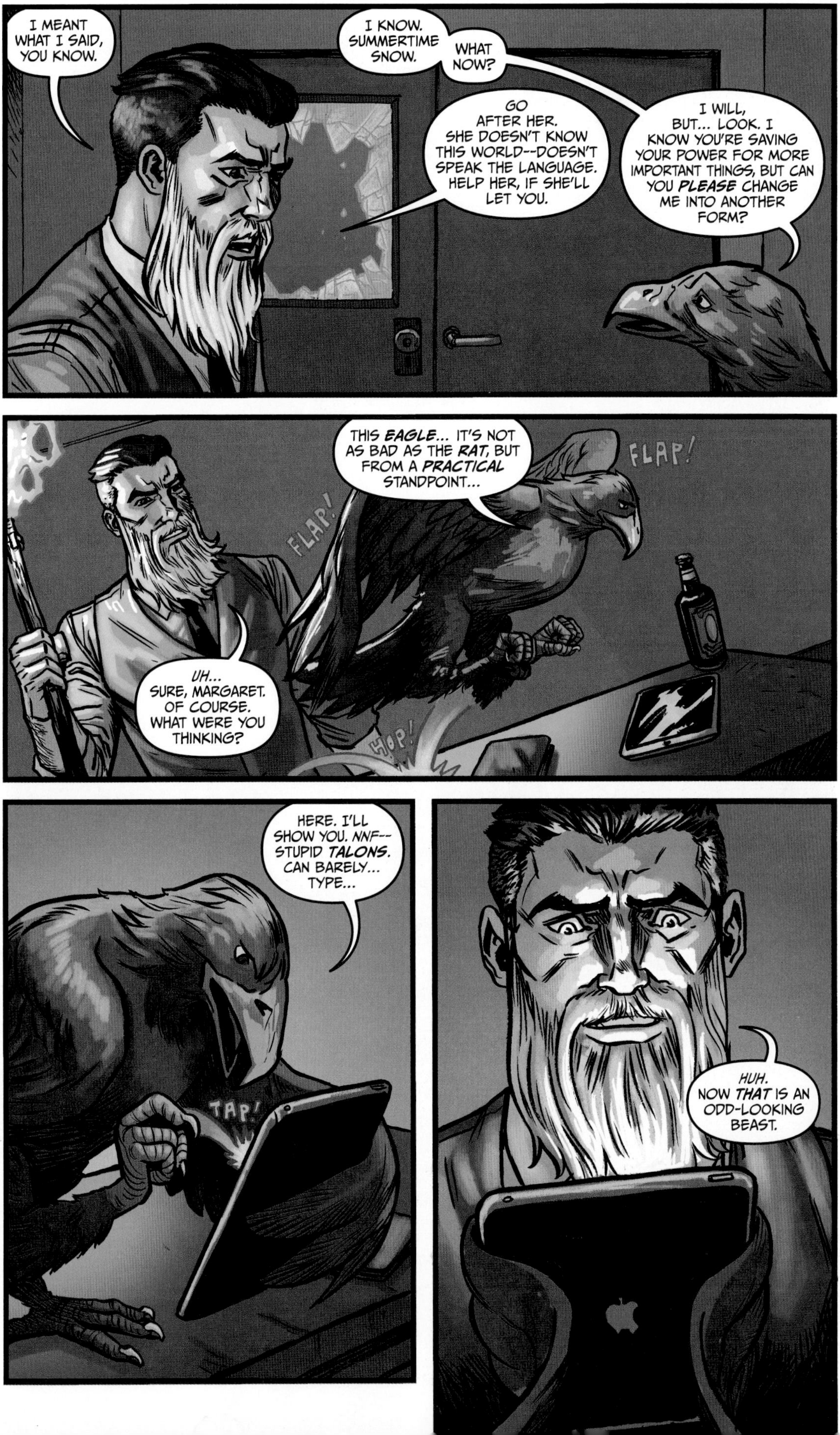
I MEANT WHAT I SAID, YOU KNOW.
I KNOW. SUMMERTIME SNOW.
WHAT NOW?
GO AFTER HER. SHE DOESN'T KNOW THIS WORLD--DOESN'T SPEAK THE LANGUAGE. HELP HER, IF SHE'LL LET YOU.
I WILL, BUT... LOOK. I KNOW YOU'RE SAVING YOUR POWER FOR MORE IMPORTANT THINGS, BUT CAN YOU PLEASE CHANGE ME INTO ANOTHER FORM?
FLAP!
THIS EAGLE... IT'S NOT AS BAD AS THE RAT, BUT FROM A PRACTICAL STANDPOINT...
FLAP!
UH... SURE, MARGARET. OF COURSE. WHAT WERE YOU THINKING?
HOP!
HERE. I'LL SHOW YOU. NNF-- STUPID TALONS. CAN BARELY... TYPE...
TAP!
HUH. NOW THAT IS AN ODD-LOOKING BEAST.

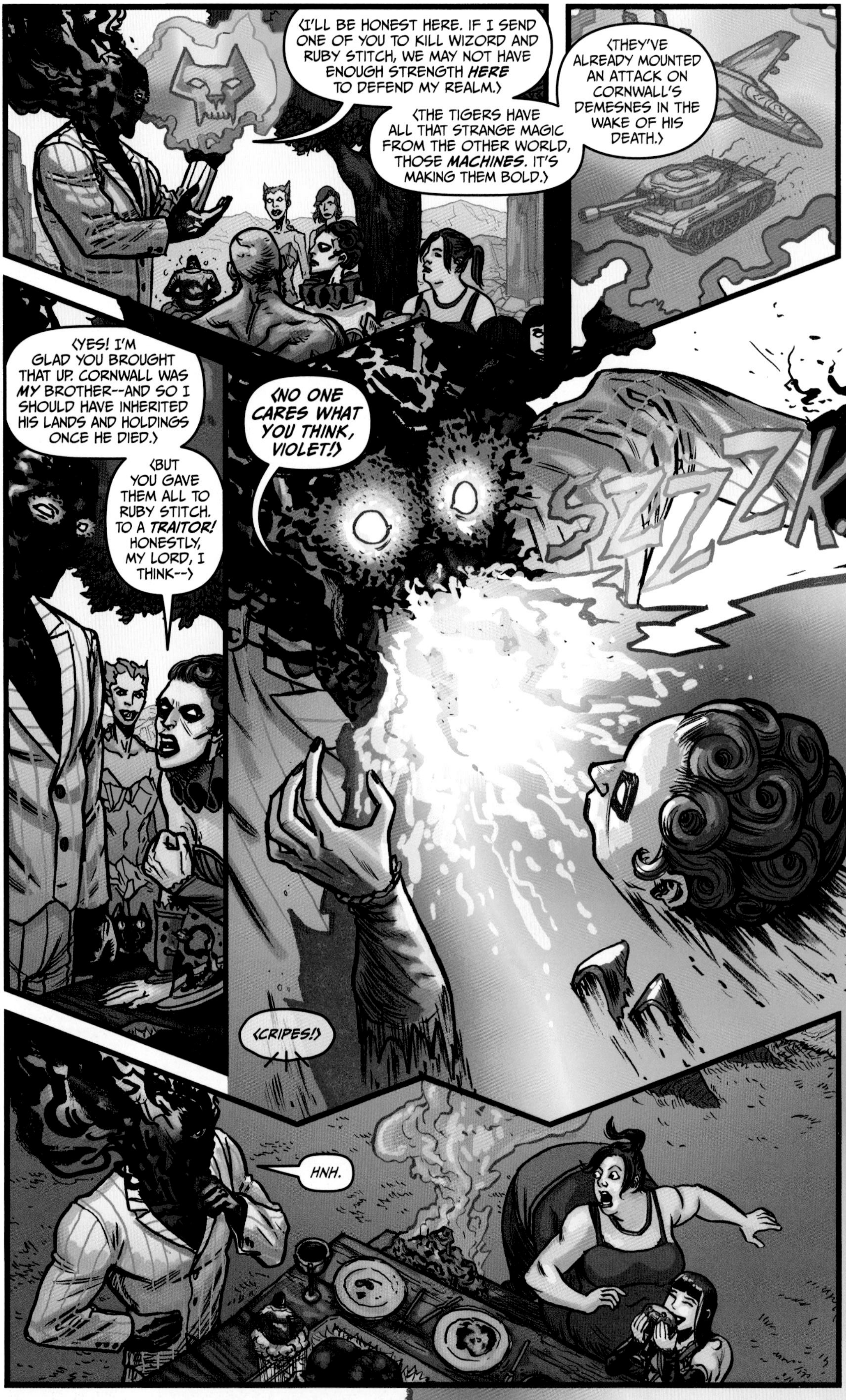

‹I'LL BE HONEST HERE. IF I SEND ONE OF YOU TO KILL WIZORD AND RUBY STITCH, WE MAY NOT HAVE ENOUGH STRENGTH *HERE* TO DEFEND MY REALM.›
‹THE TIGERS HAVE ALL THAT STRANGE MAGIC FROM THE OTHER WORLD, THOSE *MACHINES*. IT'S MAKING THEM BOLD.›
‹THEY'VE ALREADY MOUNTED AN ATTACK ON CORNWALL'S DEMESNES IN THE WAKE OF HIS DEATH.›
‹YES! I'M GLAD YOU BROUGHT THAT UP. CORNWALL WAS *MY* BROTHER--AND SO I SHOULD HAVE INHERITED HIS LANDS AND HOLDINGS ONCE HE DIED.›
‹BUT YOU GAVE THEM ALL TO RUBY STITCH. TO A *TRAITOR!* HONESTLY, MY LORD, I THINK--›
‹NO ONE CARES WHAT YOU THINK, VIOLET!›
SZZZK
‹CRIPES!›
HNH.

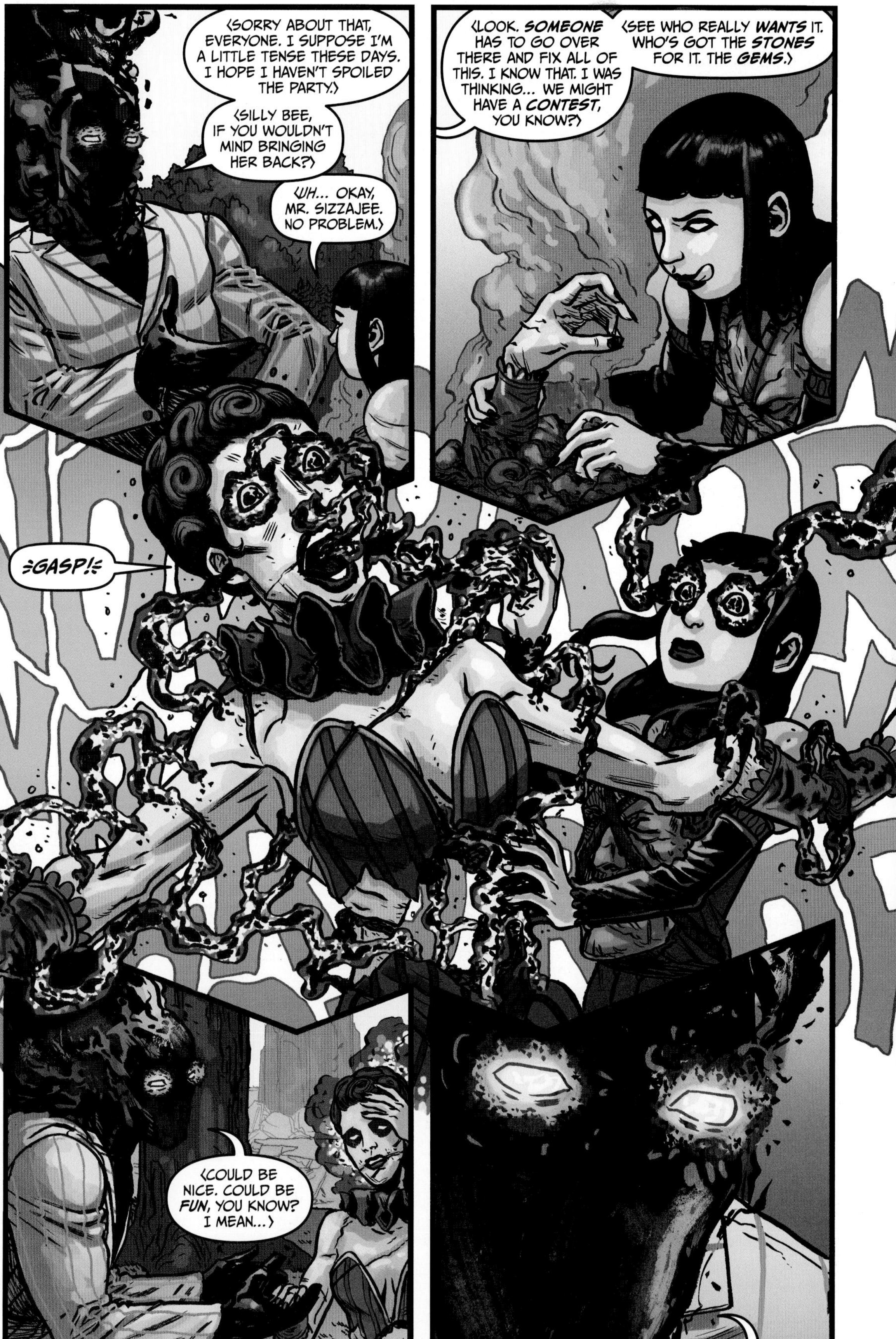
⟨SORRY ABOUT THAT, EVERYONE. I SUPPOSE I'M A LITTLE TENSE THESE DAYS. I HOPE I HAVEN'T SPOILED THE PARTY.⟩
⟨SILLY BEE, IF YOU WOULDN'T MIND BRINGING HER BACK?⟩
⟨UH... OKAY, MR. SIZZAJEE. NO PROBLEM.⟩
⟨LOOK. SOMEONE HAS TO GO OVER THERE AND FIX ALL OF THIS. I KNOW THAT. I WAS THINKING... WE MIGHT HAVE A CONTEST, YOU KNOW?⟩
⟨SEE WHO REALLY WANTS IT. WHO'S GOT THE STONES FOR IT. THE GEMS.⟩
GASP!
⟨COULD BE NICE. COULD BE FUN, YOU KNOW? I MEAN...⟩
⟨...I THINK WE'RE ALL READY FOR A GOOD TIME.⟩

OUR AGENT'S ON HIS WAY, SIR. SHOULD BE ON-SITE IN WIZORD'S OFFICE IN A FEW MINUTES.

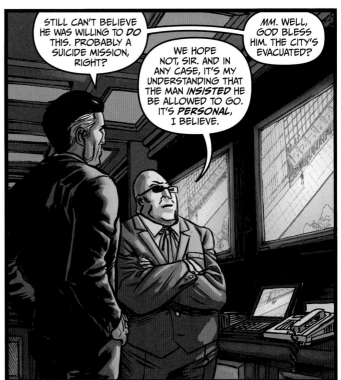

STILL CAN'T BELIEVE HE WAS WILLING TO *DO* THIS. PROBABLY A SUICIDE MISSION, RIGHT?

WE HOPE NOT, SIR. AND IN ANY CASE, IT'S MY UNDERSTANDING THAT THE MAN *INSISTED* HE BE ALLOWED TO GO. IT'S *PERSONAL*, I BELIEVE.

MM. WELL, GOD BLESS HIM. THE CITY'S EVACUATED?

YES, SIR. THE USS *SAM SPENCER'S* IN POSITION. IF WE HAVE TO LAUNCH, THE MISSILE STRIKE WILL TAKE OUT MOST OF MANHATTAN BELOW 14TH, BUT THE CITY'S BEEN CLEARED.

DO YOU SEE ANOTHER OPTION?

NOT AFTER VEGAS, NO. WIZORD'S BEEN LYING TO US SINCE THE START. WHATEVER'S *REALLY* HAPPENING... IT HAS TO STOP.

WE HAVE TO REASSERT CONTROL.

I SAY ONLY THIS: WE DO NOT KNOW WHAT THIS MAN IS CAPABLE OF. THESE MISSILES MIGHT DO NOTHING MORE THAN ANGER HIM.

AND THEN, WE HAVE NO OPTIONS LEFT. ALL RELEVANT DECISIONS BELONG TO *HIM*.

THAT'S WHY WE'LL HAVE A LITTLE *CHAT* WITH WIZORD FIRST. LET'S PRAY IT ENDS THERE.

PROCEED.

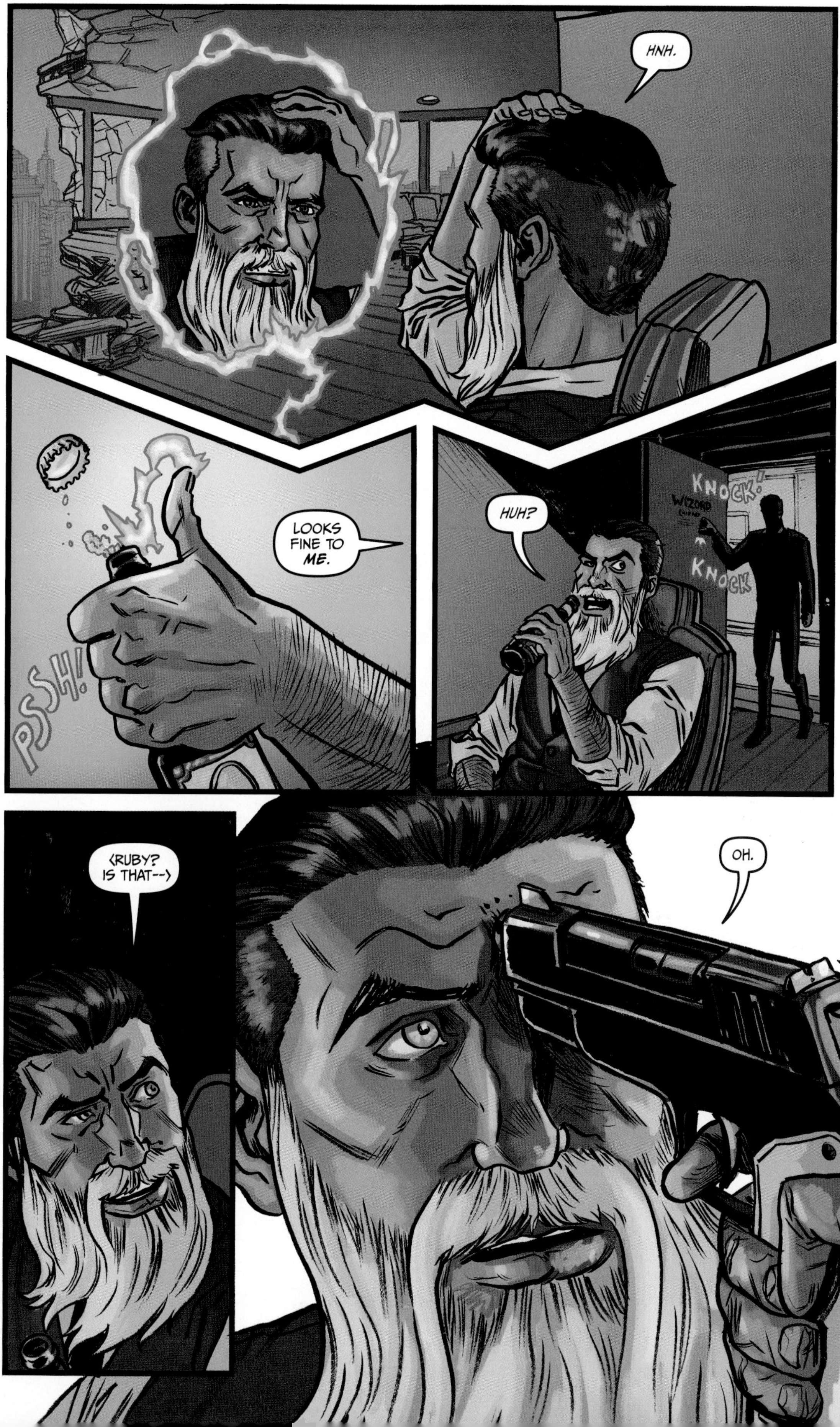
HNH.
LOOKS FINE TO ME.
PSSH!
HUH?
KNOCK!
KNOCK
<RUBY? IS THAT-->
OH.

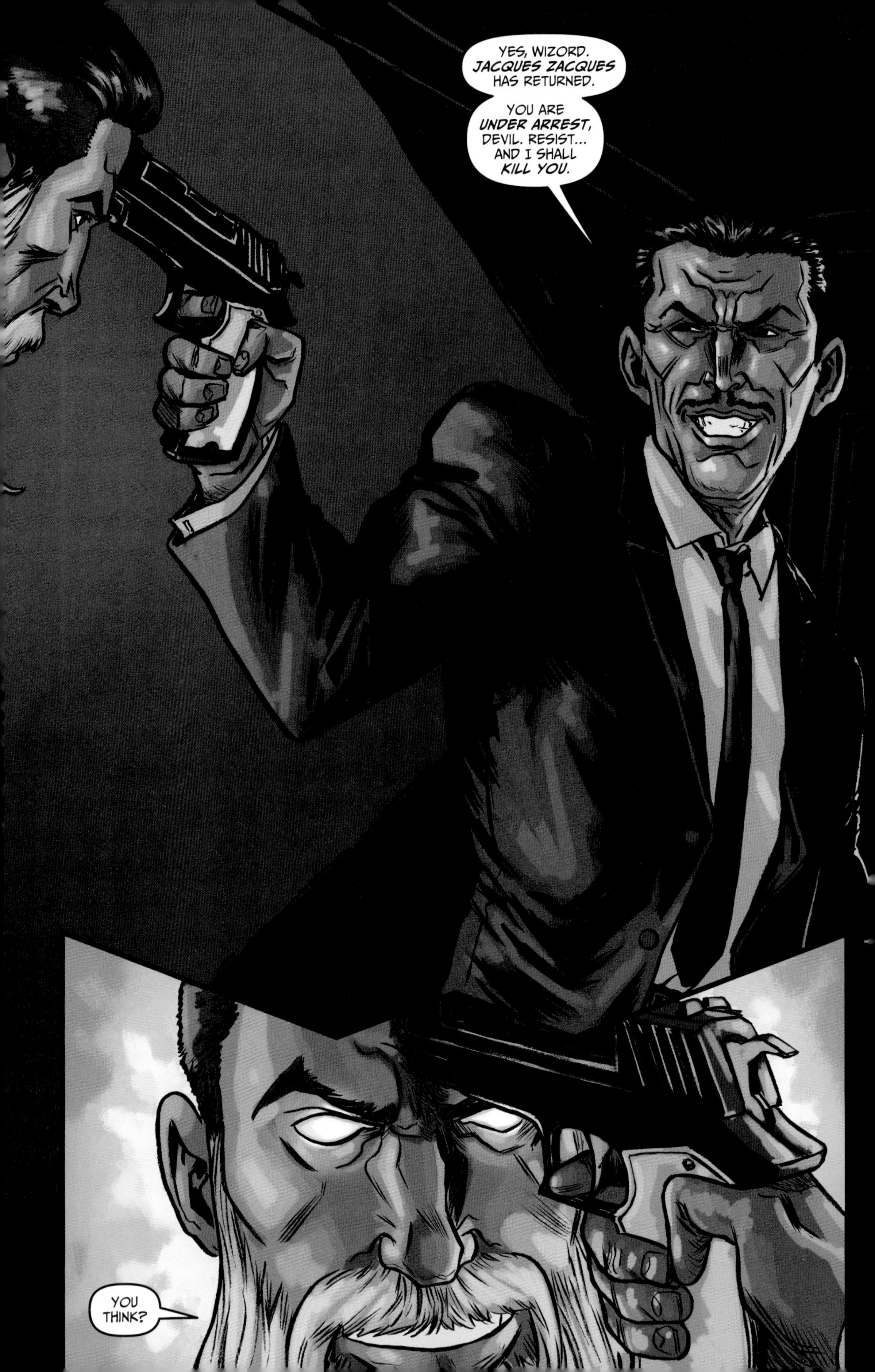
YES, WIZORD. JACQUES ZACQUES HAS RETURNED.
YOU ARE UNDER ARREST, DEVIL. RESIST... AND I SHALL KILL YOU.
YOU THINK?

SEVEN

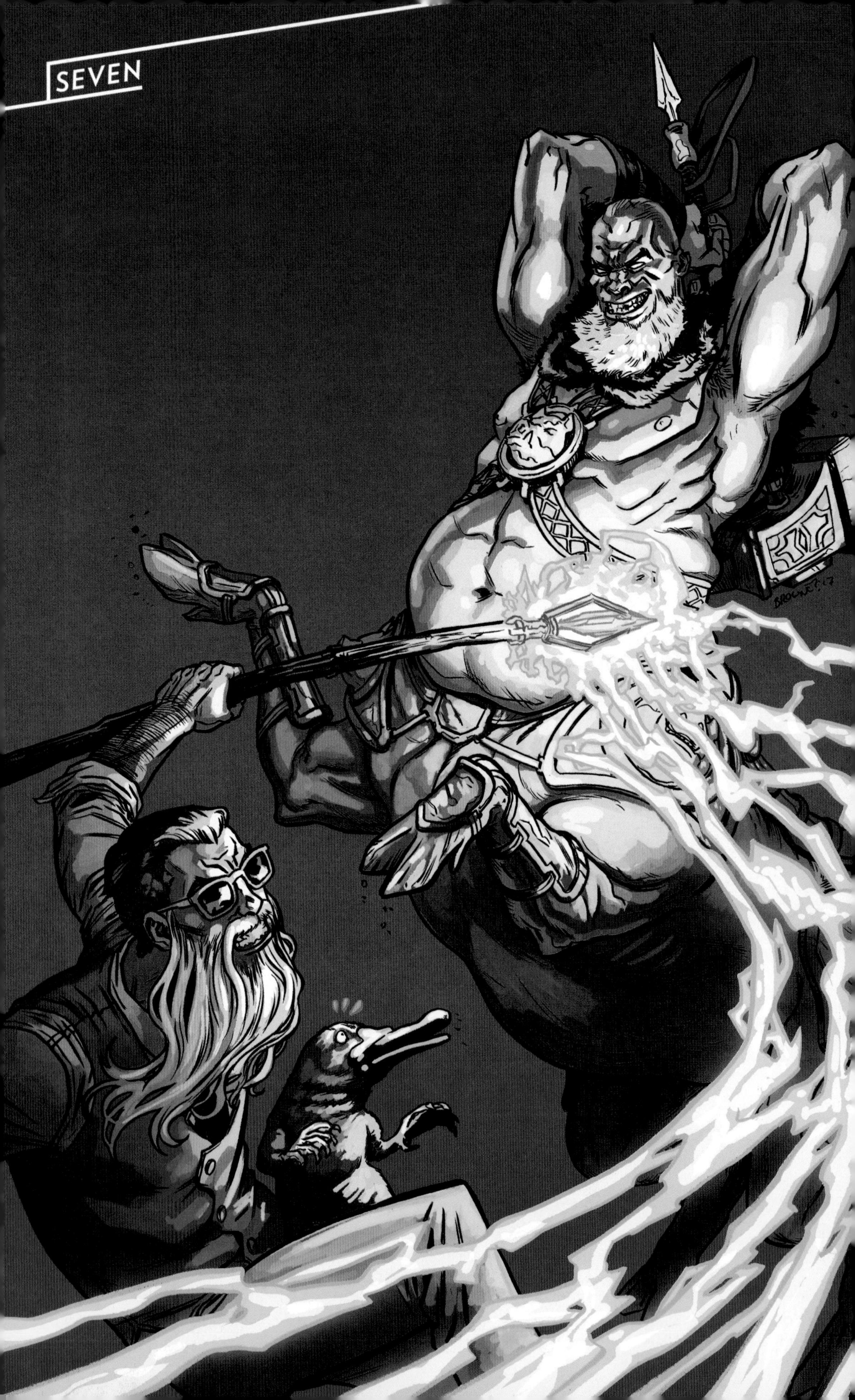

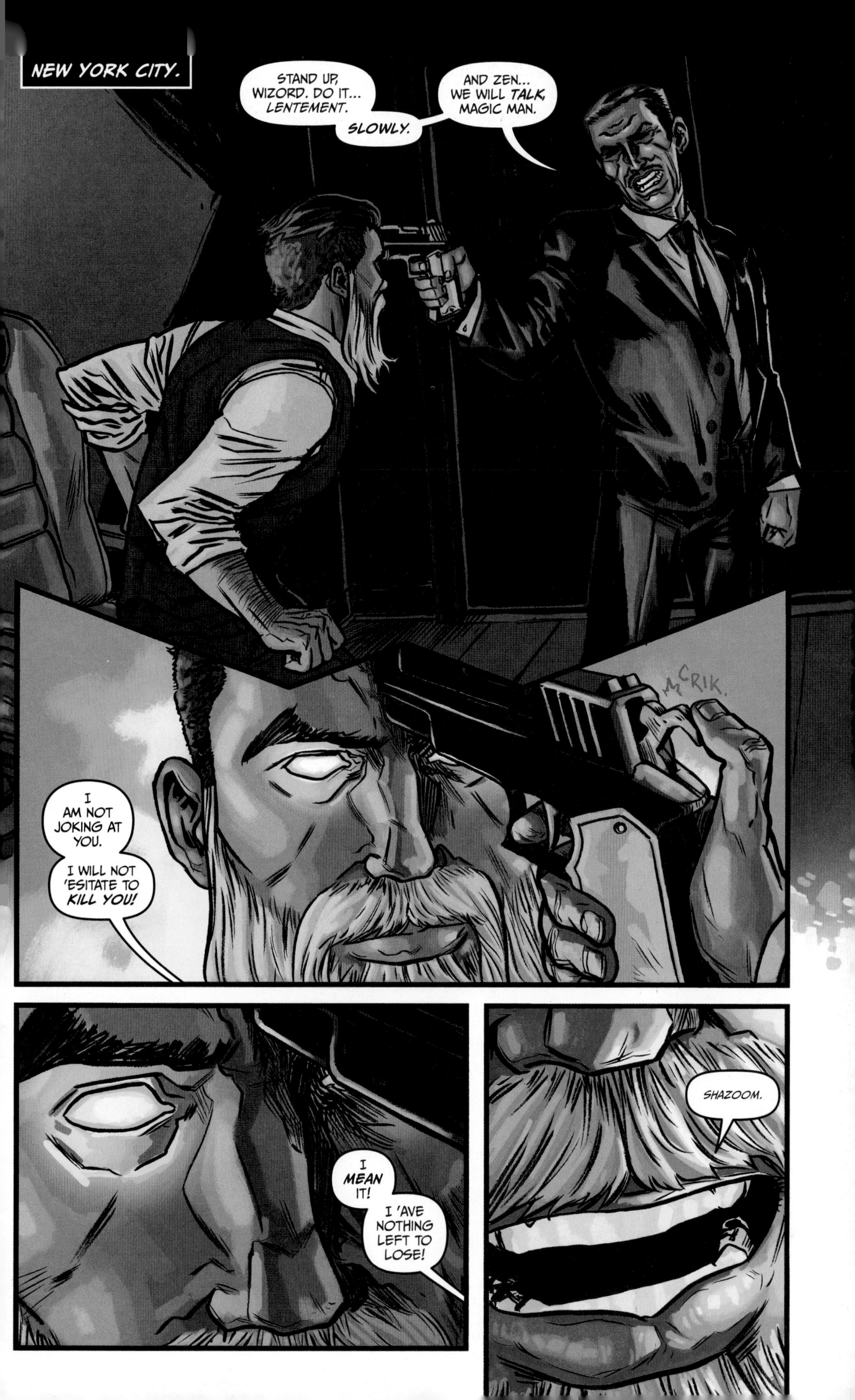
NEW YORK CITY.
STAND UP, WIZORD. DO IT... LENTEMENT.
SLOWLY.
AND ZEN... WE WILL TALK, MAGIC MAN.
CRIK.
I AM NOT JOKING AT YOU.
I WILL NOT 'ESITATE TO KILL YOU!
I MEAN IT!
I 'AVE NOTHING LEFT TO LOSE!
SHAZOOM.

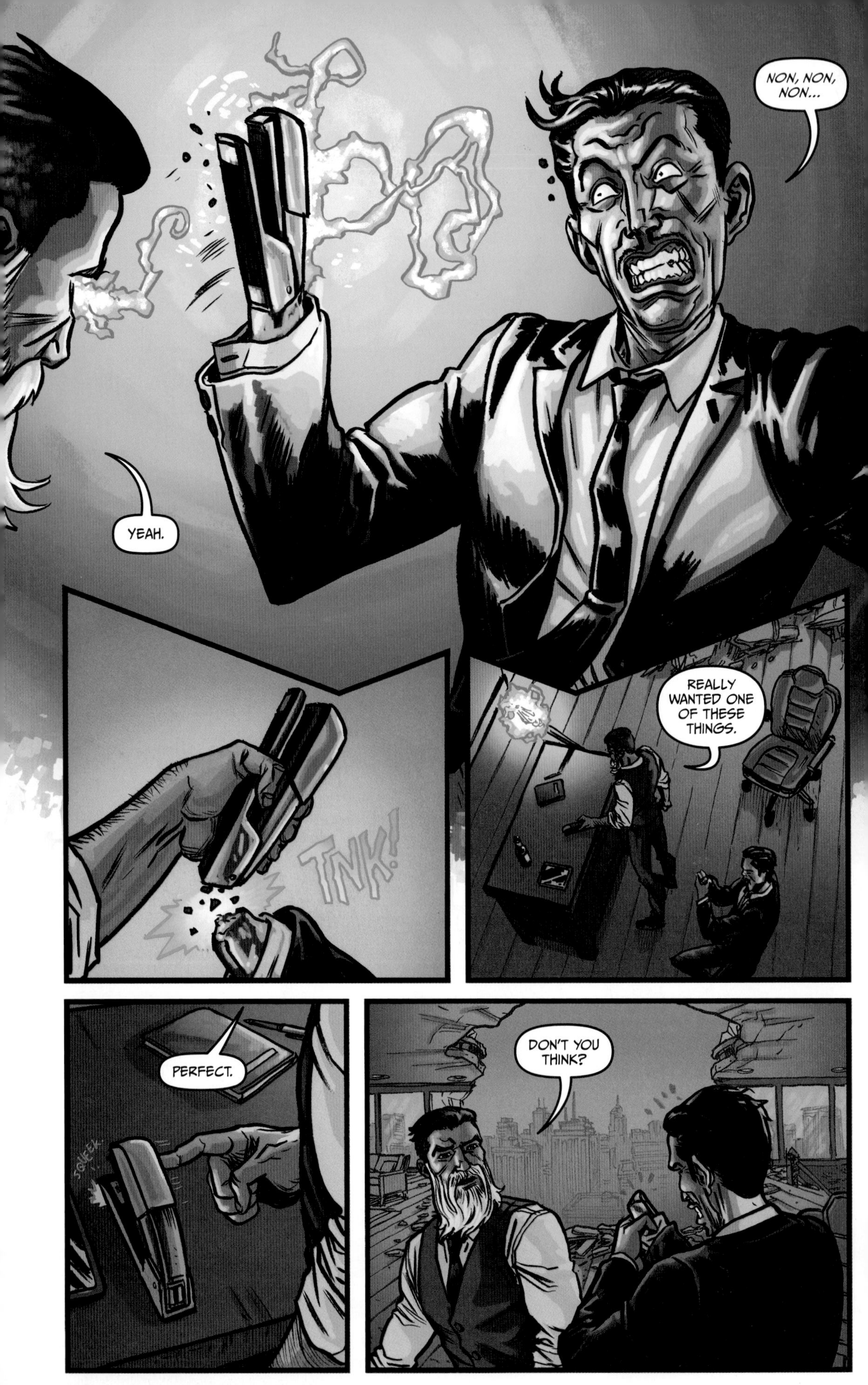
NON, NON, NON...
YEAH.
TNK!
REALLY WANTED ONE OF THESE THINGS.
PERFECT.
SQUEEK
DON'T YOU THINK?

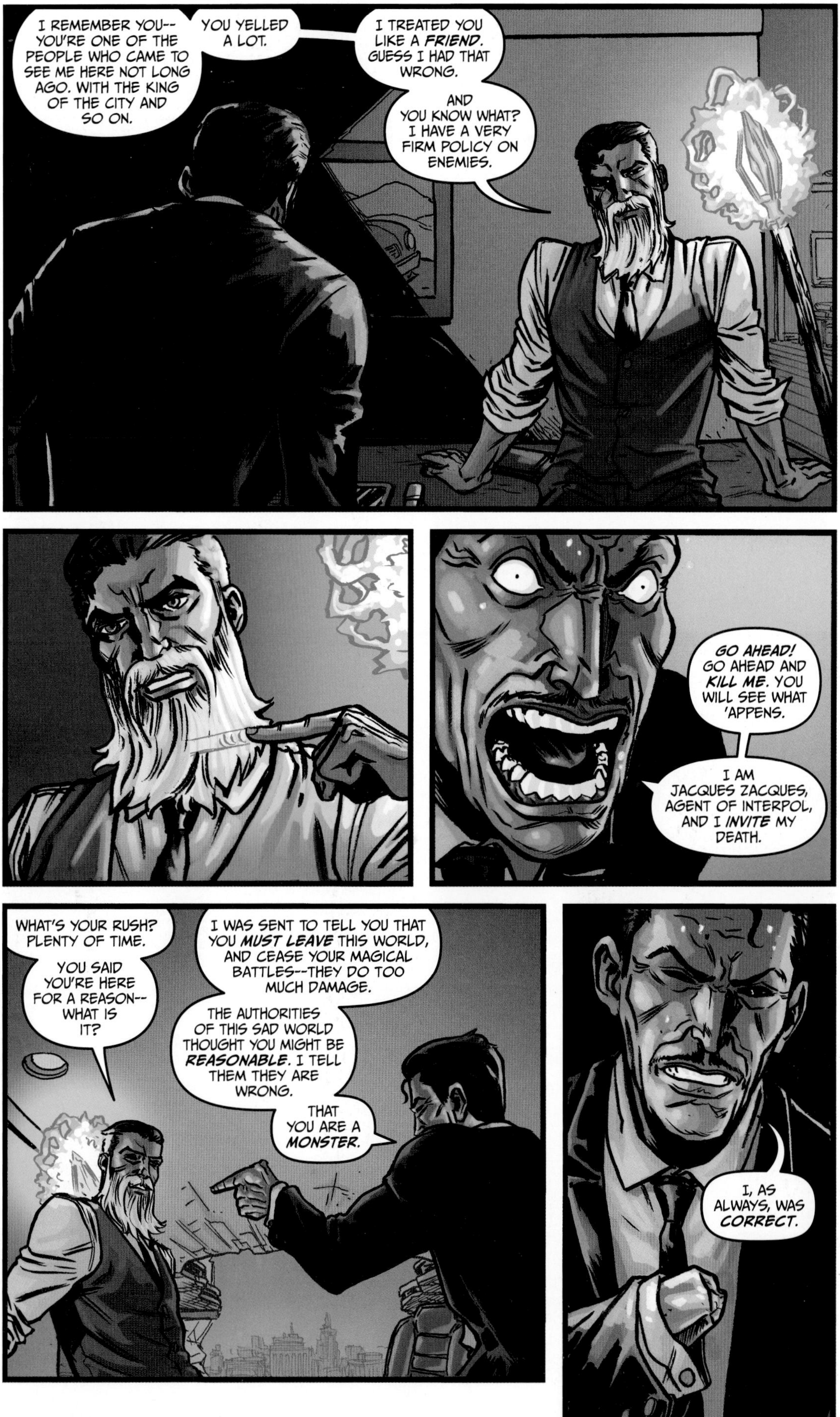
I REMEMBER YOU--YOU'RE ONE OF THE PEOPLE WHO CAME TO SEE ME HERE NOT LONG AGO. WITH THE KING OF THE CITY AND SO ON.
YOU YELLED A LOT.
I TREATED YOU LIKE A FRIEND. GUESS I HAD THAT WRONG.
AND YOU KNOW WHAT? I HAVE A VERY FIRM POLICY ON ENEMIES.
GO AHEAD! GO AHEAD AND KILL ME. YOU WILL SEE WHAT 'APPENS.
I AM JACQUES ZACQUES, AGENT OF INTERPOL, AND I INVITE MY DEATH.
WHAT'S YOUR RUSH? PLENTY OF TIME.
YOU SAID YOU'RE HERE FOR A REASON--WHAT IS IT?
I WAS SENT TO TELL YOU THAT YOU MUST LEAVE THIS WORLD, AND CEASE YOUR MAGICAL BATTLES--THEY DO TOO MUCH DAMAGE.
THE AUTHORITIES OF THIS SAD WORLD THOUGHT YOU MIGHT BE REASONABLE. I TELL THEM THEY ARE WRONG.
THAT YOU ARE A MONSTER.
I, AS ALWAYS, WAS CORRECT.

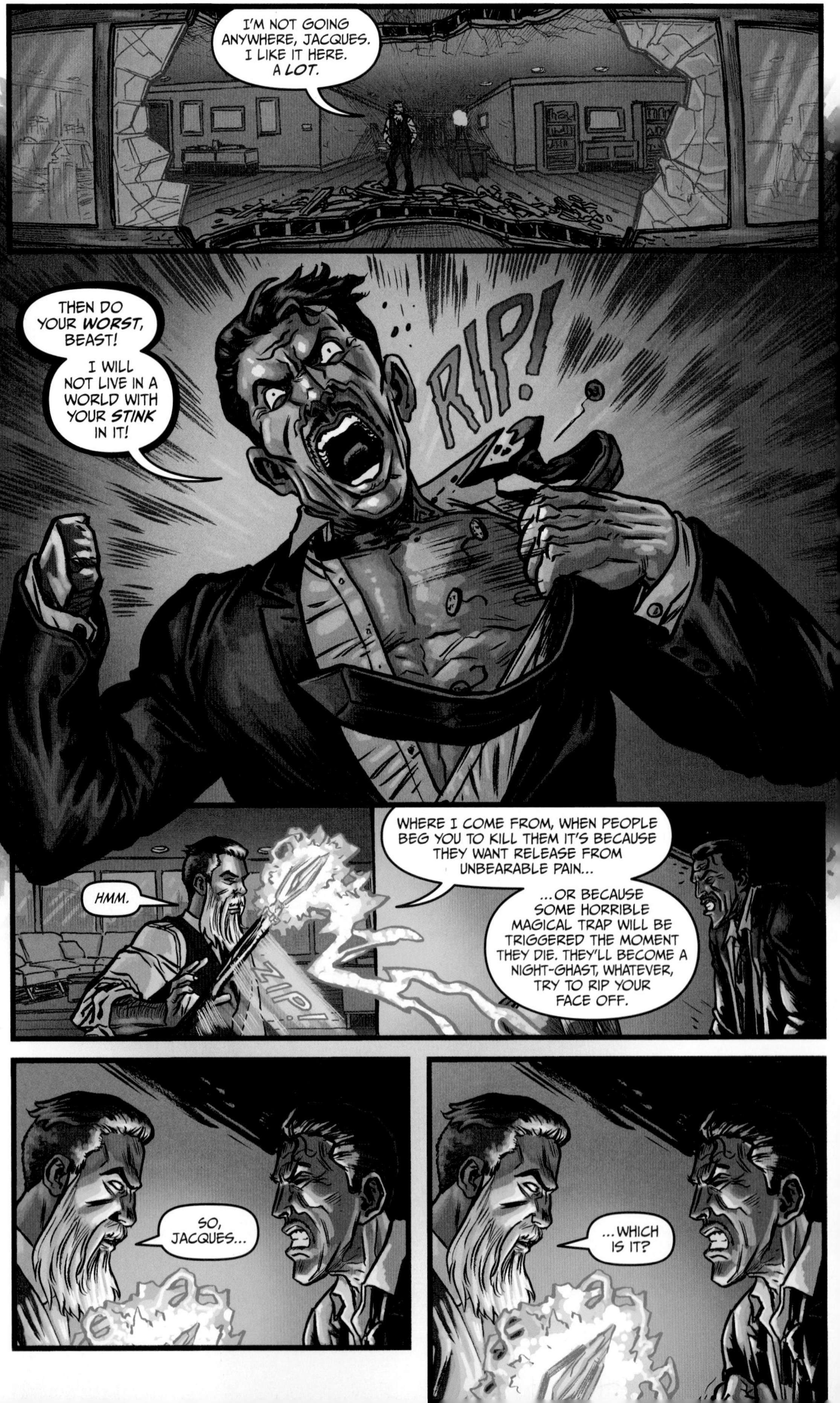
I'M NOT GOING ANYWHERE, JACQUES. I LIKE IT HERE. A LOT.
THEN DO YOUR WORST, BEAST!
I WILL NOT LIVE IN A WORLD WITH YOUR STINK IN IT!
RIP!
HMM.
WHERE I COME FROM, WHEN PEOPLE BEG YOU TO KILL THEM IT'S BECAUSE THEY WANT RELEASE FROM UNBEARABLE PAIN...
...OR BECAUSE SOME HORRIBLE MAGICAL TRAP WILL BE TRIGGERED THE MOMENT THEY DIE. THEY'LL BECOME A NIGHT-GHAST, WHATEVER, TRY TO RIP YOUR FACE OFF.
ZIP!
SO, JACQUES...
...WHICH IS IT?

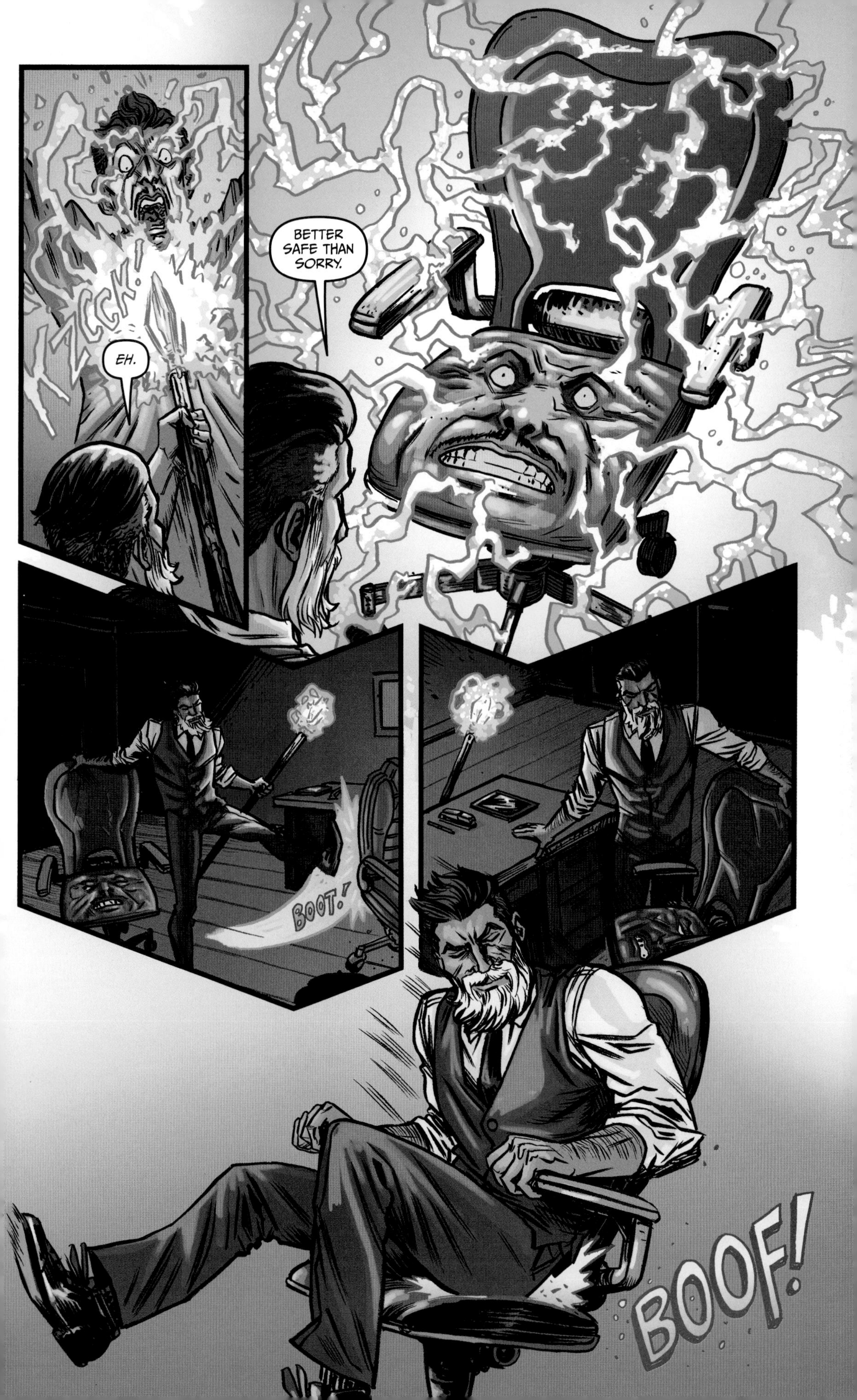
ZZCCK!
EH.
BETTER SAFE THAN SORRY.
BOOT!
BOOF!

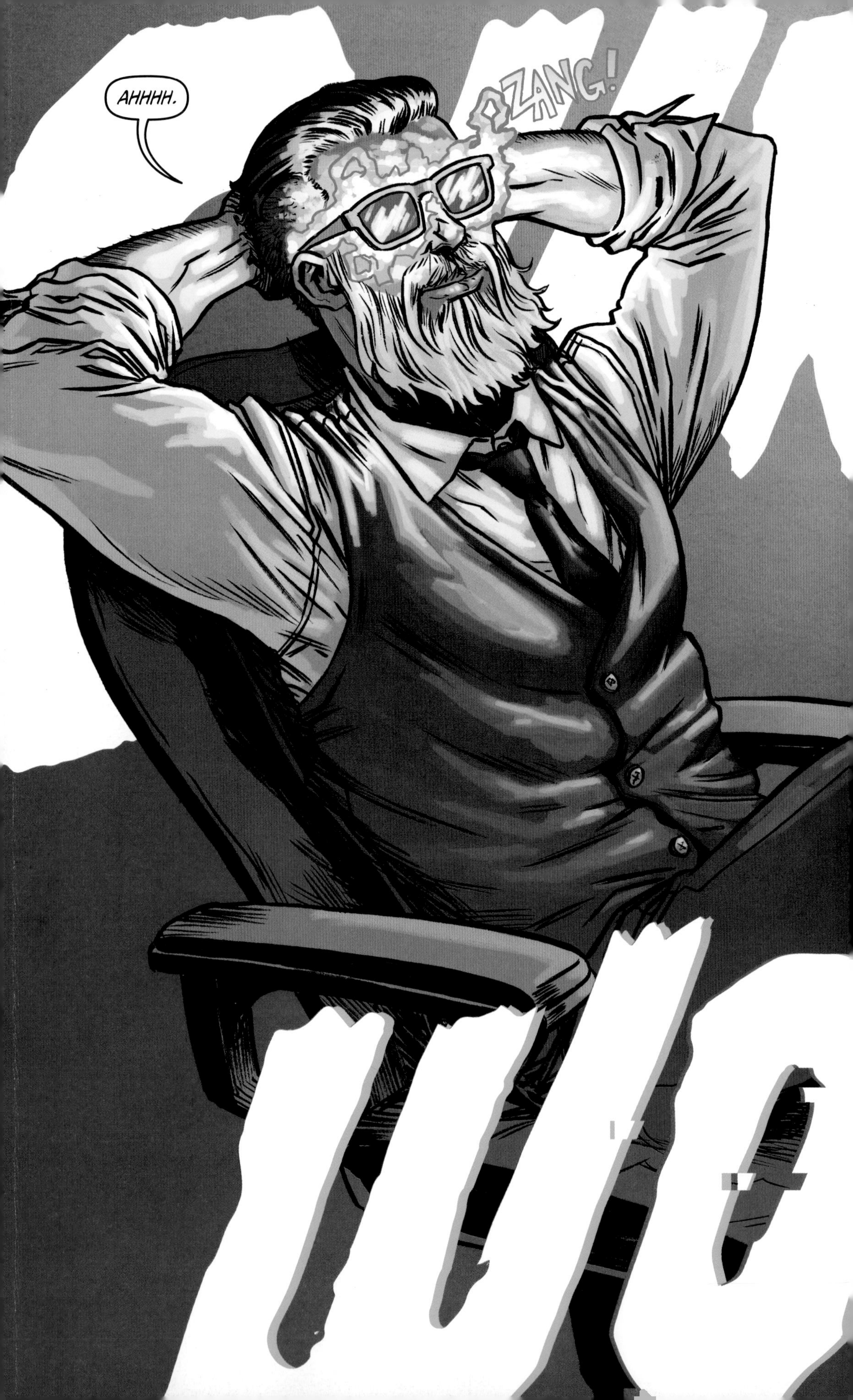
AHHHH.
ZZANG!

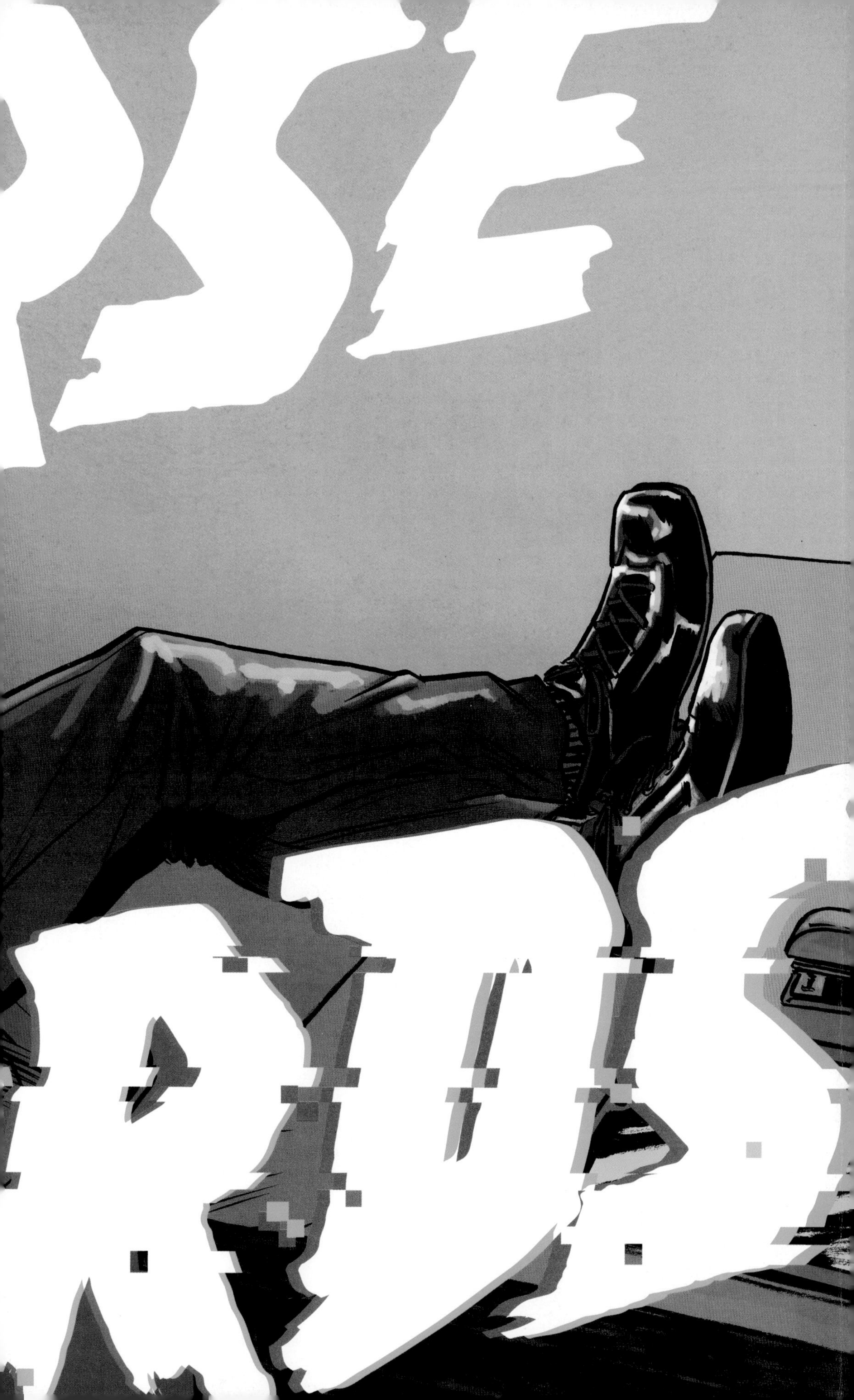

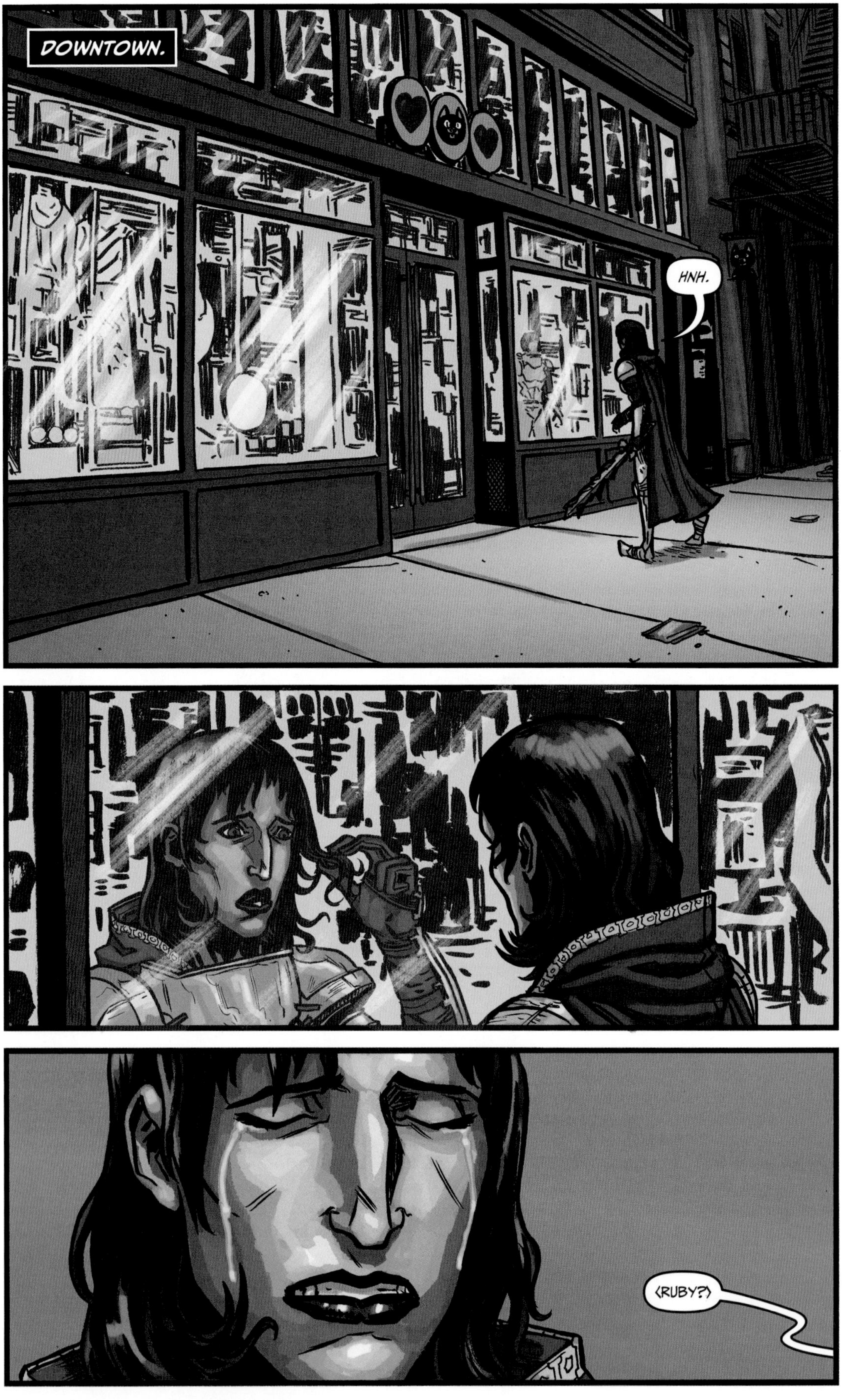
DOWNTOWN.
HNH.
‹RUBY?›

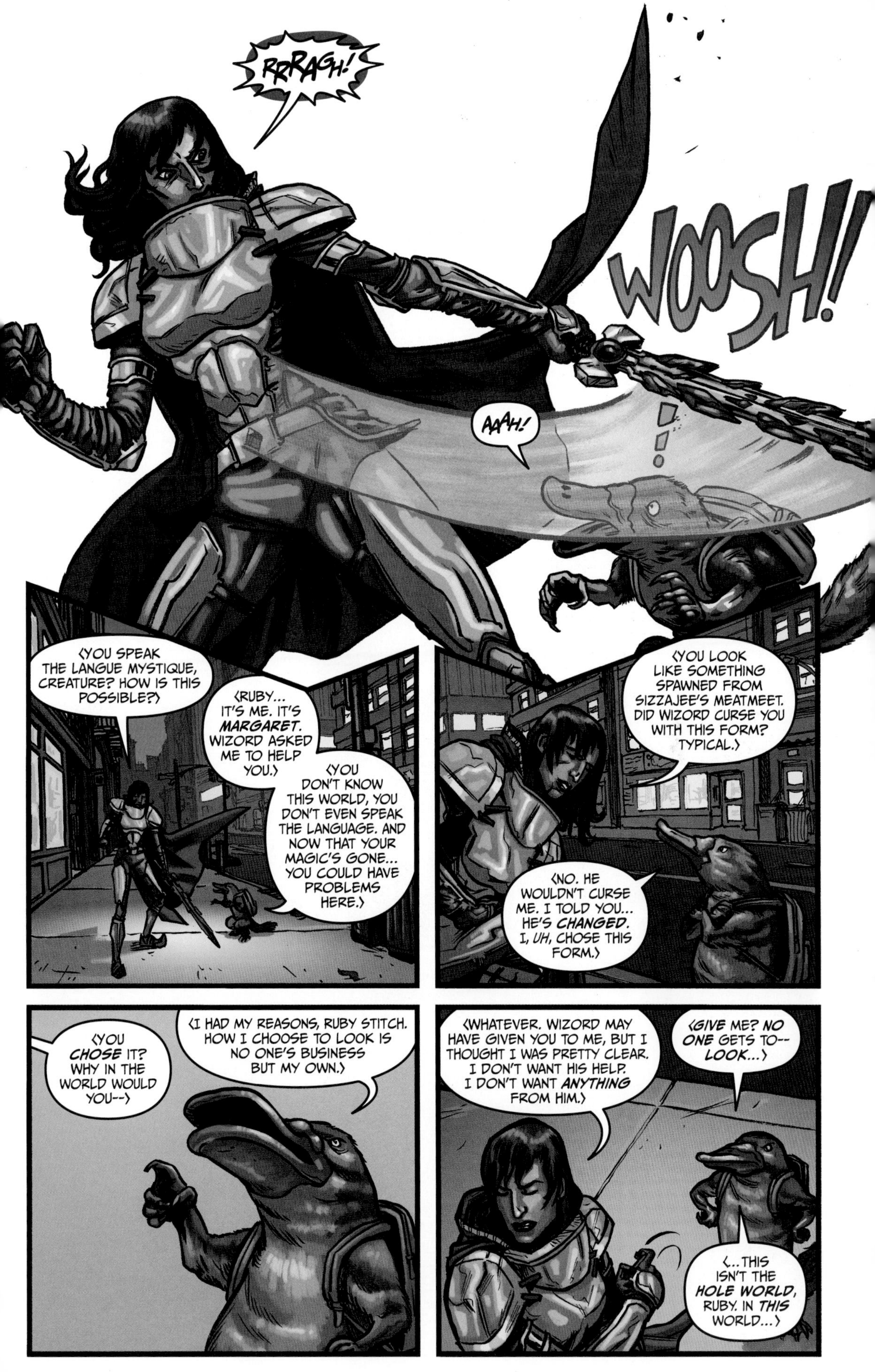
RRRAGH!
WOOSH!!
AAAH!
!
‹YOU SPEAK THE LANGUE MYSTIQUE, CREATURE? HOW IS THIS POSSIBLE?›
‹RUBY... IT'S ME. IT'S MARGARET. WIZORD ASKED ME TO HELP YOU.›
‹YOU DON'T KNOW THIS WORLD, YOU DON'T EVEN SPEAK THE LANGUAGE. AND NOW THAT YOUR MAGIC'S GONE... YOU COULD HAVE PROBLEMS HERE.›
‹YOU LOOK LIKE SOMETHING SPAWNED FROM SIZZAJEE'S MEATMEET. DID WIZORD CURSE YOU WITH THIS FORM? TYPICAL.›
‹NO. HE WOULDN'T CURSE ME. I TOLD YOU... HE'S CHANGED. I, UH, CHOSE THIS FORM.›
‹YOU CHOSE IT? WHY IN THE WORLD WOULD YOU--›
‹I HAD MY REASONS, RUBY STITCH. HOW I CHOOSE TO LOOK IS NO ONE'S BUSINESS BUT MY OWN.›
‹WHATEVER. WIZORD MAY HAVE GIVEN YOU TO ME, BUT I THOUGHT I WAS PRETTY CLEAR. I DON'T WANT HIS HELP. I DON'T WANT ANYTHING FROM HIM.›
‹GIVE ME? NO ONE GETS TO-- LOOK...›
‹...THIS ISN'T THE HOLE WORLD, RUBY. IN THIS WORLD...›

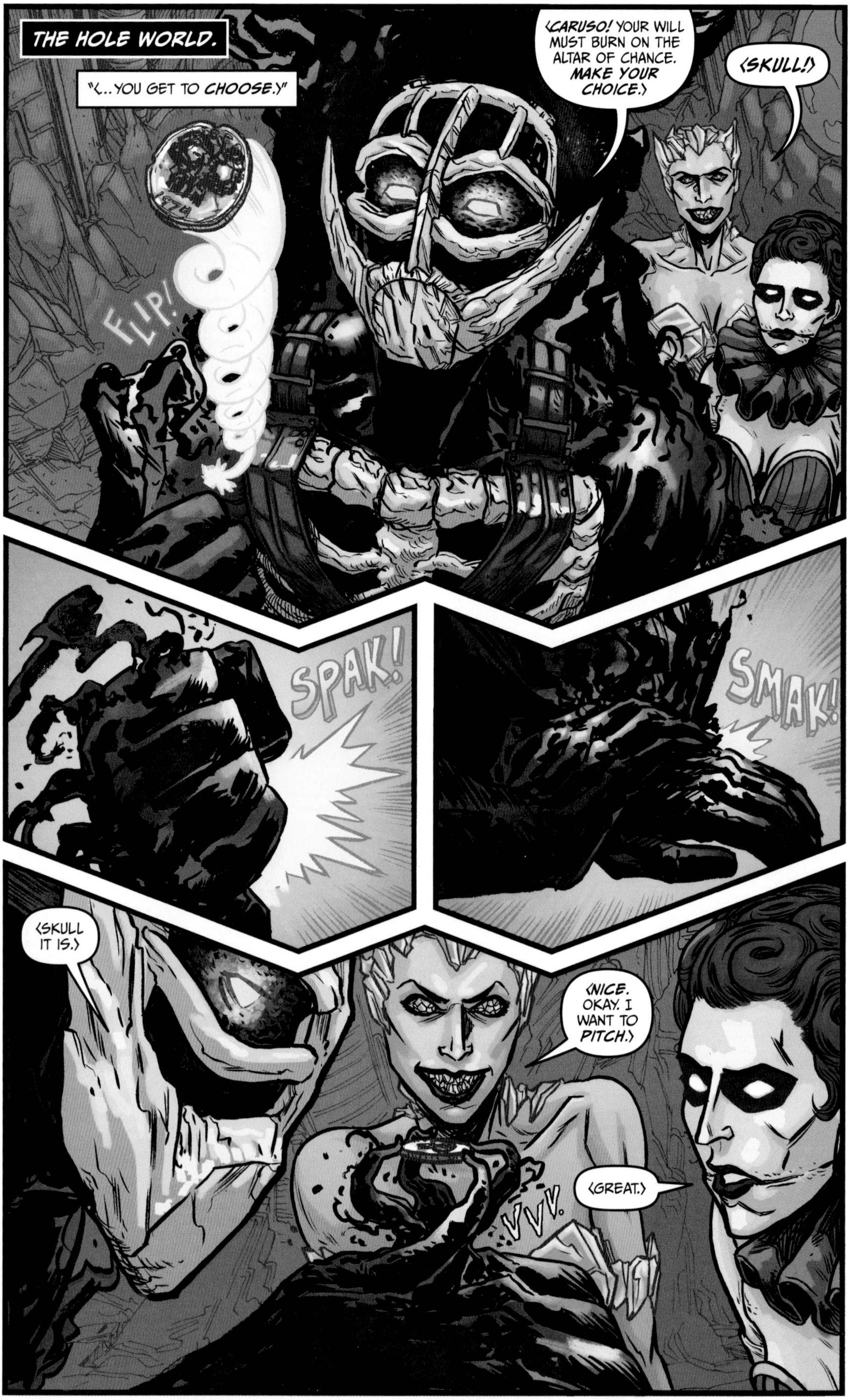
THE HOLE WORLD.
"‹...YOU GET TO CHOOSE.›"
‹CARUSO! YOUR WILL MUST BURN ON THE ALTAR OF CHANCE. MAKE YOUR CHOICE.›
‹SKULL!›
FLIP!
SPAK!
SMAK!
‹SKULL IT IS.›
‹NICE. OKAY. I WANT TO PITCH.›
‹GREAT.›
VVV.

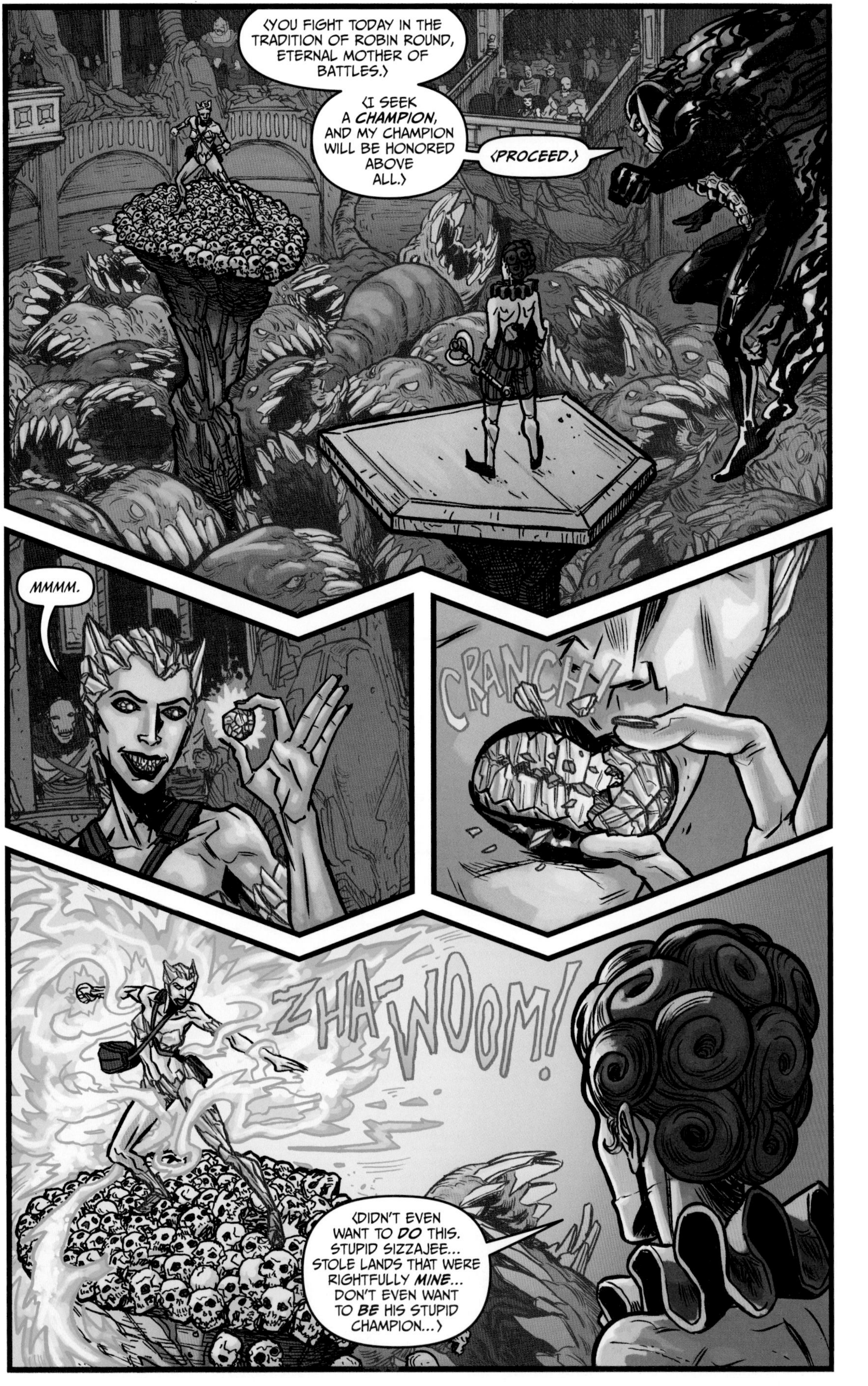
⟨YOU FIGHT TODAY IN THE TRADITION OF ROBIN ROUND, ETERNAL MOTHER OF BATTLES.⟩
⟨I SEEK A *CHAMPION*, AND MY CHAMPION WILL BE HONORED ABOVE ALL.⟩
⟨*PROCEED.*⟩
MMMM.
CRANCH!
ZHA-WOOM!
⟨DIDN'T EVEN WANT TO *DO* THIS. STUPID SIZZAJEE... STOLE LANDS THAT WERE RIGHTFULLY *MINE*... DON'T EVEN WANT TO *BE* HIS STUPID CHAMPION...⟩

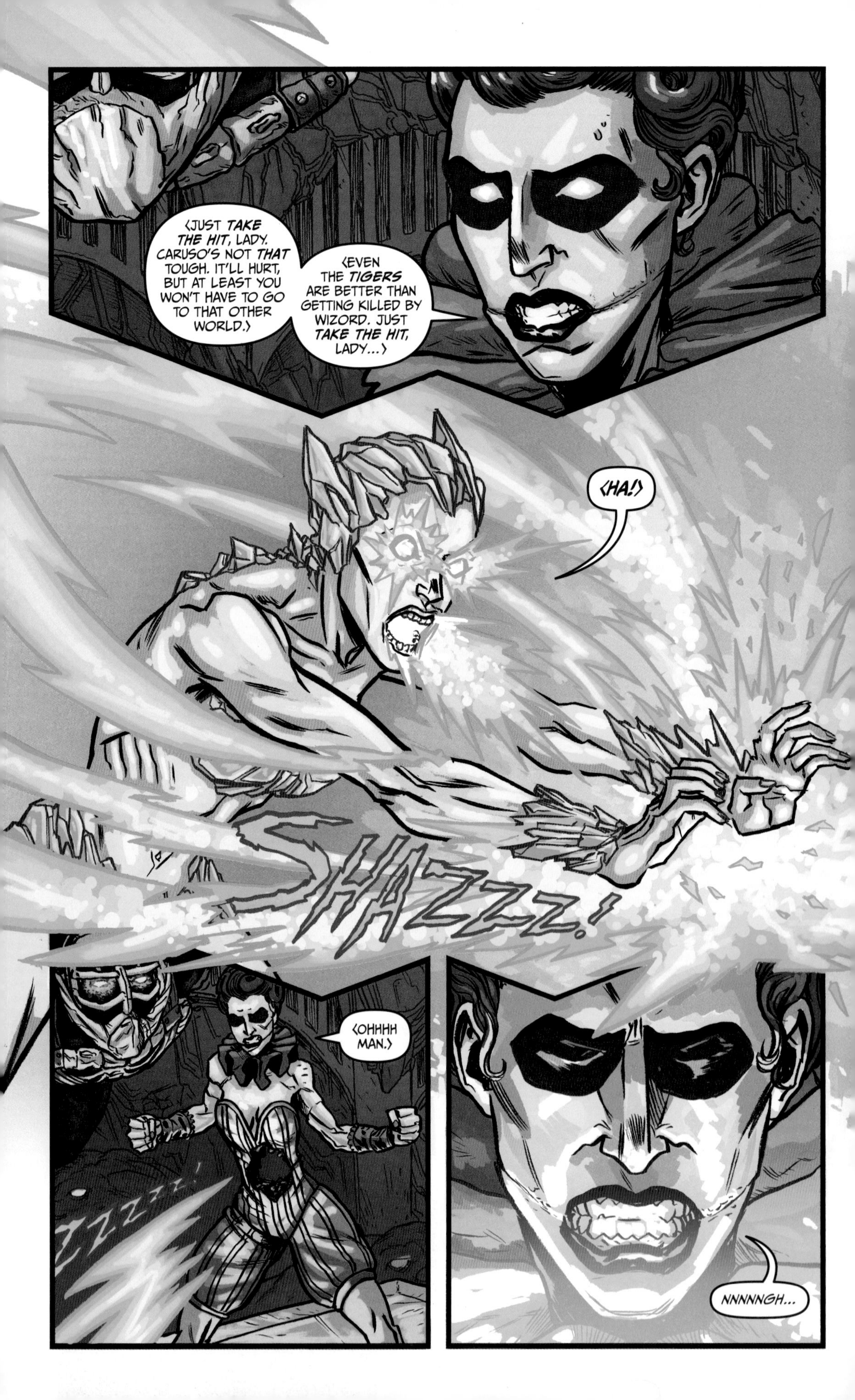
⟨JUST TAKE THE HIT, LADY. CARUSO'S NOT THAT TOUGH. IT'LL HURT, BUT AT LEAST YOU WON'T HAVE TO GO TO THAT OTHER WORLD.⟩
⟨EVEN THE TIGERS ARE BETTER THAN GETTING KILLED BY WIZORD. JUST TAKE THE HIT, LADY...⟩
⟨HA!⟩
SHAZZZZ!
⟨OHHHH MAN.⟩
NNNNNGH...

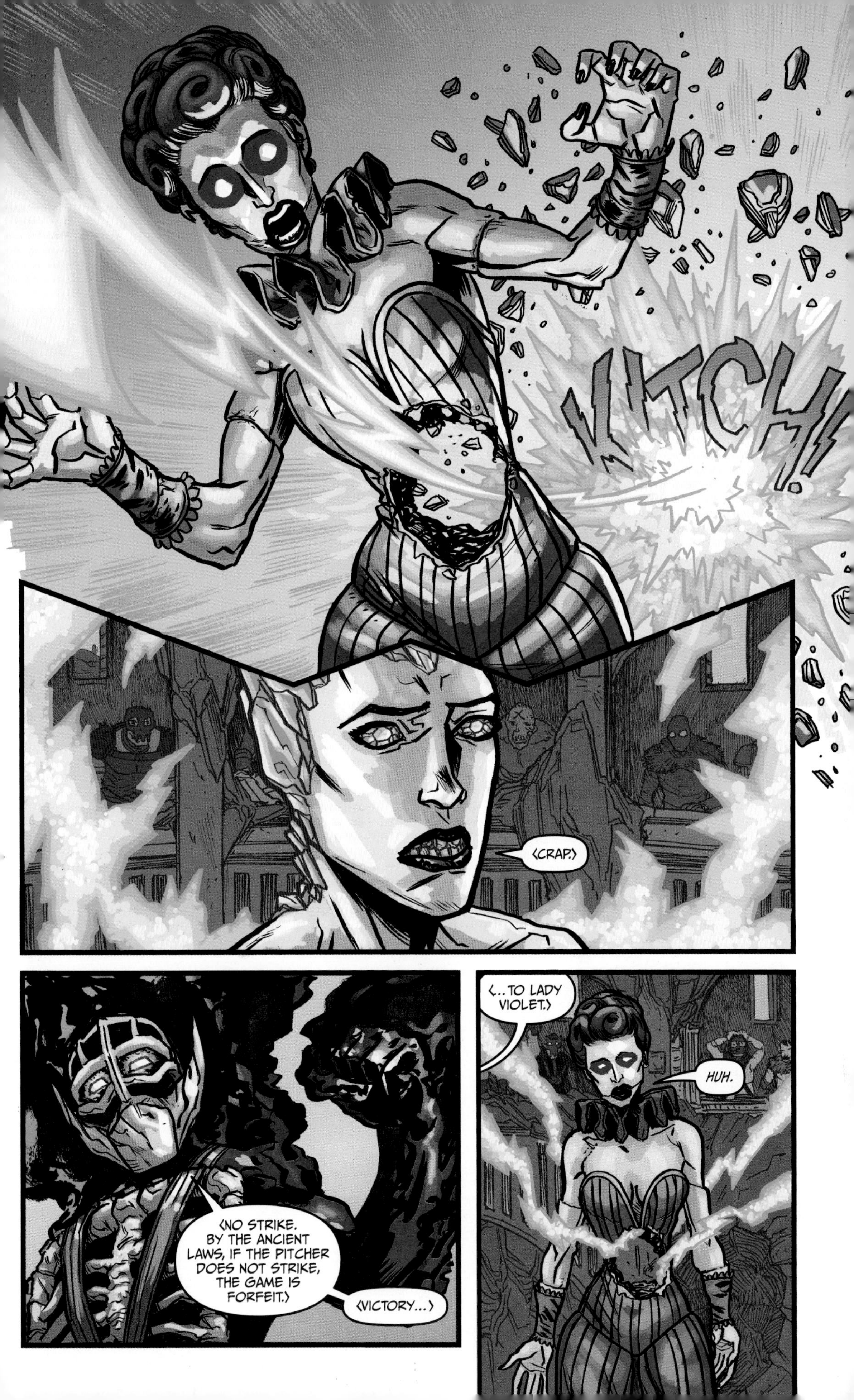
VITCH!
‹CRAP.›
‹NO STRIKE. BY THE ANCIENT LAWS, IF THE PITCHER DOES NOT STRIKE, THE GAME IS FORFEIT.›
‹VICTORY...›
‹...TO LADY VIOLET.›
HUH.

WHAT IS *HAPPENING* IN THERE?

ZACQUES IS ALIVE, MR. PRESIDENT--WE'RE STILL GETTING HIS BIOMETRIC READINGS. BUT BEYOND THAT, WE CAN'T SAY.

THE LITTLE AUDIO WE CAN PICK UP SUGGESTS THAT WIZORD IS... WELL...

WHITE HOUSE SITUATION ROOM.

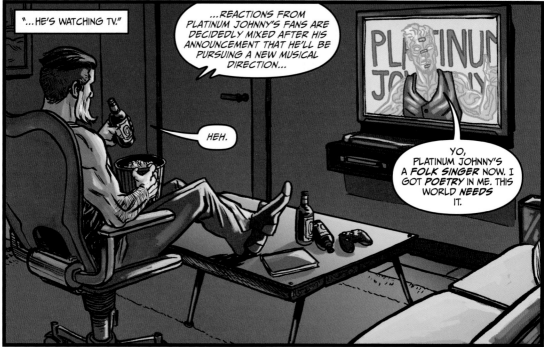

"...HE'S WATCHING TV."

...REACTIONS FROM PLATINUM JOHNNY'S FANS ARE DECIDEDLY MIXED AFTER HIS ANNOUNCEMENT THAT HE'LL BE PURSUING A NEW MUSICAL DIRECTION...

HEH.

YO, PLATINUM JOHNNY'S A *FOLK SINGER* NOW. I GOT *POETRY* IN ME. THIS WORLD *NEEDS* IT.

SIR, THE DIPLOMATIC APPROACH SEEMS TO HAVE FAILED.

THE DANGER WIZORD REPRESENTS IS CLEAR, AND THE CITY'S BEEN EVACUATED. WE MAY NEVER GET ANOTHER CHANCE LIKE THIS. IT'S YOUR CALL, BUT...

I *KNOW*, AJ. JUST... LAUNCH, ALL RIGHT?

"LAUNCH, AND MAY GOD HELP US ALL."

VOOOOOOOOSH!

RIGHT ON. RIGHT *ON*.

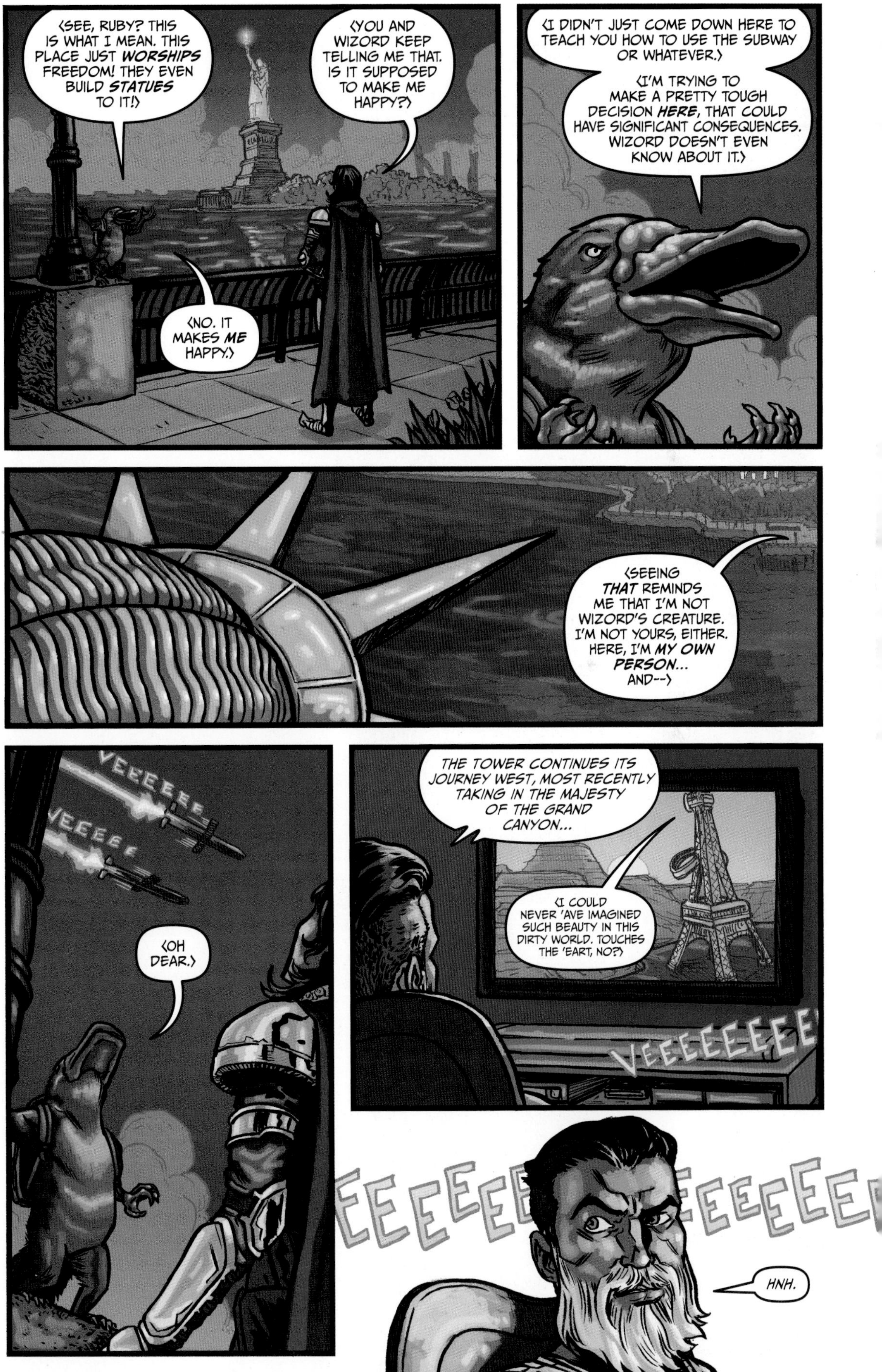

‹SEE, RUBY? THIS IS WHAT I MEAN. THIS PLACE JUST ***WORSHIPS*** FREEDOM! THEY EVEN BUILD ***STATUES*** TO IT!›
‹YOU AND WIZORD KEEP TELLING ME THAT. IS IT SUPPOSED TO MAKE ME HAPPY?›
‹NO. IT MAKES ***ME*** HAPPY.›
‹I DIDN'T JUST COME DOWN HERE TO TEACH YOU HOW TO USE THE SUBWAY OR WHATEVER.›
‹I'M TRYING TO MAKE A PRETTY TOUGH DECISION ***HERE***, THAT COULD HAVE SIGNIFICANT CONSEQUENCES. WIZORD DOESN'T EVEN KNOW ABOUT IT.›
‹SEEING ***THAT*** REMINDS ME THAT I'M NOT WIZORD'S CREATURE. I'M NOT YOURS, EITHER. HERE, I'M ***MY OWN PERSON...*** AND--›
VEEEEEEE
VEEEEEE
‹OH DEAR.›
THE TOWER CONTINUES ITS JOURNEY WEST, MOST RECENTLY TAKING IN THE MAJESTY OF THE GRAND CANYON...
‹I COULD NEVER 'AVE IMAGINED SUCH BEAUTY IN THIS DIRTY WORLD. TOUCHES THE 'EART, NO?›
VEEEEEEEEE
EEEEEEEEEEEEEEEEE
HNH.
CREEK

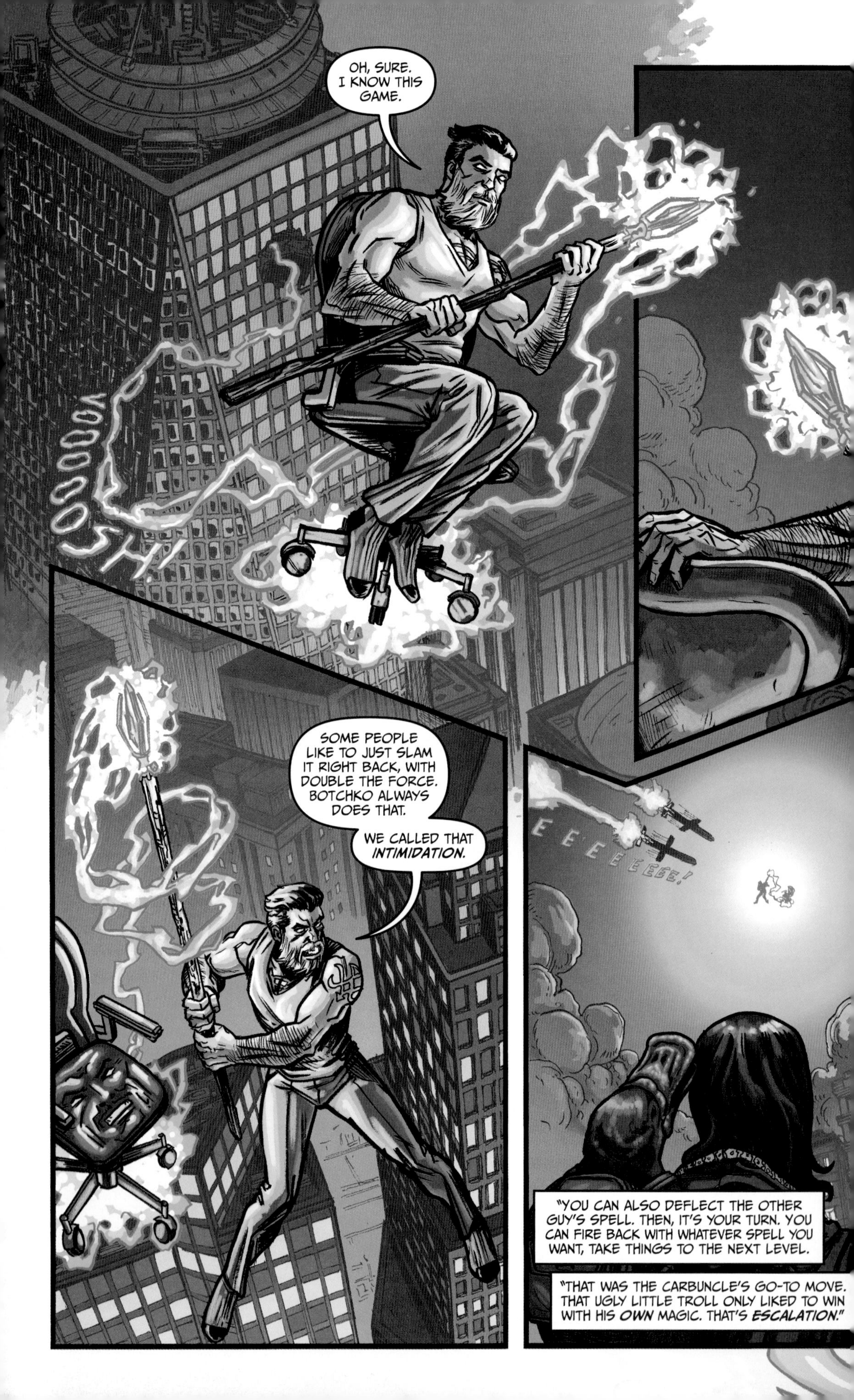

OH, SURE. I KNOW THIS GAME.
VOOOOOOSH!
SOME PEOPLE LIKE TO JUST SLAM IT RIGHT BACK, WITH DOUBLE THE FORCE. BOTCHKO ALWAYS DOES THAT.
WE CALLED THAT *INTIMIDATION.*
EEEEEEEEEE!
"YOU CAN ALSO DEFLECT THE OTHER GUY'S SPELL. THEN, IT'S YOUR TURN. YOU CAN FIRE BACK WITH WHATEVER SPELL YOU WANT, TAKE THINGS TO THE NEXT LEVEL.
"THAT WAS THE CARBUNCLE'S GO-TO MOVE. THAT UGLY LITTLE TROLL ONLY LIKED TO WIN WITH HIS ***OWN*** MAGIC. THAT'S ***ESCALATION.***"

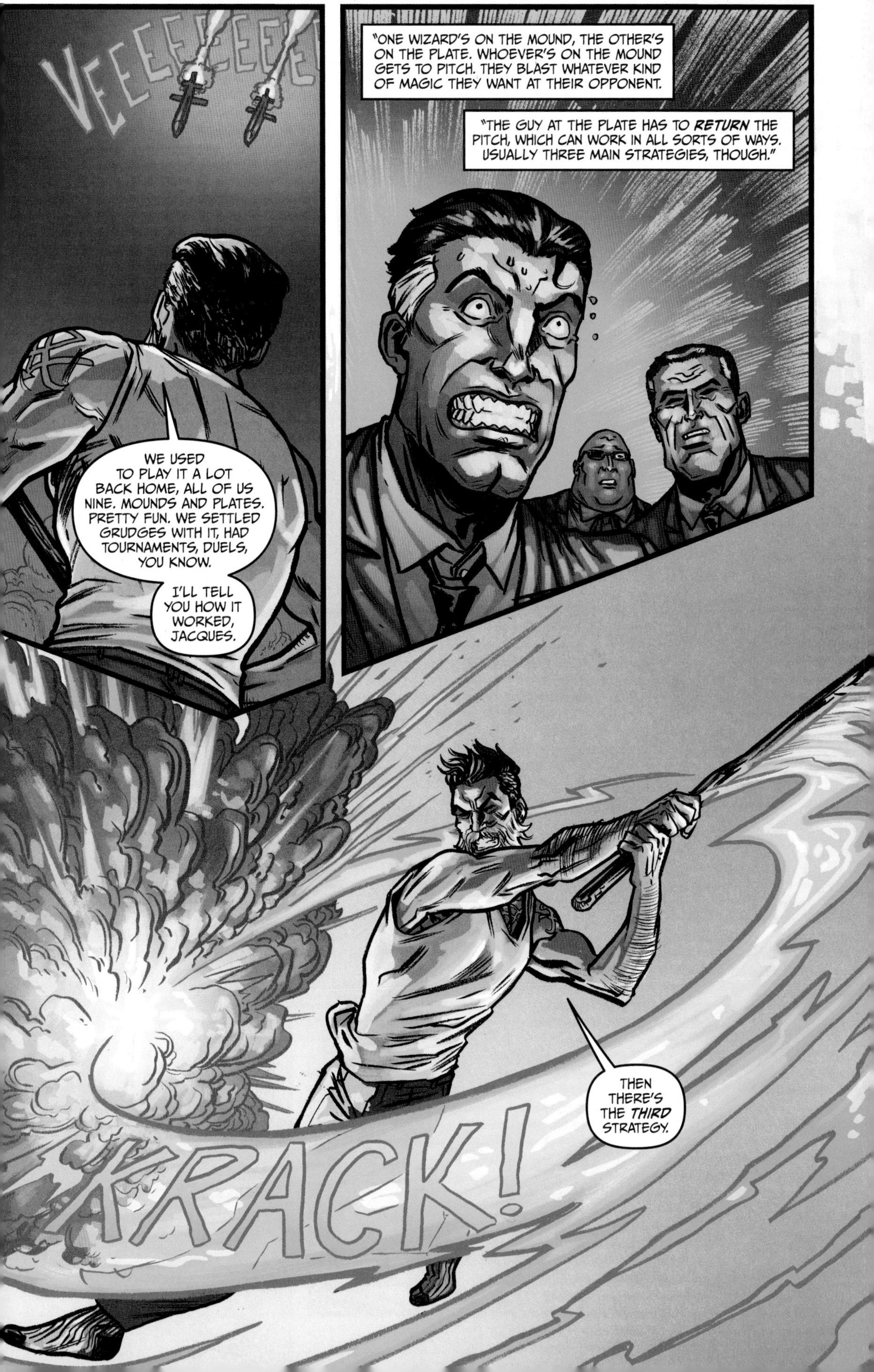
VEEEEEEEEE
WE USED TO PLAY IT A LOT BACK HOME, ALL OF US NINE. MOUNDS AND PLATES. PRETTY FUN. WE SETTLED GRUDGES WITH IT, HAD TOURNAMENTS, DUELS, YOU KNOW.
I'LL TELL YOU HOW IT WORKED, JACQUES.
"ONE WIZARD'S ON THE MOUND, THE OTHER'S ON THE PLATE. WHOEVER'S ON THE MOUND GETS TO PITCH. THEY BLAST WHATEVER KIND OF MAGIC THEY WANT AT THEIR OPPONENT.
"THE GUY AT THE PLATE HAS TO ***RETURN*** THE PITCH, WHICH CAN WORK IN ALL SORTS OF WAYS. USUALLY THREE MAIN STRATEGIES, THOUGH."
THEN THERE'S THE ***THIRD*** STRATEGY.
KRACK!

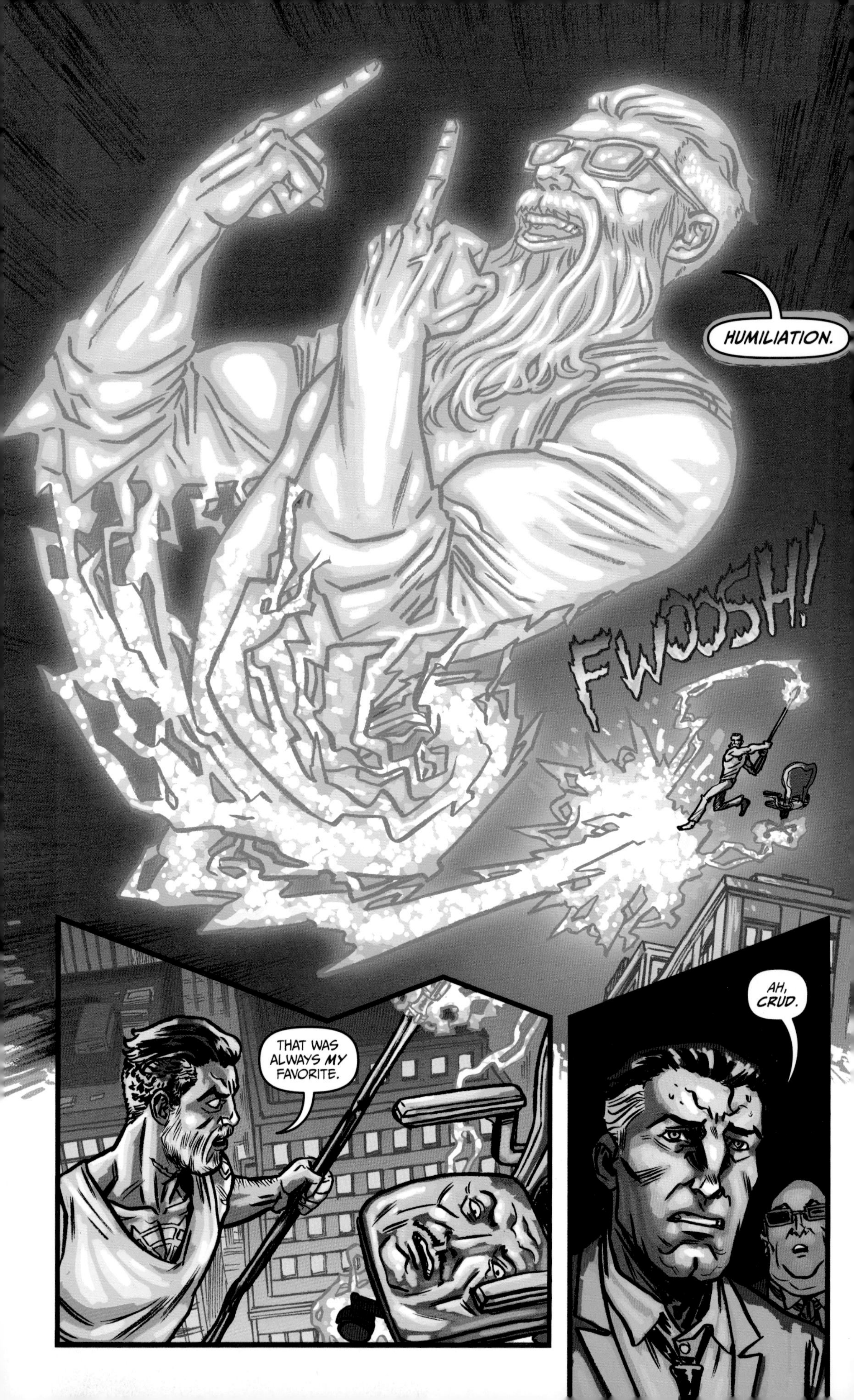
HUMILIATION.
FWOOSH!
THAT WAS ALWAYS MY FAVORITE.
AH, CRUD.

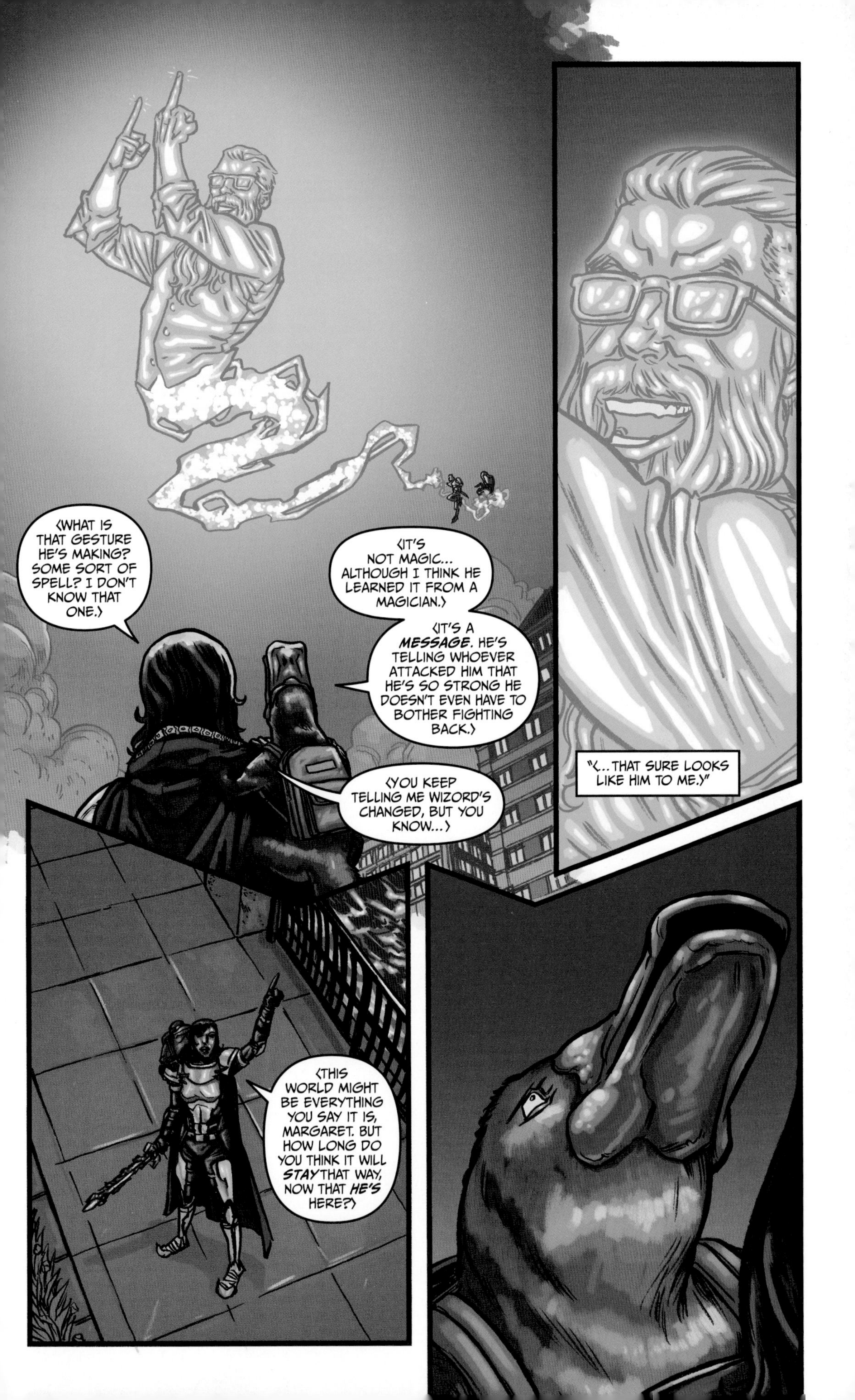

‹WHAT IS THAT GESTURE HE'S MAKING? SOME SORT OF SPELL? I DON'T KNOW THAT ONE.›
‹IT'S NOT MAGIC... ALTHOUGH I THINK HE LEARNED IT FROM A MAGICIAN.›
‹IT'S A *MESSAGE*. HE'S TELLING WHOEVER ATTACKED HIM THAT HE'S SO STRONG HE DOESN'T EVEN HAVE TO BOTHER FIGHTING BACK.›
‹YOU KEEP TELLING ME WIZORD'S CHANGED, BUT YOU KNOW...›
"‹...THAT SURE LOOKS LIKE HIM TO ME.›"
‹THIS WORLD MIGHT BE EVERYTHING YOU SAY IT IS, MARGARET. BUT HOW LONG DO YOU THINK IT WILL *STAY* THAT WAY, NOW THAT *HE'S* HERE?›

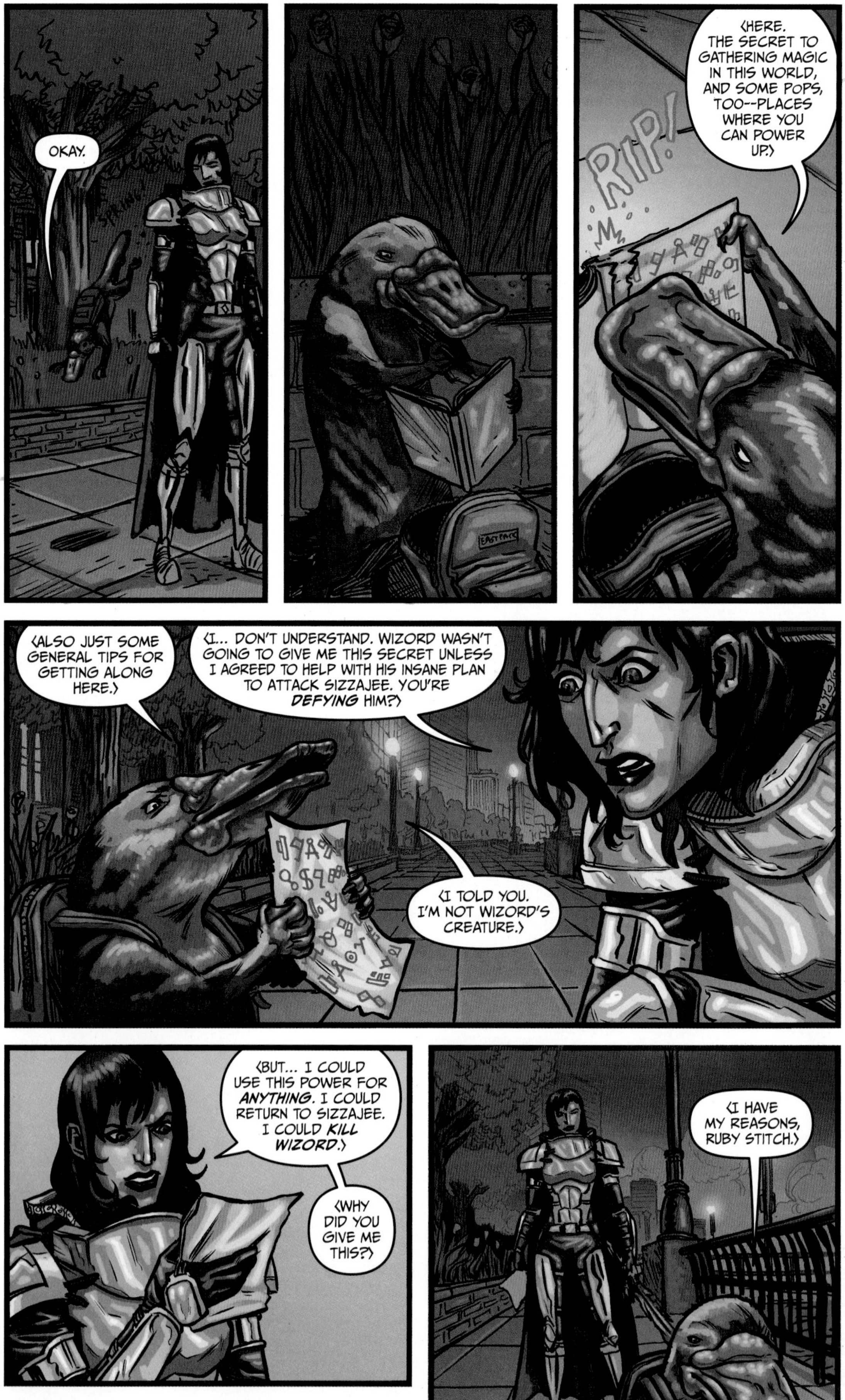
OKAY.
⟨HERE. THE SECRET TO GATHERING MAGIC IN THIS WORLD, AND SOME POPS, TOO--PLACES WHERE YOU CAN POWER UP.⟩
RIP!
⟨ALSO JUST SOME GENERAL TIPS FOR GETTING ALONG HERE.⟩
⟨I... DON'T UNDERSTAND. WIZORD WASN'T GOING TO GIVE ME THIS SECRET UNLESS I AGREED TO HELP WITH HIS INSANE PLAN TO ATTACK SIZZAJEE. YOU'RE *DEFYING* HIM?⟩
⟨I TOLD YOU. I'M NOT WIZORD'S CREATURE.⟩
⟨BUT... I COULD USE THIS POWER FOR *ANYTHING*. I COULD RETURN TO SIZZAJEE. I COULD *KILL WIZORD*.⟩
⟨WHY DID YOU GIVE ME THIS?⟩
⟨I HAVE MY REASONS, RUBY STITCH.⟩

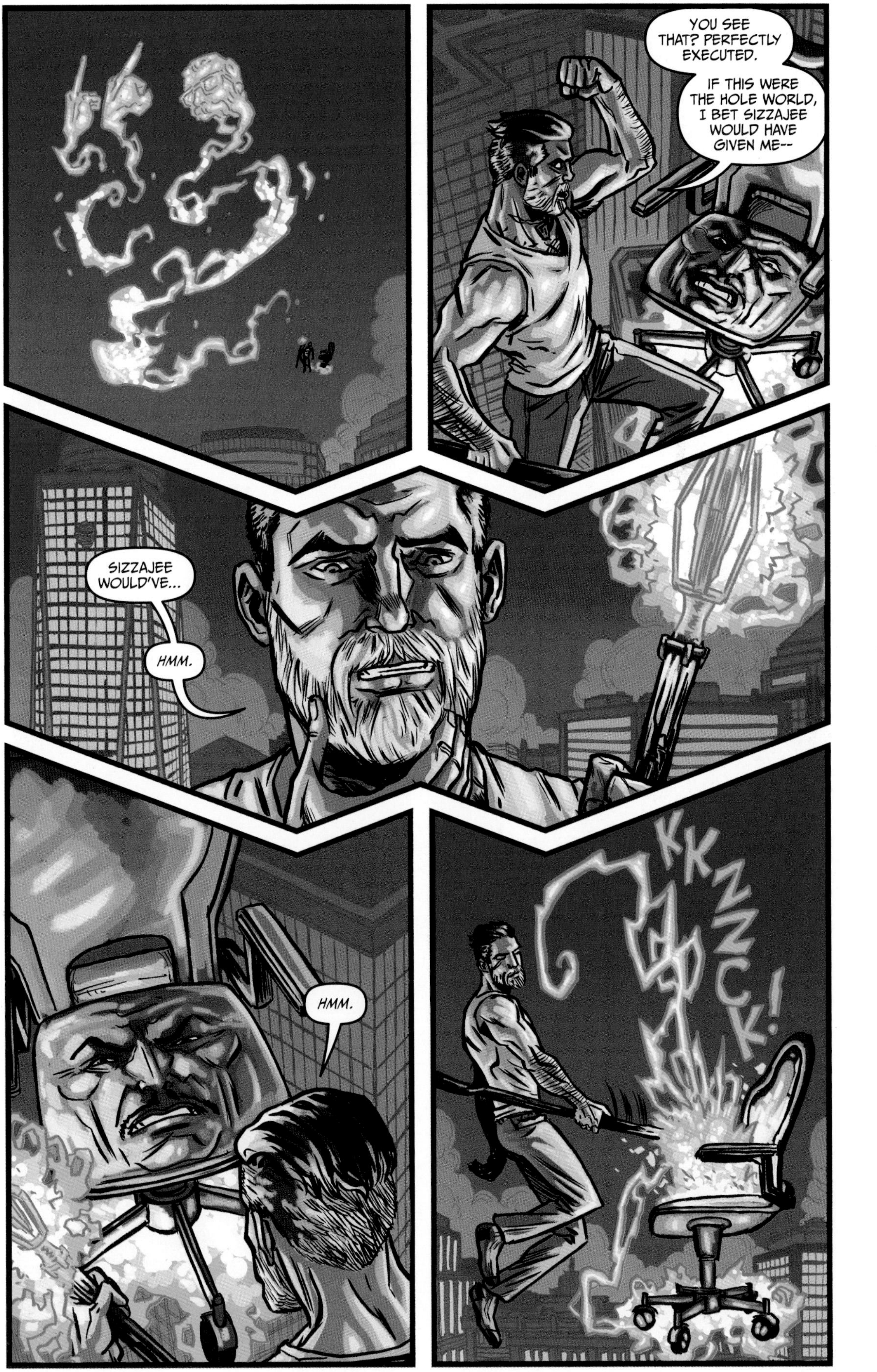
YOU SEE THAT? PERFECTLY EXECUTED.
IF THIS WERE THE HOLE WORLD, I BET SIZZAJEE WOULD HAVE GIVEN ME--
SIZZAJEE WOULD'VE...
HMM.
HMM.
KKZNZCK!

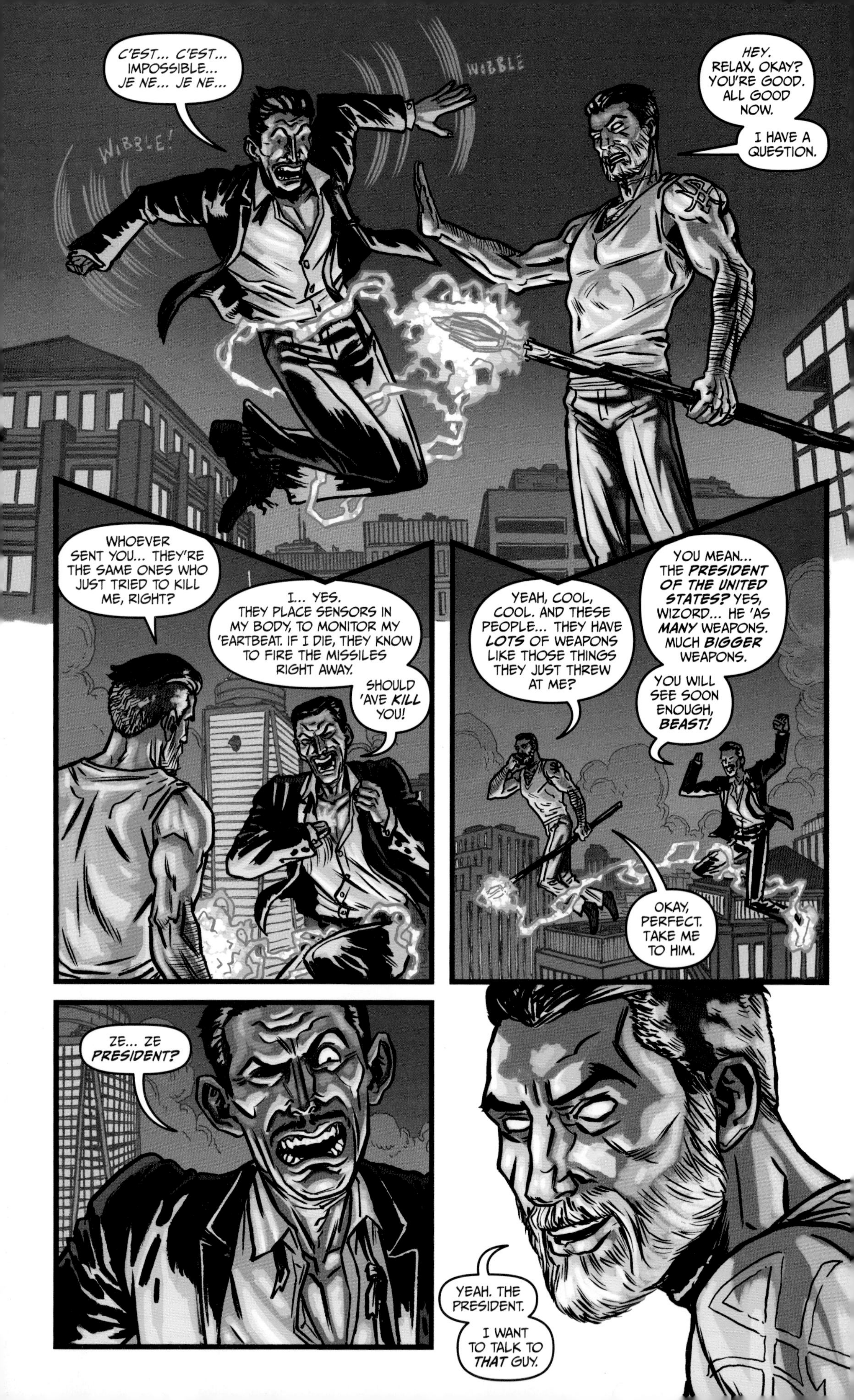
C'EST... C'EST... IMPOSSIBLE... JE NE... JE NE...
WIBBLE
WIBBLE!
HEY. RELAX, OKAY? YOU'RE GOOD. ALL GOOD NOW.
I HAVE A QUESTION.
WHOEVER SENT YOU... THEY'RE THE SAME ONES WHO JUST TRIED TO KILL ME, RIGHT?
I... YES. THEY PLACE SENSORS IN MY BODY, TO MONITOR MY 'EARTBEAT. IF I DIE, THEY KNOW TO FIRE THE MISSILES RIGHT AWAY.
SHOULD 'AVE KILL YOU!
YEAH, COOL, COOL. AND THESE PEOPLE... THEY HAVE LOTS OF WEAPONS LIKE THOSE THINGS THEY JUST THREW AT ME?
YOU MEAN... THE PRESIDENT OF THE UNITED STATES? YES, WIZORD... HE 'AS MANY WEAPONS. MUCH BIGGER WEAPONS.
YOU WILL SEE SOON ENOUGH, BEAST!
OKAY, PERFECT. TAKE ME TO HIM.
ZE... ZE PRESIDENT?
YEAH. THE PRESIDENT.
I WANT TO TALK TO THAT GUY.

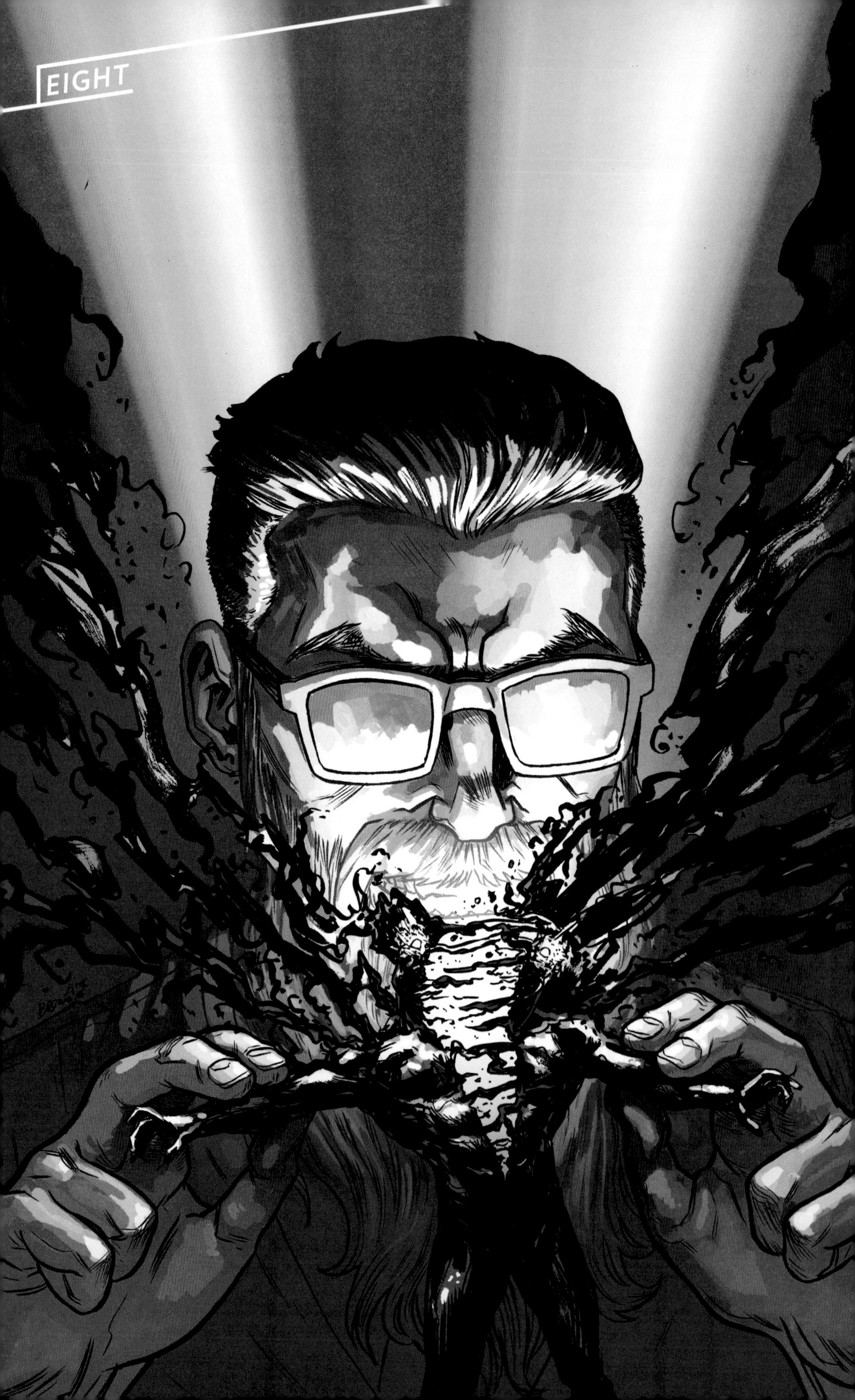
EIGHT

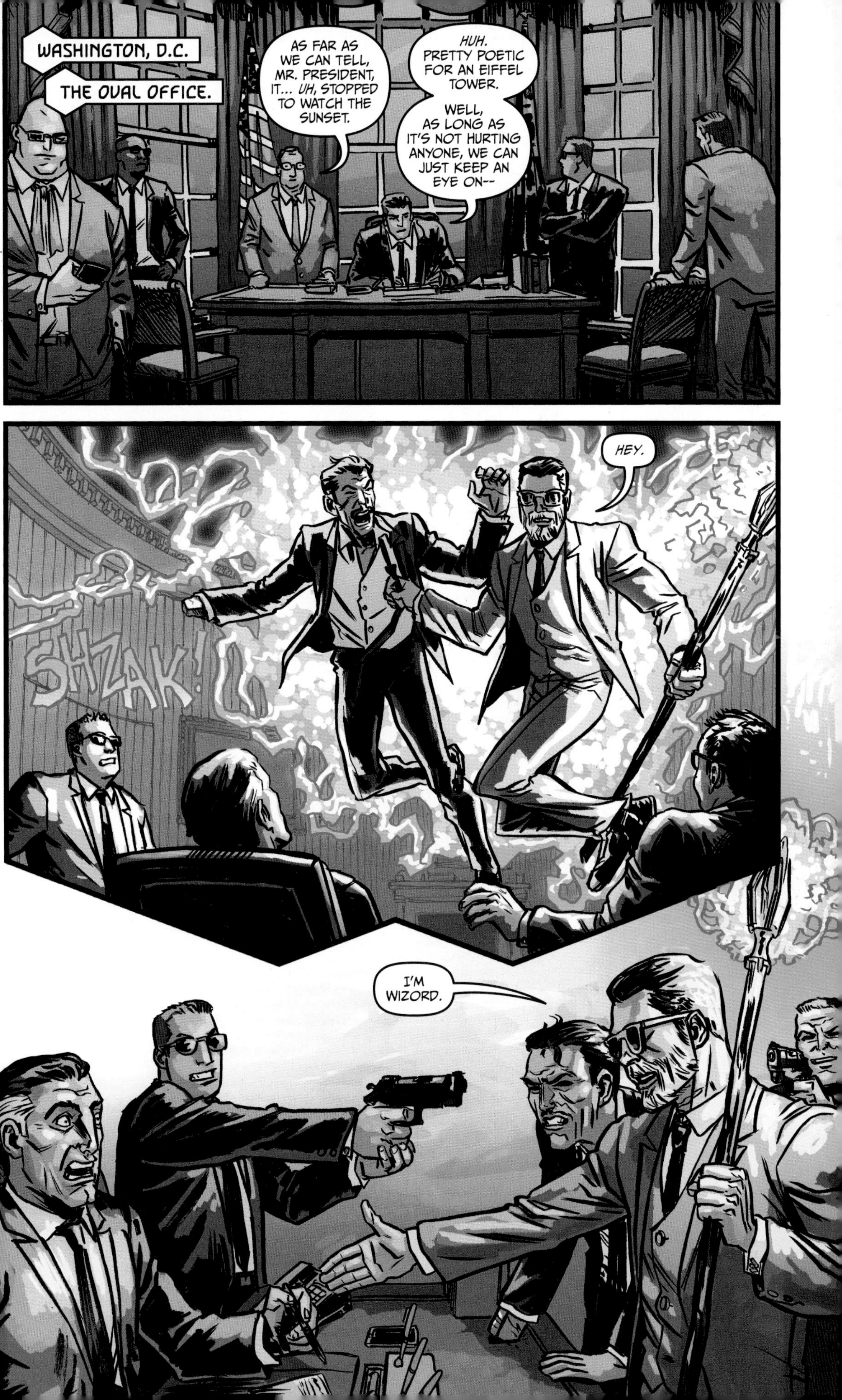
WASHINGTON, D.C.
THE OVAL OFFICE.
AS FAR AS WE CAN TELL, MR. PRESIDENT, IT... UH, STOPPED TO WATCH THE SUNSET.
HUH. PRETTY POETIC FOR AN EIFFEL TOWER.
WELL, AS LONG AS IT'S NOT HURTING ANYONE, WE CAN JUST KEEP AN EYE ON--
HEY.
SHZAK!
I'M WIZORD.

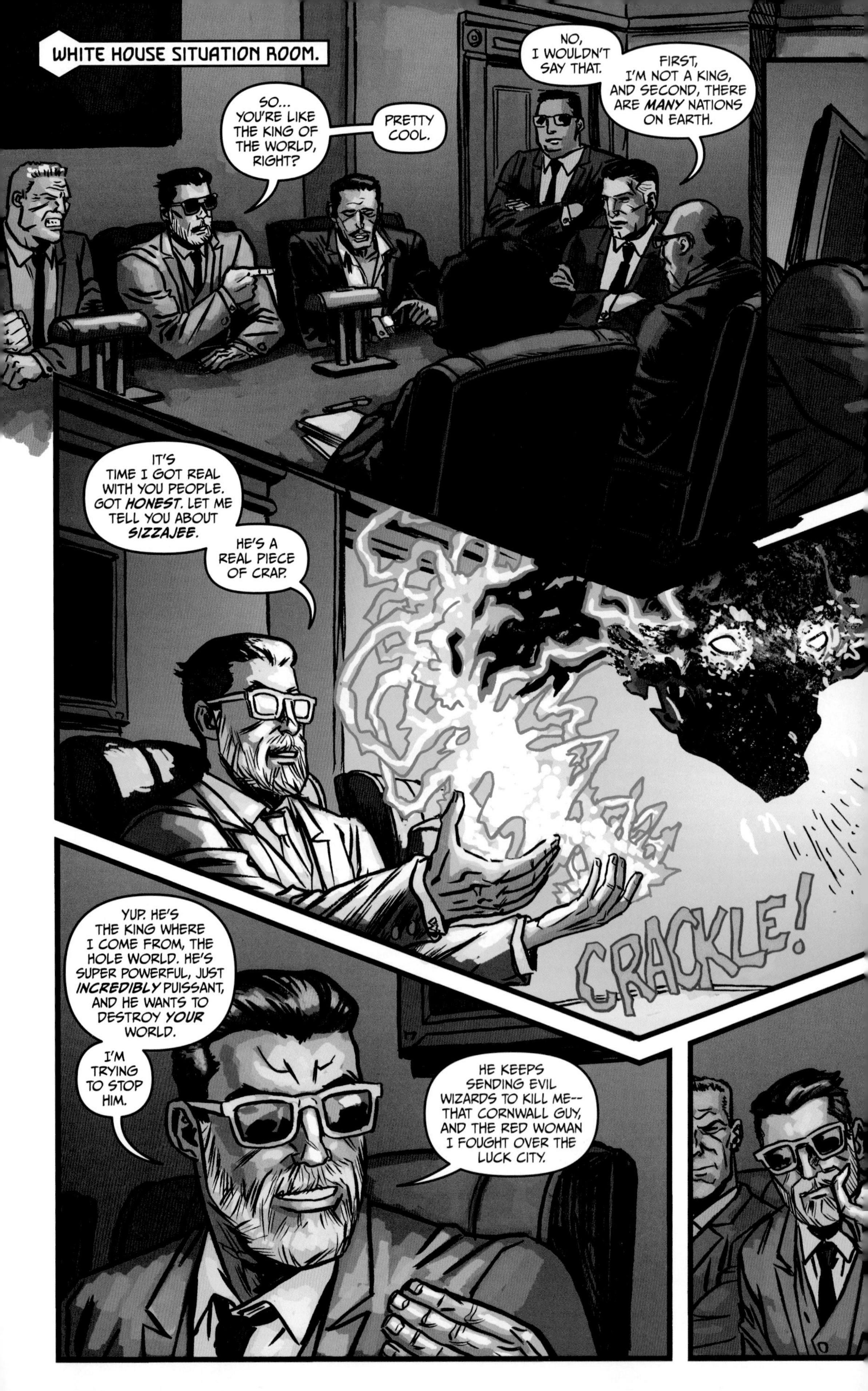
WHITE HOUSE SITUATION ROOM.
SO... YOU'RE LIKE THE KING OF THE WORLD, RIGHT?
PRETTY COOL.
NO, I WOULDN'T SAY THAT.
FIRST, I'M NOT A KING, AND SECOND, THERE ARE MANY NATIONS ON EARTH.
IT'S TIME I GOT REAL WITH YOU PEOPLE. GOT HONEST. LET ME TELL YOU ABOUT SIZZAJEE.
HE'S A REAL PIECE OF CRAP.
CRACKLE!
YUP. HE'S THE KING WHERE I COME FROM, THE HOLE WORLD. HE'S SUPER POWERFUL, JUST INCREDIBLY PUISSANT, AND HE WANTS TO DESTROY YOUR WORLD.
I'M TRYING TO STOP HIM.
HE KEEPS SENDING EVIL WIZARDS TO KILL ME-- THAT CORNWALL GUY, AND THE RED WOMAN I FOUGHT OVER THE LUCK CITY.

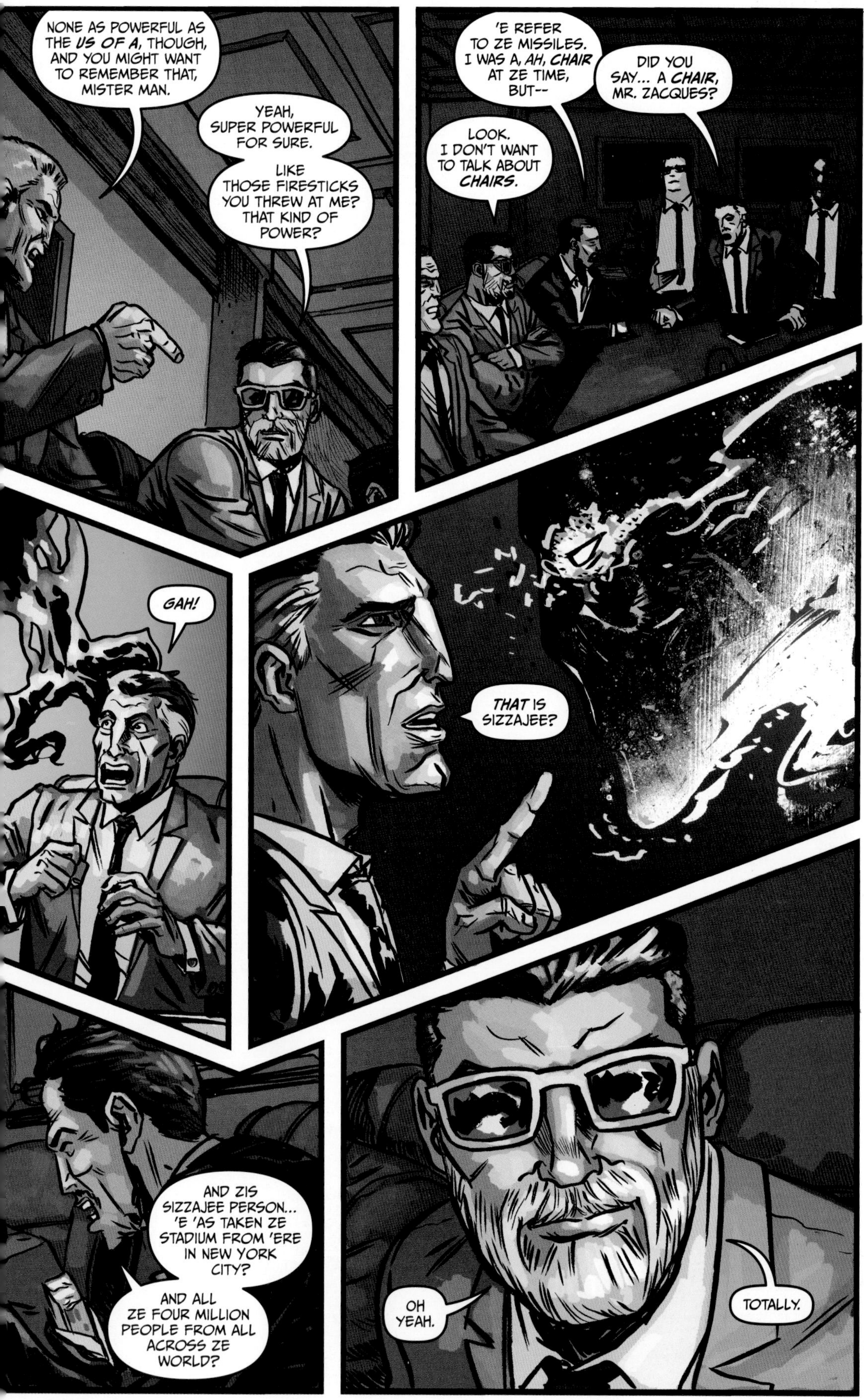
NONE AS POWERFUL AS THE US OF A, THOUGH, AND YOU MIGHT WANT TO REMEMBER THAT, MISTER MAN.
YEAH, SUPER POWERFUL FOR SURE.
LIKE THOSE FIRESTICKS YOU THREW AT ME? THAT KIND OF POWER?
'E REFER TO ZE MISSILES. I WAS A, AH, CHAIR AT ZE TIME, BUT--
DID YOU SAY... A CHAIR, MR. ZACQUES?
LOOK. I DON'T WANT TO TALK ABOUT CHAIRS.
GAH!
THAT IS SIZZAJEE?
AND ZIS SIZZAJEE PERSON... 'E 'AS TAKEN ZE STADIUM FROM 'ERE IN NEW YORK CITY?
AND ALL ZE FOUR MILLION PEOPLE FROM ALL ACROSS ZE WORLD?
OH YEAH.
TOTALLY.

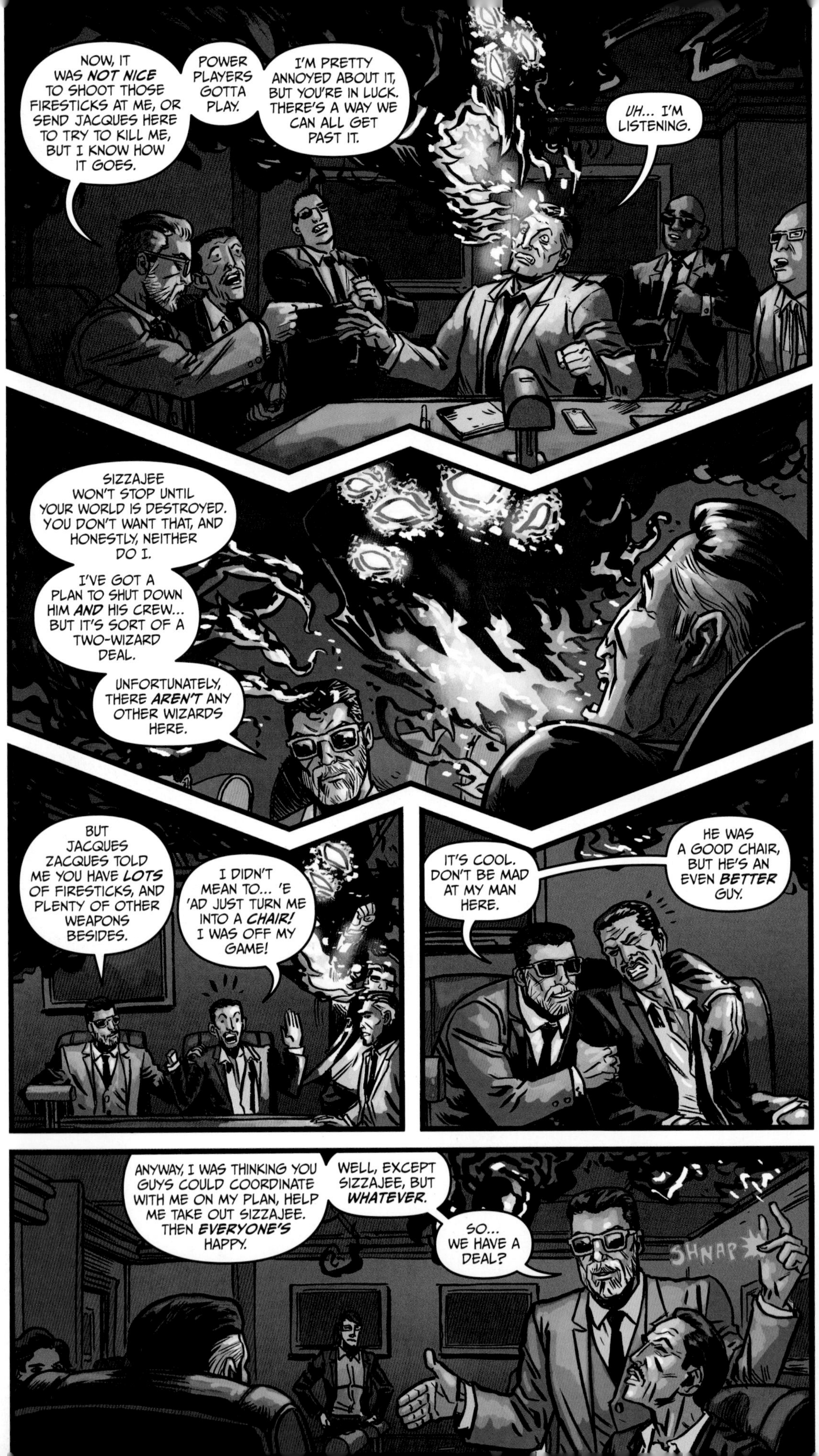
NOW, IT WAS NOT NICE TO SHOOT THOSE FIRESTICKS AT ME, OR SEND JACQUES HERE TO TRY TO KILL ME, BUT I KNOW HOW IT GOES.
POWER PLAYERS GOTTA PLAY.
I'M PRETTY ANNOYED ABOUT IT, BUT YOU'RE IN LUCK. THERE'S A WAY WE CAN ALL GET PAST IT.
UH... I'M LISTENING.
SIZZAJEE WON'T STOP UNTIL YOUR WORLD IS DESTROYED. YOU DON'T WANT THAT, AND HONESTLY, NEITHER DO I.
I'VE GOT A PLAN TO SHUT DOWN HIM AND HIS CREW... BUT IT'S SORT OF A TWO-WIZARD DEAL.
UNFORTUNATELY, THERE AREN'T ANY OTHER WIZARDS HERE.
BUT JACQUES ZACQUES TOLD ME YOU HAVE LOTS OF FIRESTICKS, AND PLENTY OF OTHER WEAPONS BESIDES.
I DIDN'T MEAN TO... 'E 'AD JUST TURN ME INTO A CHAIR! I WAS OFF MY GAME!
IT'S COOL. DON'T BE MAD AT MY MAN HERE.
HE WAS A GOOD CHAIR, BUT HE'S AN EVEN BETTER GUY.
ANYWAY, I WAS THINKING YOU GUYS COULD COORDINATE WITH ME ON MY PLAN, HELP ME TAKE OUT SIZZAJEE. THEN EVERYONE'S HAPPY.
WELL, EXCEPT SIZZAJEE, BUT WHATEVER.
SO... WE HAVE A DEAL?
SHNAP

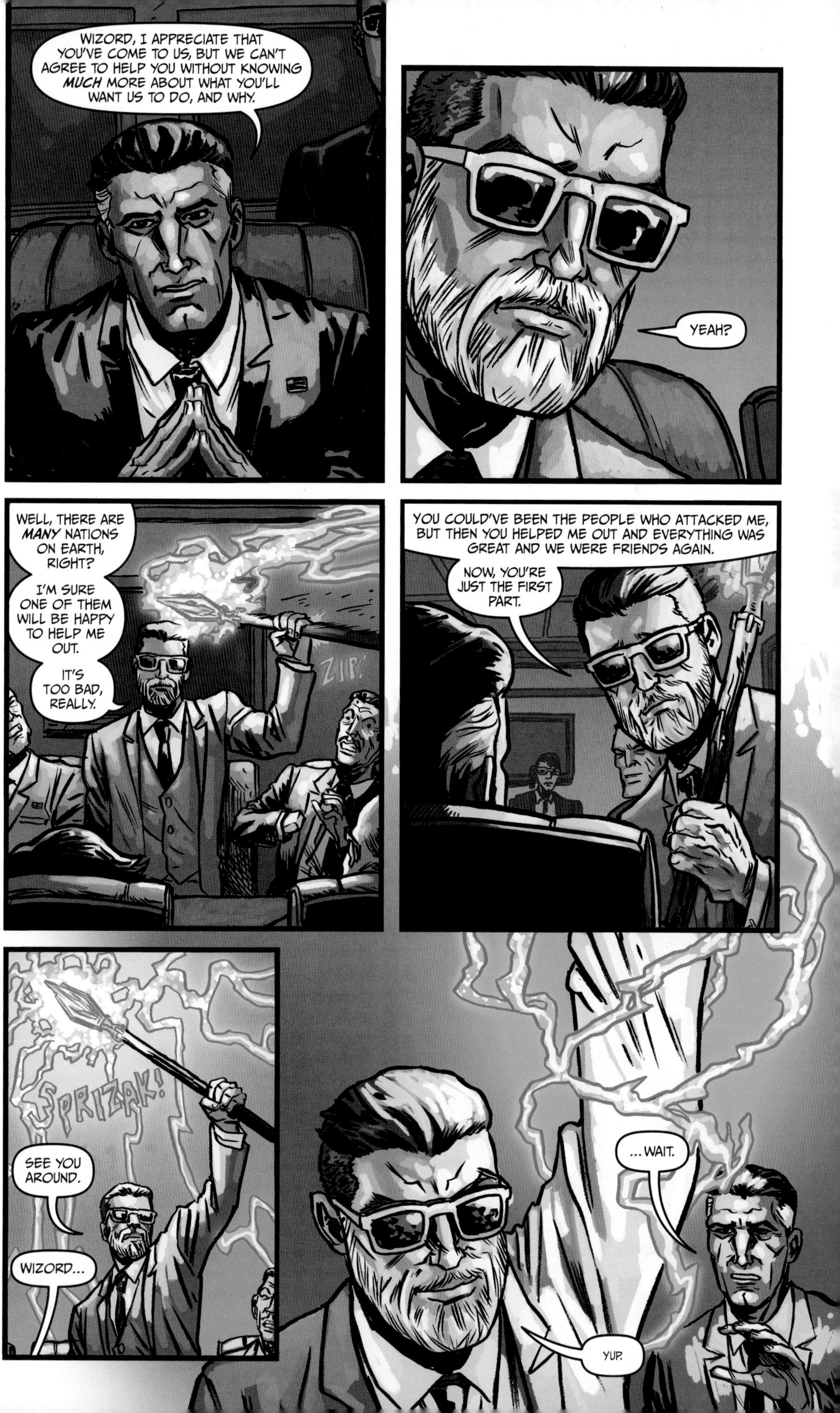
WIZORD, I APPRECIATE THAT YOU'VE COME TO US, BUT WE CAN'T AGREE TO HELP YOU WITHOUT KNOWING *MUCH* MORE ABOUT WHAT YOU'LL WANT US TO DO, AND WHY.
YEAH?
WELL, THERE ARE *MANY* NATIONS ON EARTH, RIGHT?
I'M SURE ONE OF THEM WILL BE HAPPY TO HELP ME OUT.
IT'S TOO BAD, REALLY.
ZIP!
YOU COULD'VE BEEN THE PEOPLE WHO ATTACKED ME, BUT THEN YOU HELPED ME OUT AND EVERYTHING WAS GREAT AND WE WERE FRIENDS AGAIN.
NOW, YOU'RE JUST THE FIRST PART.
SPRIZAK!
SEE YOU AROUND.
WIZORD...
...WAIT.
YUP.

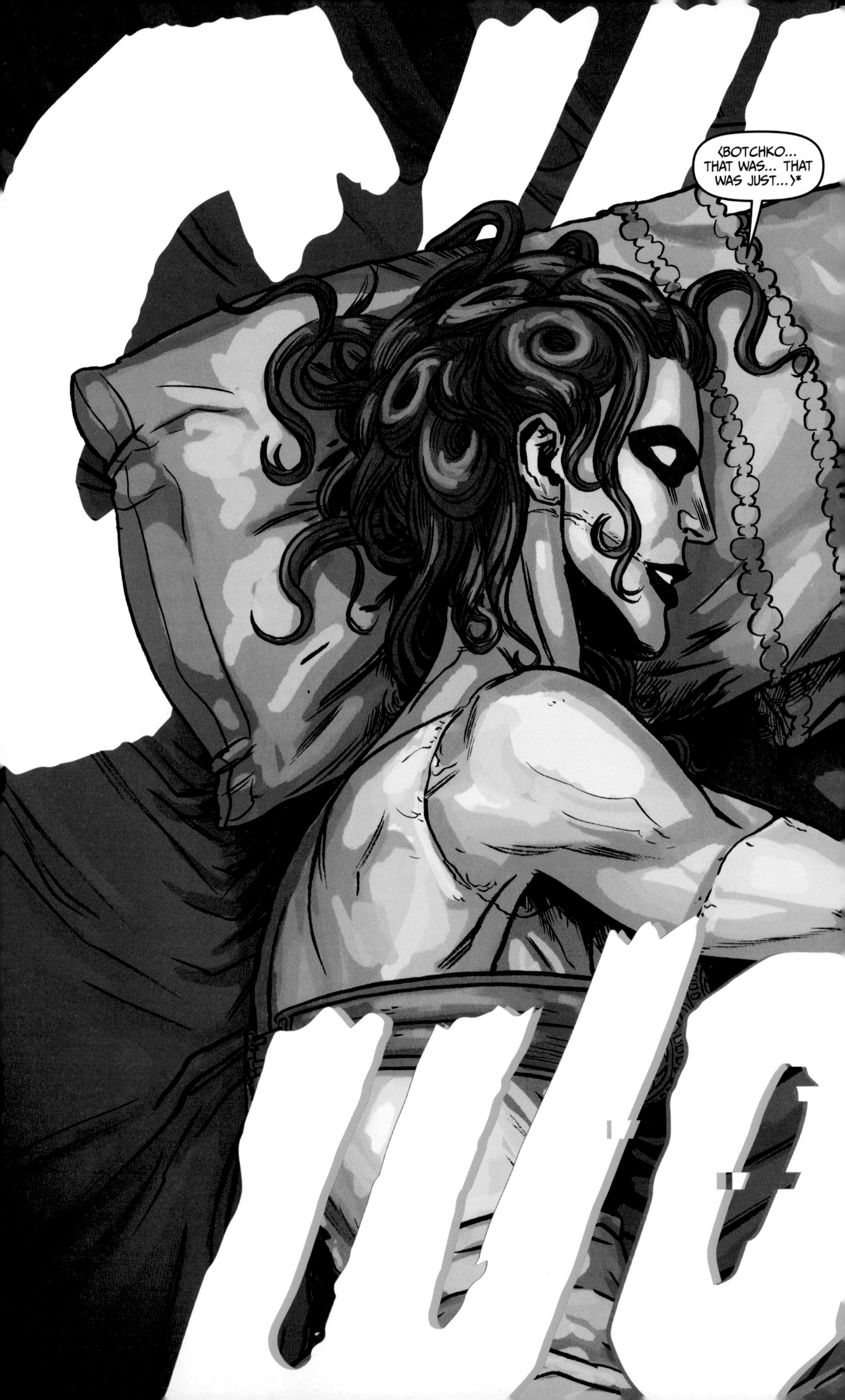
‹BOTCHKO... THAT WAS... THAT WAS JUST...›*

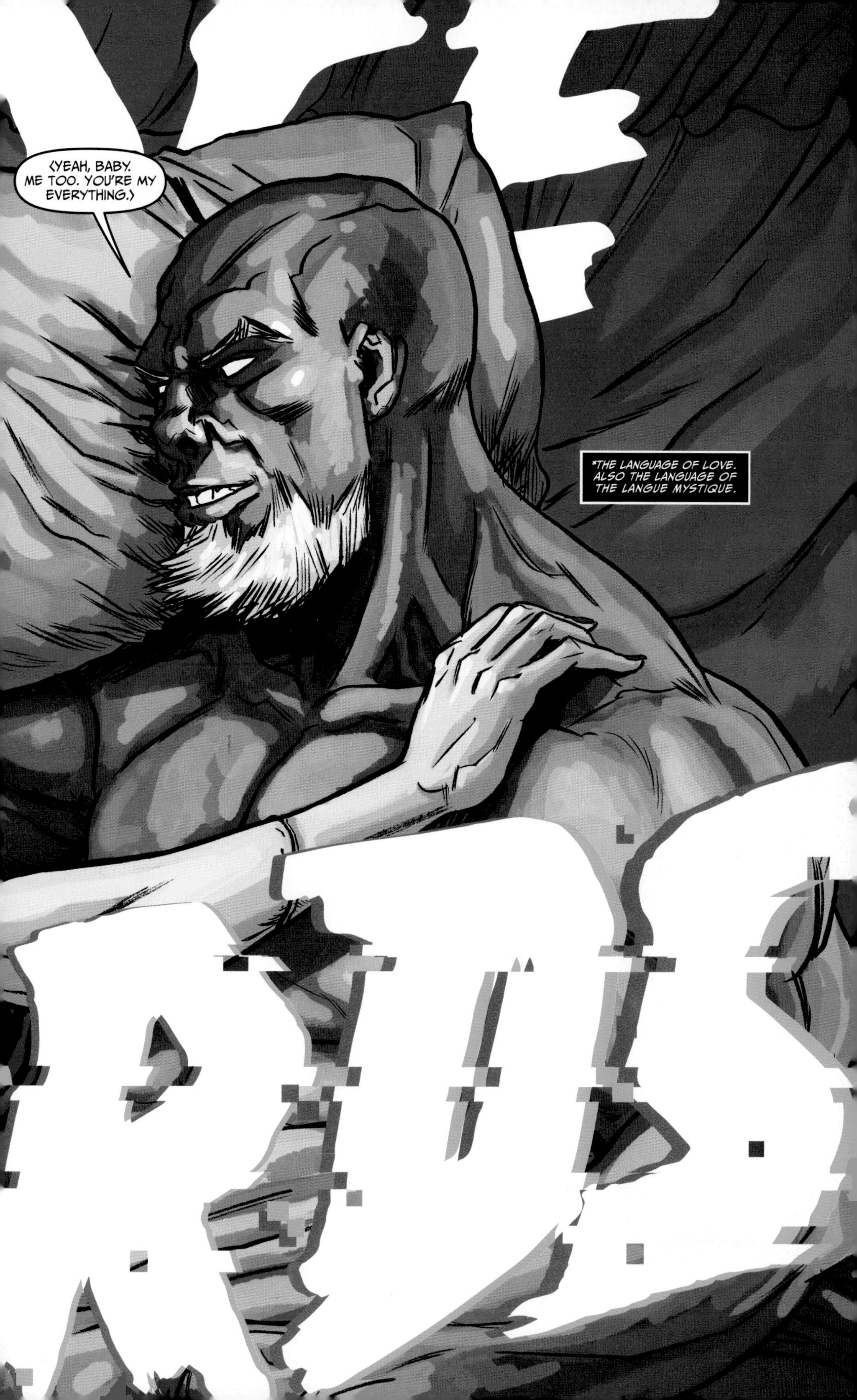
‹YEAH, BABY. ME TOO. YOU'RE MY EVERYTHING.›
*THE LANGUAGE OF LOVE. ALSO THE LANGUAGE OF THE LANGUE MYSTIQUE.

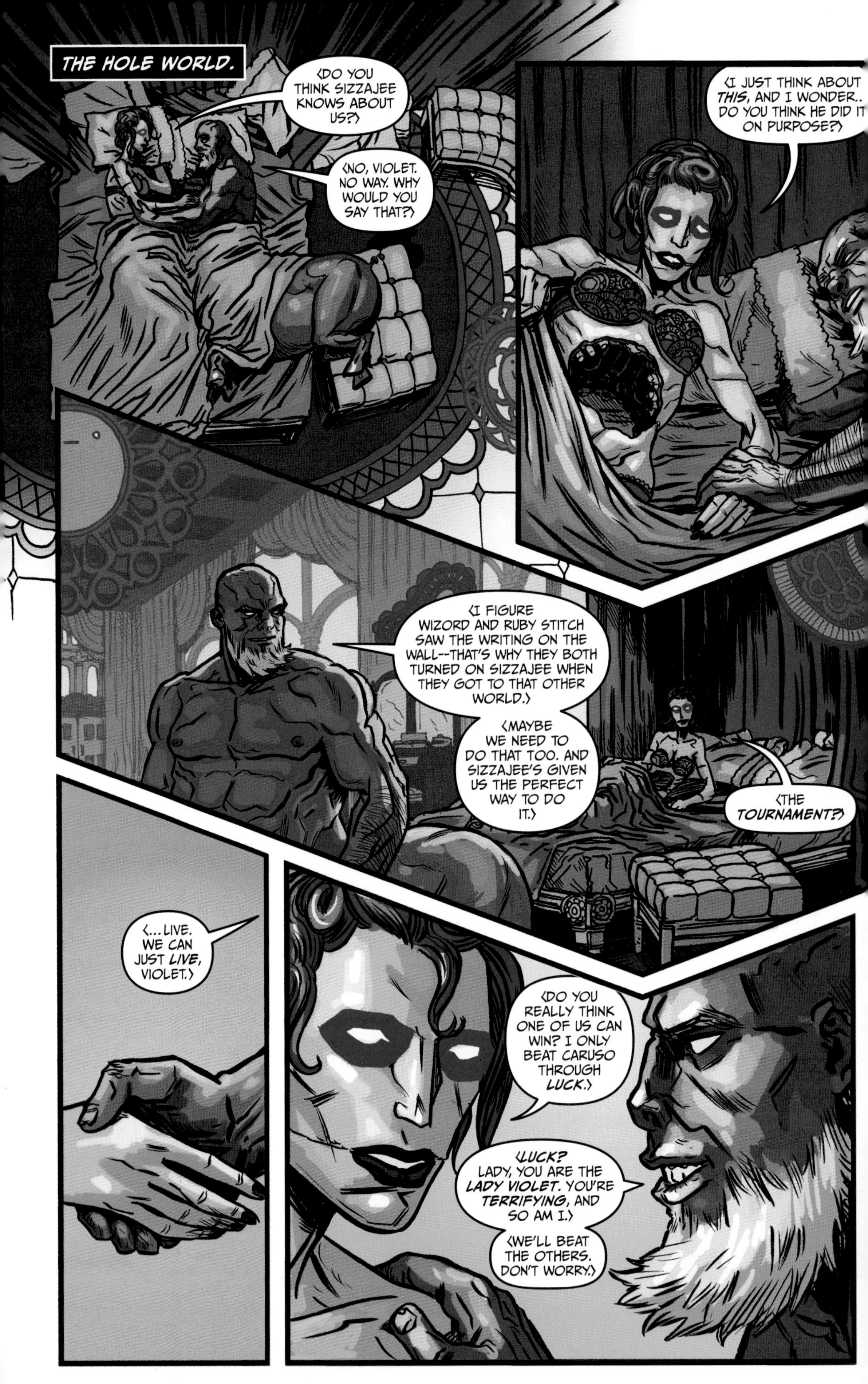
THE HOLE WORLD.
⟨DO YOU THINK SIZZAJEE KNOWS ABOUT US?⟩
⟨NO, VIOLET. NO WAY. WHY WOULD YOU SAY THAT?⟩
⟨I JUST THINK ABOUT THIS, AND I WONDER.. DO YOU THINK HE DID IT ON PURPOSE?⟩
⟨I FIGURE WIZORD AND RUBY STITCH SAW THE WRITING ON THE WALL--THAT'S WHY THEY BOTH TURNED ON SIZZAJEE WHEN THEY GOT TO THAT OTHER WORLD.⟩
⟨MAYBE WE NEED TO DO THAT TOO. AND SIZZAJEE'S GIVEN US THE PERFECT WAY TO DO IT.⟩
⟨THE TOURNAMENT?⟩
⟨...LIVE. WE CAN JUST LIVE, VIOLET.⟩
⟨DO YOU REALLY THINK ONE OF US CAN WIN? I ONLY BEAT CARUSO THROUGH LUCK.⟩
⟨LUCK? LADY, YOU ARE THE LADY VIOLET. YOU'RE TERRIFYING, AND SO AM I.⟩
⟨WE'LL BEAT THE OTHERS. DON'T WORRY.⟩

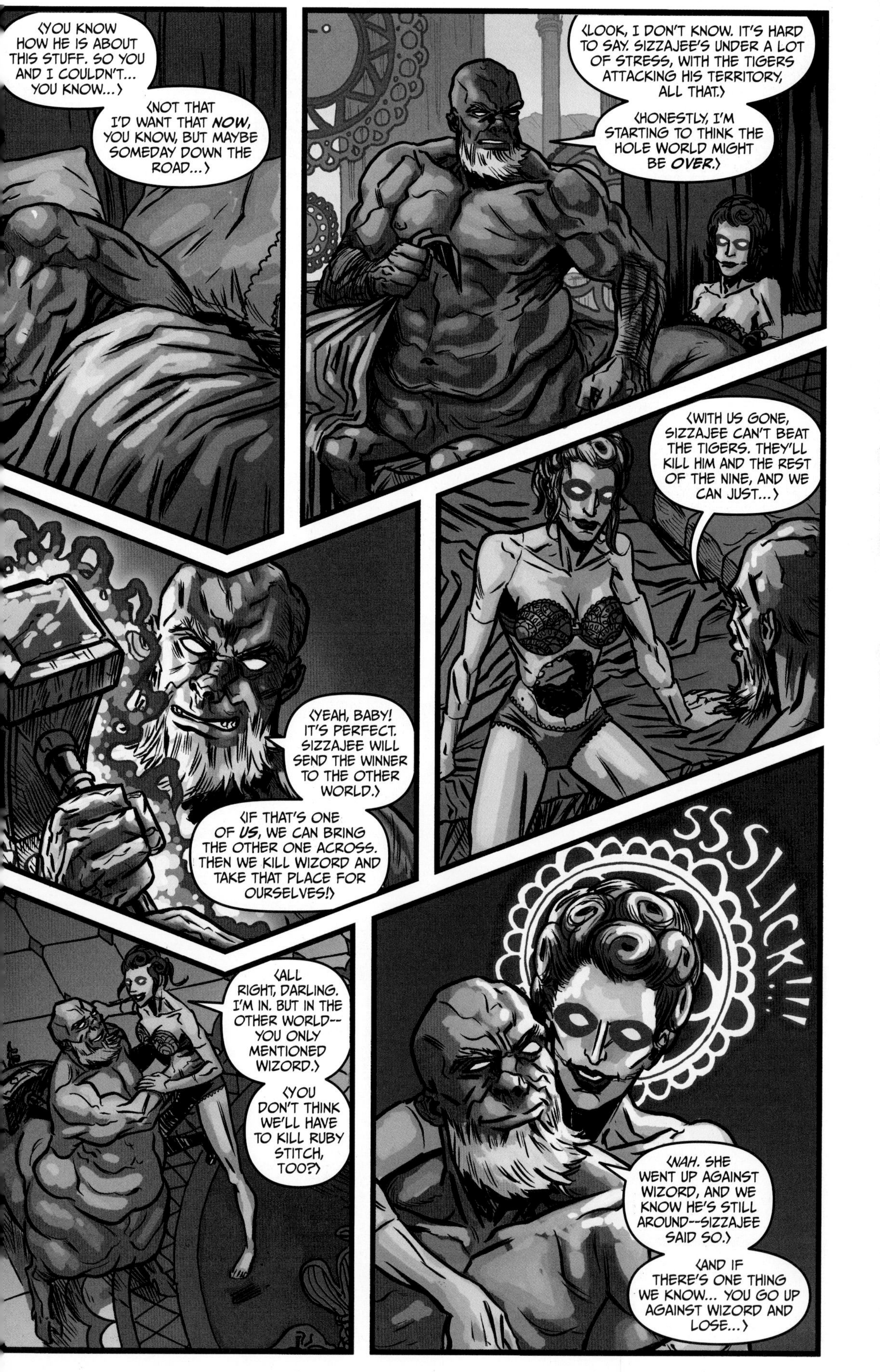
⟨YOU KNOW HOW HE IS ABOUT THIS STUFF. SO YOU AND I COULDN'T... YOU KNOW...⟩
⟨NOT THAT I'D WANT THAT *NOW*, YOU KNOW, BUT MAYBE SOMEDAY DOWN THE ROAD...⟩
⟨LOOK, I DON'T KNOW. IT'S HARD TO SAY. SIZZAJEE'S UNDER A LOT OF STRESS, WITH THE TIGERS ATTACKING HIS TERRITORY, ALL THAT.⟩
⟨HONESTLY, I'M STARTING TO THINK THE HOLE WORLD MIGHT BE *OVER*.⟩
⟨WITH US GONE, SIZZAJEE CAN'T BEAT THE TIGERS. THEY'LL KILL HIM AND THE REST OF THE NINE, AND WE CAN JUST...⟩
⟨YEAH, BABY! IT'S PERFECT. SIZZAJEE WILL SEND THE WINNER TO THE OTHER WORLD.⟩
⟨IF THAT'S ONE OF *US*, WE CAN BRING THE OTHER ONE ACROSS. THEN WE KILL WIZORD AND TAKE THAT PLACE FOR OURSELVES!⟩
⟨ALL RIGHT, DARLING. I'M IN. BUT IN THE OTHER WORLD-- YOU ONLY MENTIONED WIZORD.⟩
⟨YOU DON'T THINK WE'LL HAVE TO KILL RUBY STITCH, TOO?⟩
SSSLICK!!!
⟨*NAH*. SHE WENT UP AGAINST WIZORD, AND WE KNOW HE'S STILL AROUND--SIZZAJEE SAID SO.⟩
⟨AND IF THERE'S ONE THING WE KNOW... YOU GO UP AGAINST WIZORD AND LOSE...⟩

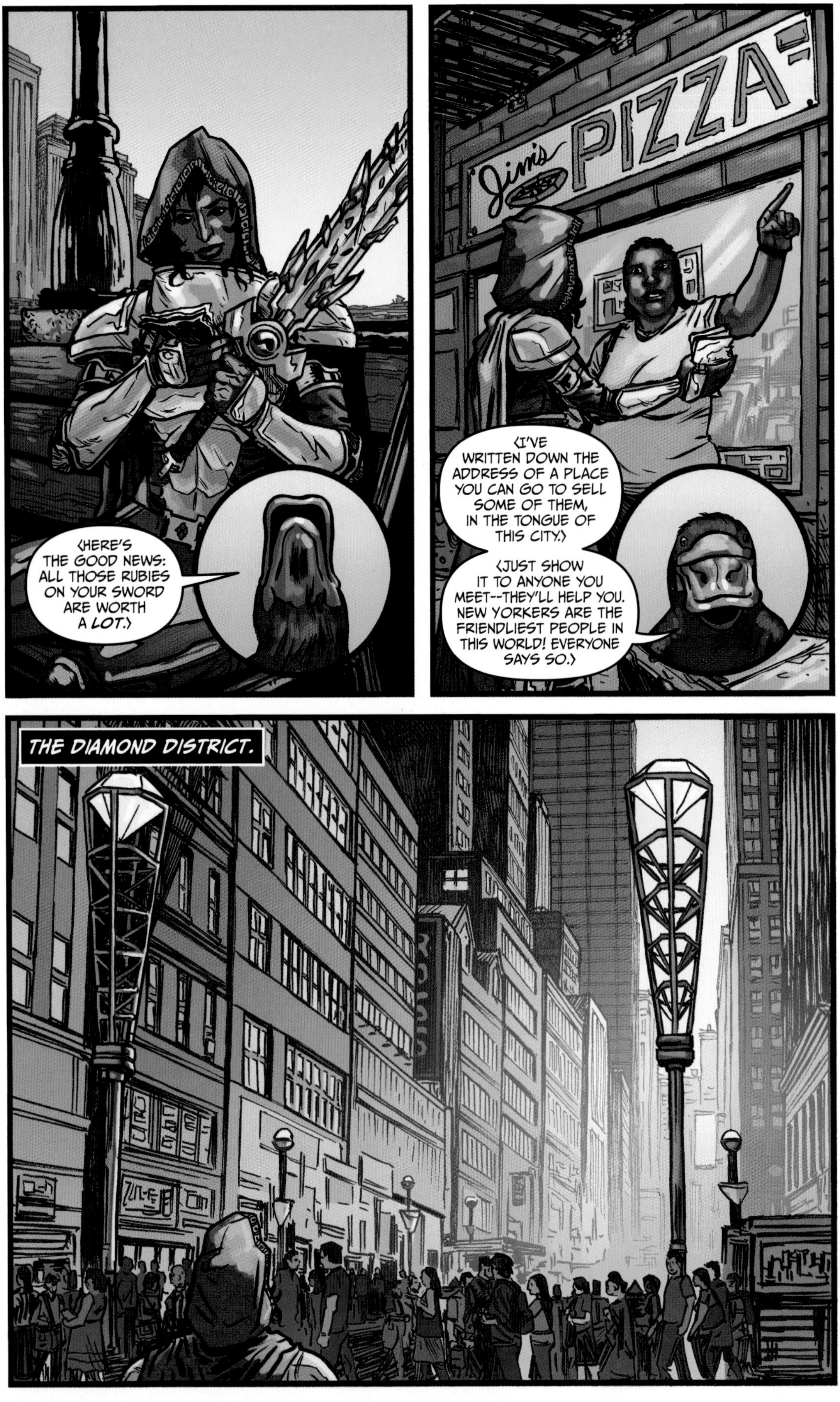
‹HERE'S THE GOOD NEWS: ALL THOSE RUBIES ON YOUR SWORD ARE WORTH A LOT.›
Jim's PIZZA
‹I'VE WRITTEN DOWN THE ADDRESS OF A PLACE YOU CAN GO TO SELL SOME OF THEM, IN THE TONGUE OF THIS CITY.›
‹JUST SHOW IT TO ANYONE YOU MEET--THEY'LL HELP YOU. NEW YORKERS ARE THE FRIENDLIEST PEOPLE IN THIS WORLD! EVERYONE SAYS SO.›
THE DIAMOND DISTRICT.

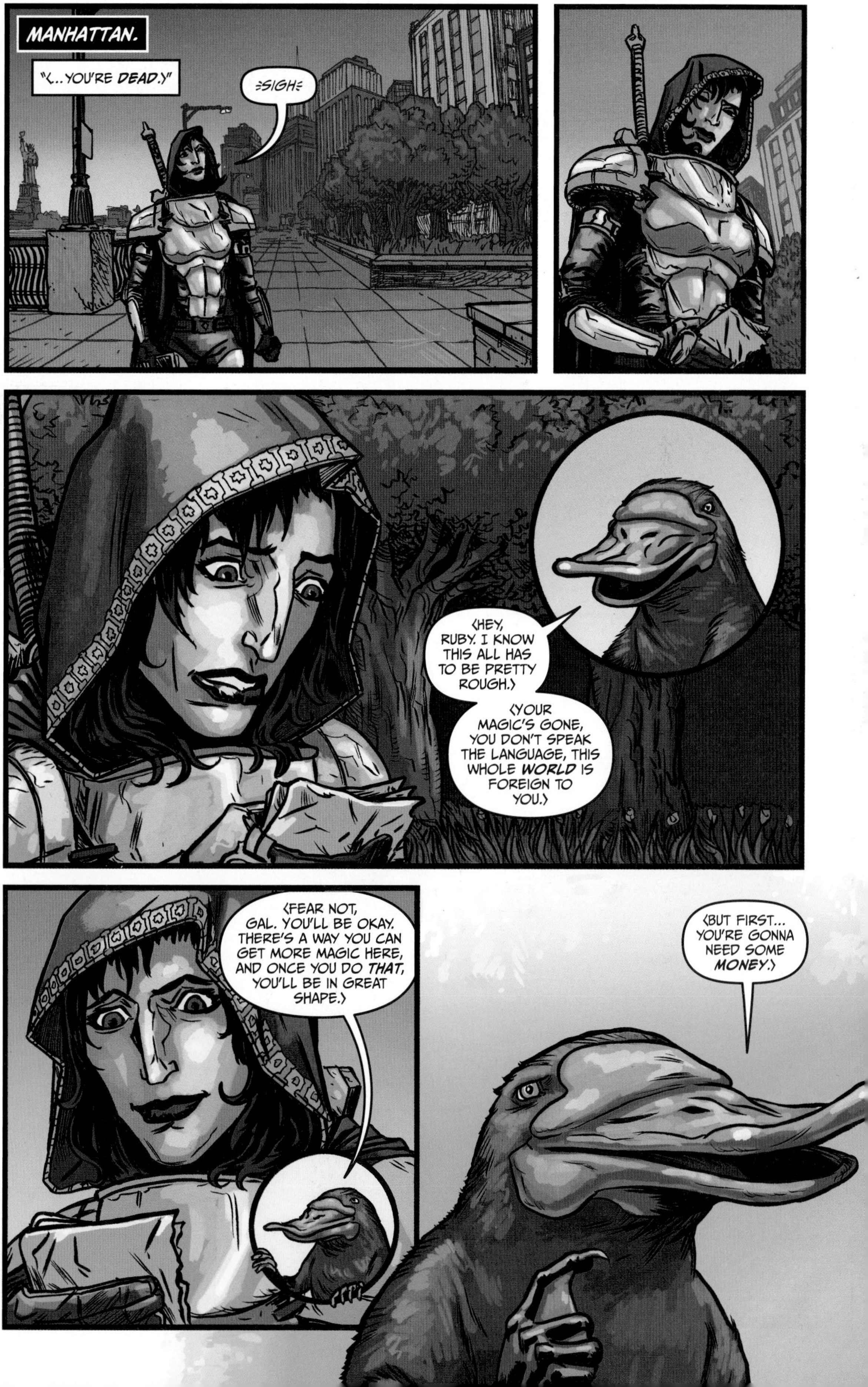
MANHATTAN.
"〈...YOU'RE DEAD.〉"
SIGH
〈HEY, RUBY. I KNOW THIS ALL HAS TO BE PRETTY ROUGH.〉
〈YOUR MAGIC'S GONE, YOU DON'T SPEAK THE LANGUAGE, THIS WHOLE WORLD IS FOREIGN TO YOU.〉
〈FEAR NOT, GAL. YOU'LL BE OKAY. THERE'S A WAY YOU CAN GET MORE MAGIC HERE, AND ONCE YOU DO THAT, YOU'LL BE IN GREAT SHAPE.〉
〈BUT FIRST... YOU'RE GONNA NEED SOME MONEY.〉

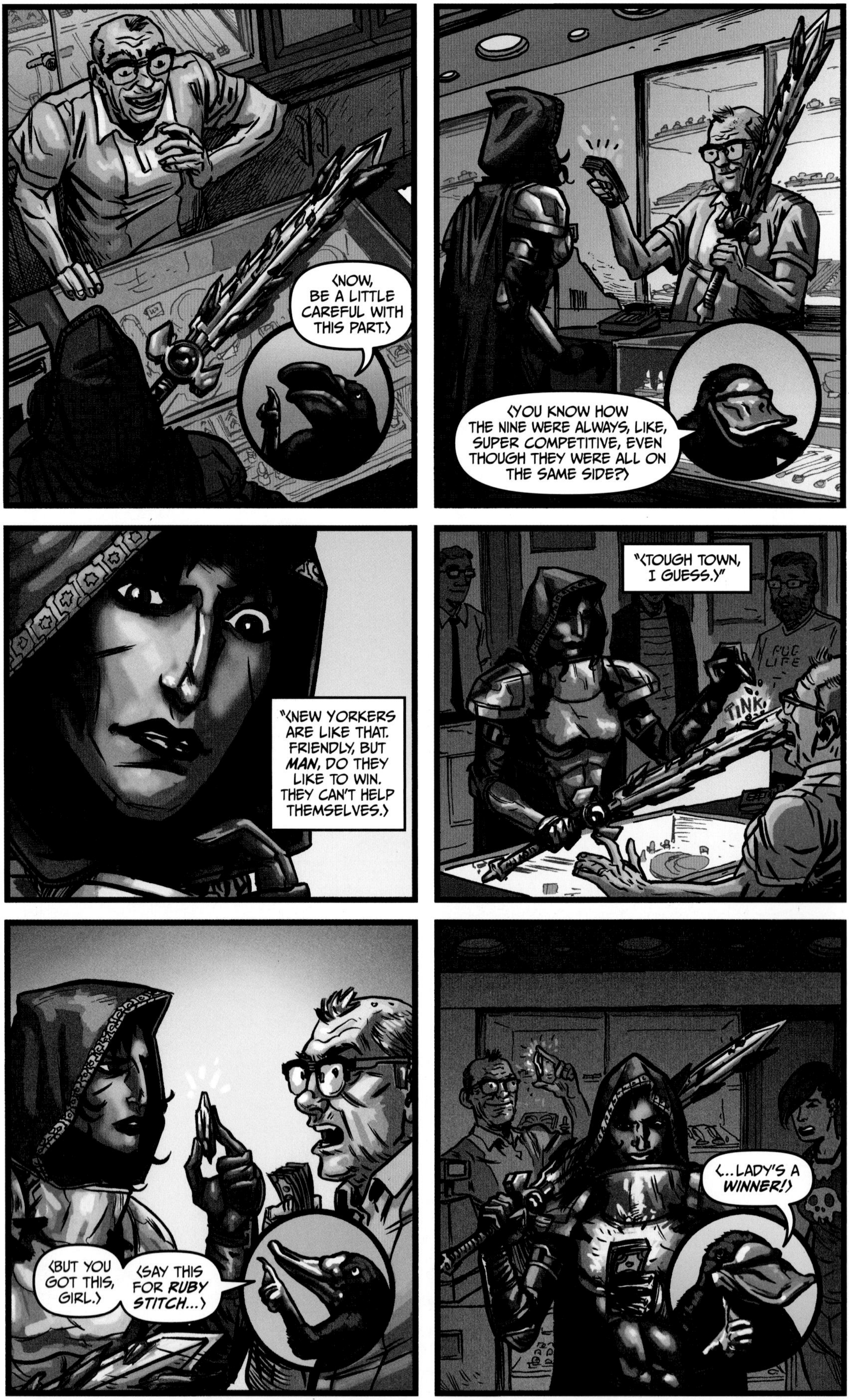

‹NOW, BE A LITTLE CAREFUL WITH THIS PART.›
‹YOU KNOW HOW THE NINE WERE ALWAYS, LIKE, SUPER COMPETITIVE, EVEN THOUGH THEY WERE ALL ON THE SAME SIDE?›
"‹NEW YORKERS ARE LIKE THAT. FRIENDLY, BUT *MAN*, DO THEY LIKE TO WIN. THEY CAN'T HELP THEMSELVES.›
"‹TOUGH TOWN, I GUESS.›"
TINK
‹BUT YOU GOT THIS, GIRL.›
‹SAY THIS FOR *RUBY STITCH*...›
‹...LADY'S A *WINNER!*›

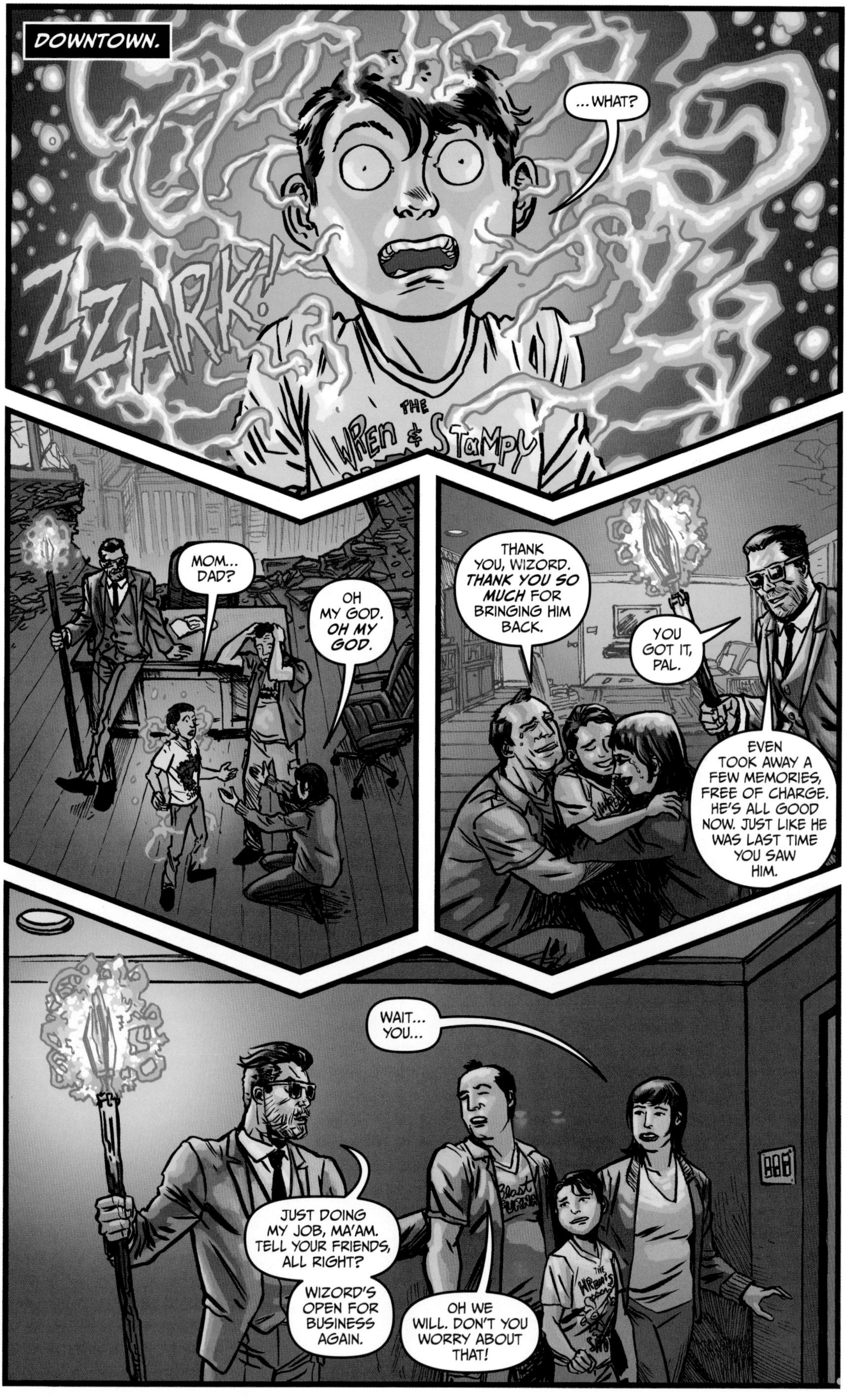
DOWNTOWN.
...WHAT?
ZZARK!
THE WREN & STAMPY
MOM... DAD?
OH MY GOD. OH MY GOD.
THANK YOU, WIZORD. THANK YOU SO MUCH FOR BRINGING HIM BACK.
YOU GOT IT, PAL.
EVEN TOOK AWAY A FEW MEMORIES, FREE OF CHARGE. HE'S ALL GOOD NOW. JUST LIKE HE WAS LAST TIME YOU SAW HIM.
WAIT... YOU...
JUST DOING MY JOB, MA'AM. TELL YOUR FRIENDS, ALL RIGHT?
WIZORD'S OPEN FOR BUSINESS AGAIN.
OH WE WILL. DON'T YOU WORRY ABOUT THAT!

OH, HEY, MARGARET. WAS WONDERING WHAT HAPPENED TO YOU.

WIZORD
(WIZARD)

HEY. WHO ARE THESE NICE-LOOKING FOLKS?

SOME FAMILY. THE KID WENT MISSING, I BROUGHT HIM BACK. PRETTY STANDARD STUFF, DIDN'T TAKE MUCH MAGIC TO PULL OFF.

THEY... THEY SEEM SO *HAPPY*.

YEAH, WELL...

...SO AM I.

WAIT, YOU DID THAT FOR PAY? YOU'RE WORKING AGAIN?

YEAH. I'VE GOT SOMETHING *BIG* COMING UP. I'LL NEED ALL THE SAPPHIRES I CAN GET.

I'M GLAD TO SEE IT. TAKING CLIENTS IS GOOD FOR YOU. KEEPS YOU FROM GETTING TOO FAR INTO YOUR OWN HEAD.

ANYWAY, I DON'T HAVE ANY SAPPHIRES, BUT I WAS WONDERING... ANY CHANCE YOU MIGHT CHANGE ME AGAIN?

CHANGE YOU? I JUST DID! YOU DIDN'T WANT TO BE THAT BIG BIRD, AND NOW YOU'RE... WHATEVER YOU ARE NOW.

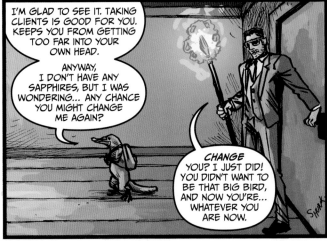

I KNOW... IT'S JUST... THIS DOESN'T FEEL RIGHT. I THOUGHT IT WOULD, BUT SOMETHING ABOUT IT...

THIS ISN'T WHO I AM. SOMETHING'S JUST *OFF*.

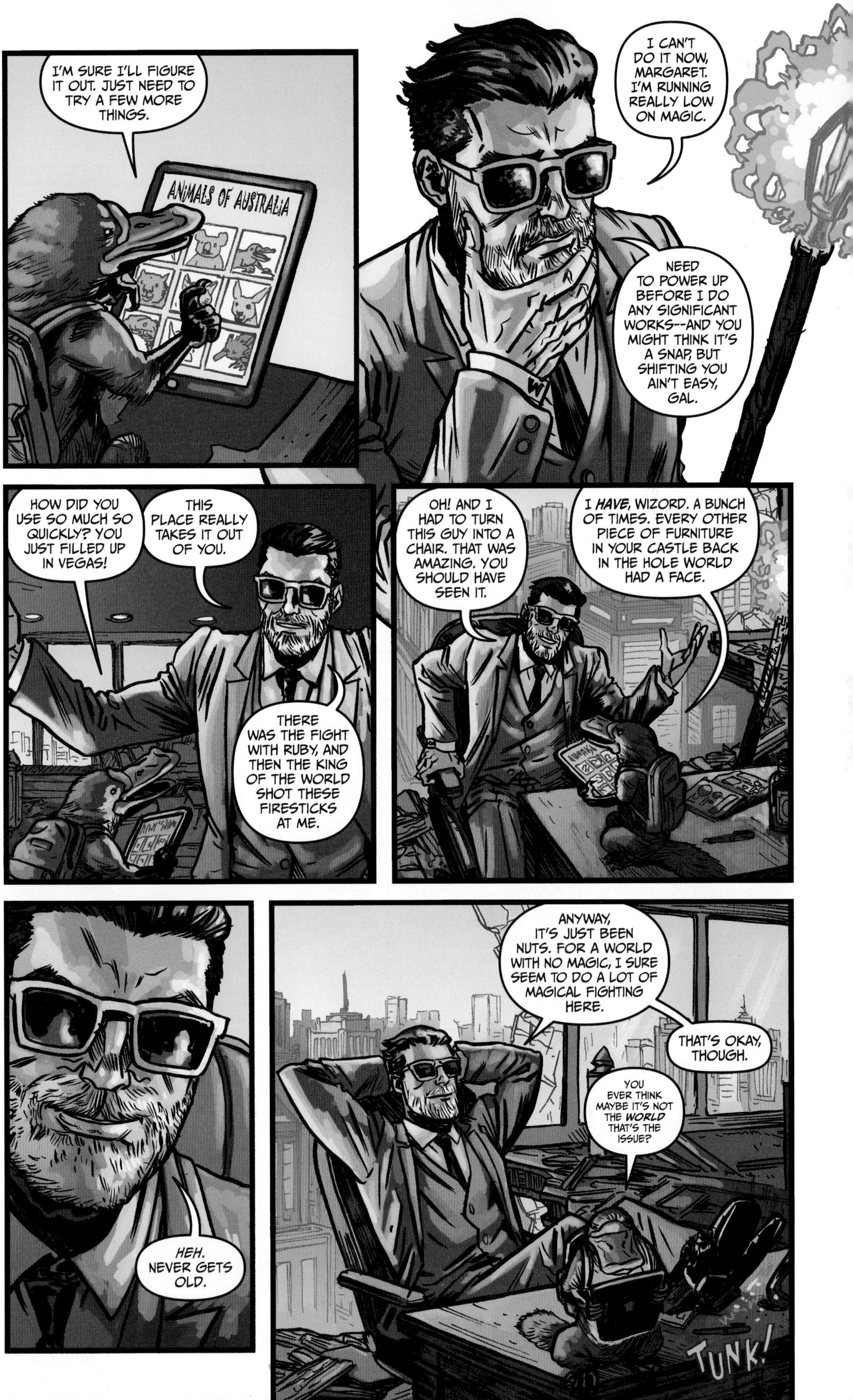
I'M SURE I'LL FIGURE IT OUT. JUST NEED TO TRY A FEW MORE THINGS.
ANIMALS OF AUSTRALIA
I CAN'T DO IT NOW, MARGARET. I'M RUNNING REALLY LOW ON MAGIC.
NEED TO POWER UP BEFORE I DO ANY SIGNIFICANT WORKS--AND YOU MIGHT THINK IT'S A SNAP, BUT SHIFTING YOU AIN'T EASY, GAL.
HOW DID YOU USE SO MUCH SO QUICKLY? YOU JUST FILLED UP IN VEGAS!
THIS PLACE REALLY TAKES IT OUT OF YOU.
THERE WAS THE FIGHT WITH RUBY, AND THEN THE KING OF THE WORLD SHOT THESE FIRESTICKS AT ME.
OH! AND I HAD TO TURN THIS GUY INTO A CHAIR. THAT WAS AMAZING. YOU SHOULD HAVE SEEN IT.
I *HAVE*, WIZORD. A BUNCH OF TIMES. EVERY OTHER PIECE OF FURNITURE IN YOUR CASTLE BACK IN THE HOLE WORLD HAD A FACE.
HEH. NEVER GETS OLD.
ANYWAY, IT'S JUST BEEN NUTS. FOR A WORLD WITH NO MAGIC, I SURE SEEM TO DO A LOT OF MAGICAL FIGHTING HERE.
THAT'S OKAY, THOUGH.
YOU EVER THINK MAYBE IT'S NOT THE *WORLD* THAT'S THE ISSUE?
TUNK!

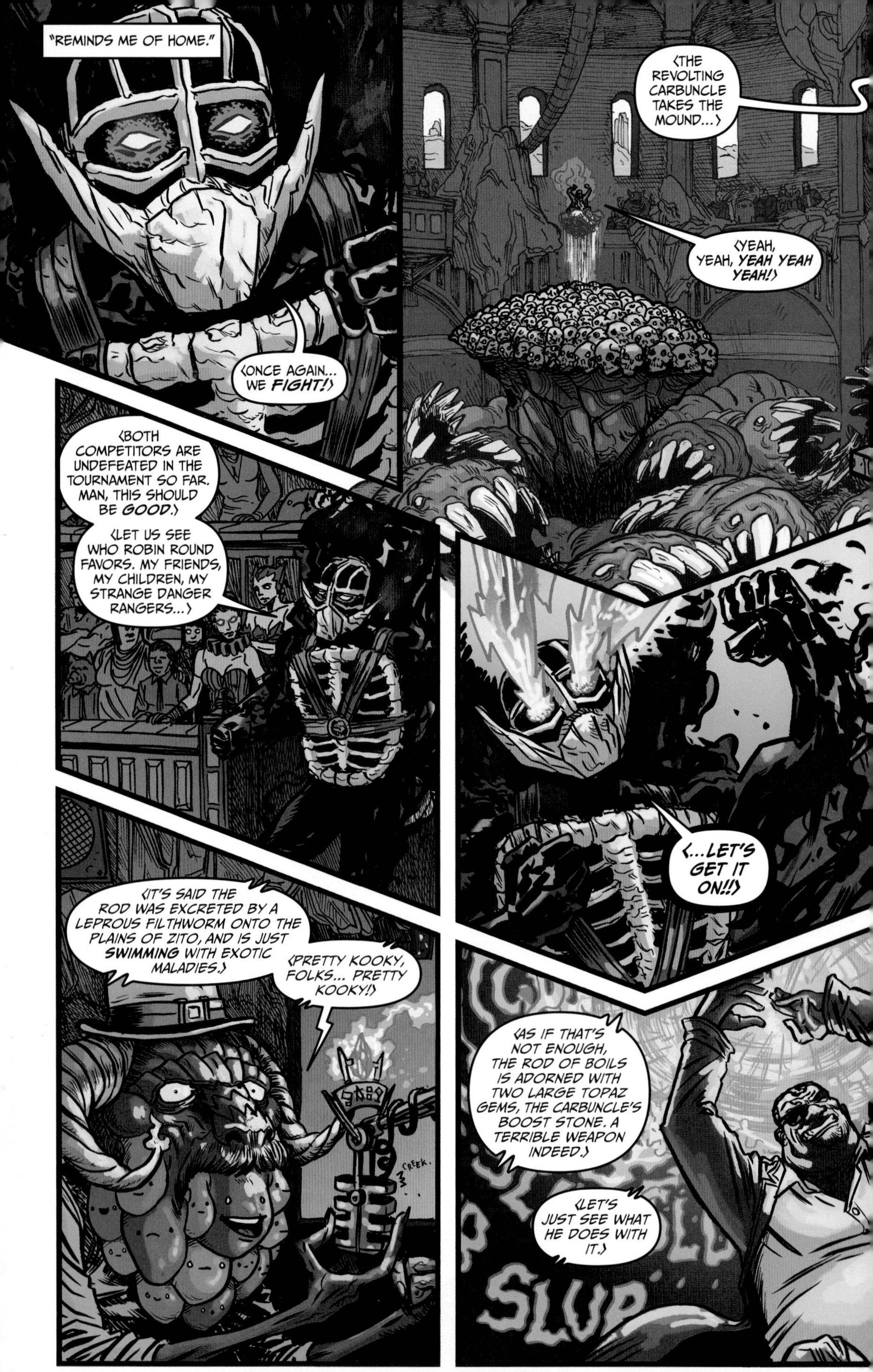
"REMINDS ME OF HOME."
‹ONCE AGAIN... WE FIGHT!›
‹THE REVOLTING CARBUNCLE TAKES THE MOUND...›
‹YEAH, YEAH, YEAH YEAH YEAH!›
‹BOTH COMPETITORS ARE UNDEFEATED IN THE TOURNAMENT SO FAR. MAN, THIS SHOULD BE GOOD.›
‹LET US SEE WHO ROBIN ROUND FAVORS. MY FRIENDS, MY CHILDREN, MY STRANGE DANGER RANGERS...›
‹...LET'S GET IT ON!!›
‹IT'S SAID THE ROD WAS EXCRETED BY A LEPROUS FILTHWORM ONTO THE PLAINS OF ZITO, AND IS JUST SWIMMING WITH EXOTIC MALADIES.›
‹PRETTY KOOKY, FOLKS... PRETTY KOOKY!›
CREEK.
‹AS IF THAT'S NOT ENOUGH, THE ROD OF BOILS IS ADORNED WITH TWO LARGE TOPAZ GEMS, THE CARBUNCLE'S BOOST STONE. A TERRIBLE WEAPON INDEED.›
‹LET'S JUST SEE WHAT HE DOES WITH IT.›
SLUP

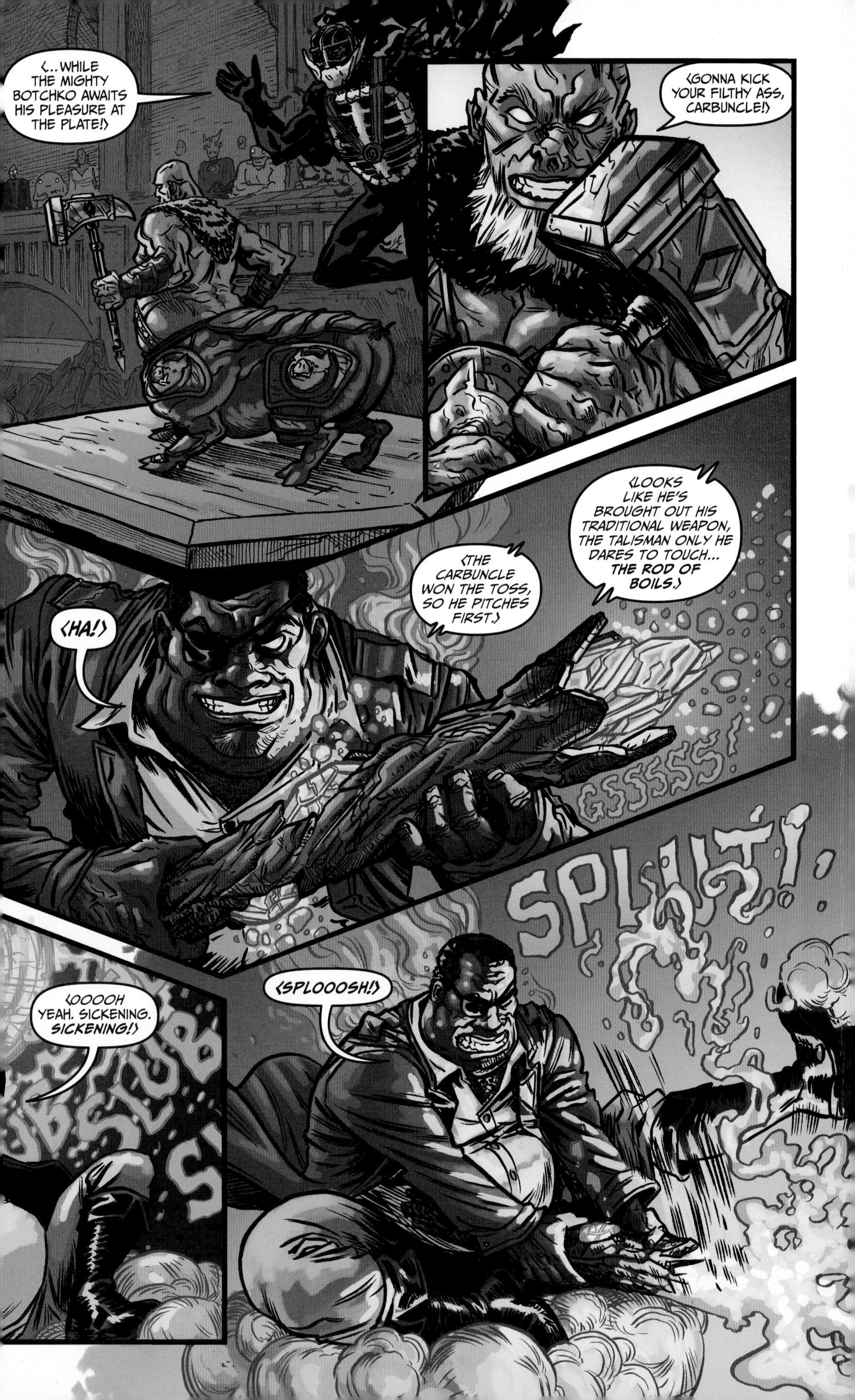
‹...WHILE THE MIGHTY BOTCHKO AWAITS HIS PLEASURE AT THE PLATE!›
‹GONNA KICK YOUR FILTHY ASS, CARBUNCLE!›
‹HA!›
‹THE CARBUNCLE WON THE TOSS, SO HE PITCHES FIRST.›
‹LOOKS LIKE HE'S BROUGHT OUT HIS TRADITIONAL WEAPON, THE TALISMAN ONLY HE DARES TO TOUCH... **THE ROD OF BOILS.**›
GSSSSS!
SPLUT!
‹OOOOH YEAH. SICKENING. **SICKENING!**›
‹SPLOOOSH!›

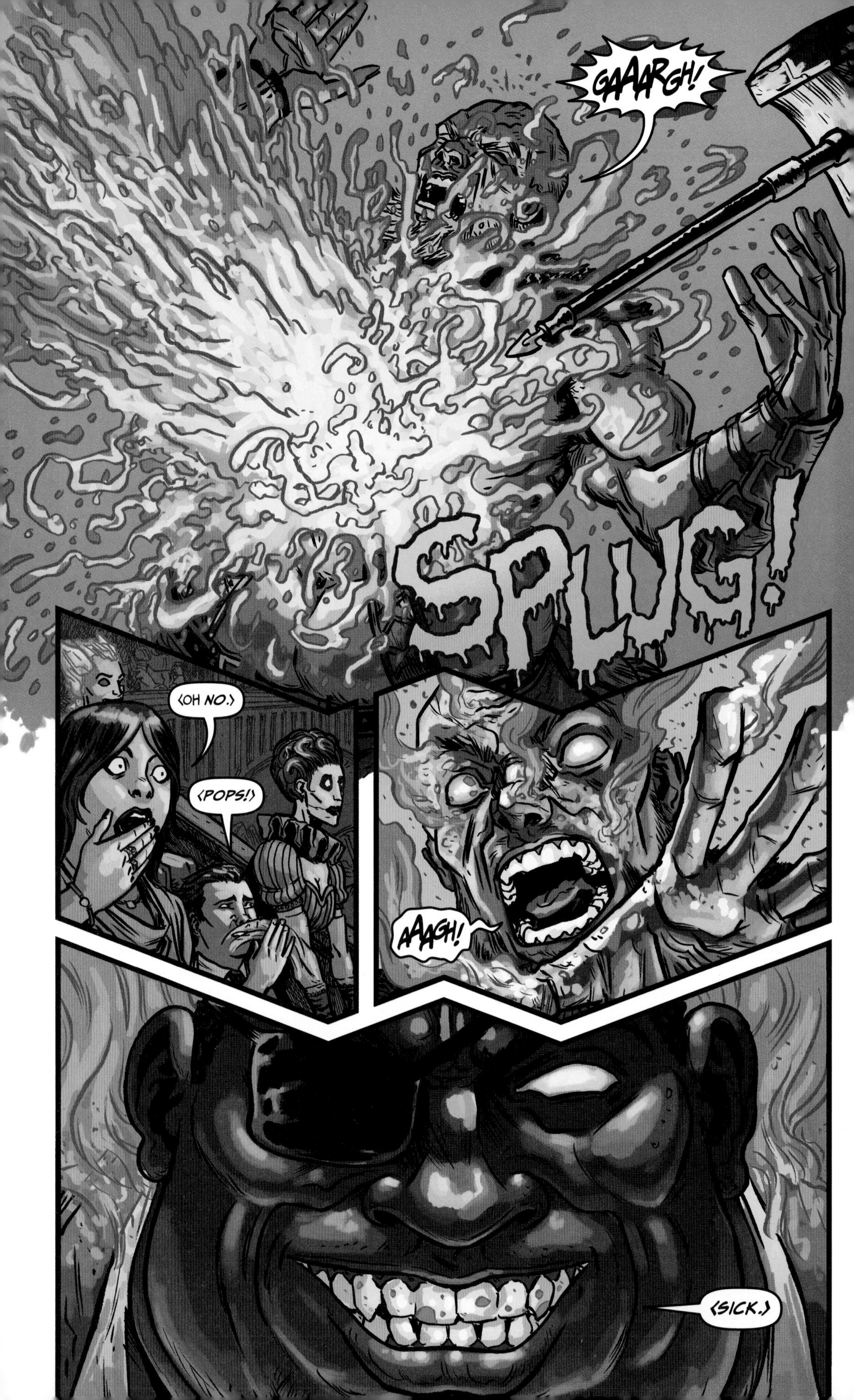
GAAARGH!
SPLUG!
⟨OH NO.⟩
⟨POPS!⟩
AAAGH!
⟨SICK.⟩

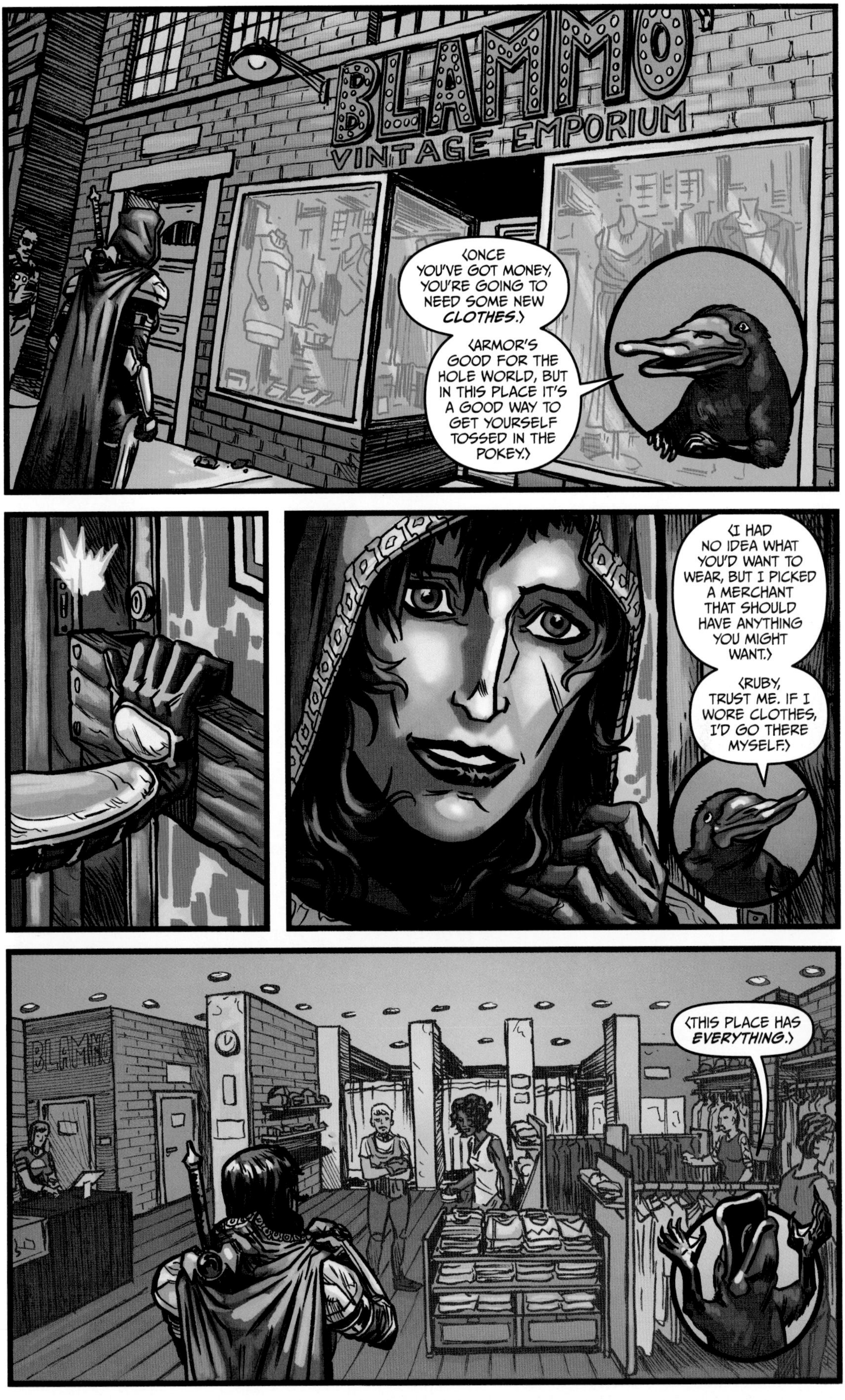
BLAMMO
VINTAGE EMPORIUM
⟨ONCE YOU'VE GOT MONEY, YOU'RE GOING TO NEED SOME NEW *CLOTHES*.⟩
⟨ARMOR'S GOOD FOR THE HOLE WORLD, BUT IN THIS PLACE IT'S A GOOD WAY TO GET YOURSELF TOSSED IN THE POKEY.⟩
⟨I HAD NO IDEA WHAT YOU'D WANT TO WEAR, BUT I PICKED A MERCHANT THAT SHOULD HAVE ANYTHING YOU MIGHT WANT.⟩
⟨RUBY, TRUST ME. IF I WORE CLOTHES, I'D GO THERE MYSELF.⟩
BLAMMO
⟨THIS PLACE HAS *EVERYTHING*.⟩

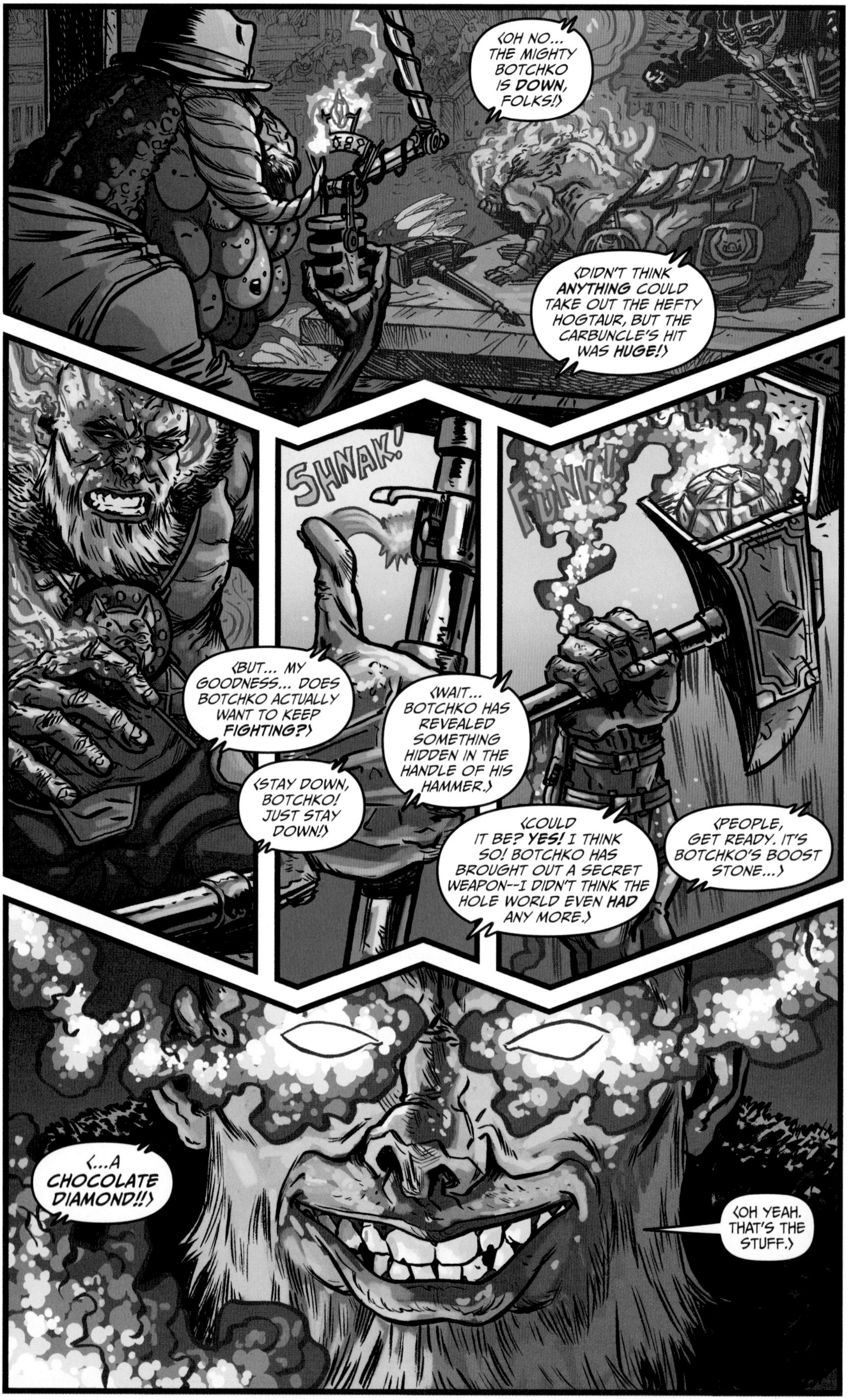
‹OH NO... THE MIGHTY BOTCHKO IS DOWN, FOLKS!›
‹DIDN'T THINK ANYTHING COULD TAKE OUT THE HEFTY HOGTAUR, BUT THE CARBUNCLE'S HIT WAS HUGE!›
SHNAK!
FUNK!
‹BUT... MY GOODNESS... DOES BOTCHKO ACTUALLY WANT TO KEEP FIGHTING?›
‹STAY DOWN, BOTCHKO! JUST STAY DOWN!›
‹WAIT... BOTCHKO HAS REVEALED SOMETHING HIDDEN IN THE HANDLE OF HIS HAMMER.›
‹COULD IT BE? YES! I THINK SO! BOTCHKO HAS BROUGHT OUT A SECRET WEAPON--I DIDN'T THINK THE HOLE WORLD EVEN HAD ANY MORE.›
‹PEOPLE, GET READY. IT'S BOTCHKO'S BOOST STONE...›
‹...A CHOCOLATE DIAMOND!!›
‹OH YEAH. THAT'S THE STUFF.›

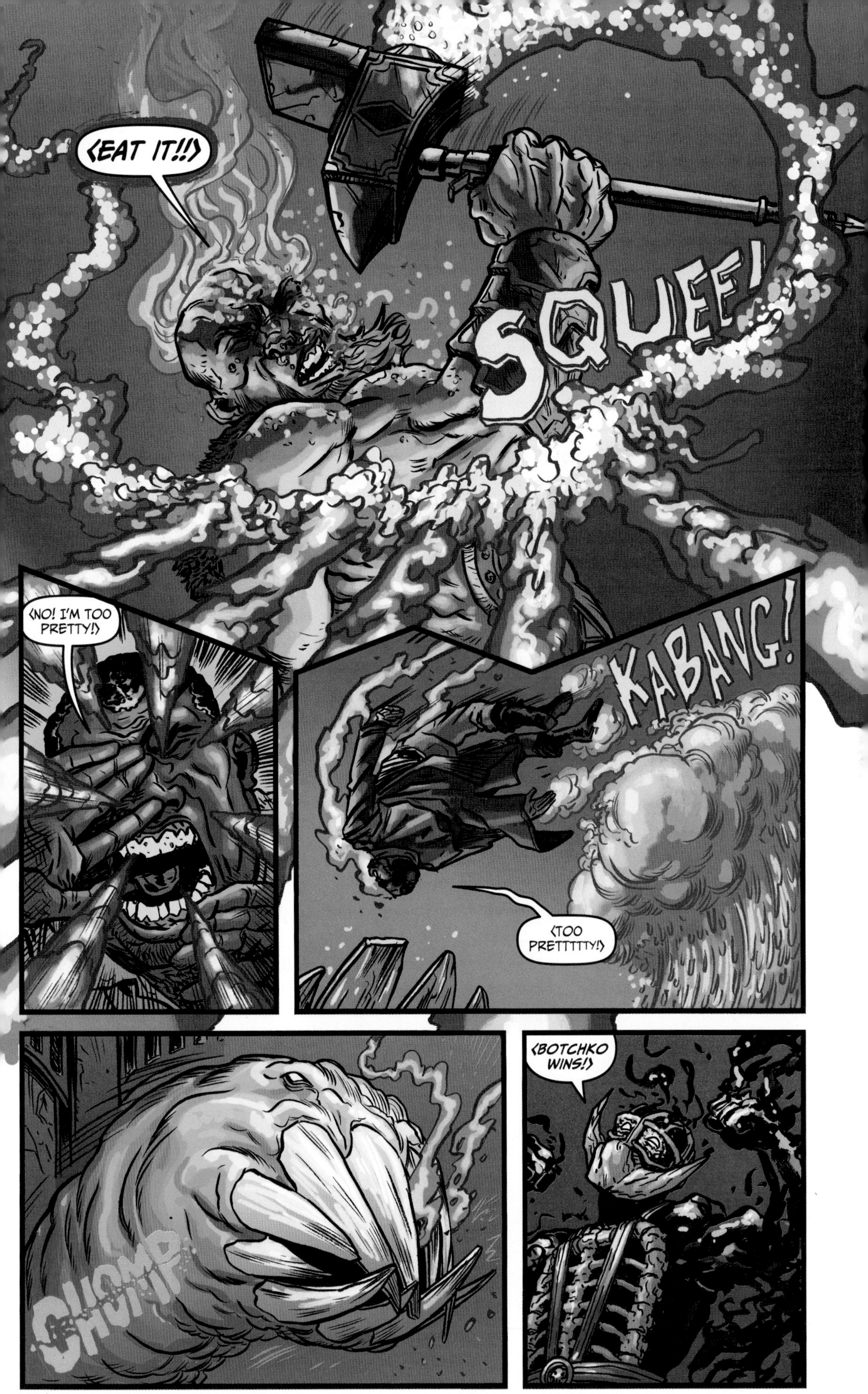
⟨EAT IT!!⟩
SQUEE!
⟨NO! I'M TOO PRETTY!⟩
KABANG!
⟨TOO PRETTTTTY!⟩
CHOMP
⟨BOTCHKO WINS!⟩

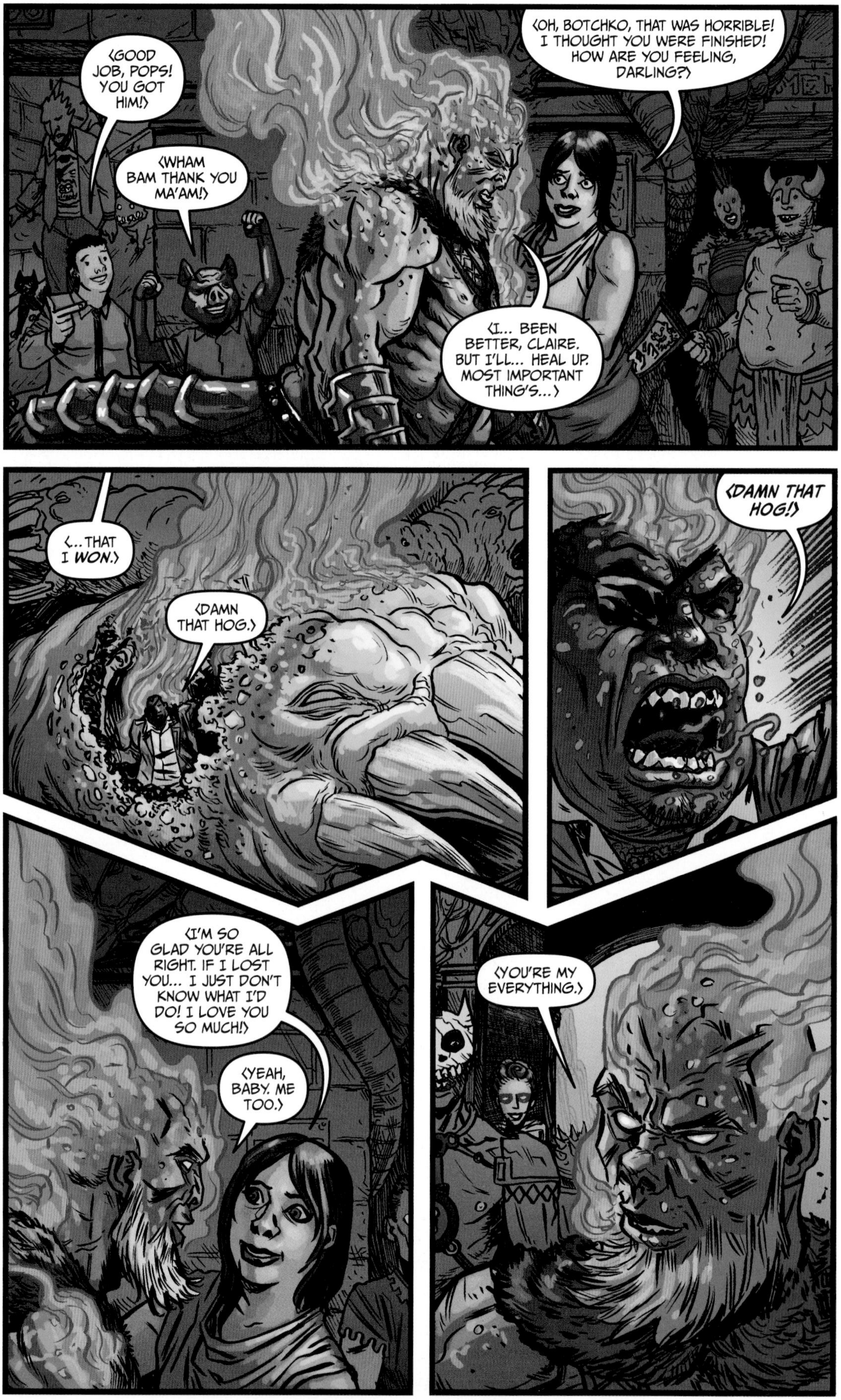

⟨GOOD JOB, POPS! YOU GOT HIM!⟩
⟨WHAM BAM THANK YOU MA'AM!⟩
⟨OH, BOTCHKO, THAT WAS HORRIBLE! I THOUGHT YOU WERE FINISHED! HOW ARE YOU FEELING, DARLING?⟩
⟨I... BEEN BETTER, CLAIRE. BUT I'LL... HEAL UP. MOST IMPORTANT THING'S...⟩
⟨...THAT I *WON.*⟩
⟨DAMN THAT HOG.⟩
⟨*DAMN THAT HOG!*⟩
⟨I'M SO GLAD YOU'RE ALL RIGHT. IF I LOST YOU... I JUST DON'T KNOW WHAT I'D DO! I LOVE YOU SO MUCH!⟩
⟨YEAH, BABY. ME TOO.⟩
⟨YOU'RE MY EVERYTHING.⟩

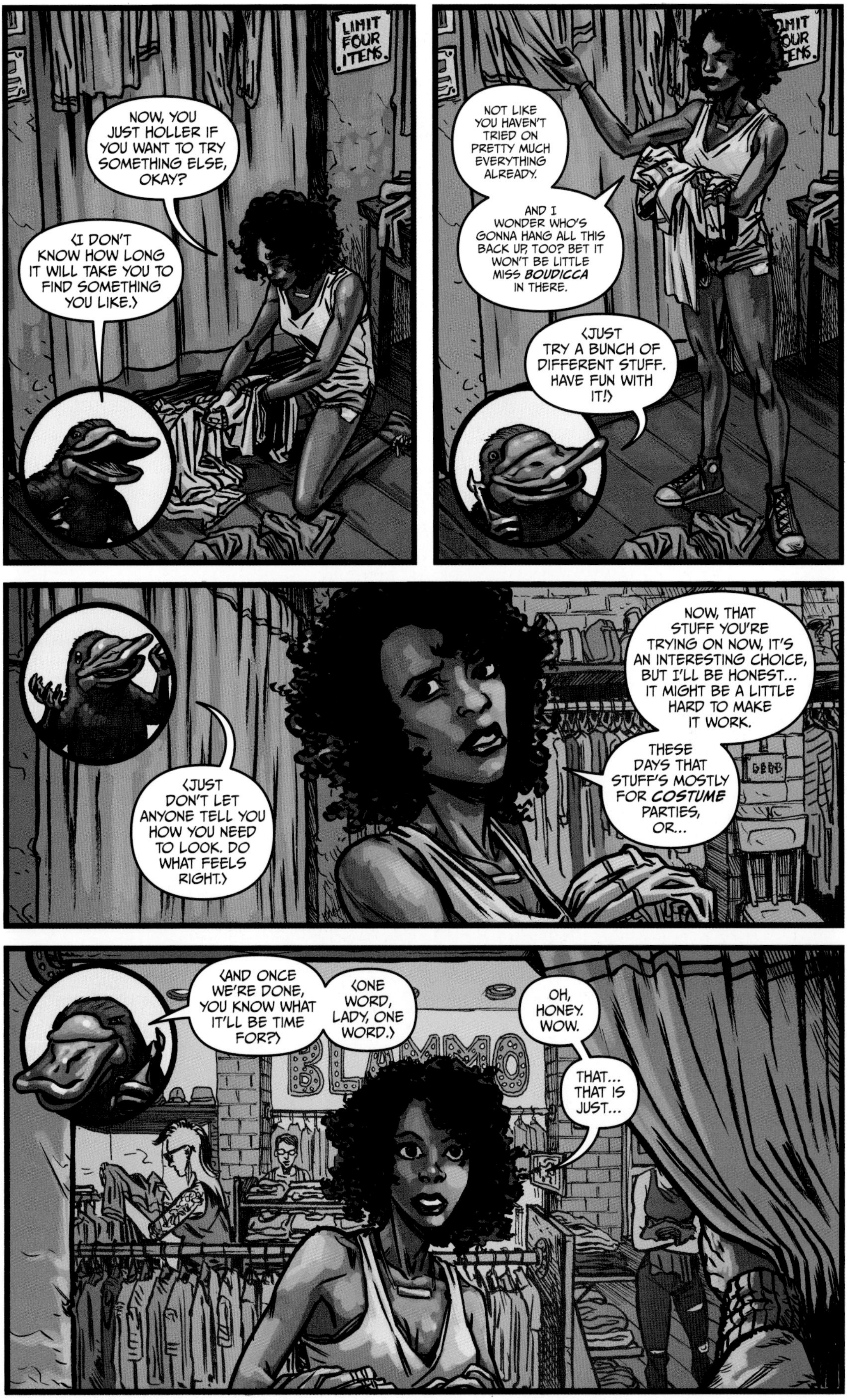
LIMIT FOUR ITEMS.
NOW, YOU JUST HOLLER IF YOU WANT TO TRY SOMETHING ELSE, OKAY?
<I DON'T KNOW HOW LONG IT WILL TAKE YOU TO FIND SOMETHING YOU LIKE.>
LIMIT FOUR ITEMS.
NOT LIKE YOU HAVEN'T TRIED ON PRETTY MUCH EVERYTHING ALREADY.
AND I WONDER WHO'S GONNA HANG ALL THIS BACK UP, TOO? BET IT WON'T BE LITTLE MISS *BOUDICCA* IN THERE.
<JUST TRY A BUNCH OF DIFFERENT STUFF. HAVE FUN WITH IT!>
<JUST DON'T LET ANYONE TELL YOU HOW YOU NEED TO LOOK. DO WHAT FEELS RIGHT.>
NOW, THAT STUFF YOU'RE TRYING ON NOW, IT'S AN INTERESTING CHOICE, BUT I'LL BE HONEST... IT MIGHT BE A LITTLE HARD TO MAKE IT WORK.
THESE DAYS THAT STUFF'S MOSTLY FOR *COSTUME* PARTIES, OR...
<AND ONCE WE'RE DONE, YOU KNOW WHAT IT'LL BE TIME FOR?>
<ONE WORD, LADY, ONE WORD.>
OH, HONEY. WOW.
THAT... THAT IS JUST...
BLAMMO

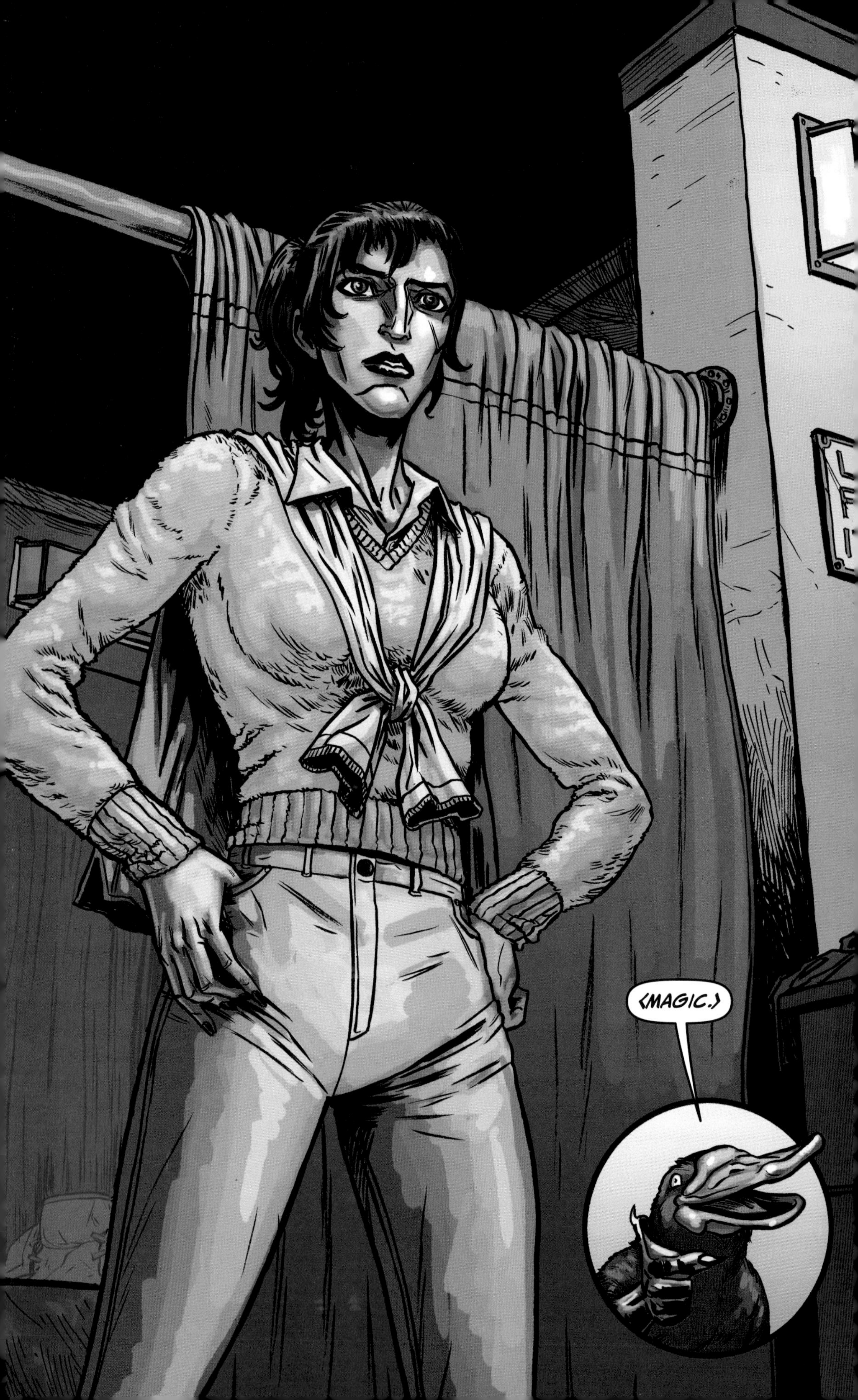
<MAGIC.>

NINE

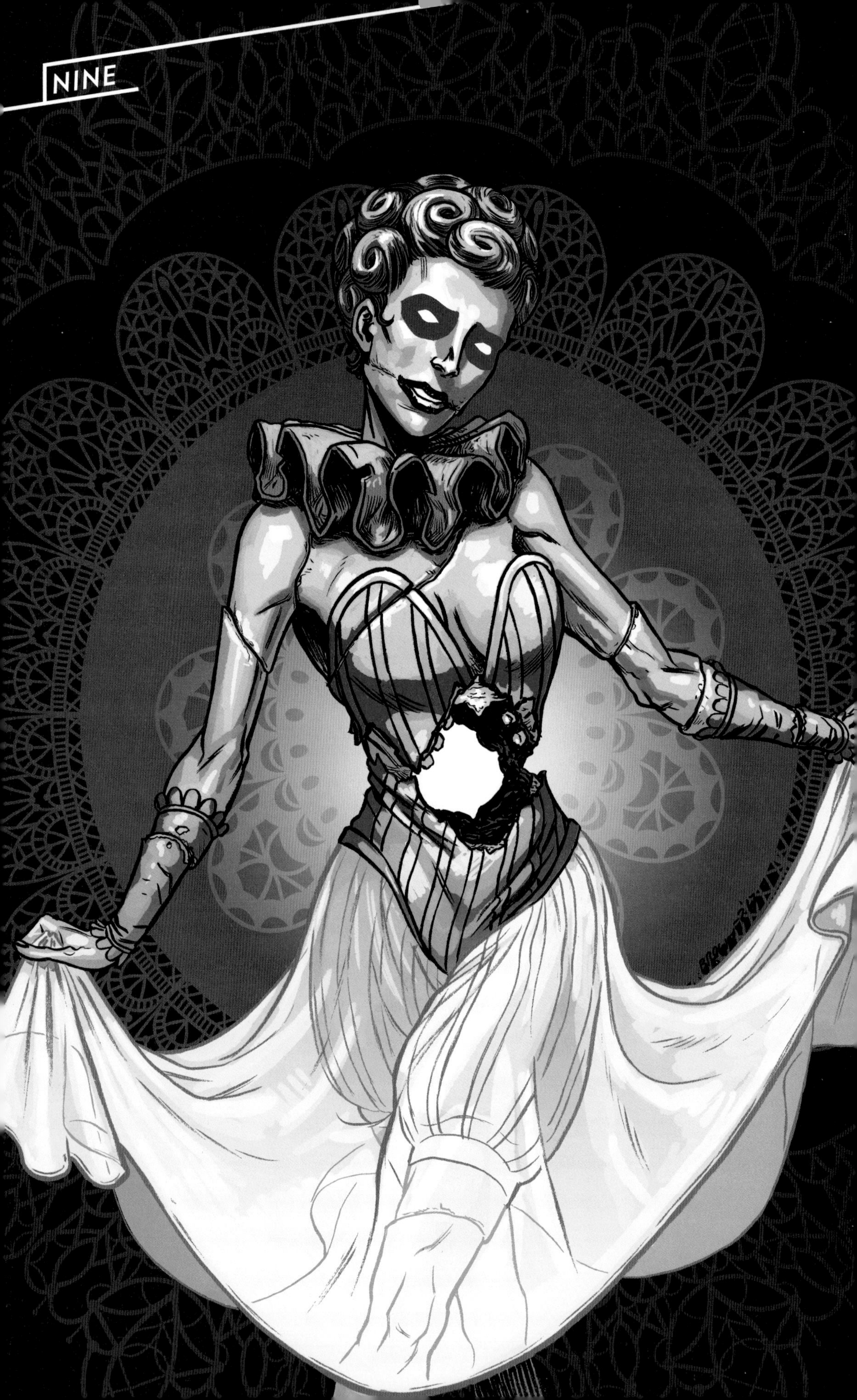

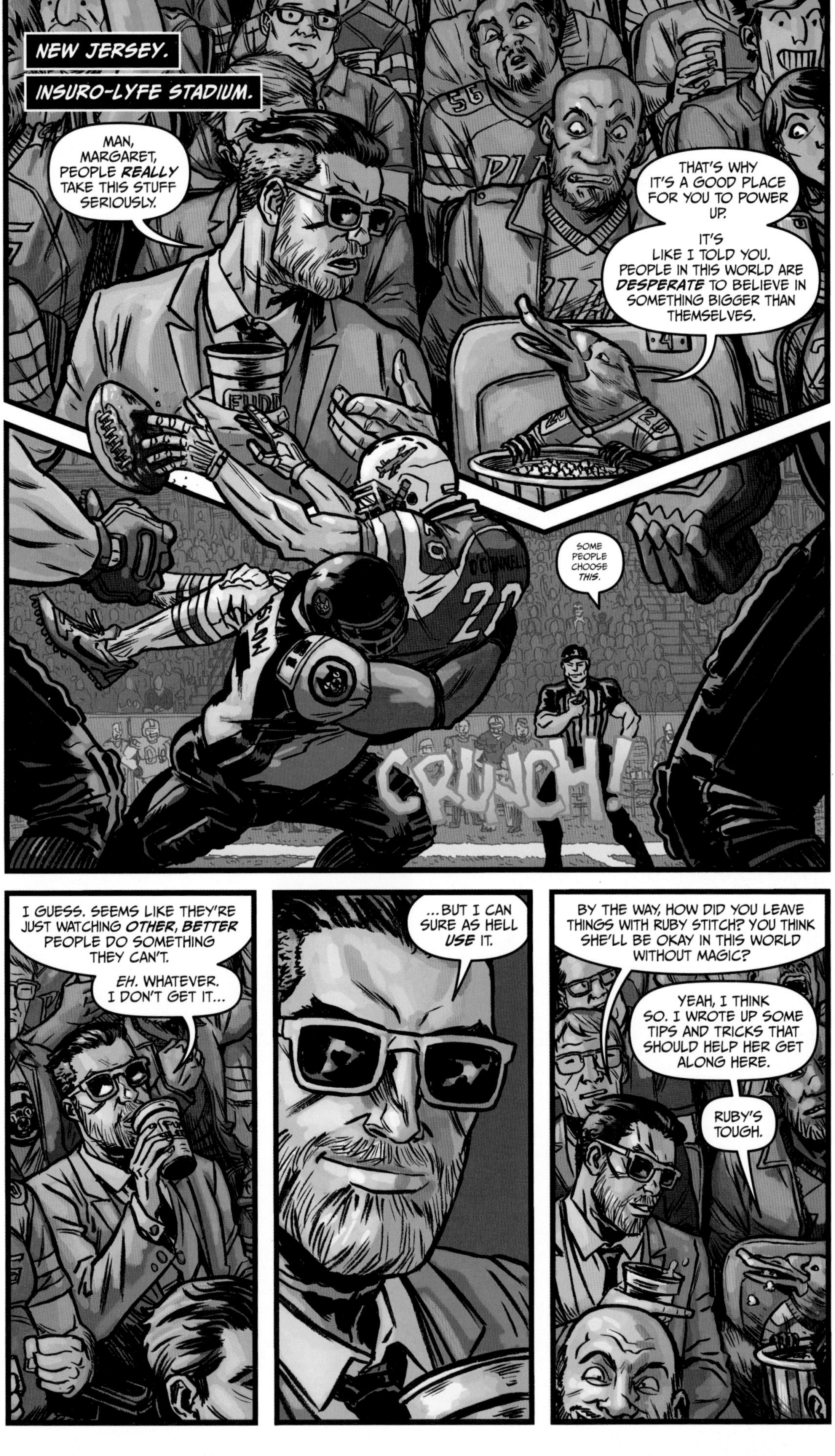
NEW JERSEY.
INSURO-LYFE STADIUM.
MAN, MARGARET, PEOPLE *REALLY* TAKE THIS STUFF SERIOUSLY.
THAT'S WHY IT'S A GOOD PLACE FOR YOU TO POWER UP.
IT'S LIKE I TOLD YOU. PEOPLE IN THIS WORLD ARE *DESPERATE* TO BELIEVE IN SOMETHING BIGGER THAN THEMSELVES.
SOME PEOPLE CHOOSE *THIS*.
CRUNCH!
I GUESS. SEEMS LIKE THEY'RE JUST WATCHING *OTHER, BETTER* PEOPLE DO SOMETHING THEY CAN'T.
EH. WHATEVER. I DON'T GET IT...
...BUT I CAN SURE AS HELL *USE* IT.
BY THE WAY, HOW DID YOU LEAVE THINGS WITH RUBY STITCH? YOU THINK SHE'LL BE OKAY IN THIS WORLD WITHOUT MAGIC?
YEAH, I THINK SO. I WROTE UP SOME TIPS AND TRICKS THAT SHOULD HELP HER GET ALONG HERE.
RUBY'S TOUGH.

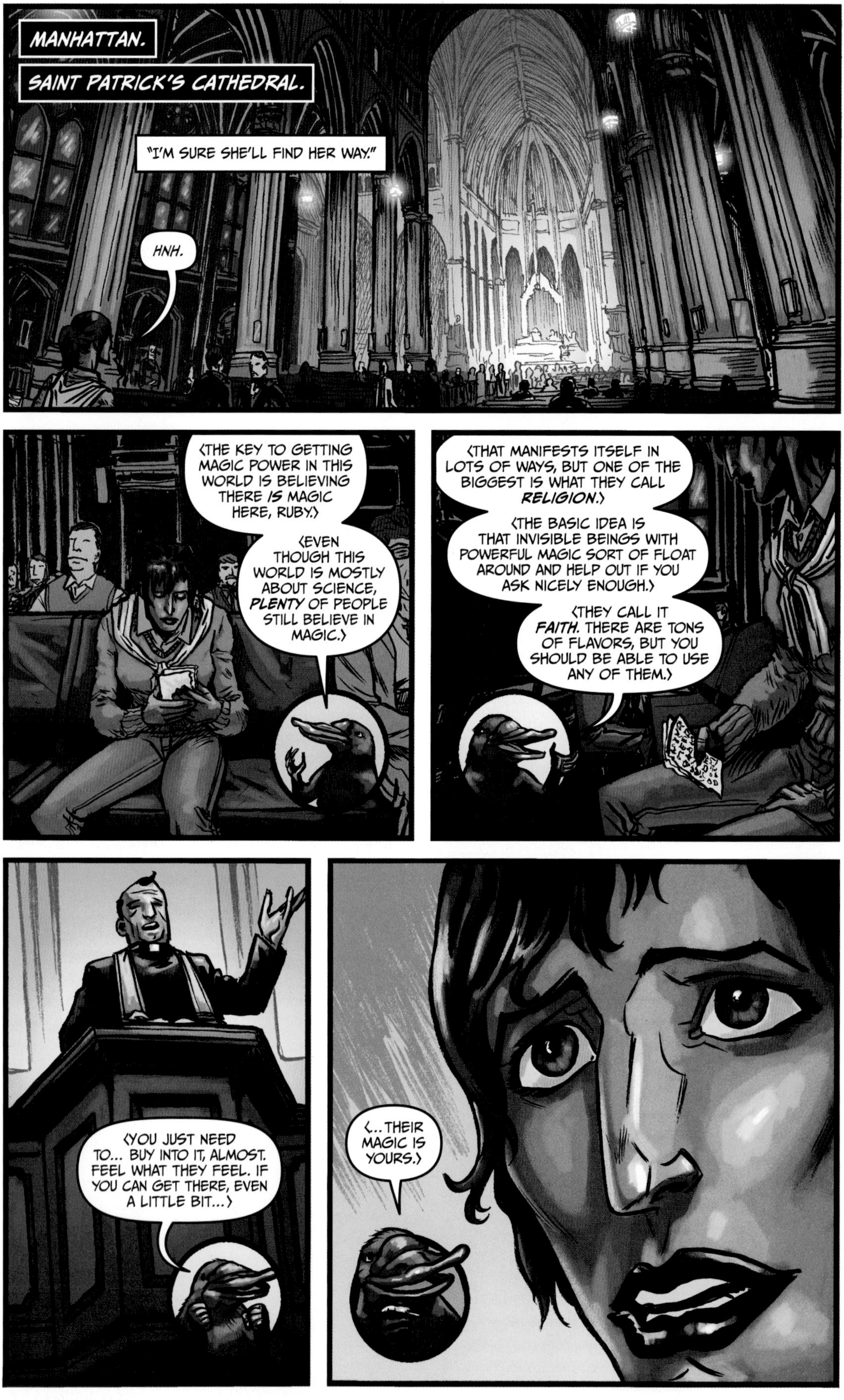
MANHATTAN.
SAINT PATRICK'S CATHEDRAL.
"I'M SURE SHE'LL FIND HER WAY."
HNH.
‹THE KEY TO GETTING MAGIC POWER IN THIS WORLD IS BELIEVING THERE *IS* MAGIC HERE, RUBY.›
‹EVEN THOUGH THIS WORLD IS MOSTLY ABOUT SCIENCE, *PLENTY* OF PEOPLE STILL BELIEVE IN MAGIC.›
‹THAT MANIFESTS ITSELF IN LOTS OF WAYS, BUT ONE OF THE BIGGEST IS WHAT THEY CALL *RELIGION*.›
‹THE BASIC IDEA IS THAT INVISIBLE BEINGS WITH POWERFUL MAGIC SORT OF FLOAT AROUND AND HELP OUT IF YOU ASK NICELY ENOUGH.›
‹THEY CALL IT *FAITH*. THERE ARE TONS OF FLAVORS, BUT YOU SHOULD BE ABLE TO USE ANY OF THEM.›
‹YOU JUST NEED TO... BUY INTO IT, ALMOST. FEEL WHAT THEY FEEL. IF YOU CAN GET THERE, EVEN A LITTLE BIT...›
‹...THEIR MAGIC IS YOURS.›

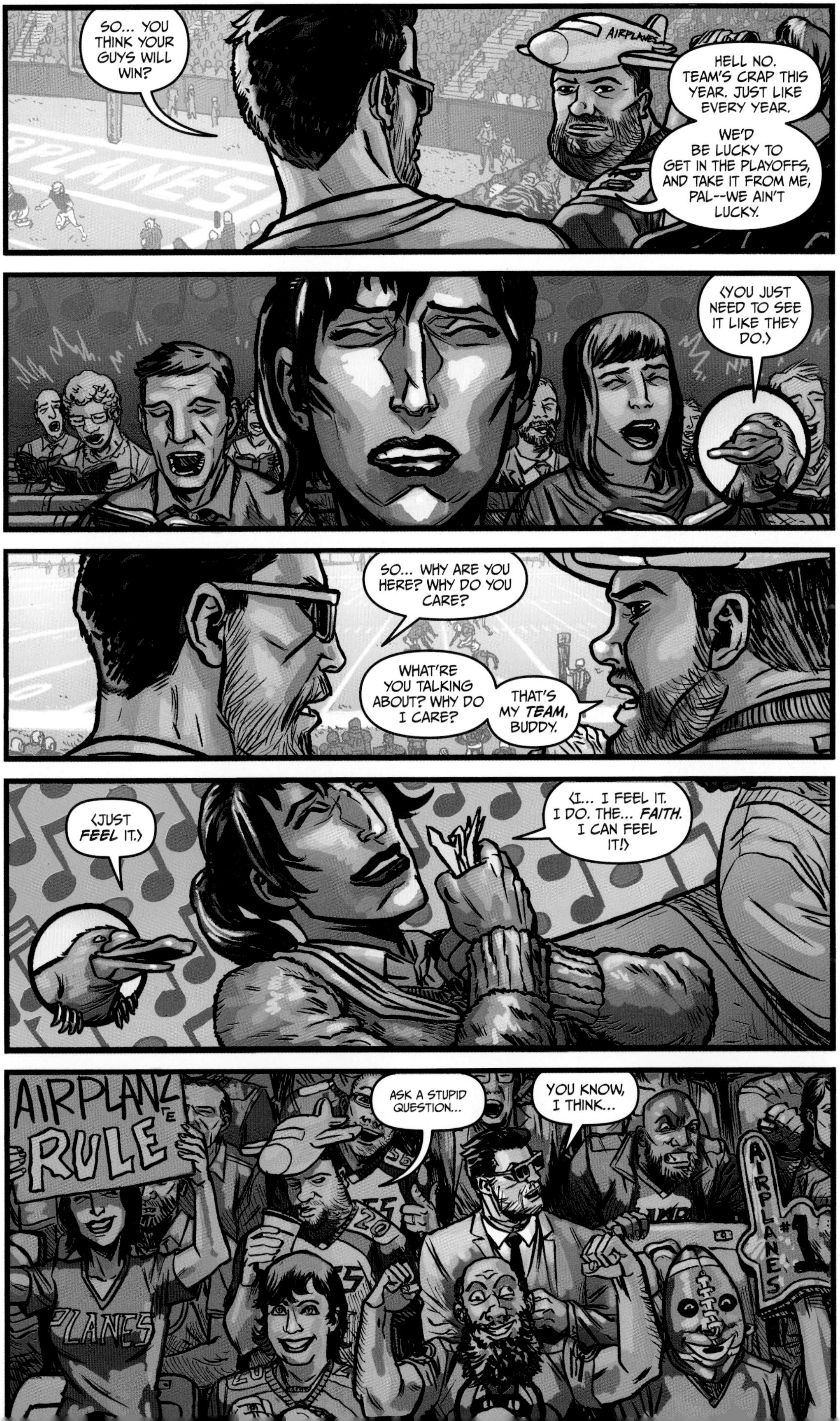
SO... YOU THINK YOUR GUYS WILL WIN?
AIRPLANES
HELL NO. TEAM'S CRAP THIS YEAR. JUST LIKE EVERY YEAR.
WE'D BE LUCKY TO GET IN THE PLAYOFFS, AND TAKE IT FROM ME, PAL--WE AIN'T LUCKY.
PLANES
‹YOU JUST NEED TO SEE IT LIKE THEY DO.›
SO... WHY ARE YOU HERE? WHY DO YOU CARE?
WHAT'RE YOU TALKING ABOUT? WHY DO I CARE?
THAT'S MY *TEAM*, BUDDY.
‹JUST *FEEL* IT.›
‹I... I FEEL IT. I DO. THE... *FAITH*. I CAN FEEL IT!›
AIRPLANZ E RULE
ASK A STUPID QUESTION...
YOU KNOW, I THINK...
AIRPLANES #1
PLANES

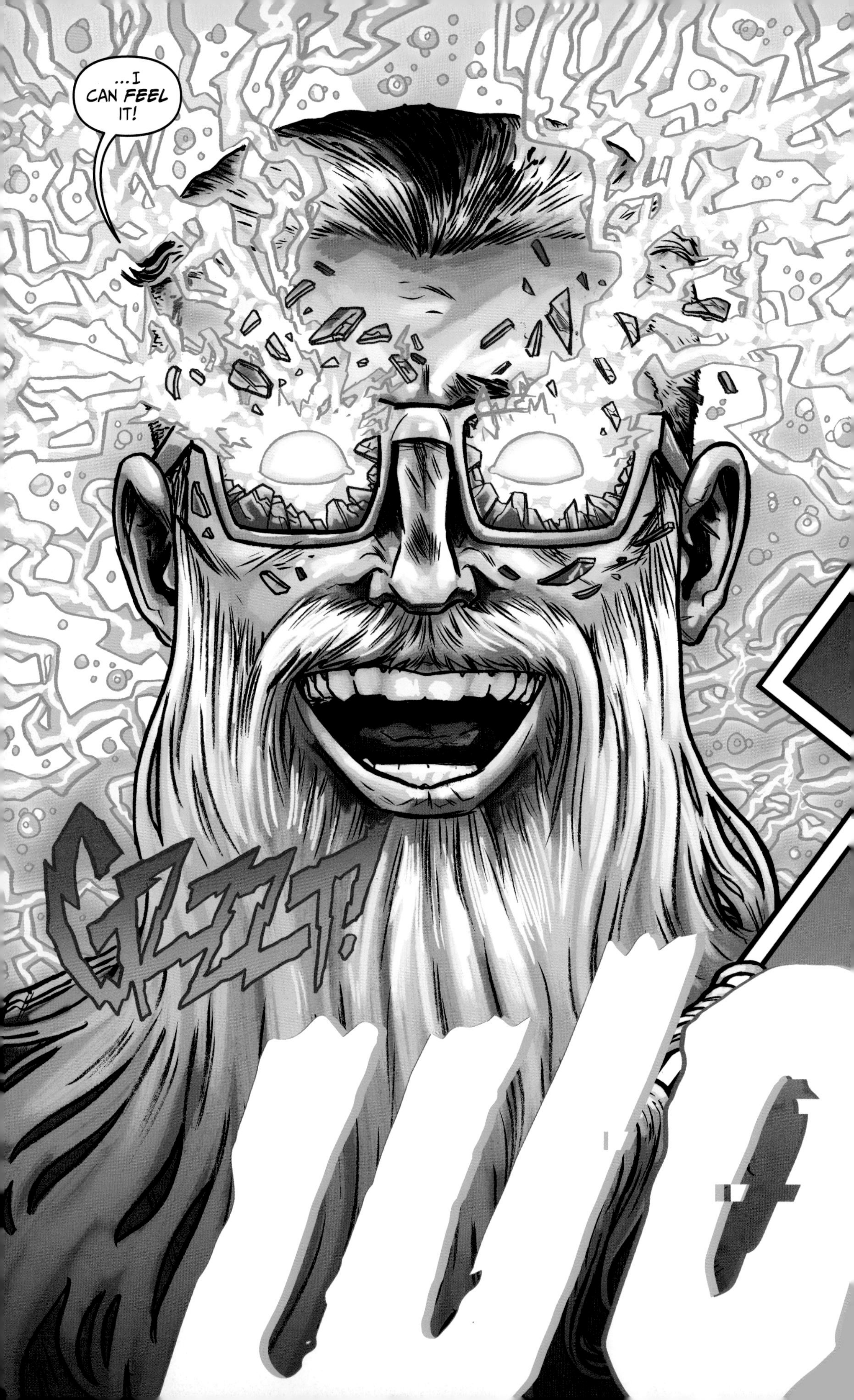
...I CAN FEEL IT!
GZZZT!

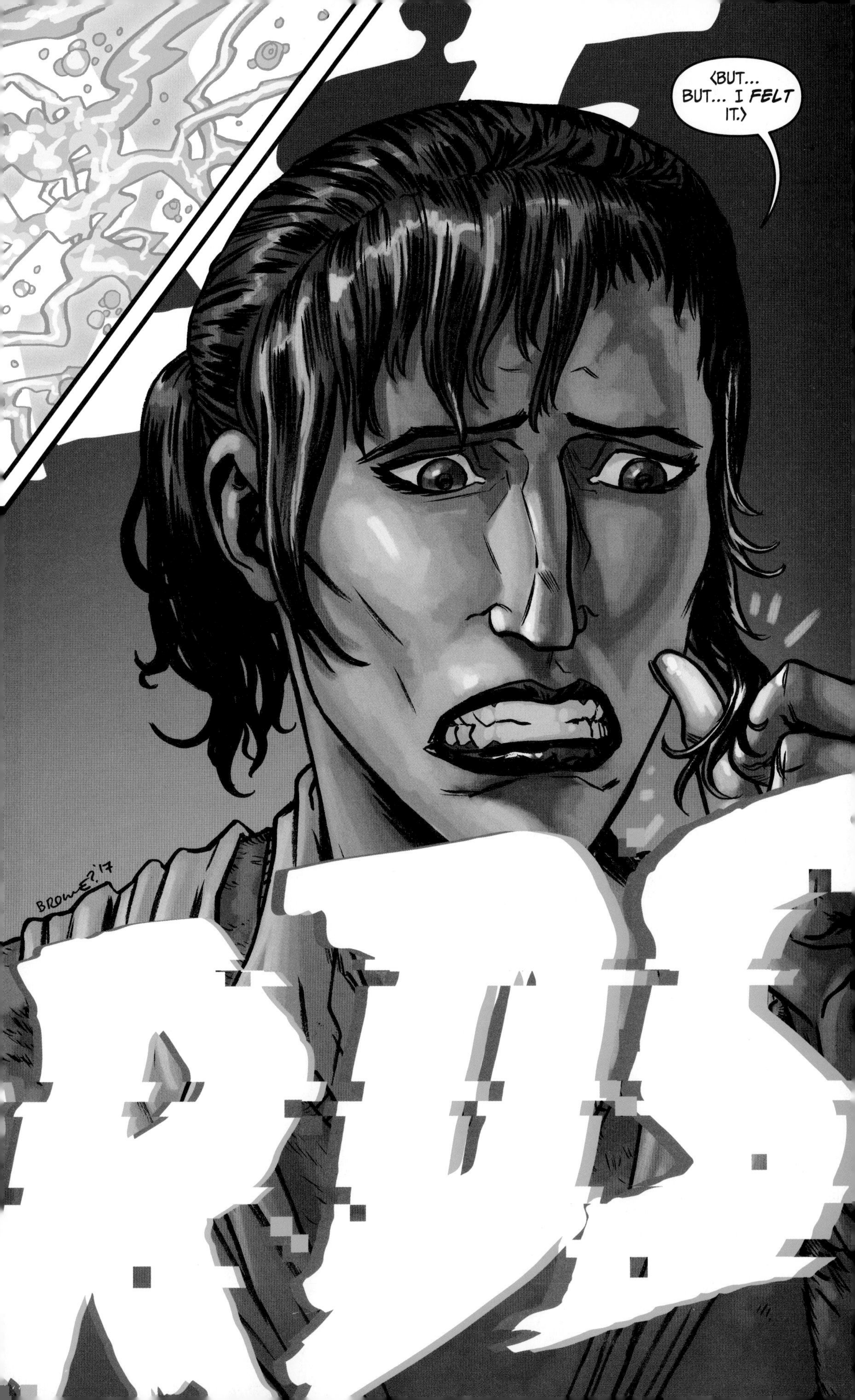
<BUT... BUT... I FELT IT.>

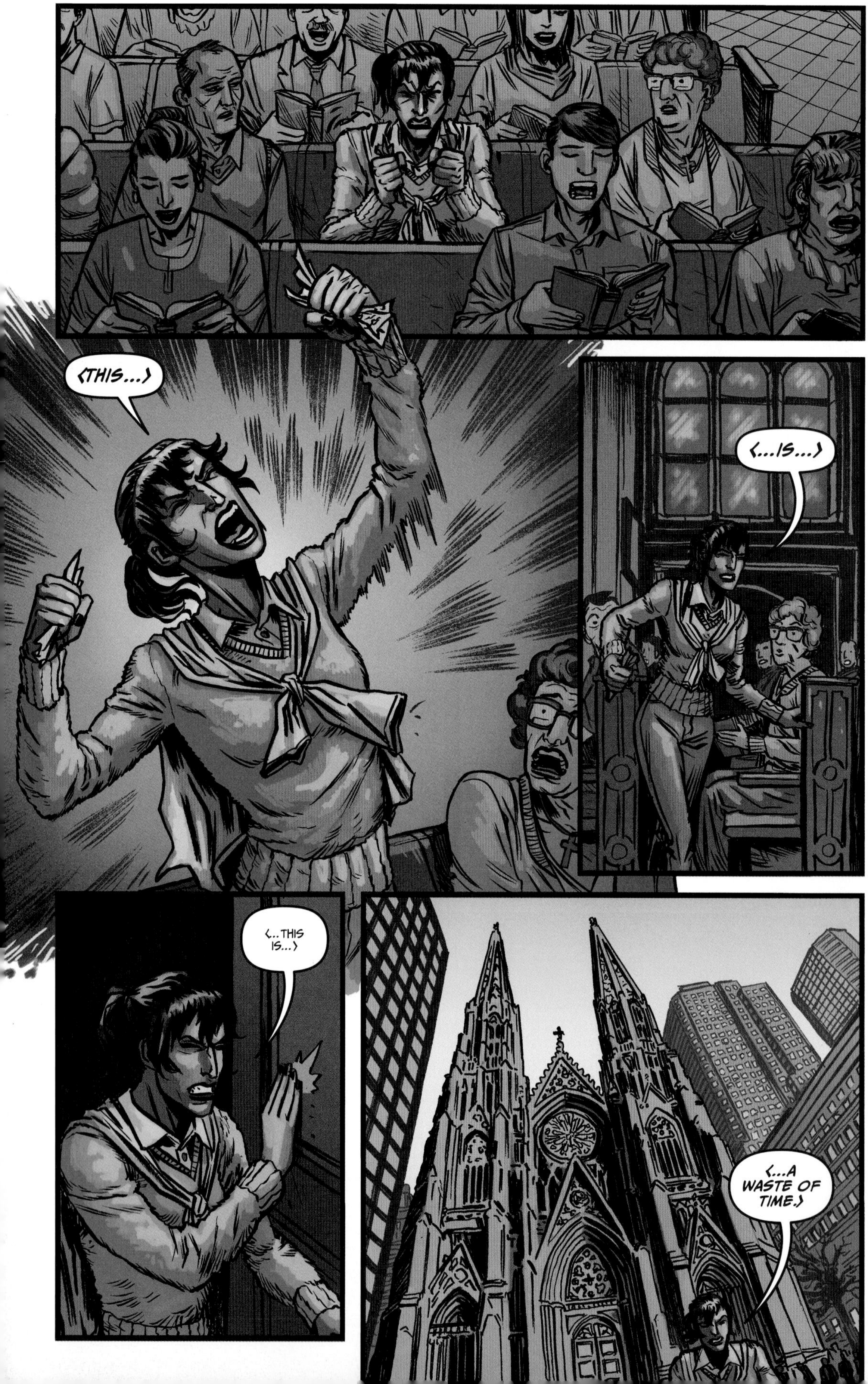
‹THIS...›
‹...IS...›
‹..THIS IS...›
‹...A WASTE OF TIME.›

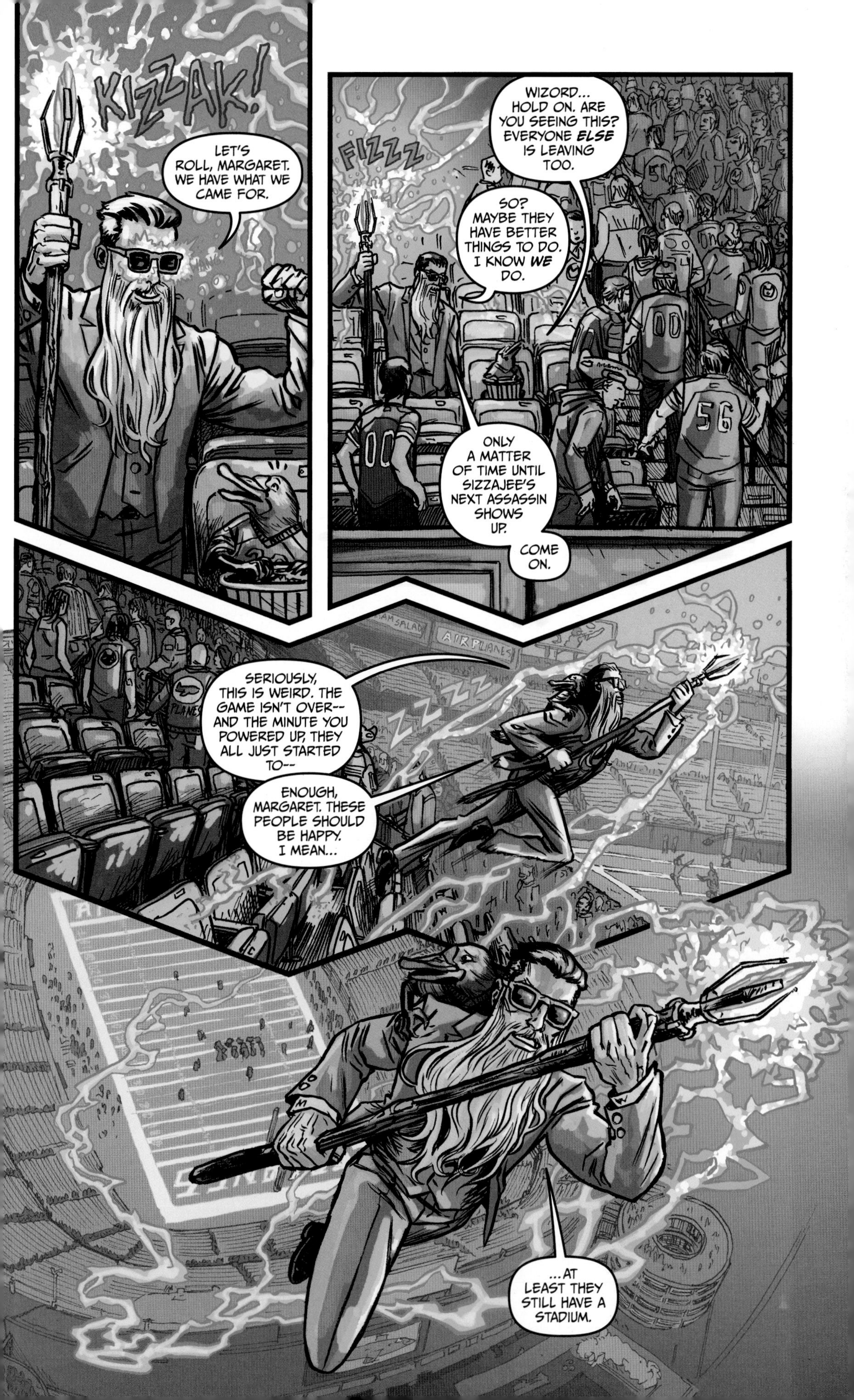
KIZZAK!
LET'S ROLL, MARGARET. WE HAVE WHAT WE CAME FOR.
FIZZZ
WIZORD... HOLD ON. ARE YOU SEEING THIS? EVERYONE *ELSE* IS LEAVING TOO.
SO? MAYBE THEY HAVE BETTER THINGS TO DO. I KNOW *WE* DO.
ONLY A MATTER OF TIME UNTIL SIZZAJEE'S NEXT ASSASSIN SHOWS UP.
COME ON.
ZZZZ
SERIOUSLY, THIS IS WEIRD. THE GAME ISN'T OVER-- AND THE MINUTE YOU POWERED UP, THEY ALL JUST STARTED TO--
ENOUGH, MARGARET. THESE PEOPLE SHOULD BE HAPPY. I MEAN...
...AT LEAST THEY STILL HAVE A STADIUM.

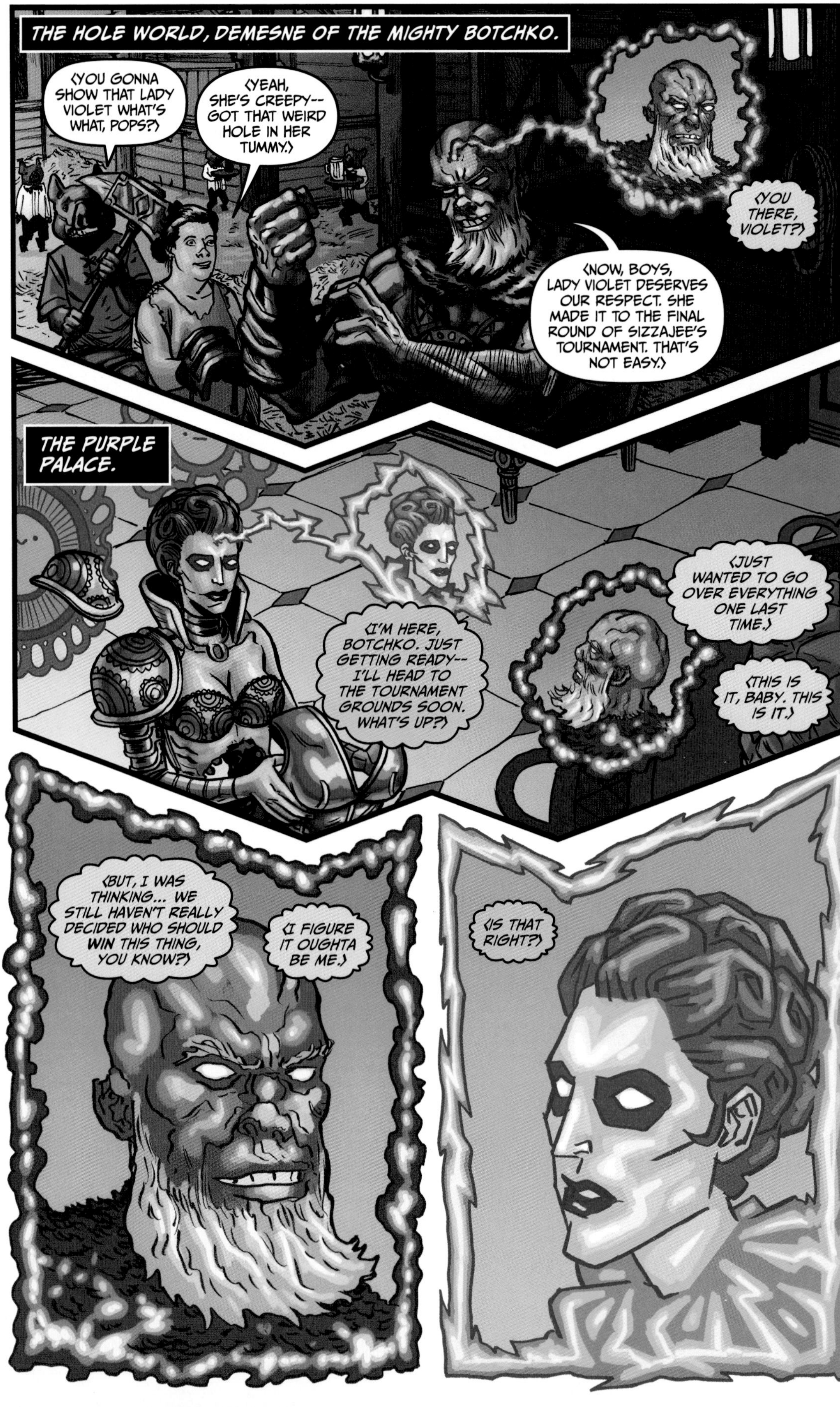

THE HOLE WORLD, DEMESNE OF THE MIGHTY BOTCHKO.
‹YOU GONNA SHOW THAT LADY VIOLET WHAT'S WHAT, POPS?›
‹YEAH, SHE'S CREEPY-- GOT THAT WEIRD HOLE IN HER TUMMY.›
‹NOW, BOYS, LADY VIOLET DESERVES OUR RESPECT. SHE MADE IT TO THE FINAL ROUND OF SIZZAJEE'S TOURNAMENT. THAT'S NOT EASY.›
‹YOU THERE, VIOLET?›
THE PURPLE PALACE.
‹I'M HERE, BOTCHKO. JUST GETTING READY-- I'LL HEAD TO THE TOURNAMENT GROUNDS SOON. WHAT'S UP?›
‹JUST WANTED TO GO OVER EVERYTHING ONE LAST TIME.›
‹THIS IS IT, BABY. THIS IS IT.›
‹BUT, I WAS THINKING... WE STILL HAVEN'T REALLY DECIDED WHO SHOULD WIN THIS THING, YOU KNOW?›
‹I FIGURE IT OUGHTA BE ME.›
‹IS THAT RIGHT?›

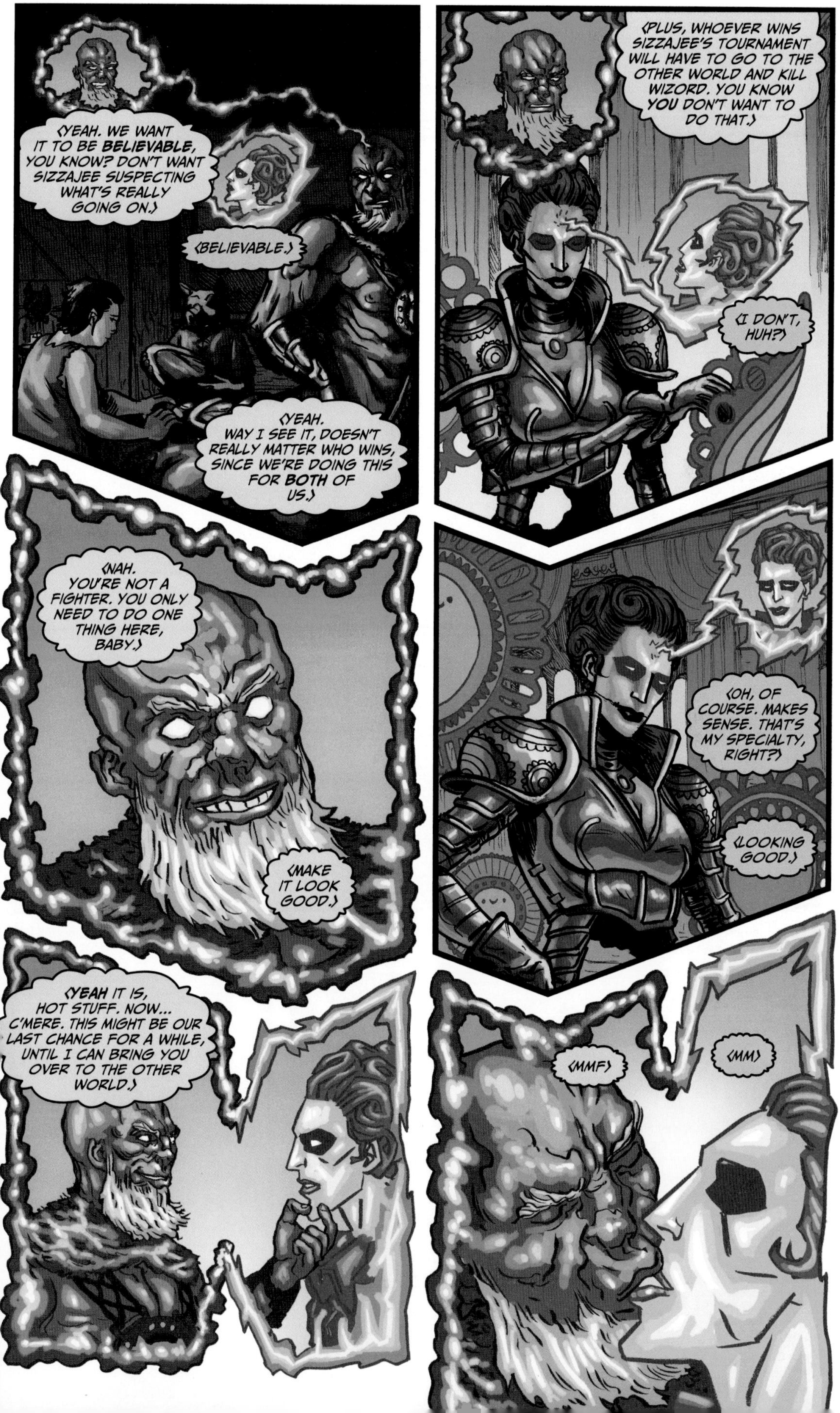

⟨YEAH. WE WANT IT TO BE BELIEVABLE, YOU KNOW? DON'T WANT SIZZAJEE SUSPECTING WHAT'S REALLY GOING ON.⟩
⟨BELIEVABLE.⟩
⟨YEAH. WAY I SEE IT, DOESN'T REALLY MATTER WHO WINS, SINCE WE'RE DOING THIS FOR BOTH OF US.⟩
⟨PLUS, WHOEVER WINS SIZZAJEE'S TOURNAMENT WILL HAVE TO GO TO THE OTHER WORLD AND KILL WIZORD. YOU KNOW YOU DON'T WANT TO DO THAT.⟩
⟨I DON'T, HUH?⟩
⟨NAH. YOU'RE NOT A FIGHTER. YOU ONLY NEED TO DO ONE THING HERE, BABY.⟩
⟨MAKE IT LOOK GOOD.⟩
⟨OH, OF COURSE. MAKES SENSE. THAT'S MY SPECIALTY, RIGHT?⟩
⟨LOOKING GOOD.⟩
⟨YEAH IT IS, HOT STUFF. NOW... C'MERE. THIS MIGHT BE OUR LAST CHANCE FOR A WHILE, UNTIL I CAN BRING YOU OVER TO THE OTHER WORLD.⟩
⟨MMF⟩
⟨MM⟩

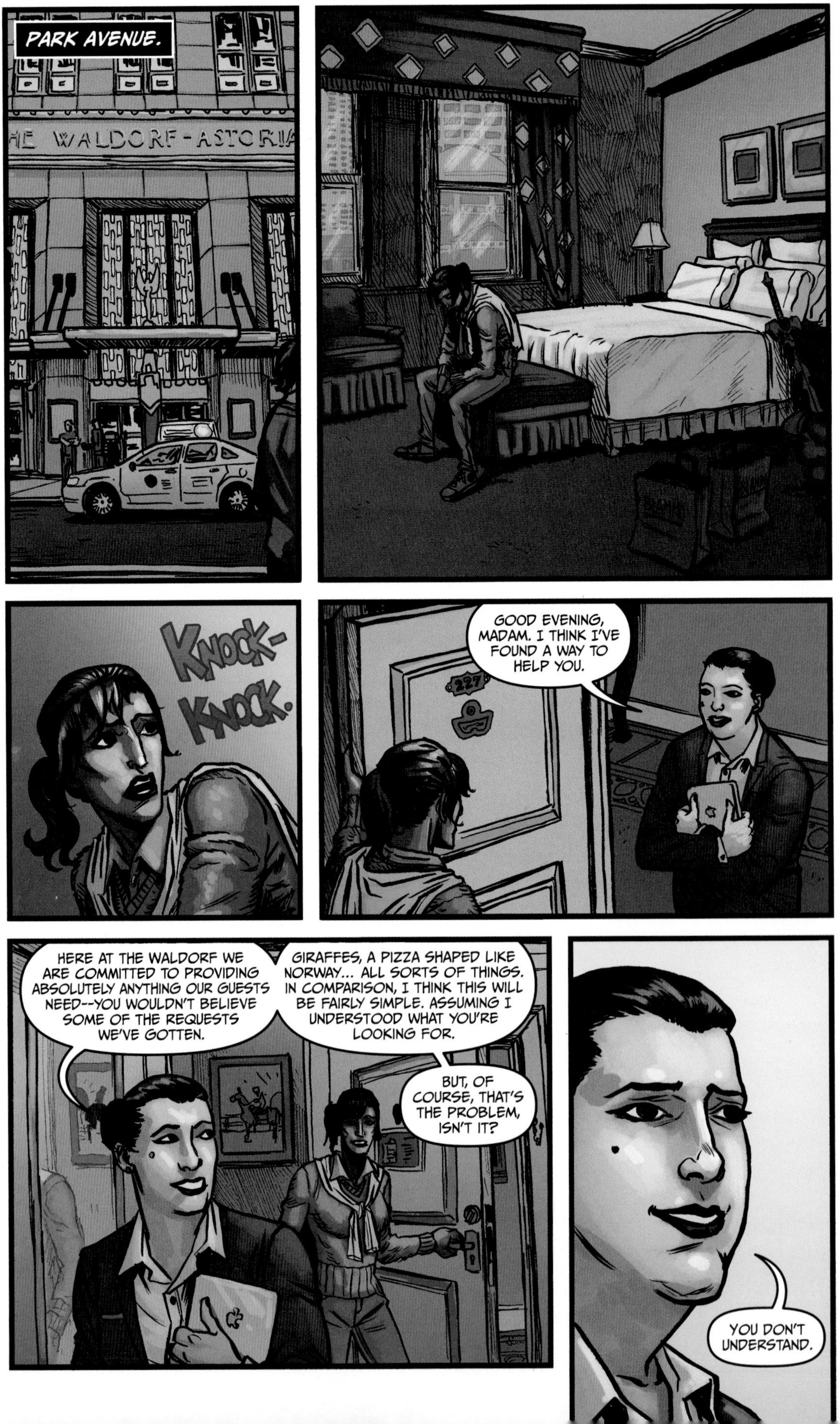
PARK AVENUE.
THE WALDORF-ASTORIA
KNOCK-KNOCK.
227
GOOD EVENING, MADAM. I THINK I'VE FOUND A WAY TO HELP YOU.
HERE AT THE WALDORF WE ARE COMMITTED TO PROVIDING ABSOLUTELY ANYTHING OUR GUESTS NEED--YOU WOULDN'T BELIEVE SOME OF THE REQUESTS WE'VE GOTTEN.
GIRAFFES, A PIZZA SHAPED LIKE NORWAY... ALL SORTS OF THINGS. IN COMPARISON, I THINK THIS WILL BE FAIRLY SIMPLE. ASSUMING I UNDERSTOOD WHAT YOU'RE LOOKING FOR.
BUT, OF COURSE, THAT'S THE PROBLEM, ISN'T IT?
YOU DON'T UNDERSTAND.

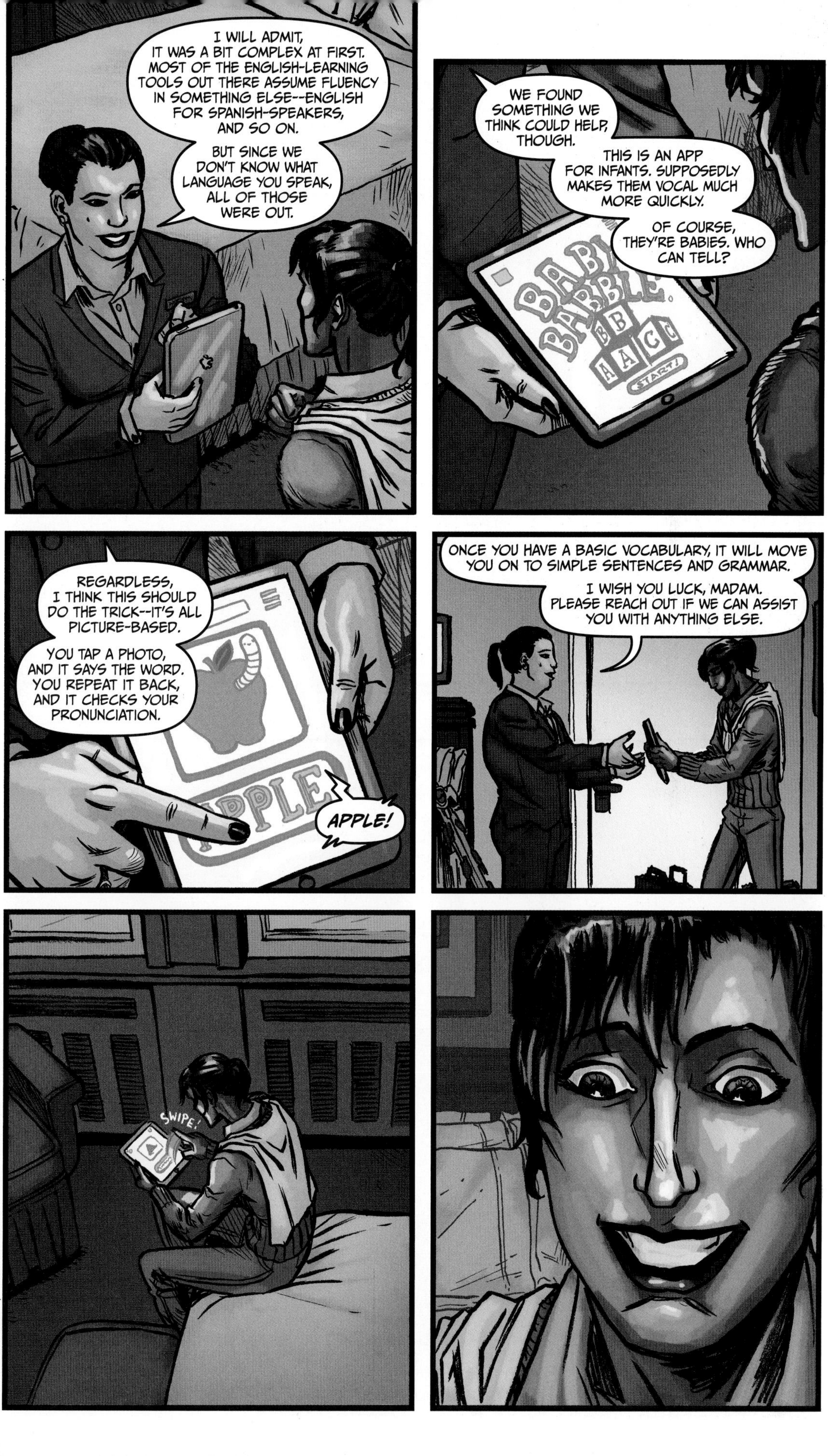

I WILL ADMIT, IT WAS A BIT COMPLEX AT FIRST. MOST OF THE ENGLISH-LEARNING TOOLS OUT THERE ASSUME FLUENCY IN SOMETHING ELSE--ENGLISH FOR SPANISH-SPEAKERS, AND SO ON.
BUT SINCE WE DON'T KNOW WHAT LANGUAGE YOU SPEAK, ALL OF THOSE WERE OUT.
WE FOUND SOMETHING WE THINK COULD HELP, THOUGH.
THIS IS AN APP FOR INFANTS. SUPPOSEDLY MAKES THEM VOCAL MUCH MORE QUICKLY.
OF COURSE, THEY'RE BABIES. WHO CAN TELL?
BABBLE
START!
REGARDLESS, I THINK THIS SHOULD DO THE TRICK--IT'S ALL PICTURE-BASED.
YOU TAP A PHOTO, AND IT SAYS THE WORD. YOU REPEAT IT BACK, AND IT CHECKS YOUR PRONUNCIATION.
APPLE!
ONCE YOU HAVE A BASIC VOCABULARY, IT WILL MOVE YOU ON TO SIMPLE SENTENCES AND GRAMMAR.
I WISH YOU LUCK, MADAM. PLEASE REACH OUT IF WE CAN ASSIST YOU WITH ANYTHING ELSE.
SWIPE!

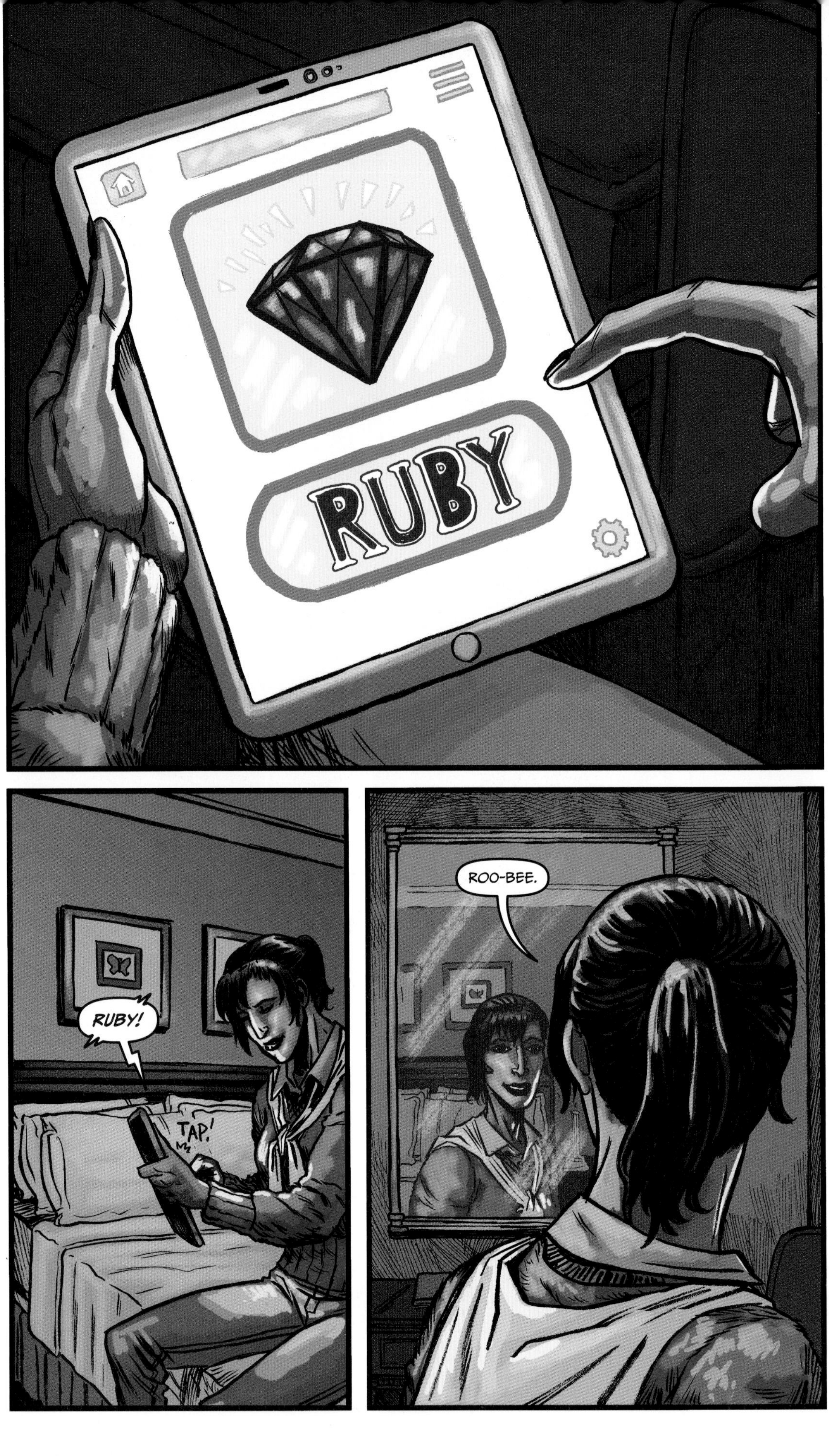
RUBY
RUBY!
TAP!
ROO-BEE.

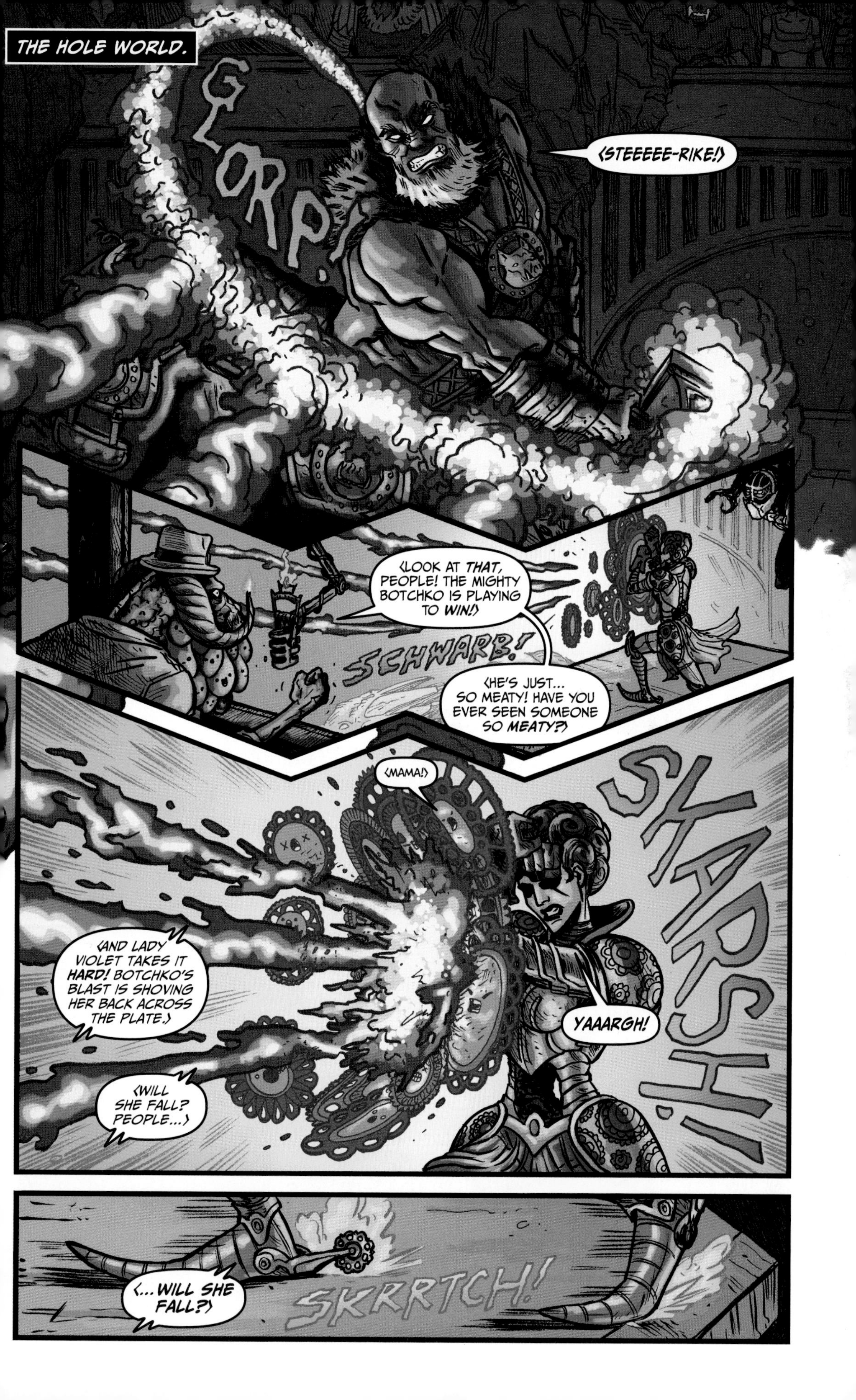
THE HOLE WORLD.
GLORP!
‹STEEEEE-RIKE!›
‹LOOK AT THAT, PEOPLE! THE MIGHTY BOTCHKO IS PLAYING TO WIN!›
SCHWARB!
‹HE'S JUST... SO MEATY! HAVE YOU EVER SEEN SOMEONE SO MEATY?›
‹MAMA!›
SKARSH!
‹AND LADY VIOLET TAKES IT HARD! BOTCHKO'S BLAST IS SHOVING HER BACK ACROSS THE PLATE.›
YAAARGH!
‹WILL SHE FALL? PEOPLE...›
‹...WILL SHE FALL?›
SKRRTCH!

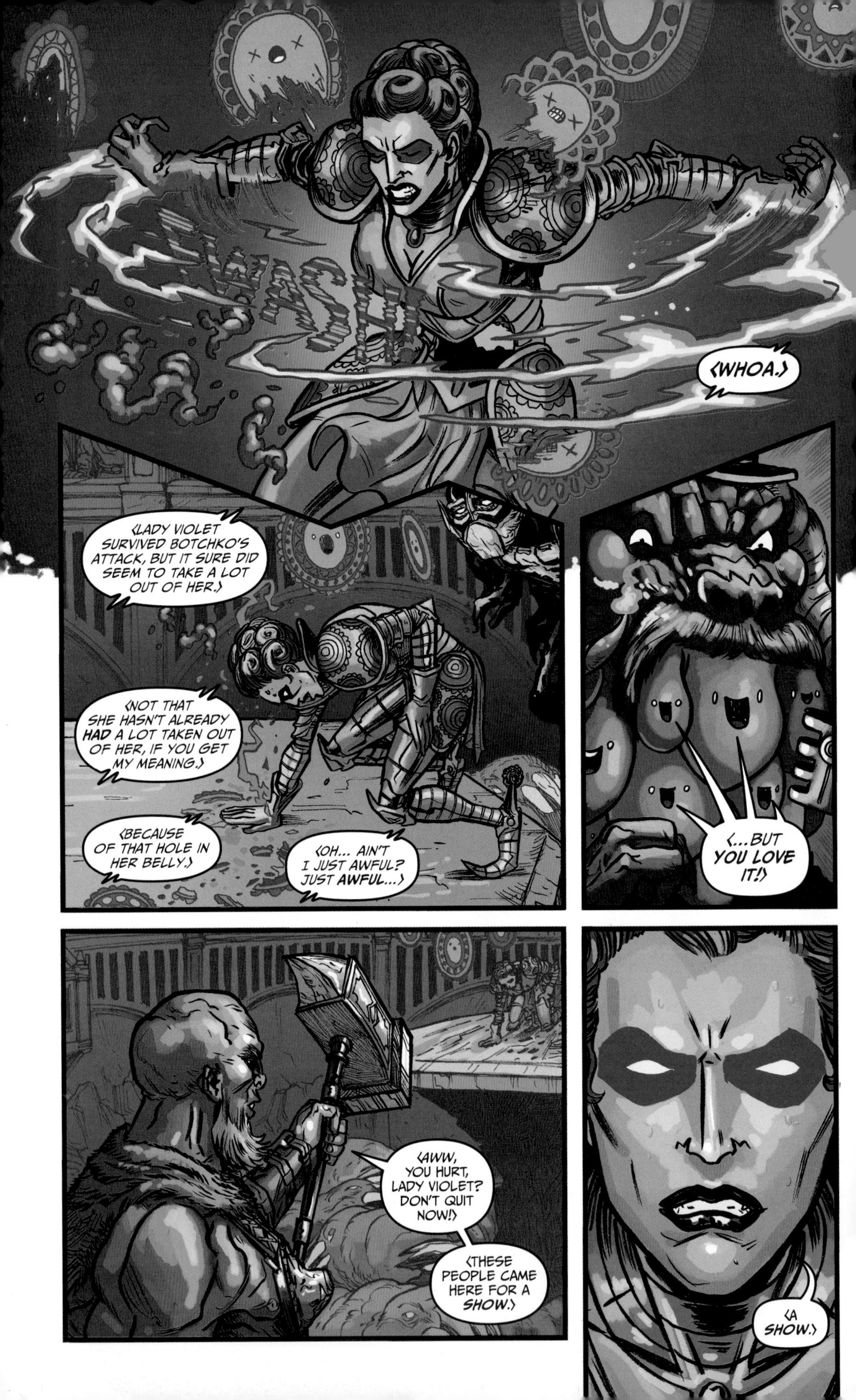
SHASH!
‹WHOA.›
‹LADY VIOLET SURVIVED BOTCHKO'S ATTACK, BUT IT SURE DID SEEM TO TAKE A LOT OUT OF HER.›
‹NOT THAT SHE HASN'T ALREADY **HAD** A LOT TAKEN OUT OF HER, IF YOU GET MY MEANING.›
‹BECAUSE OF THAT HOLE IN HER BELLY.›
‹OH... AIN'T I JUST AWFUL? JUST **AWFUL**...›
‹...BUT **YOU LOVE** IT!›
‹AWW, YOU HURT, LADY VIOLET? DON'T QUIT NOW!›
‹THESE PEOPLE CAME HERE FOR A ***SHOW.***›
‹A ***SHOW.***›

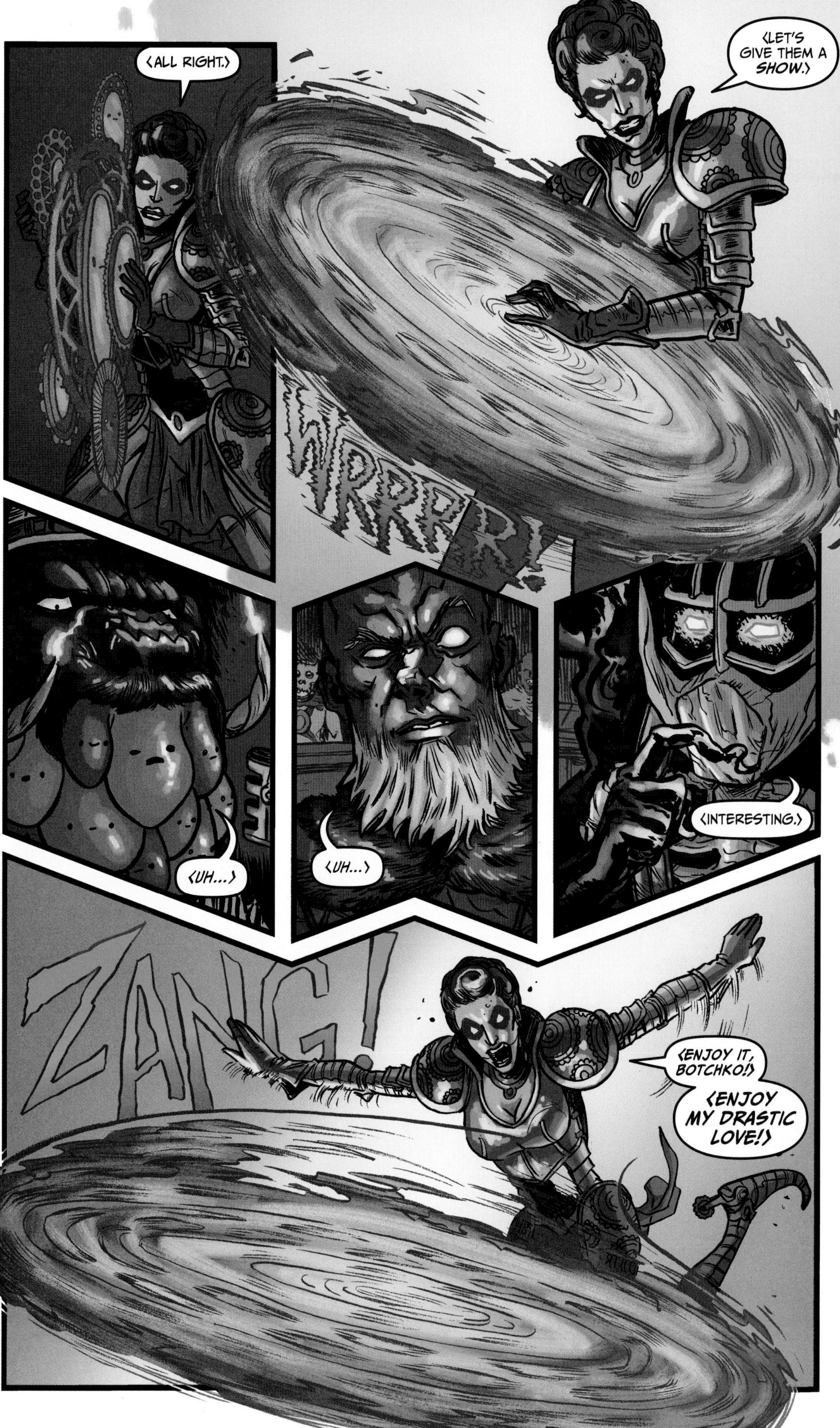
<ALL RIGHT.>
<LET'S GIVE THEM A SHOW.>
WRRRR!
<UH...>
<UH...>
<INTERESTING.>
ZANG!
<ENJOY IT, BOTCHKO!>
<ENJOY MY DRASTIC LOVE!>

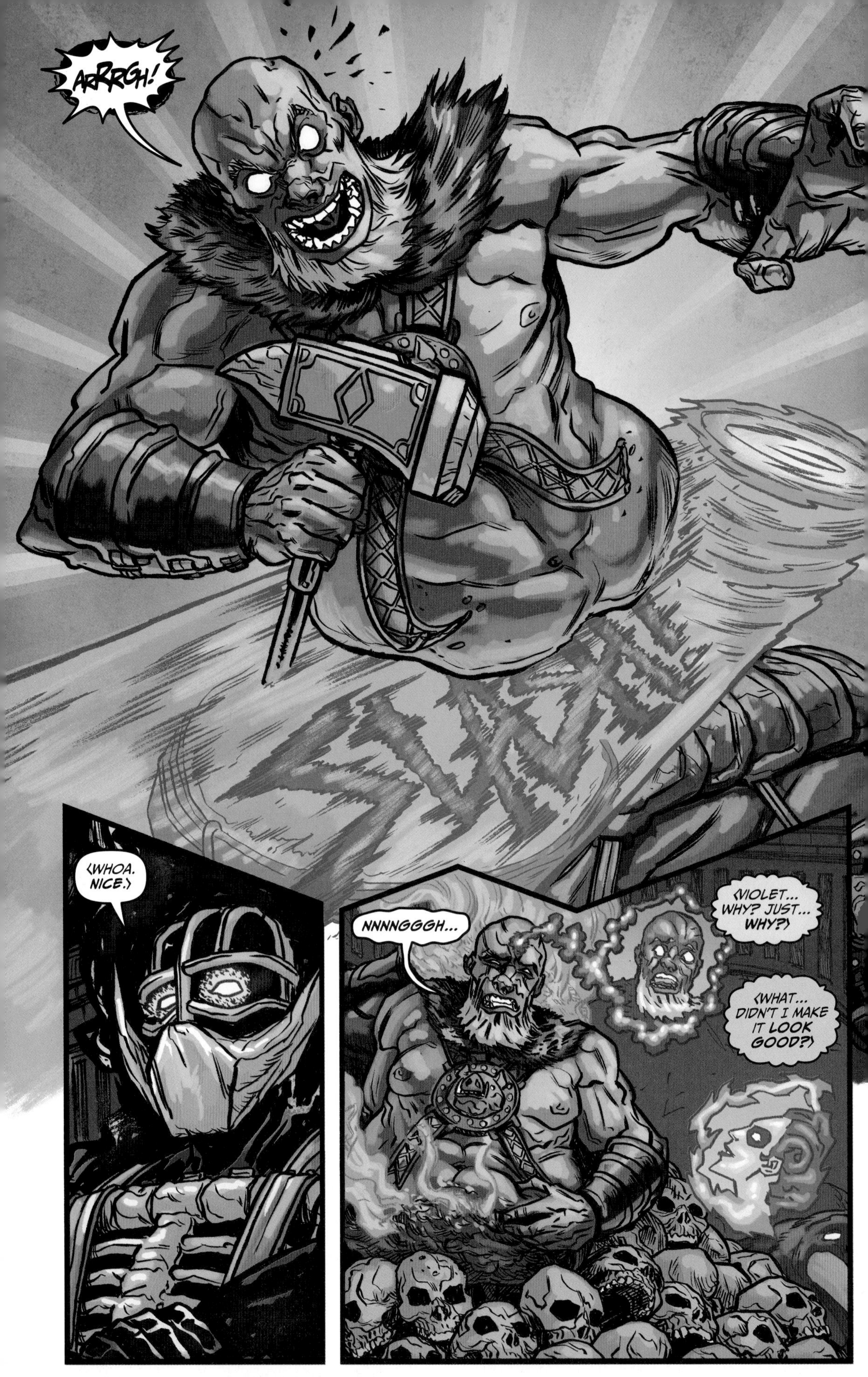
ARRRGH!
⟨WHOA. NICE.⟩
NNNNGGGH...
⟨VIOLET... WHY? JUST... WHY?⟩
⟨WHAT... DIDN'T I MAKE IT LOOK GOOD?⟩

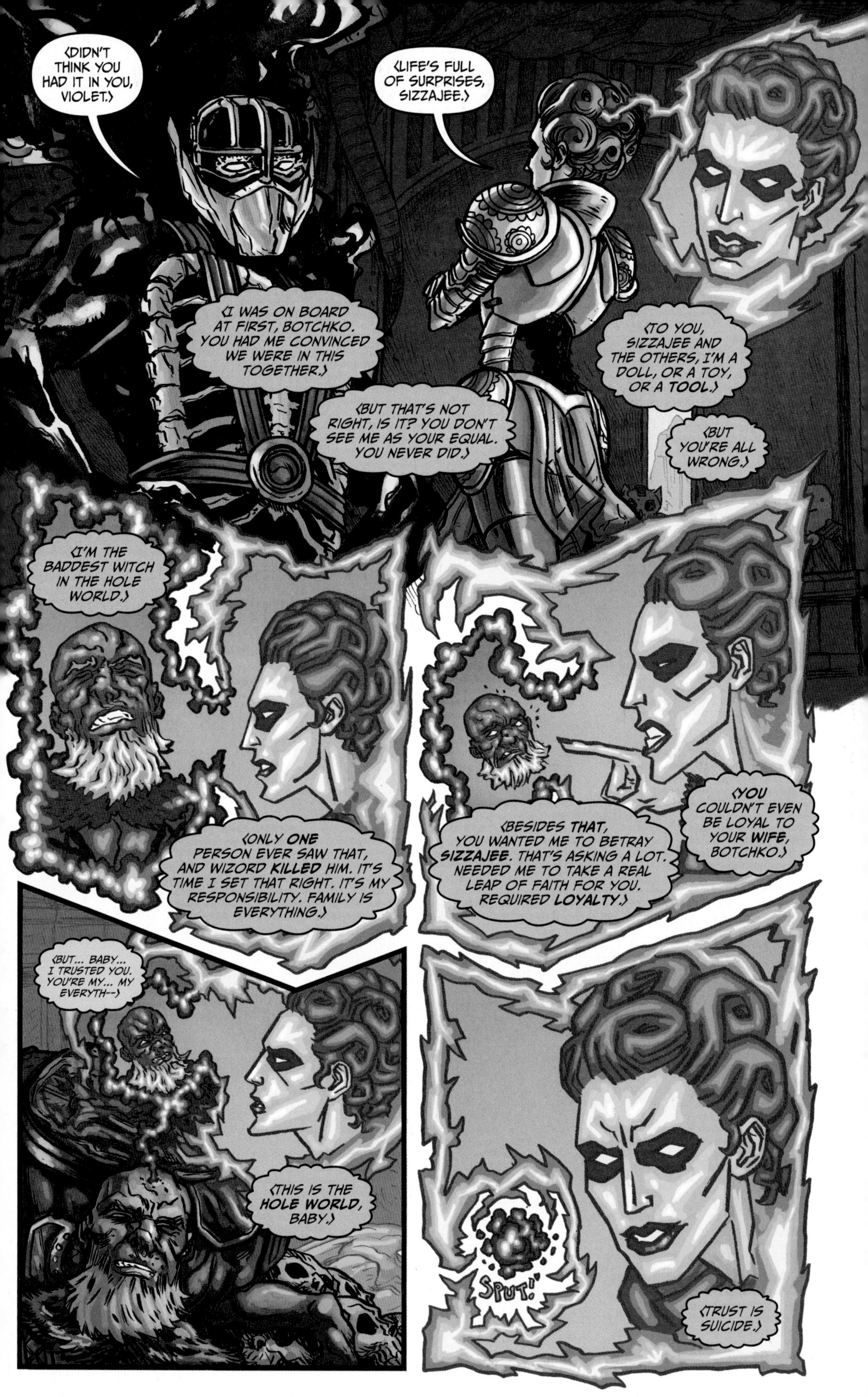

<DIDN'T THINK YOU HAD IT IN YOU, VIOLET.>
<LIFE'S FULL OF SURPRISES, SIZZAJEE.>
<I WAS ON BOARD AT FIRST, BOTCHKO. YOU HAD ME CONVINCED WE WERE IN THIS TOGETHER.>
<BUT THAT'S NOT RIGHT, IS IT? YOU DON'T SEE ME AS YOUR EQUAL. YOU NEVER DID.>
<TO YOU, SIZZAJEE AND THE OTHERS, I'M A DOLL, OR A TOY, OR A **TOOL**.>
<BUT YOU'RE ALL WRONG.>
<I'M THE BADDEST WITCH IN THE HOLE WORLD.>
<ONLY **ONE** PERSON EVER SAW THAT, AND WIZORD **KILLED** HIM. IT'S TIME I SET THAT RIGHT. IT'S MY RESPONSIBILITY. FAMILY IS EVERYTHING.>
<BESIDES **THAT**, YOU WANTED ME TO BETRAY **SIZZAJEE**. THAT'S ASKING A LOT. NEEDED ME TO TAKE A REAL LEAP OF FAITH FOR YOU. REQUIRED **LOYALTY**.>
<**YOU** COULDN'T EVEN BE LOYAL TO YOUR **WIFE**, BOTCHKO.>
<BUT... BABY... I TRUSTED YOU. YOU'RE MY... MY EVERYTH-->
<THIS IS THE **HOLE WORLD**, BABY.>
SPUT!
<TRUST IS SUICIDE.>

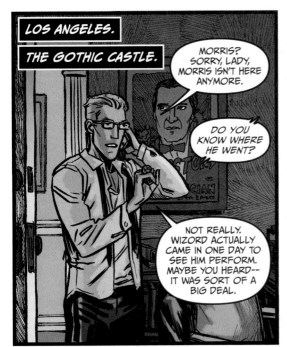

LOS ANGELES.

THE GOTHIC CASTLE.

MORRIS? SORRY, LADY, MORRIS ISN'T HERE ANYMORE.

DO YOU KNOW WHERE HE WENT?

NOT REALLY. WIZORD ACTUALLY CAME IN ONE DAY TO SEE HIM PERFORM. MAYBE YOU HEARD-- IT WAS SORT OF A BIG DEAL.

YEAH, I MIGHT HAVE HEARD SOMETHING ABOUT THAT. BUT YOU WERE SAYING... ABOUT MORRIS?

YEAH. HE LEFT RIGHT AFTER THAT SHOW. JUST TOOK THAT WAND WIZORD GAVE HIM AND BAILED. HAVEN'T HEARD FROM HIM SINCE.

ROLL!

HMM. DO YOU HAVE ANY IDEA WHY?

HE DIDN'T SAY. MAYBE HE THOUGHT HE NEEDED TO PRACTICE OR SOMETHING. LIKE HE WAS GETTING RUSTY.

RUSTY?

WELL, MAYBE OLD, ACTUALLY. HE COULDN'T REMEMBER HIS TRICKS ANYMORE.

WAIT... WHAT? WHAT DO YOU MEAN?

FLIP!

EVERY TRICK HE DID FOR WIZORD... IT WAS LIKE HE JUST FORGOT THEM. MORRIS USED TO BE ONE OF THE GREATS--IT'S SAD, REALLY.

BUT LOOK, IF YOU WANT TO HIRE A MAGICIAN, WE GOT PLENTY OF AMAZING PERFORMERS AT THE MAGIC CASTLE.

HELL, I'M PRETTY DAMN GOOD MYSELF. LOOK ME UP ON YOUTUBE. GORDO THE GRE--

FLOP!

CLICK

WHATEVER.

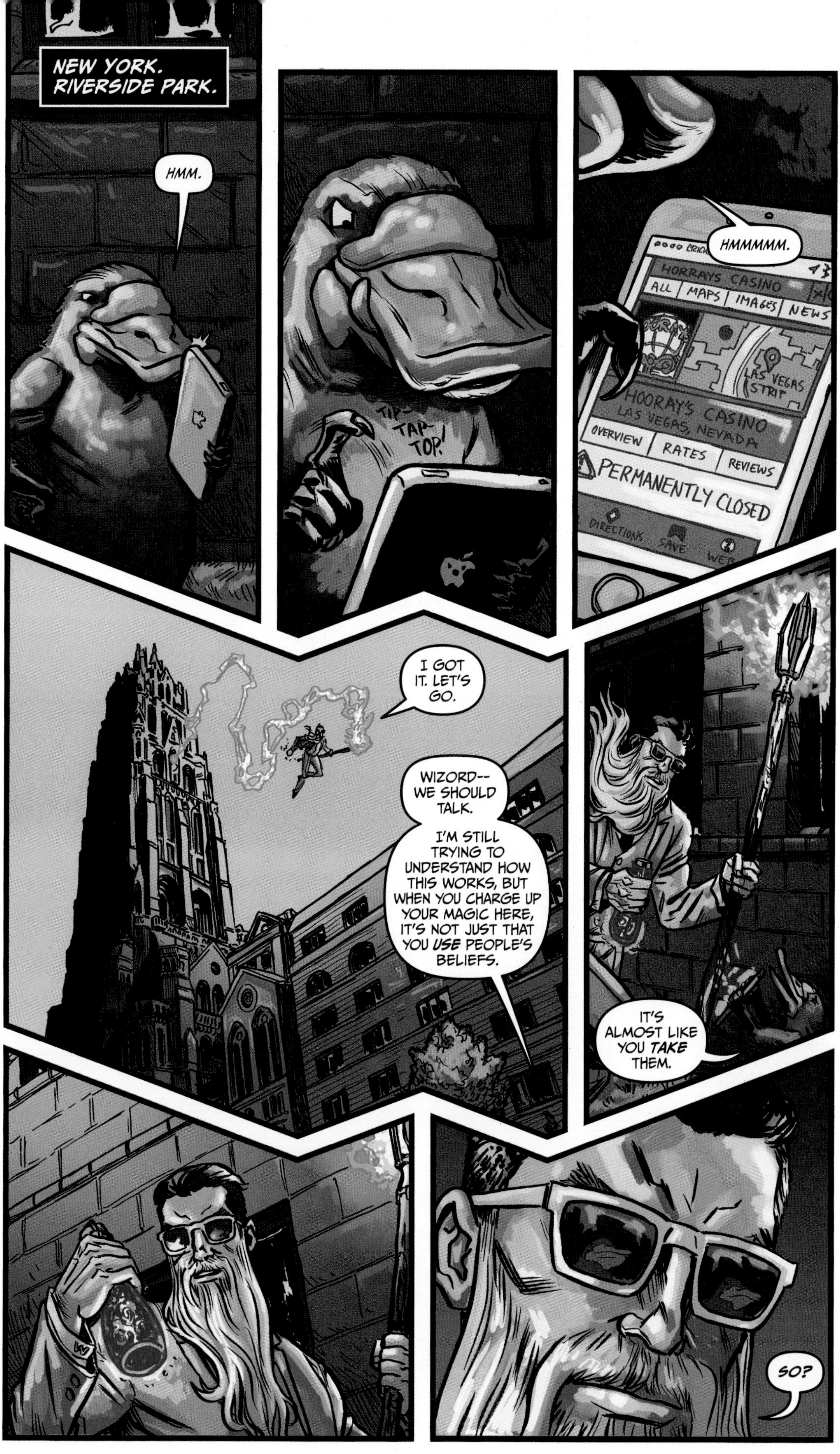
NEW YORK.
RIVERSIDE PARK.
HMM.
TIP-TAP-TOP!
HMMMMM.
HORRAYS CASINO
ALL
MAPS
IMAGES
NEWS
LAS VEGAS STRIP
HOORAY'S CASINO
LAS VEGAS, NEVADA
OVERVIEW
RATES
REVIEWS
PERMANENTLY CLOSED
DIRECTIONS
SAVE
I GOT IT. LET'S GO.
WIZORD-- WE SHOULD TALK.
I'M STILL TRYING TO UNDERSTAND HOW THIS WORKS, BUT WHEN YOU CHARGE UP YOUR MAGIC HERE, IT'S NOT JUST THAT YOU *USE* PEOPLE'S BELIEFS.
IT'S ALMOST LIKE YOU *TAKE* THEM.
SO?

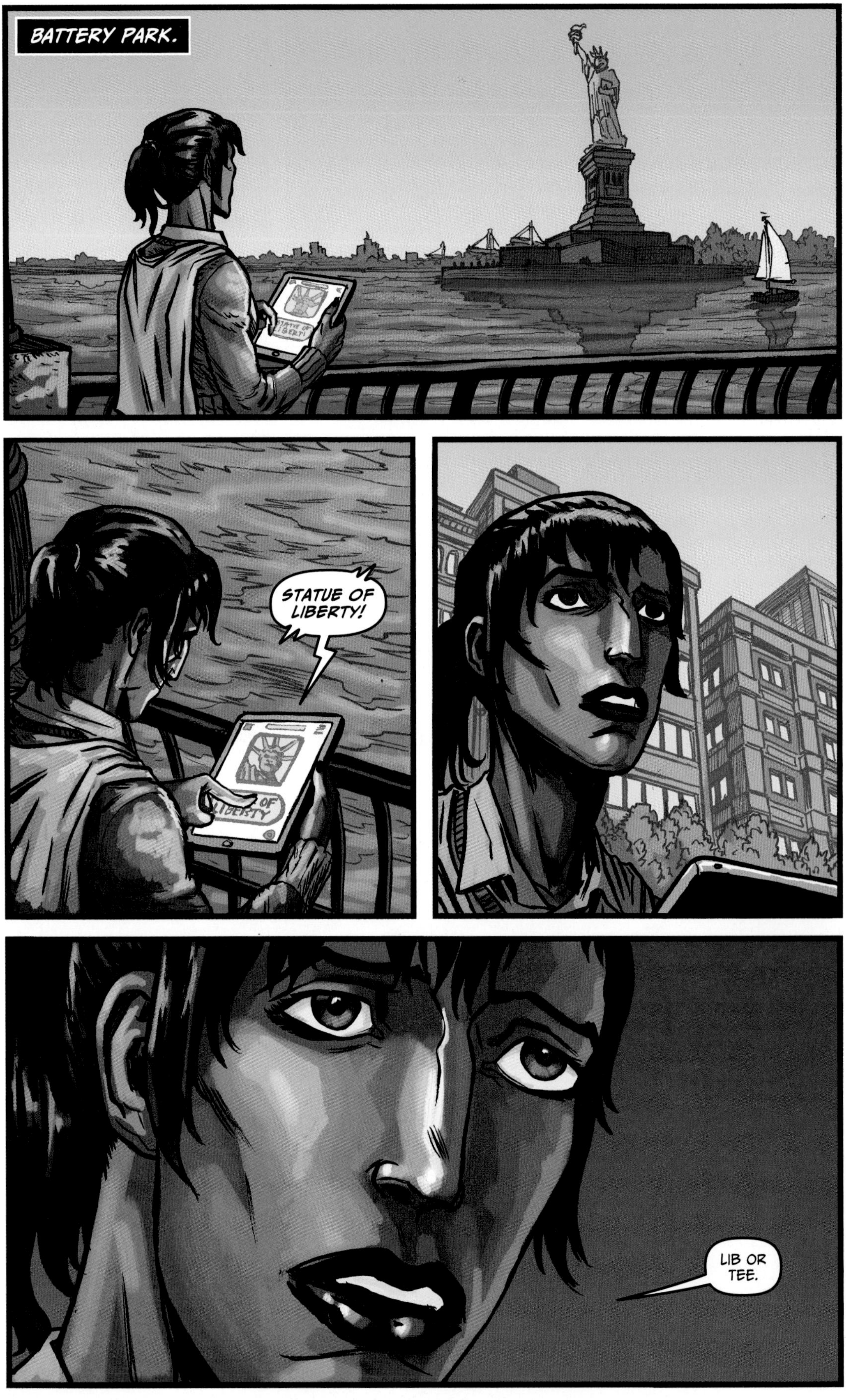
BATTERY PARK.
STATUE OF LIBERTY!
LIB OR TEE.

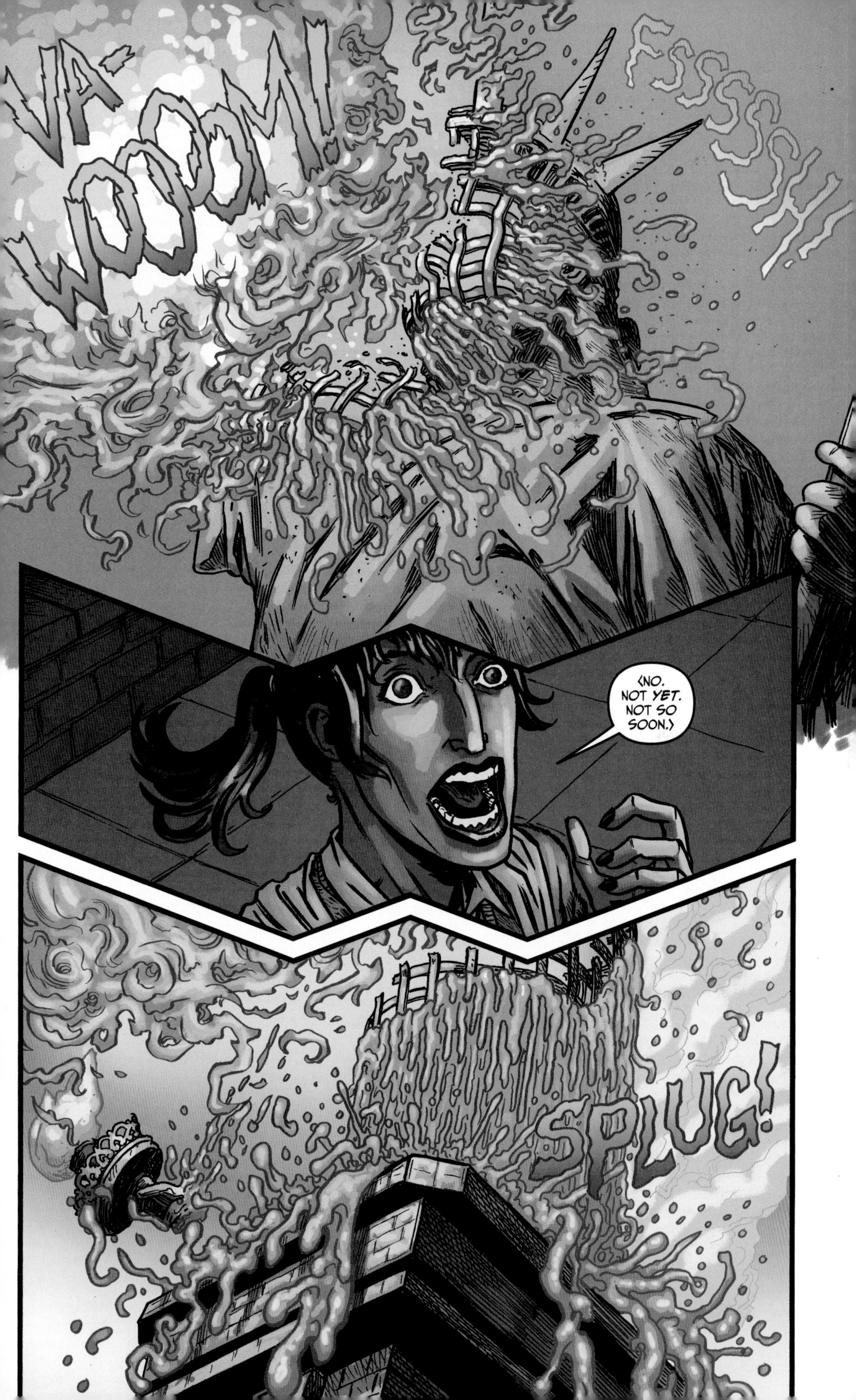
VA-WOOOM!
FSSSSH!!
<NO. NOT YET. NOT SO SOON.>
SPLUG!

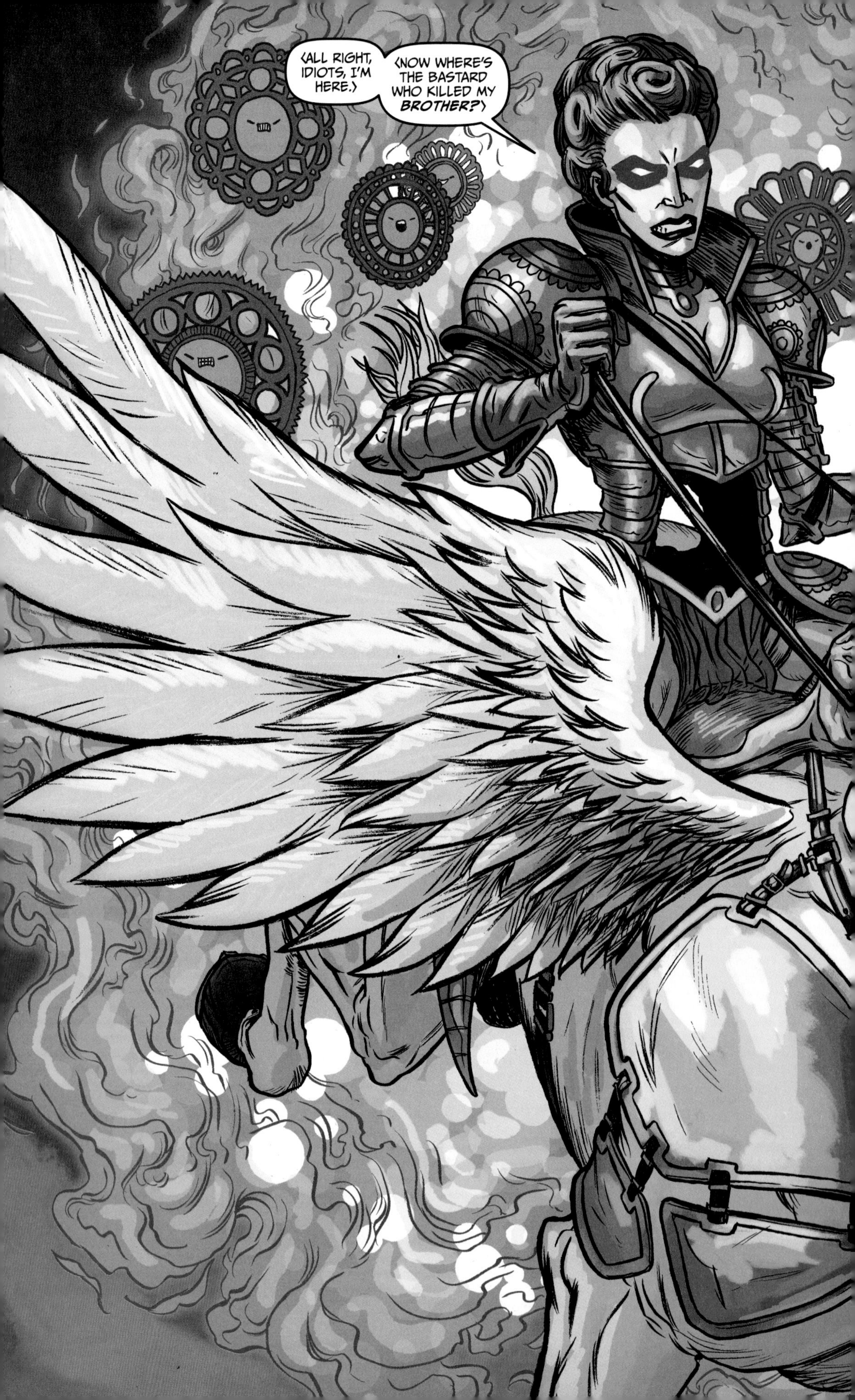

‹ALL RIGHT, IDIOTS, I'M HERE.›
‹NOW WHERE'S THE BASTARD WHO KILLED MY *BROTHER?*›

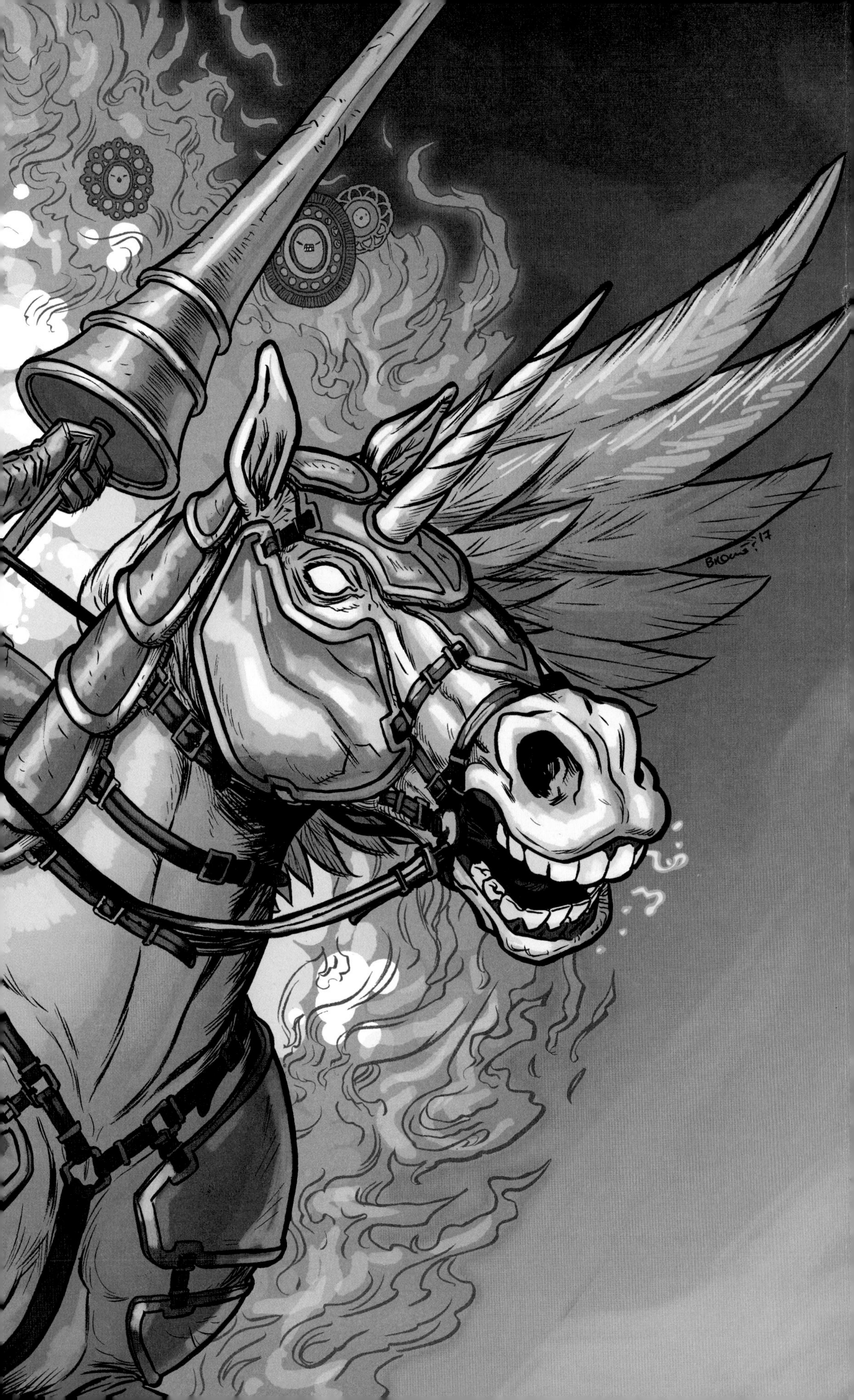

TEN

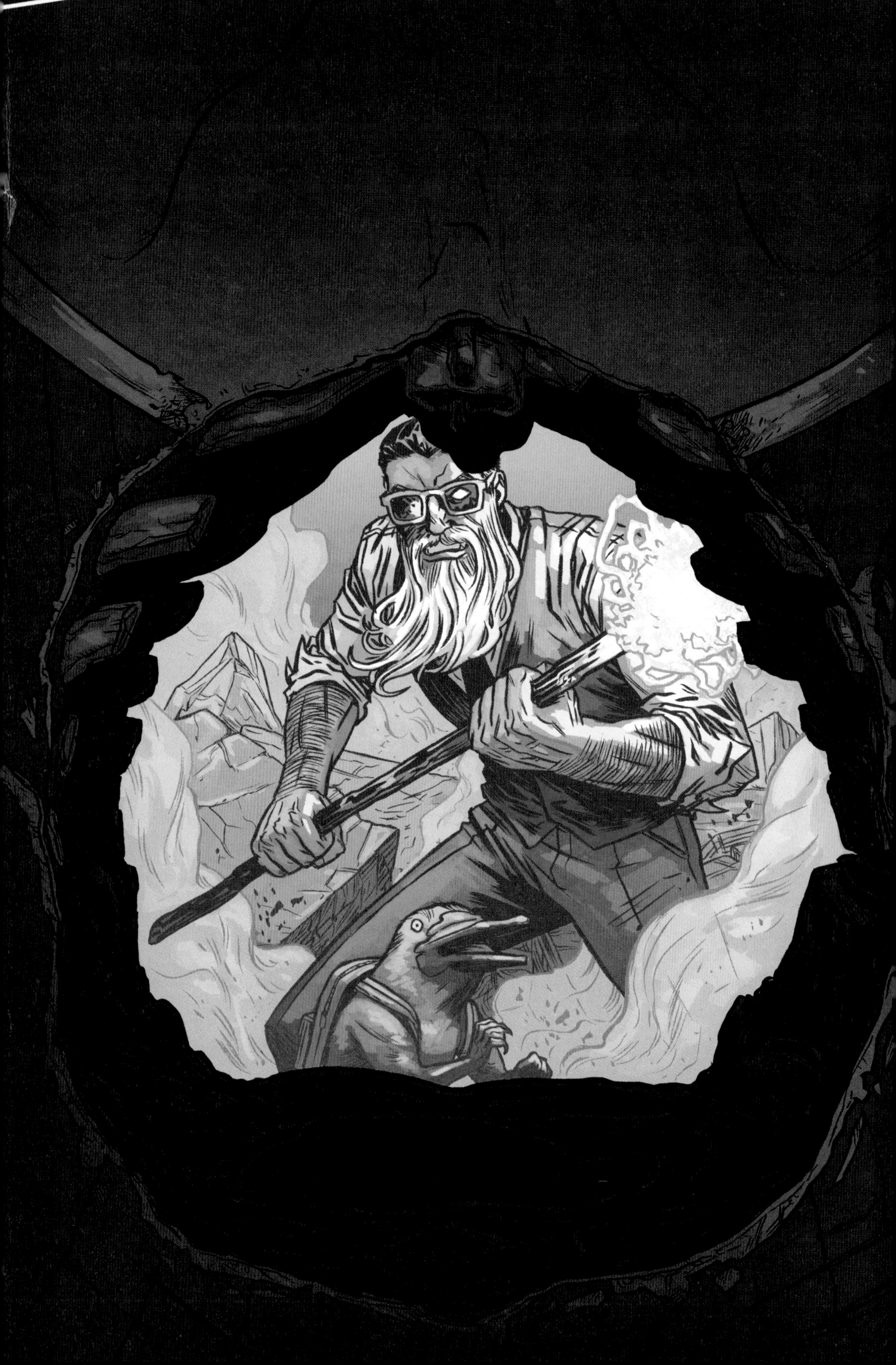

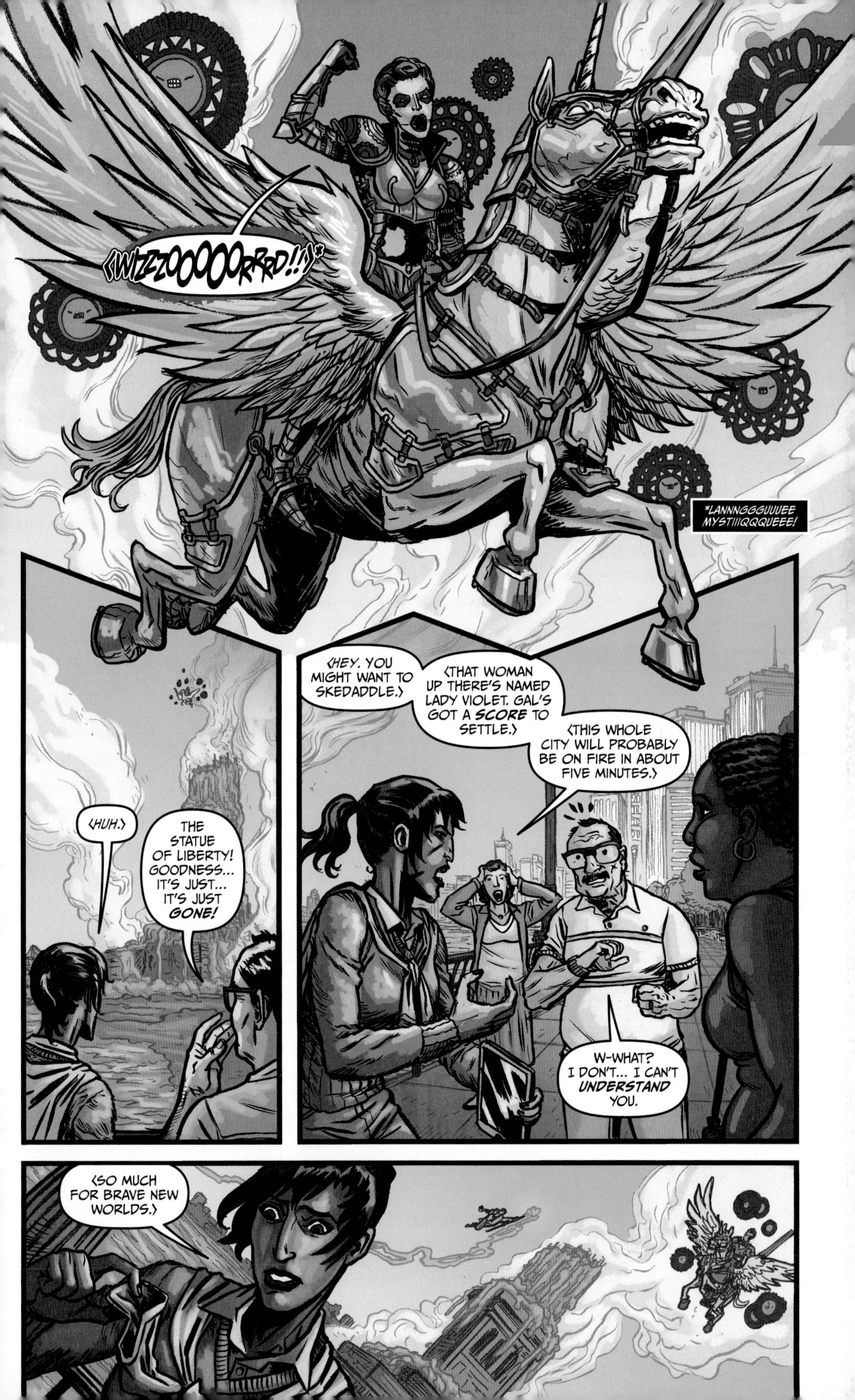

<WIZZZOOOOORRRD!!>*
*LANNNGGGUUUEE MYSTIIIQQQUEEE!
<HUH.>
THE STATUE OF LIBERTY! GOODNESS... IT'S JUST... IT'S JUST GONE!
<HEY. YOU MIGHT WANT TO SKEDADDLE.>
<THAT WOMAN UP THERE'S NAMED LADY VIOLET. GAL'S GOT A SCORE TO SETTLE.>
<THIS WHOLE CITY WILL PROBABLY BE ON FIRE IN ABOUT FIVE MINUTES.>
W-WHAT? I DON'T... I CAN'T UNDERSTAND YOU.
<SO MUCH FOR BRAVE NEW WORLDS.>

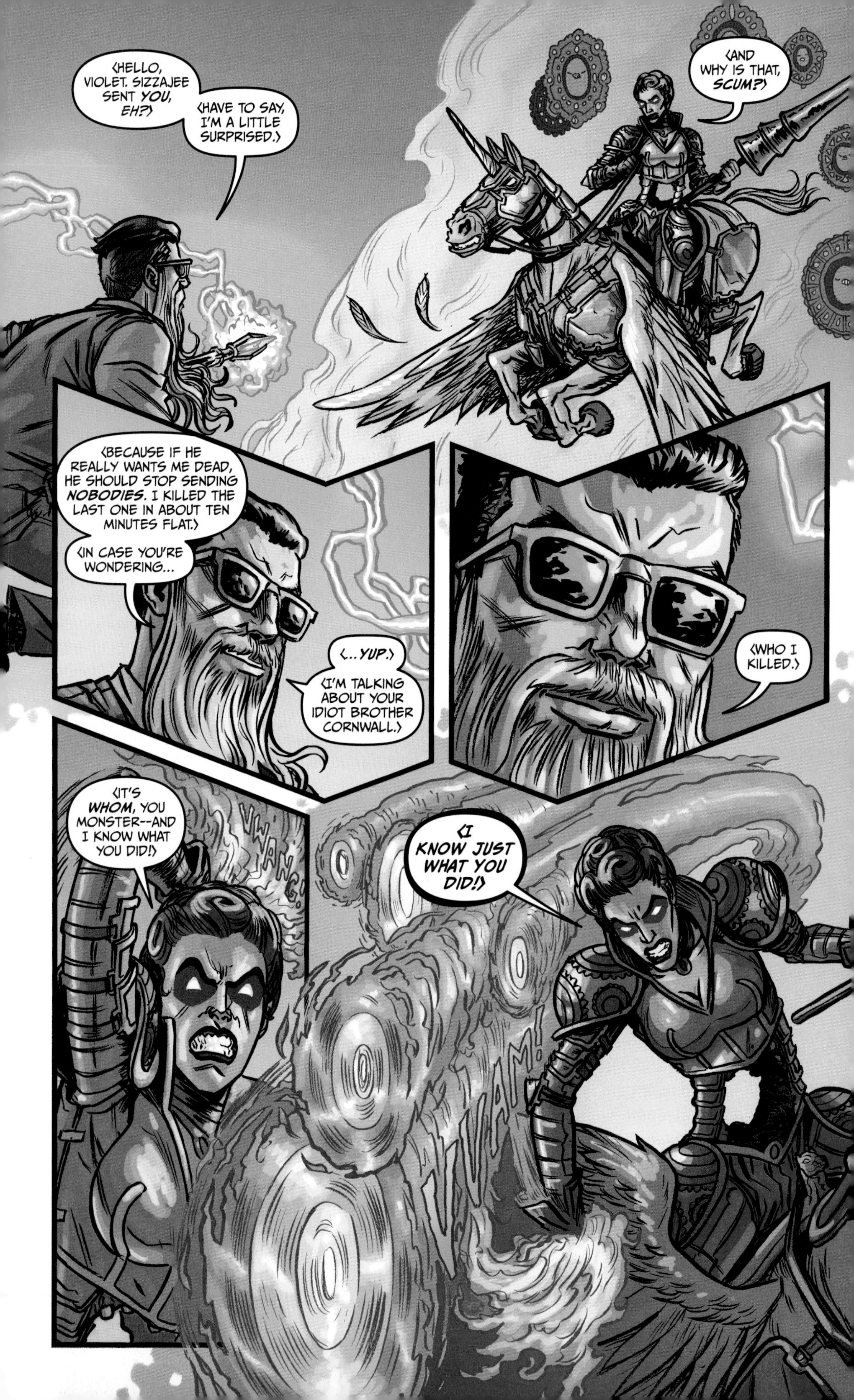
⟨HELLO, VIOLET. SIZZAJEE SENT YOU, EH?⟩
⟨HAVE TO SAY, I'M A LITTLE SURPRISED.⟩
⟨AND WHY IS THAT, SCUM?⟩
⟨BECAUSE IF HE REALLY WANTS ME DEAD, HE SHOULD STOP SENDING NOBODIES. I KILLED THE LAST ONE IN ABOUT TEN MINUTES FLAT.⟩
⟨IN CASE YOU'RE WONDERING...
⟨...YUP.⟩
⟨I'M TALKING ABOUT YOUR IDIOT BROTHER CORNWALL.⟩
⟨WHO I KILLED.⟩
⟨IT'S WHOM, YOU MONSTER--AND I KNOW WHAT YOU DID!⟩
WWANG!
⟨I KNOW JUST WHAT YOU DID!⟩
WAM!

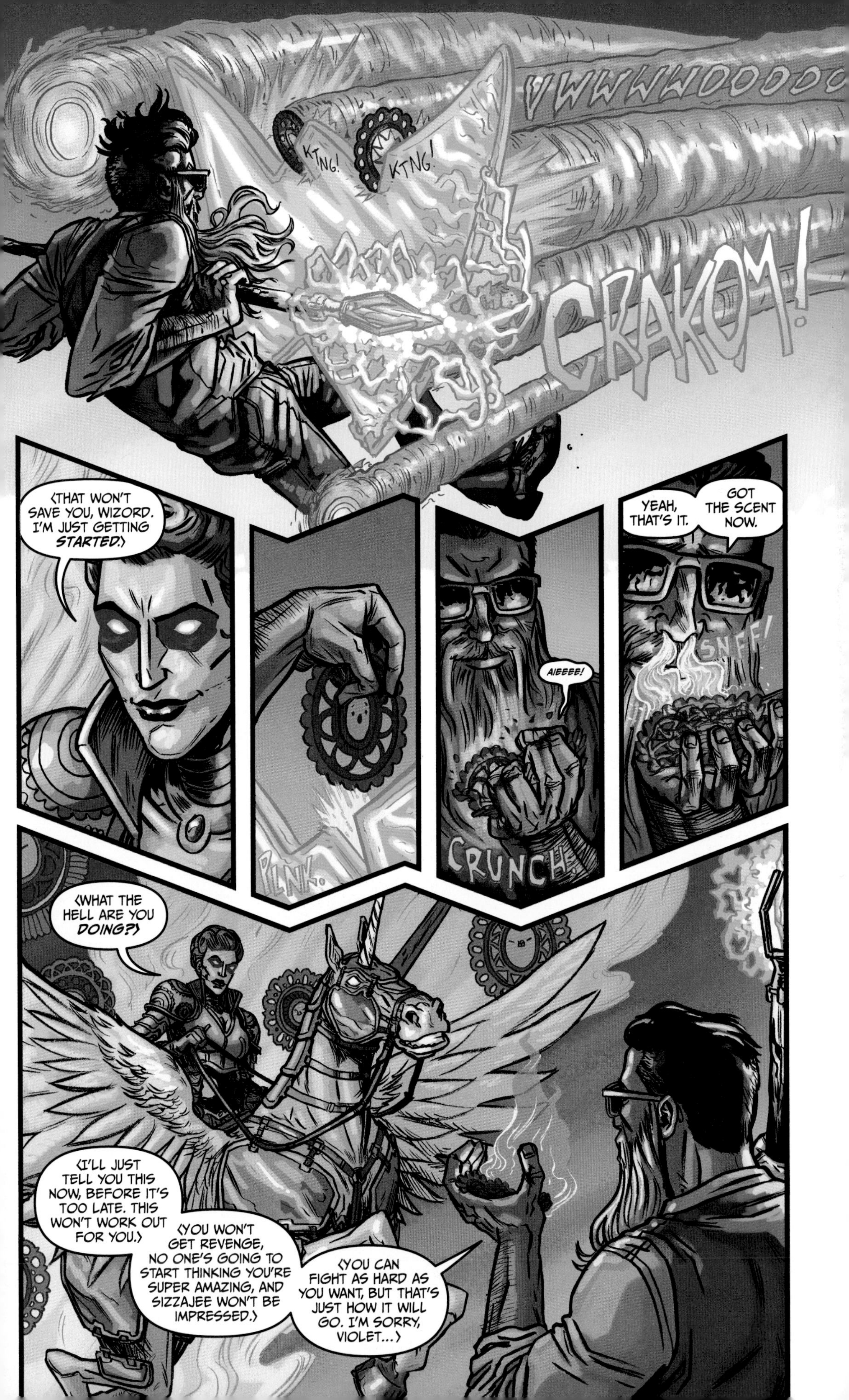
VWWWWOOOOO
KTNG!
KTNG!
CRAKOM!
‹THAT WON'T SAVE YOU, WIZORD. I'M JUST GETTING *STARTED.*›
PLNK.
AIEEEE!
CRUNCH.
YEAH, THAT'S IT.
GOT THE SCENT NOW.
SNFF!
‹WHAT THE HELL ARE YOU *DOING?*›
‹I'LL JUST TELL YOU THIS NOW, BEFORE IT'S TOO LATE. THIS WON'T WORK OUT FOR YOU.›
‹YOU WON'T GET REVENGE, NO ONE'S GOING TO START THINKING YOU'RE SUPER AMAZING, AND SIZZAJEE WON'T BE IMPRESSED.›
‹YOU CAN FIGHT AS HARD AS YOU WANT, BUT THAT'S JUST HOW IT WILL GO. I'M SORRY, VIOLET...›

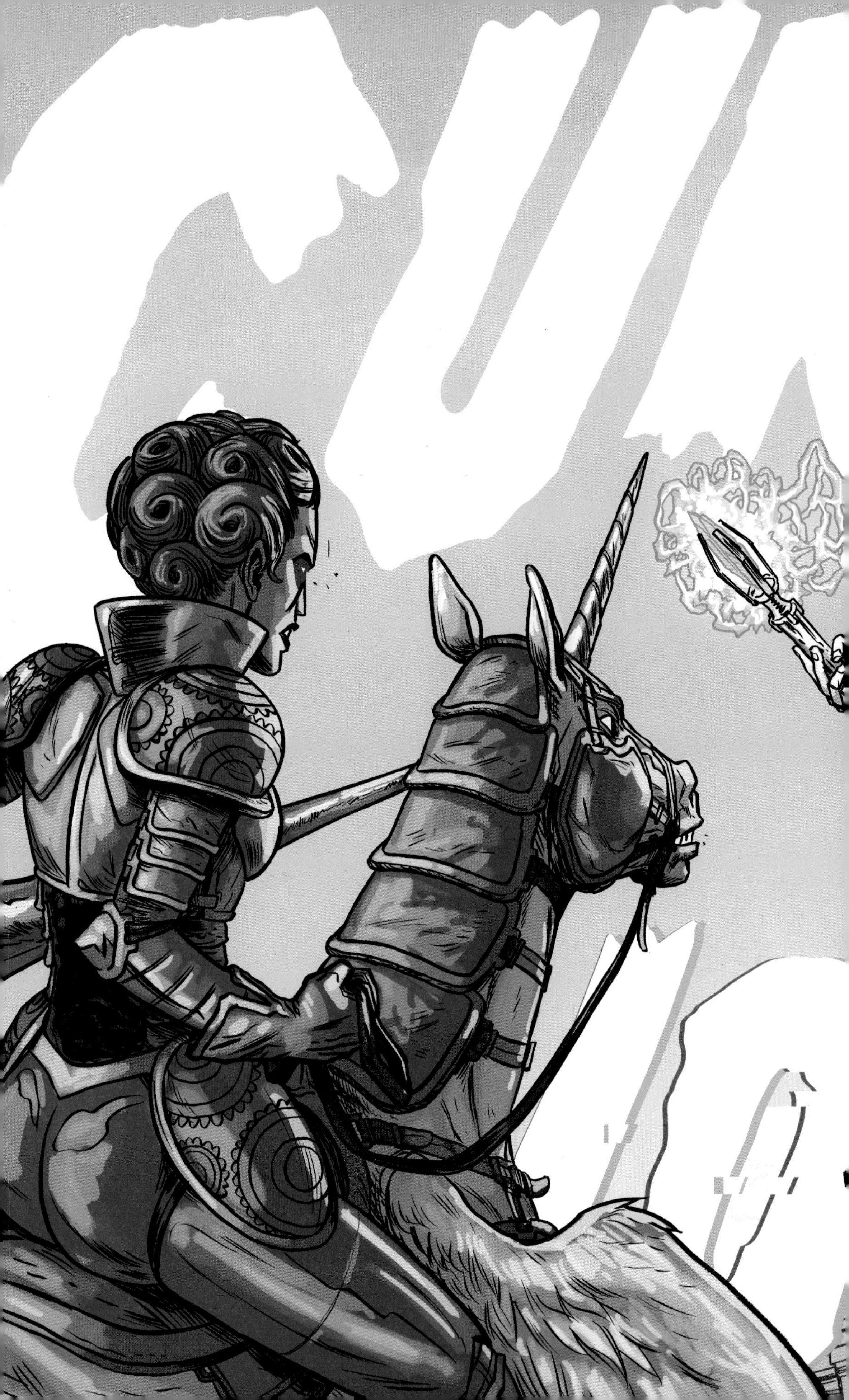

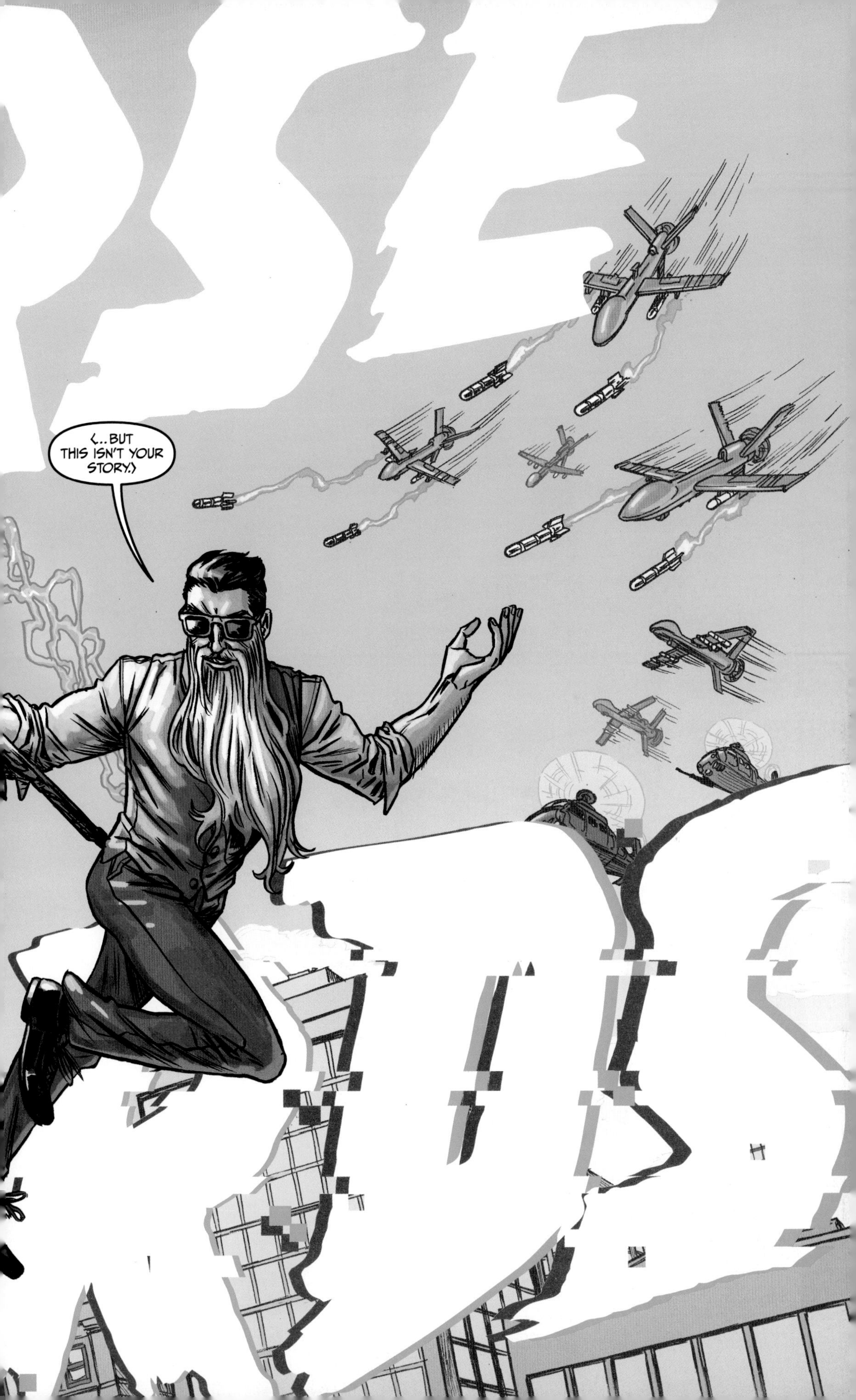
<...BUT THIS ISN'T YOUR STORY.>

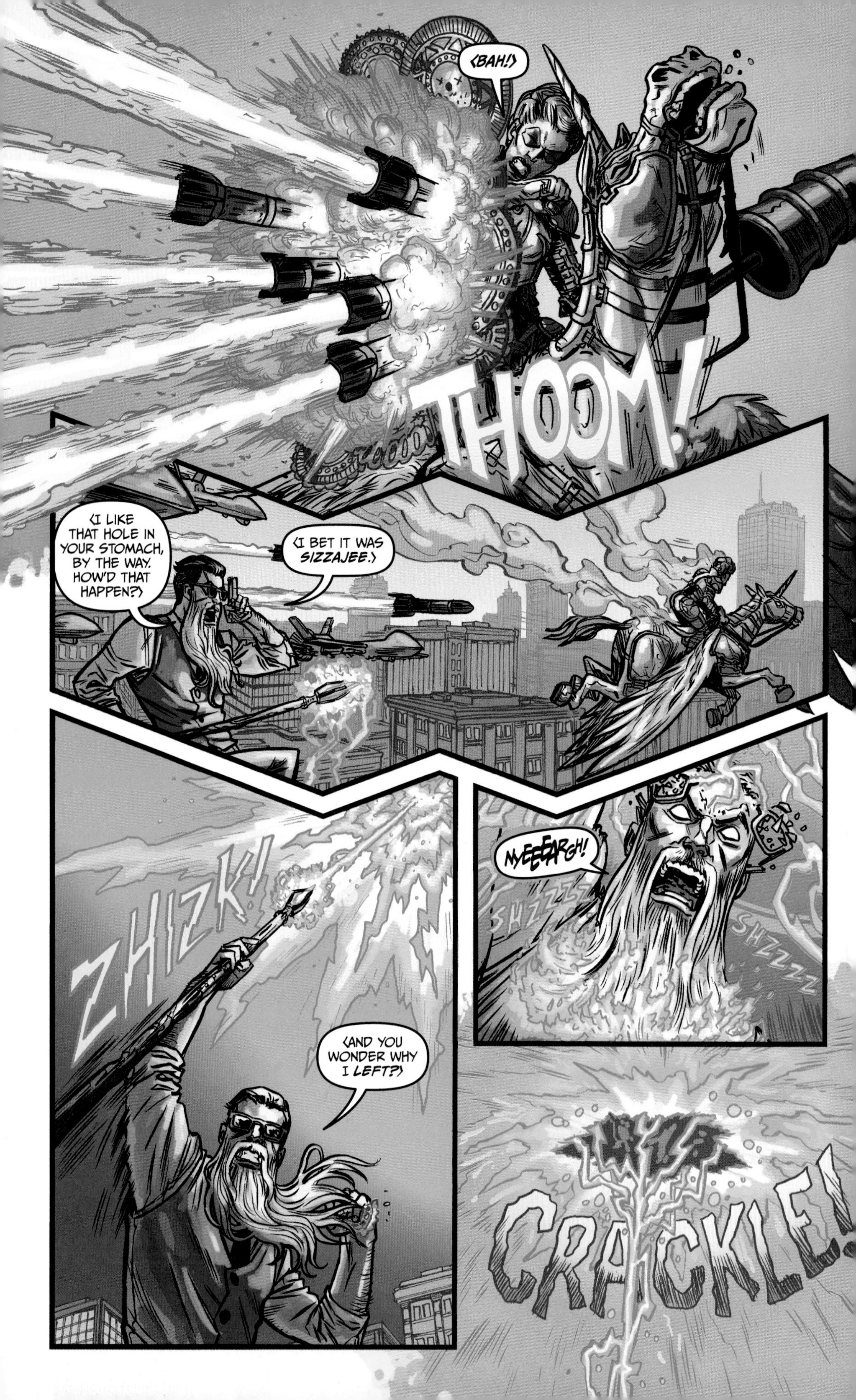
‹BAH!›
THOOM!
‹I LIKE THAT HOLE IN YOUR STOMACH, BY THE WAY. HOW'D THAT HAPPEN?›
‹I BET IT WAS SIZZAJEE.›
ZHIZK!
‹AND YOU WONDER WHY I LEFT?›
NYEEEEARGH!
SHZZZZ
SHZZZZZ
CRACKLE!

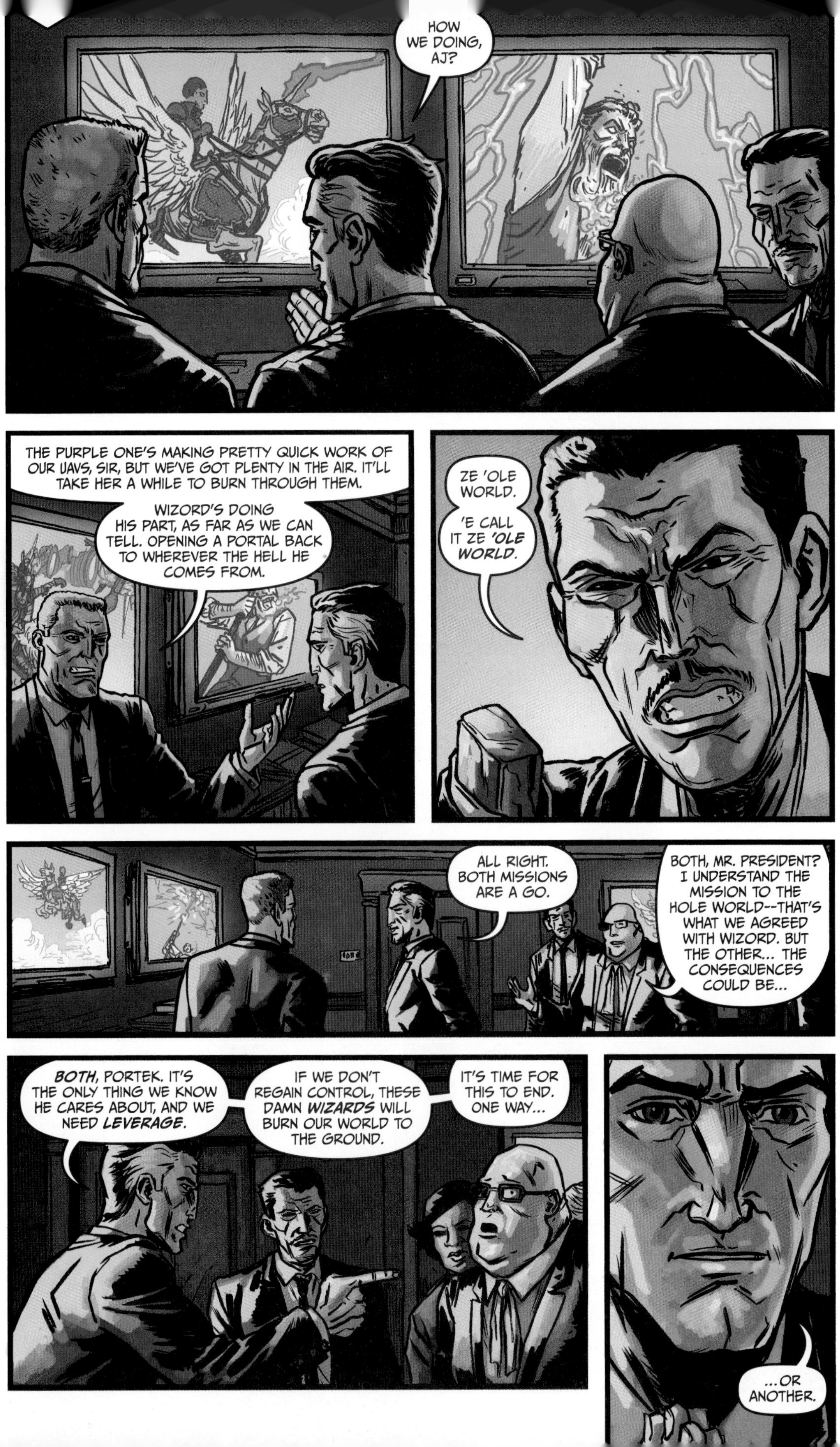
HOW WE DOING, AJ?
THE PURPLE ONE'S MAKING PRETTY QUICK WORK OF OUR UAVS, SIR, BUT WE'VE GOT PLENTY IN THE AIR. IT'LL TAKE HER A WHILE TO BURN THROUGH THEM.
WIZORD'S DOING HIS PART, AS FAR AS WE CAN TELL. OPENING A PORTAL BACK TO WHEREVER THE HELL HE COMES FROM.
ZE 'OLE WORLD.
'E CALL IT ZE *'OLE WORLD*.
ALL RIGHT. BOTH MISSIONS ARE A GO.
BOTH, MR. PRESIDENT? I UNDERSTAND THE MISSION TO THE HOLE WORLD--THAT'S WHAT WE AGREED WITH WIZORD. BUT THE OTHER... THE CONSEQUENCES COULD BE...
BOTH, PORTEK. IT'S THE ONLY THING WE KNOW HE CARES ABOUT, AND WE NEED *LEVERAGE*.
IF WE DON'T REGAIN CONTROL, THESE DAMN *WIZARDS* WILL BURN OUR WORLD TO THE GROUND.
IT'S TIME FOR THIS TO END. ONE WAY...
...OR ANOTHER.

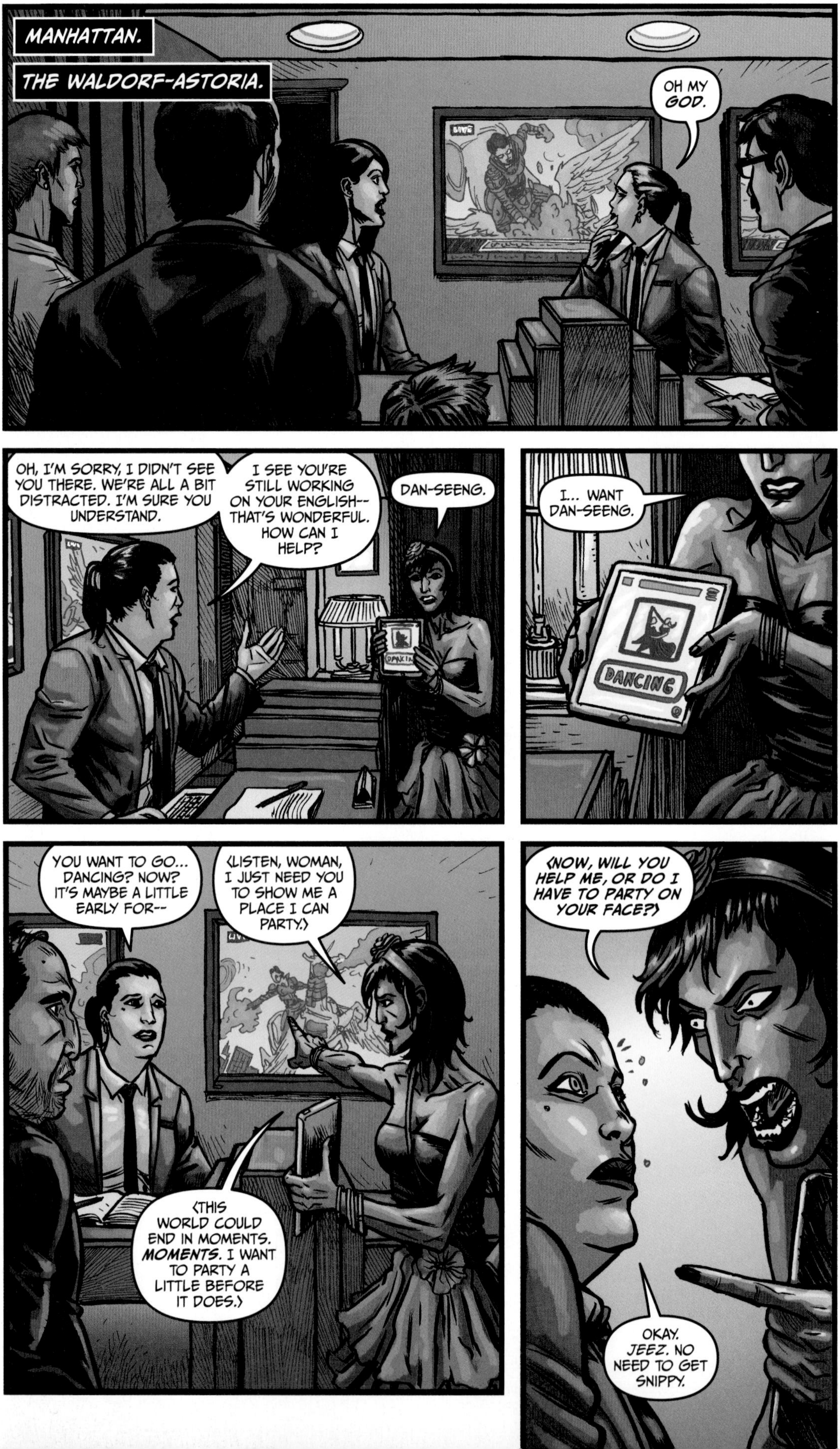
MANHATTAN.
THE WALDORF-ASTORIA.
OH MY *GOD.*
OH, I'M SORRY, I DIDN'T SEE YOU THERE. WE'RE ALL A BIT DISTRACTED. I'M SURE YOU UNDERSTAND.
I SEE YOU'RE STILL WORKING ON YOUR ENGLISH-- THAT'S WONDERFUL. HOW CAN I HELP?
DAN-SEENG.
I... WANT DAN-SEENG.
DANCING
YOU WANT TO GO... DANCING? NOW? IT'S MAYBE A LITTLE EARLY FOR--
‹LISTEN, WOMAN, I JUST NEED YOU TO SHOW ME A PLACE I CAN PARTY.›
‹THIS WORLD COULD END IN MOMENTS. *MOMENTS.* I WANT TO PARTY A LITTLE BEFORE IT DOES.›
‹NOW, WILL YOU HELP ME, OR DO I HAVE TO PARTY ON YOUR FACE?›
OKAY. JEEZ. NO NEED TO GET SNIPPY.

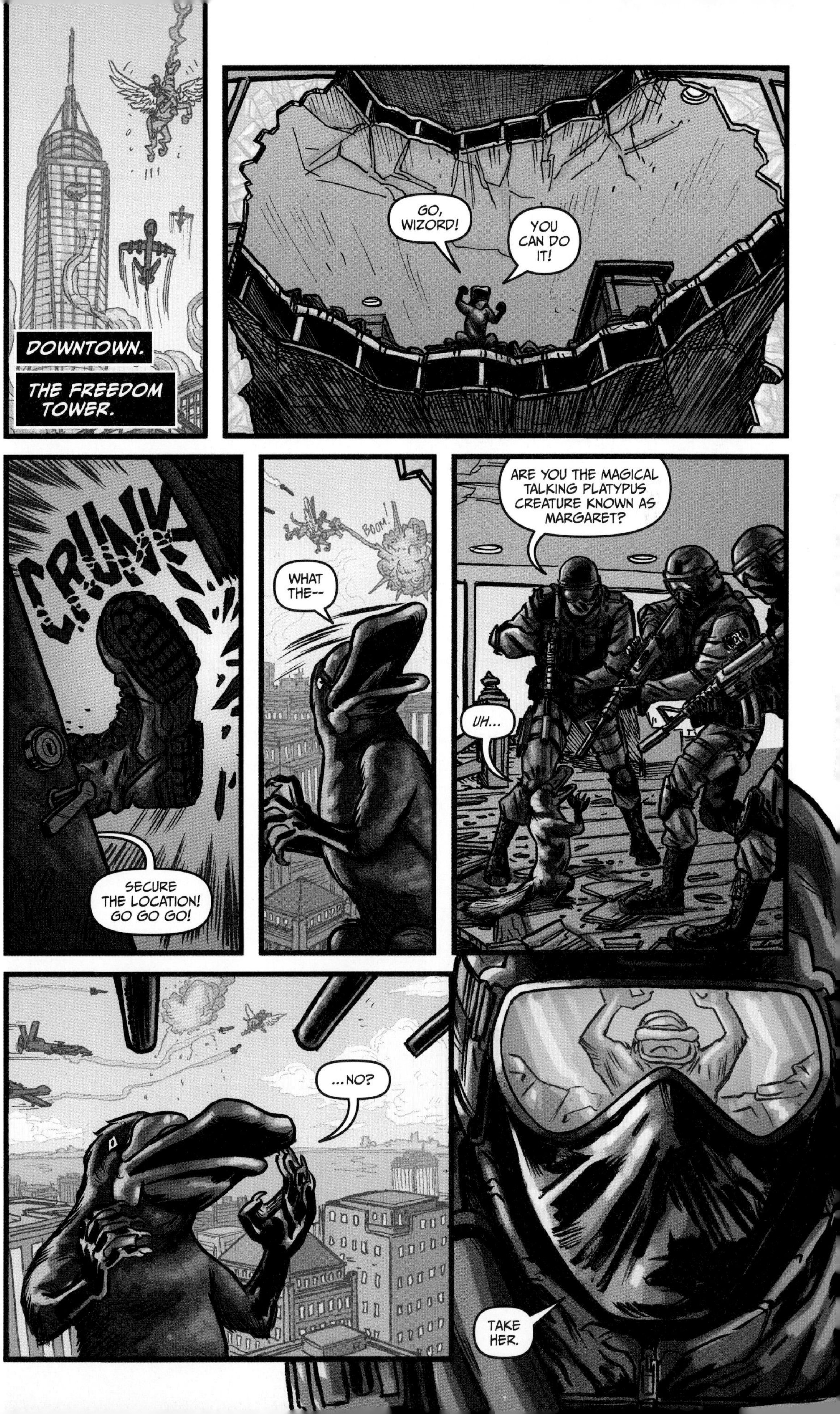
DOWNTOWN.
THE FREEDOM TOWER.
GO, WIZORD!
YOU CAN DO IT!
CRUNK
SECURE THE LOCATION! GO GO GO!
BOOM!
WHAT THE--
ARE YOU THE MAGICAL TALKING PLATYPUS CREATURE KNOWN AS MARGARET?
UH...
...NO?
TAKE HER.

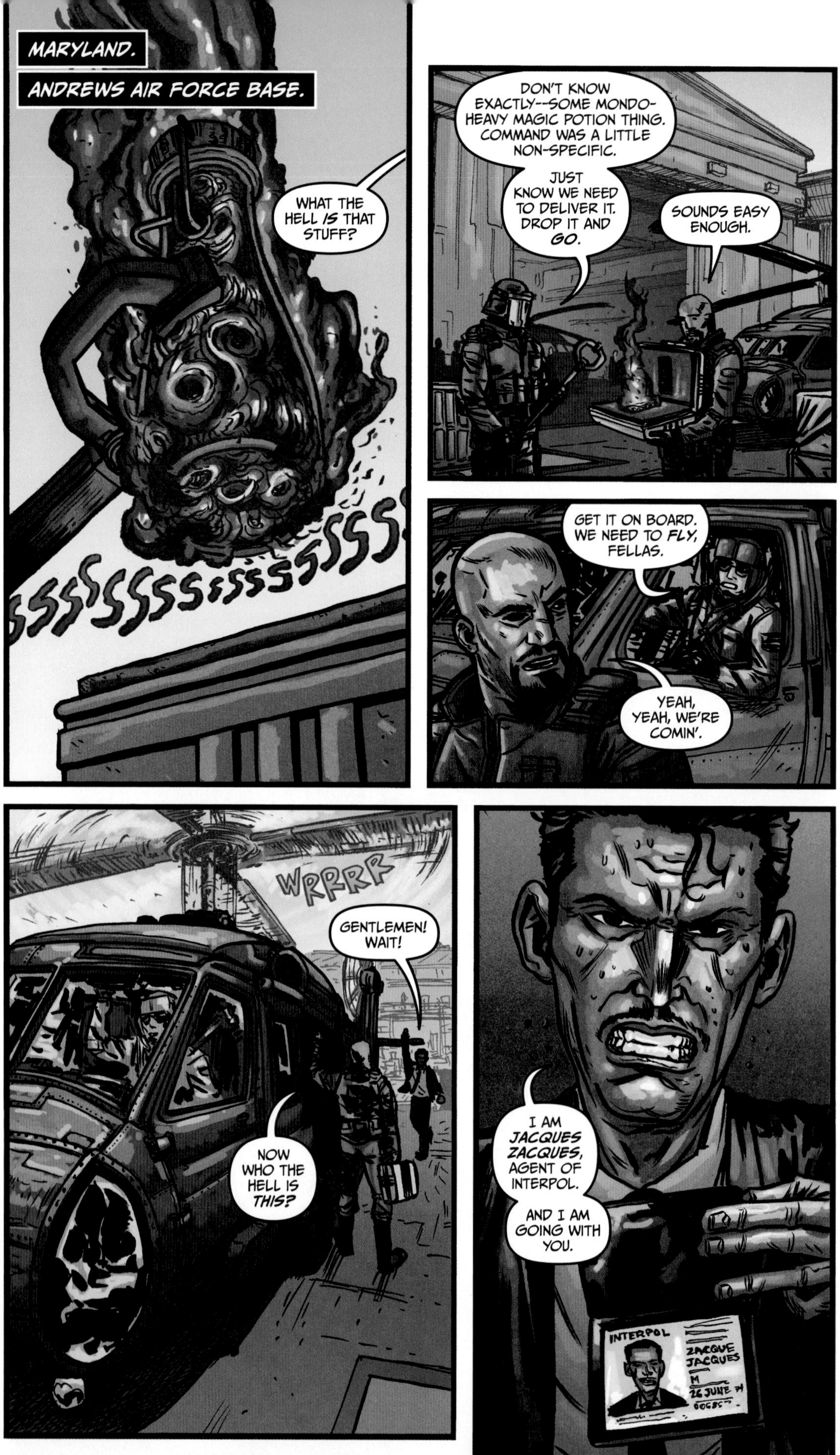
MARYLAND.
ANDREWS AIR FORCE BASE.
WHAT THE HELL *IS* THAT STUFF?
SSSSSSSSSSSSSSSSSSS
DON'T KNOW EXACTLY--SOME MONDO-HEAVY MAGIC POTION THING. COMMAND WAS A LITTLE NON-SPECIFIC.
JUST KNOW WE NEED TO DELIVER IT. DROP IT AND *GO*.
SOUNDS EASY ENOUGH.
GET IT ON BOARD. WE NEED TO *FLY*, FELLAS.
YEAH, YEAH, WE'RE COMIN'.
WRRRR
GENTLEMEN! WAIT!
NOW WHO THE HELL IS *THIS?*
I AM *JACQUES ZACQUES*, AGENT OF INTERPOL.
AND I AM GOING WITH YOU.
INTERPOL
ZACQUE JACQUES
M
26 JUNE 71

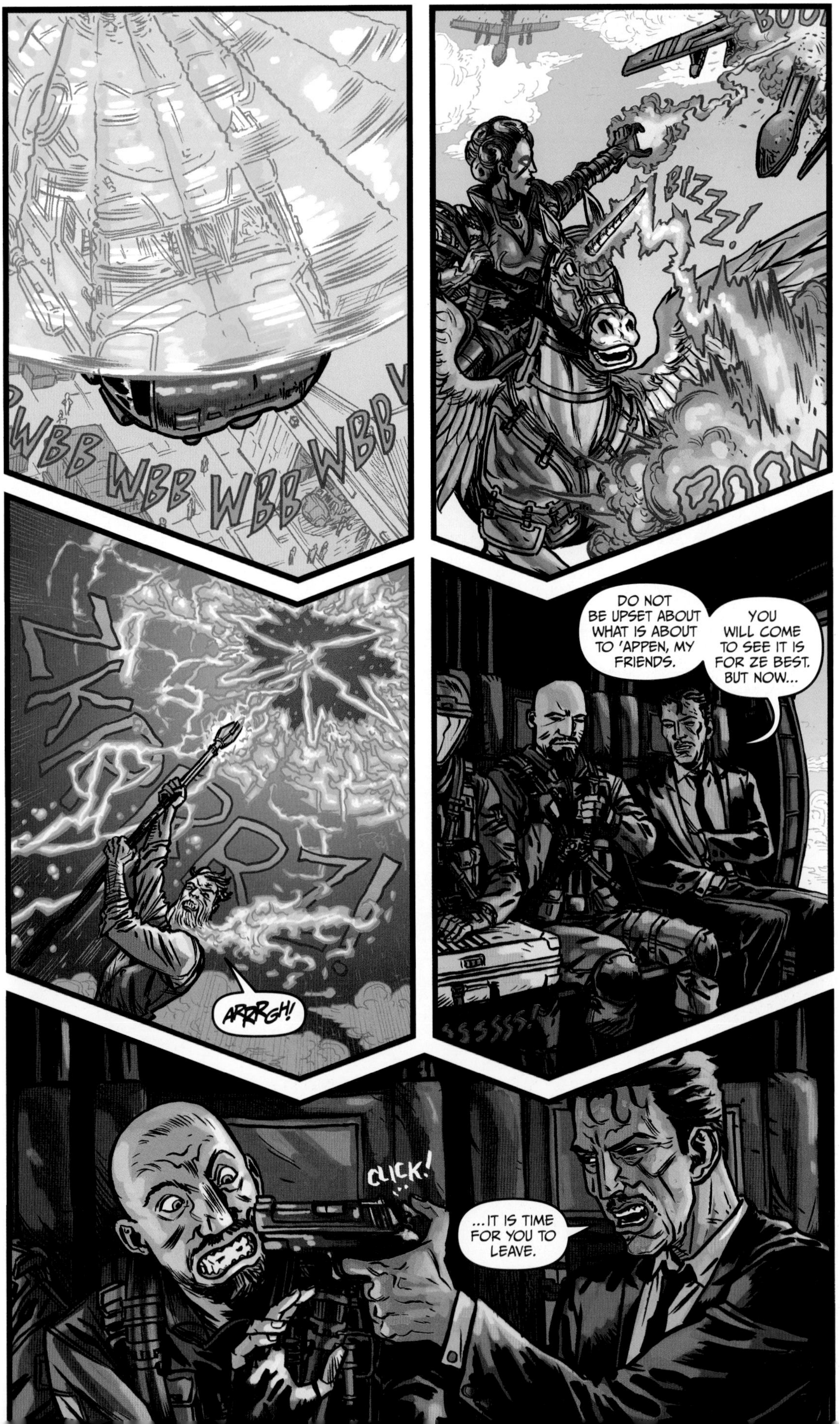
WBB WBB WBB WBB WBB
BIZZZ!
BOOM
ARRRGH!
DO NOT BE UPSET ABOUT WHAT IS ABOUT TO 'APPEN, MY FRIENDS.
YOU WILL COME TO SEE IT IS FOR ZE BEST. BUT NOW...
CLICK!
...IT IS TIME FOR YOU TO LEAVE.

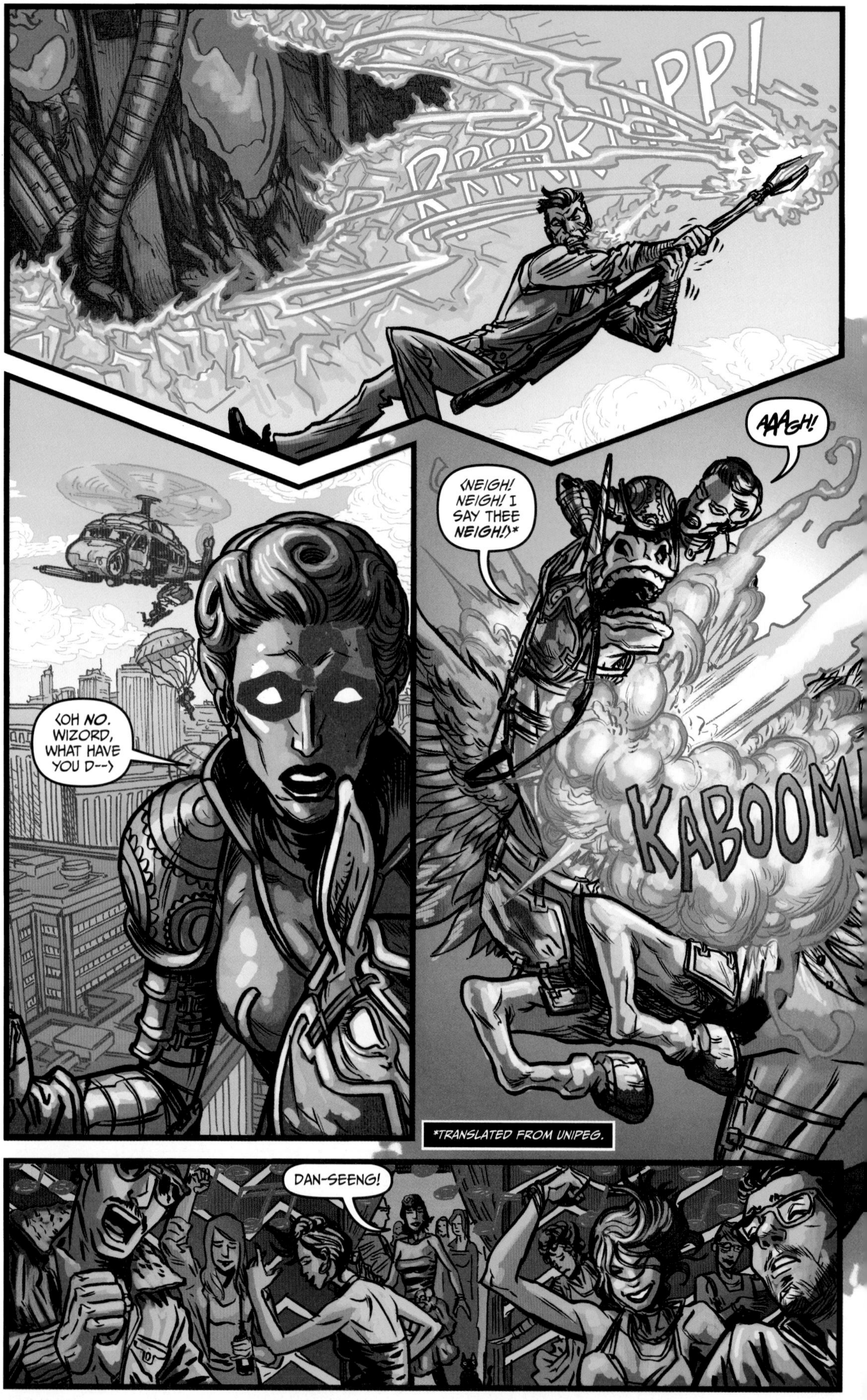
BRRRRRIIIIPP!
<NEIGH! NEIGH! I SAY THEE NEIGH!>*
AAAGH!
KABOOM!
<OH NO. WIZORD, WHAT HAVE YOU D-->
*TRANSLATED FROM UNIPEG.
DAN-SEENG!

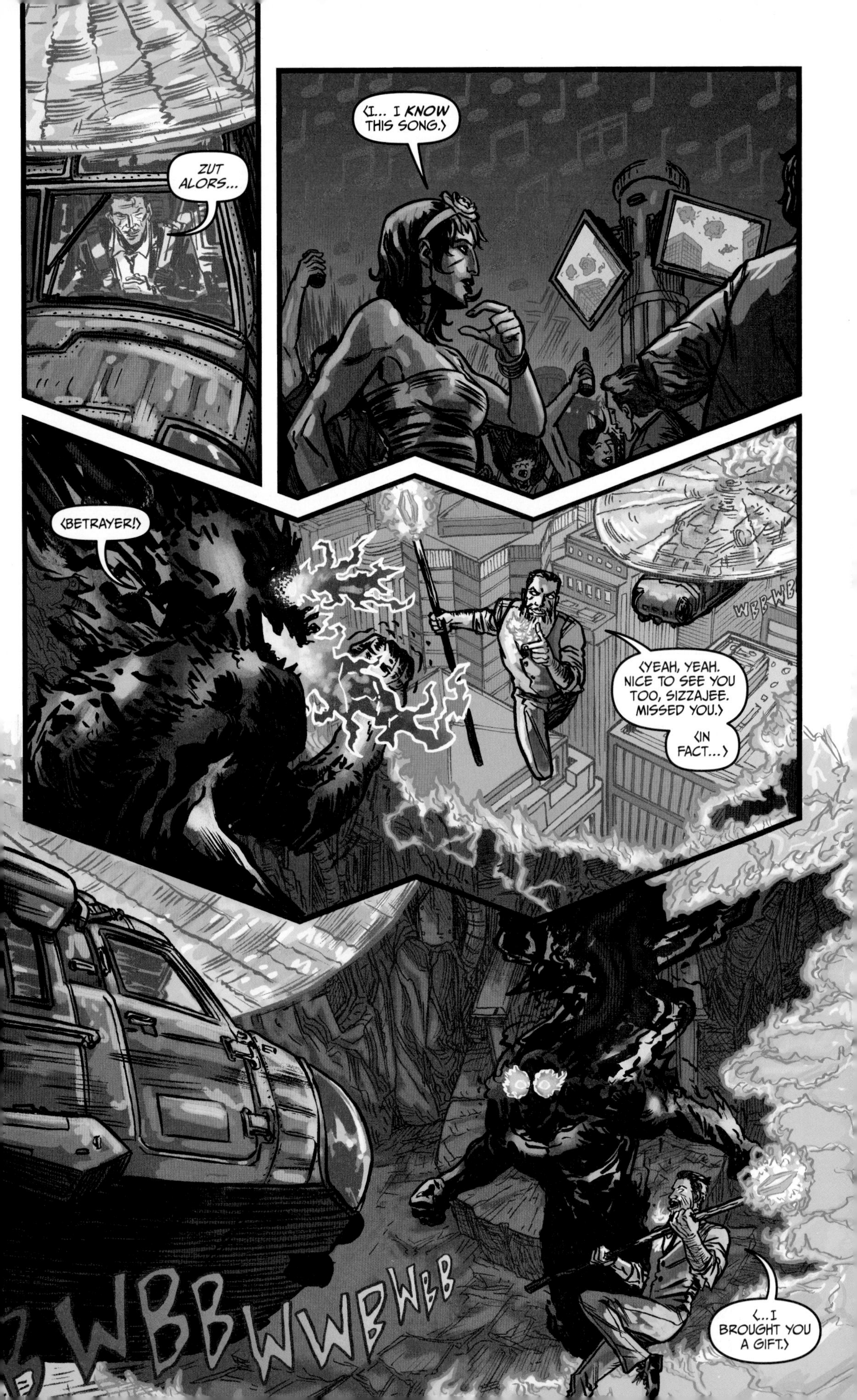
ZUT ALORS...
‹I... I *KNOW* THIS SONG.›
‹BETRAYER!›
‹YEAH, YEAH. NICE TO SEE YOU TOO, SIZZAJEE. MISSED YOU.›
‹IN FACT...›
WBBWB
‹..I BROUGHT YOU A GIFT.›
WBBWWBWBB

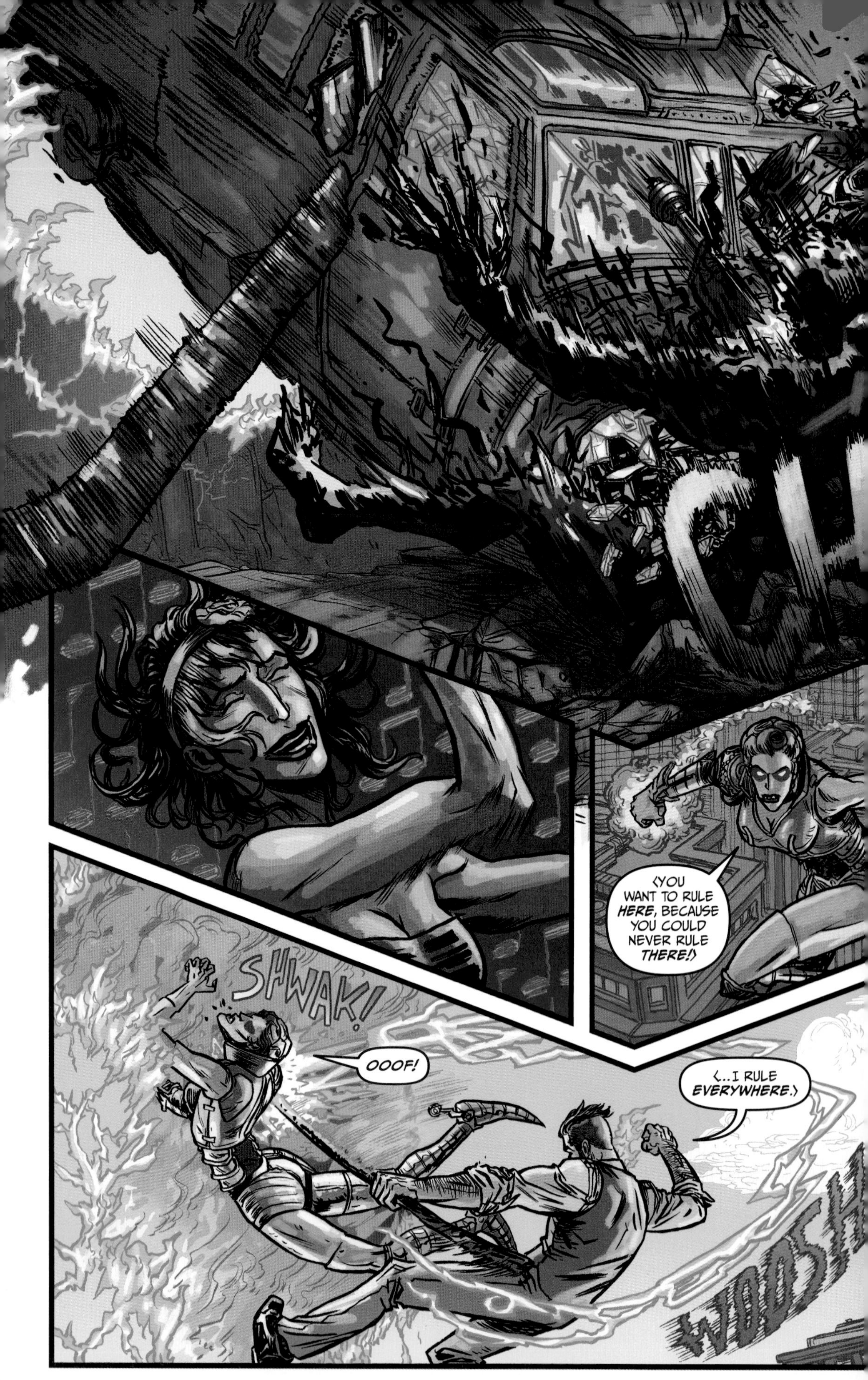
‹YOU WANT TO RULE HERE, BECAUSE YOU COULD NEVER RULE THERE!›
SHWAK!
OOOF!
‹...I RULE EVERYWHERE.›
WOOSH

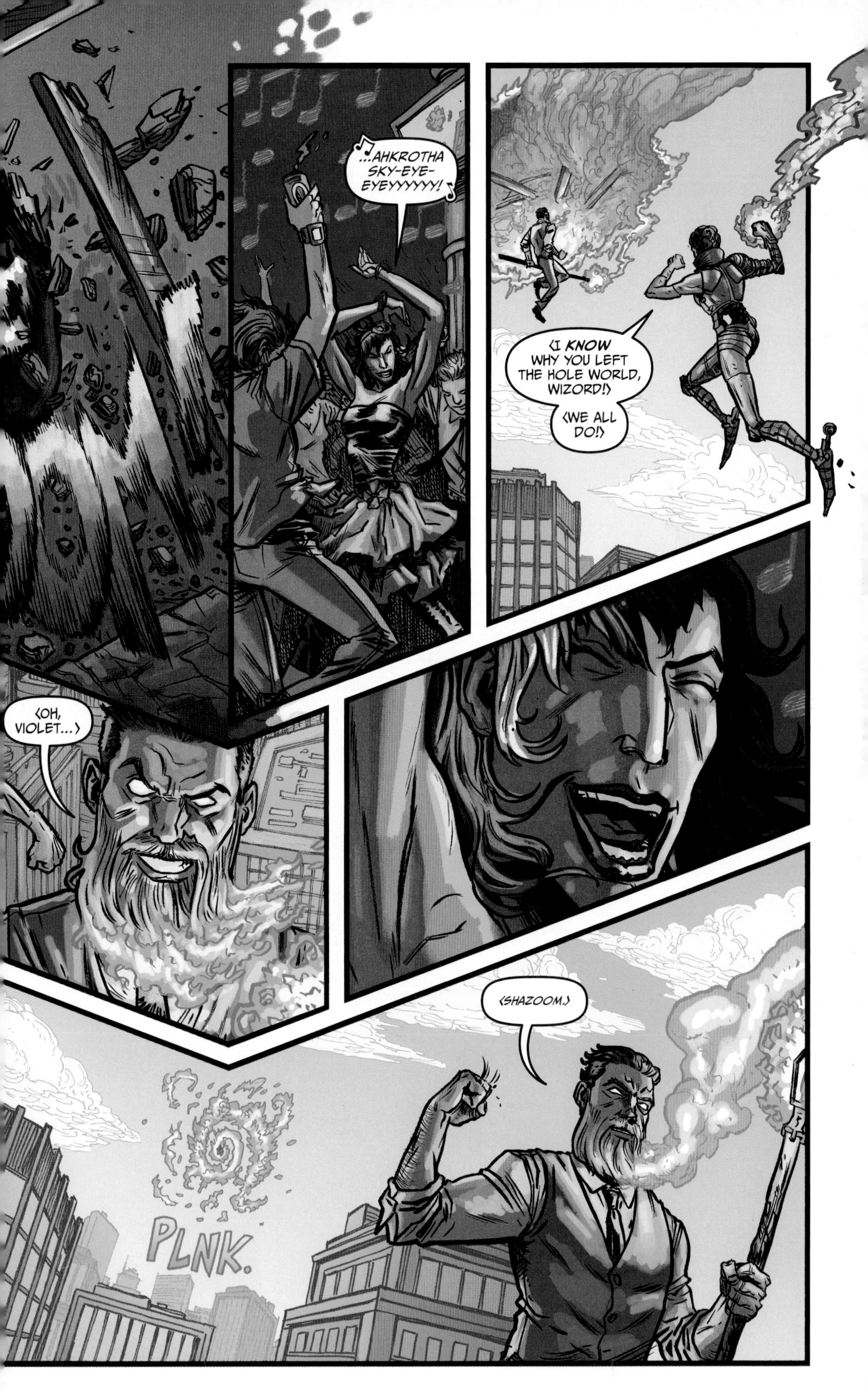
...AHKROTHA SKY-EYE-EYEYYYYYY!
‹I KNOW WHY YOU LEFT THE HOLE WORLD, WIZORD!›
‹WE ALL DO!›
‹OH, VIOLET...›
‹SHAZOOM.›
PLNK.

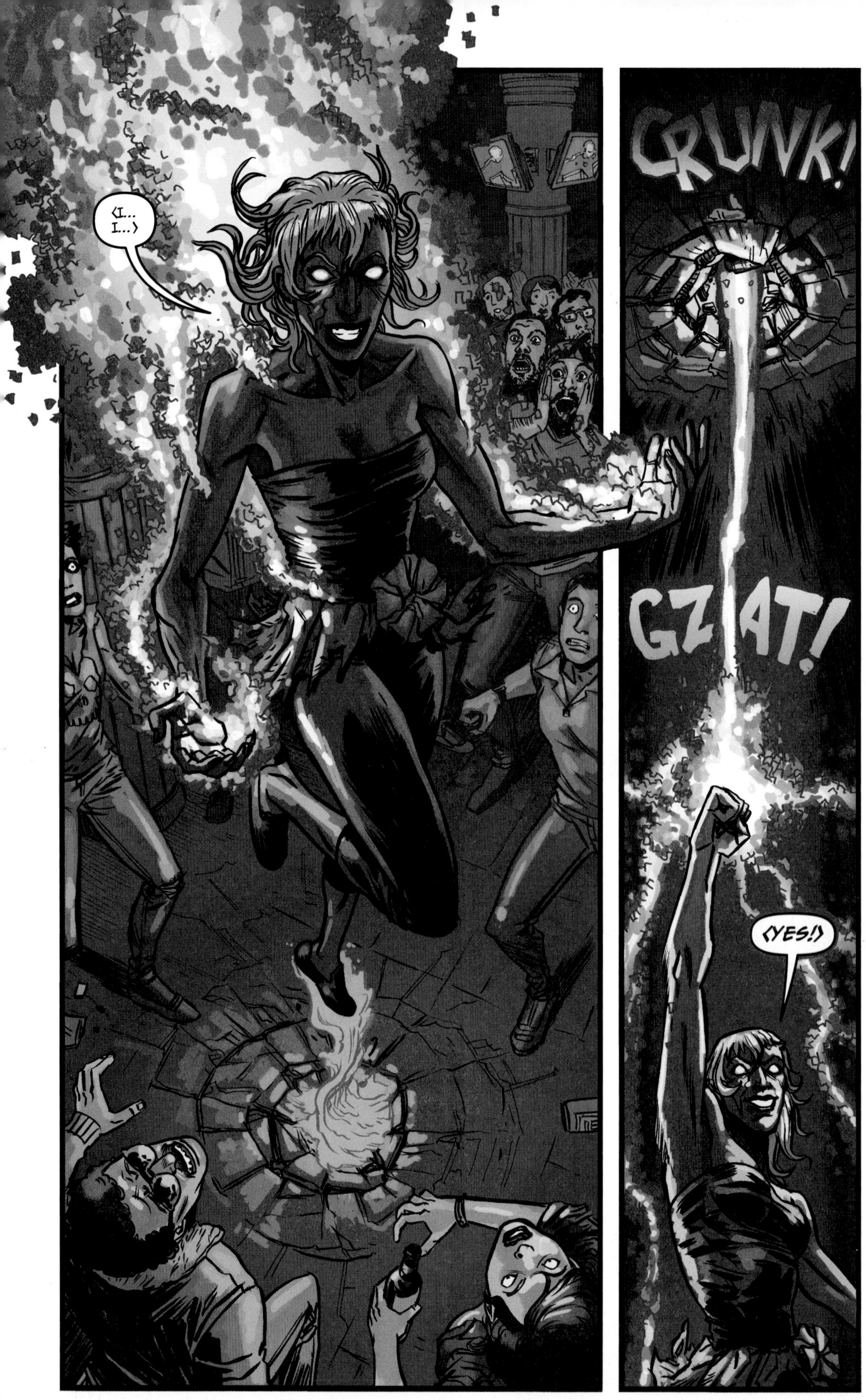
‹I...
I...›
CRUNK!
GZAT!
‹YES!›

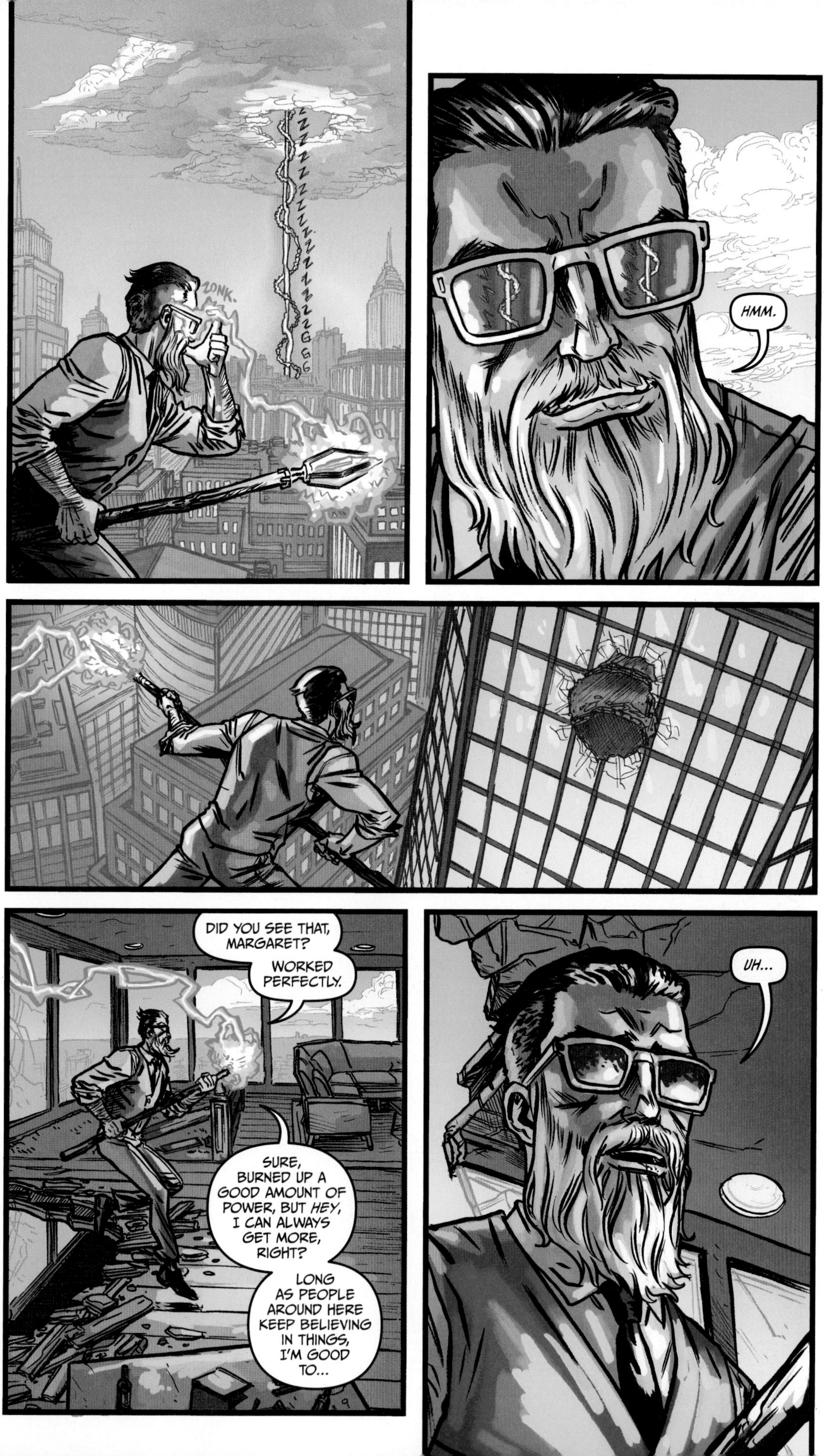
ZONK.
ZZZZZZZZZZZZZZZZZGGG
HMM.
DID YOU SEE THAT, MARGARET?
WORKED PERFECTLY.
SURE, BURNED UP A GOOD AMOUNT OF POWER, BUT *HEY*, I CAN ALWAYS GET MORE, RIGHT?
LONG AS PEOPLE AROUND HERE KEEP BELIEVING IN THINGS, I'M GOOD TO...
UH...

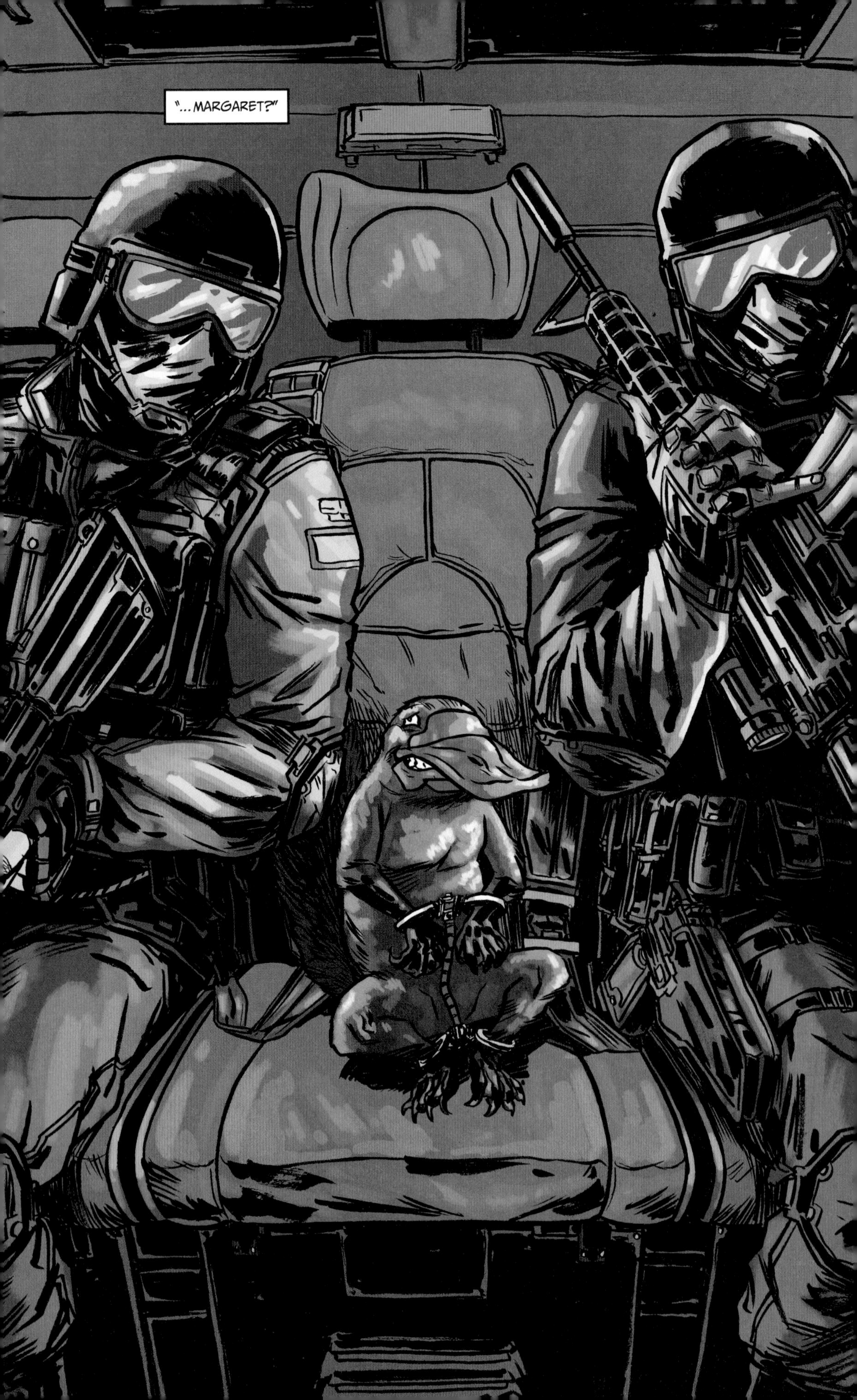
"...MARGARET?"

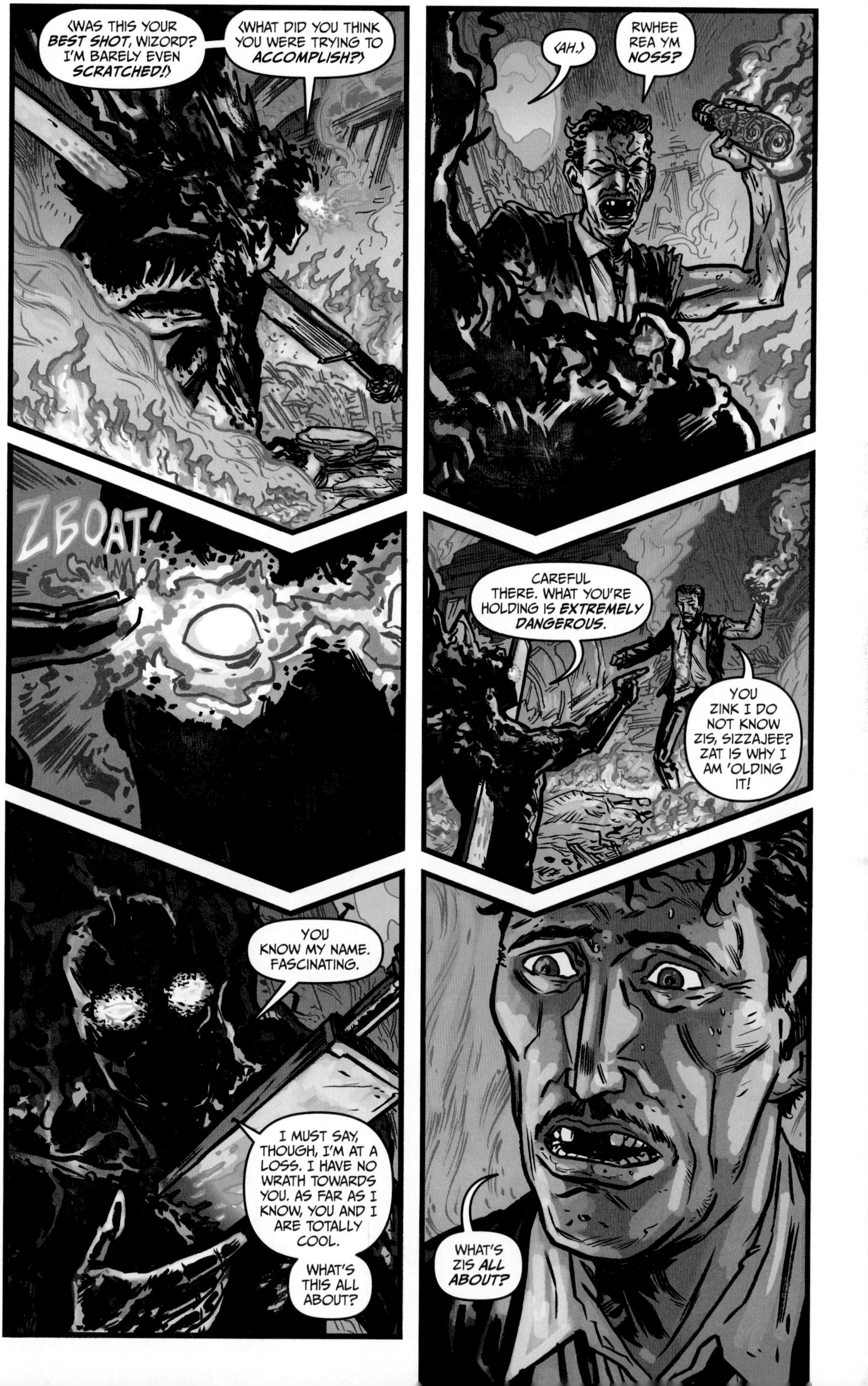

‹WAS THIS YOUR BEST SHOT, WIZORD? I'M BARELY EVEN SCRATCHED!›
‹WHAT DID YOU THINK YOU WERE TRYING TO ACCOMPLISH?›
‹AH.›
RWHEE REA YM NOSS?
ZBOAT!
CAREFUL THERE. WHAT YOU'RE HOLDING IS EXTREMELY DANGEROUS.
YOU ZINK I DO NOT KNOW ZIS, SIZZAJEE? ZAT IS WHY I AM 'OLDING IT!
YOU KNOW MY NAME. FASCINATING.
I MUST SAY, THOUGH, I'M AT A LOSS. I HAVE NO WRATH TOWARDS YOU. AS FAR AS I KNOW, YOU AND I ARE TOTALLY COOL.
WHAT'S THIS ALL ABOUT?
WHAT'S ZIS ALL ABOUT?

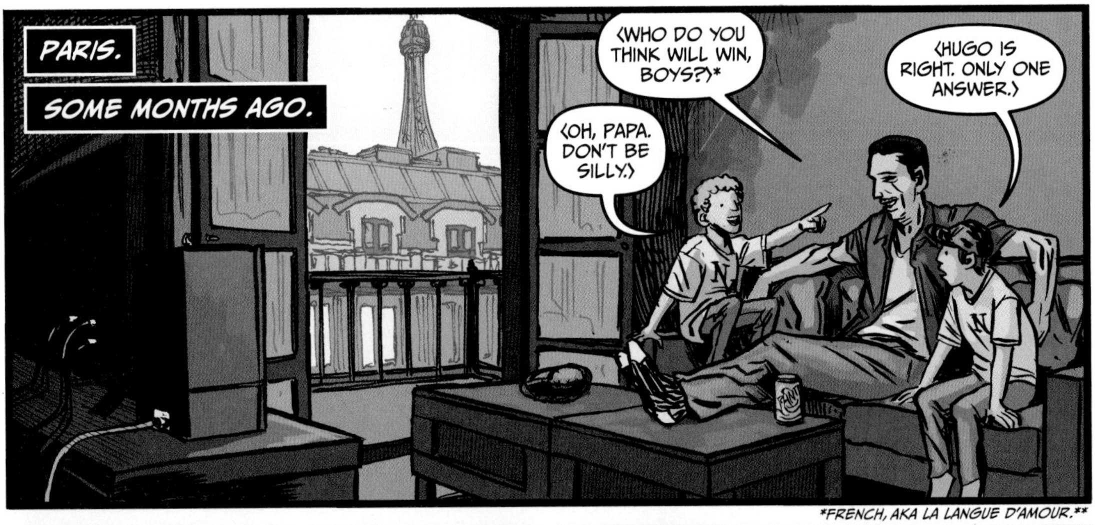
PARIS.
SOME MONTHS AGO.
‹WHO DO YOU THINK WILL WIN, BOYS?›*
‹OH, PAPA. DON'T BE SILLY.›
‹HUGO IS RIGHT. ONLY ONE ANSWER.›

*FRENCH, AKA LA LANGUE D'AMOUR.**

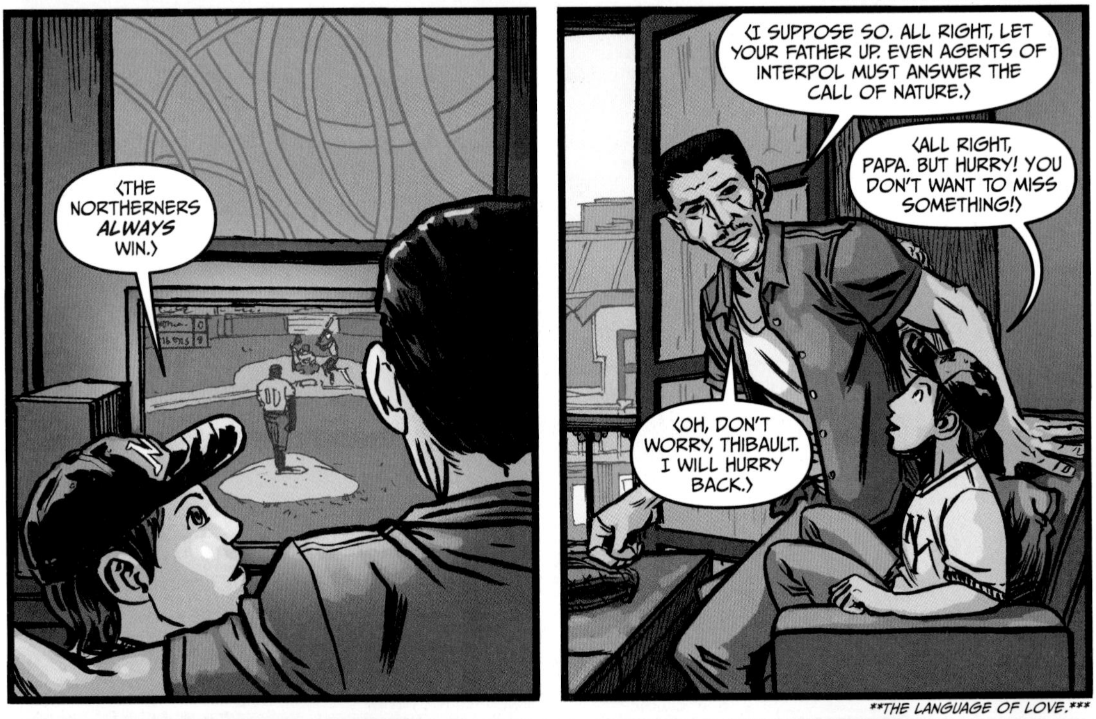
‹THE NORTHERNERS ALWAYS WIN.›
‹I SUPPOSE SO. ALL RIGHT, LET YOUR FATHER UP. EVEN AGENTS OF INTERPOL MUST ANSWER THE CALL OF NATURE.›
‹ALL RIGHT, PAPA. BUT HURRY! YOU DON'T WANT TO MISS SOMETHING!›
‹OH, DON'T WORRY, THIBAULT. I WILL HURRY BACK.›

THE LANGUAGE OF LOVE.*

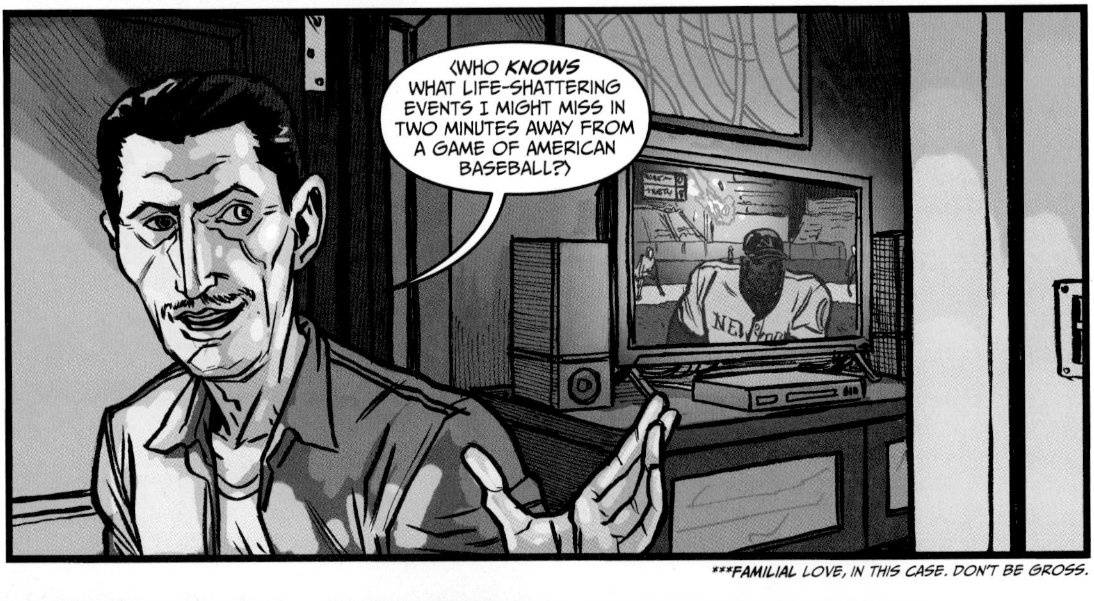
‹WHO KNOWS WHAT LIFE-SHATTERING EVENTS I MIGHT MISS IN TWO MINUTES AWAY FROM A GAME OF AMERICAN BASEBALL?›

***FAMILIAL LOVE, IN THIS CASE. DON'T BE GROSS.

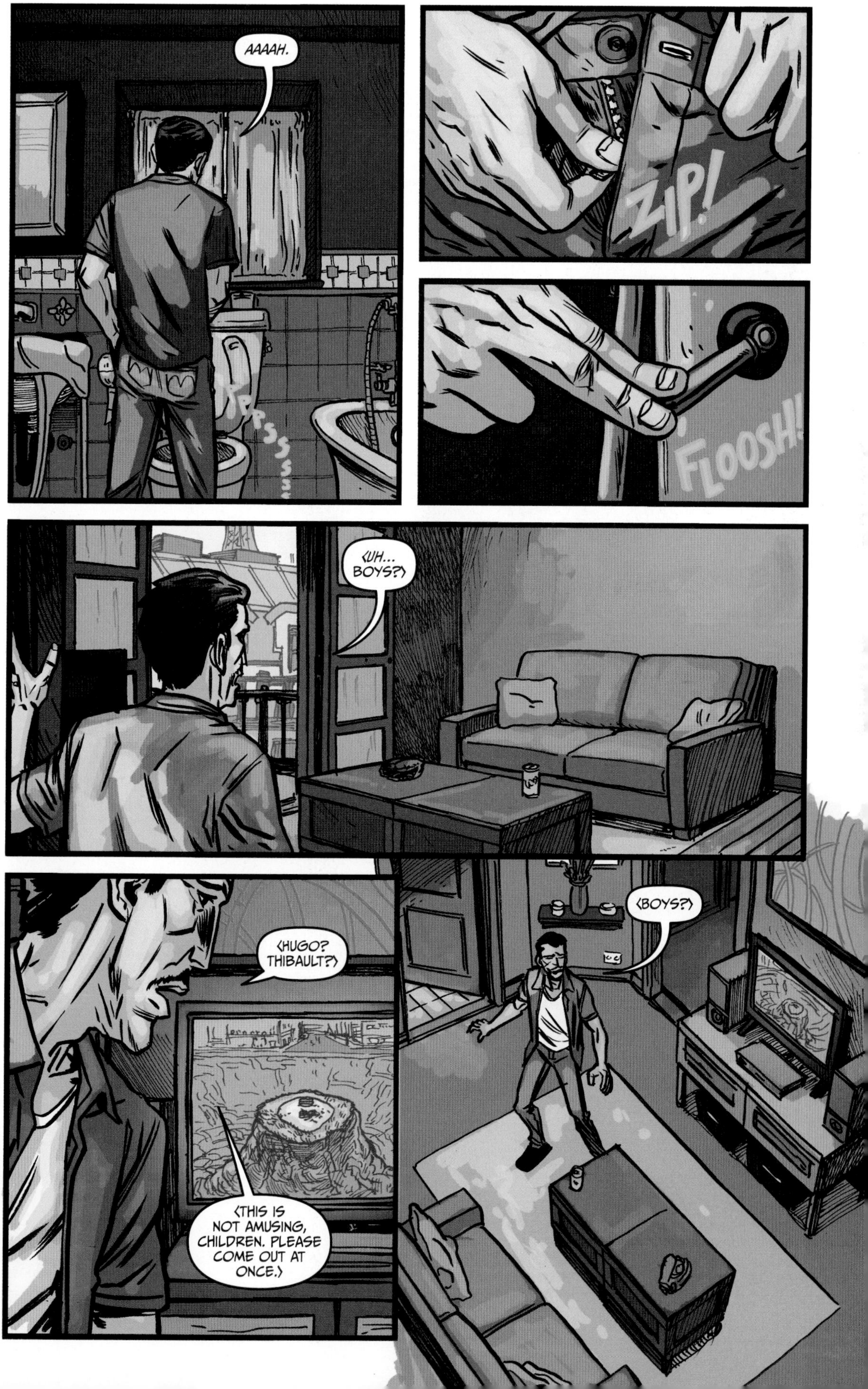

AAAAH.
PPPSSSSS
ZIP!
FLOOSH!
<UH... BOYS?>
<HUGO? THIBAULT?>
<THIS IS NOT AMUSING, CHILDREN. PLEASE COME OUT AT ONCE.>
<BOYS?>

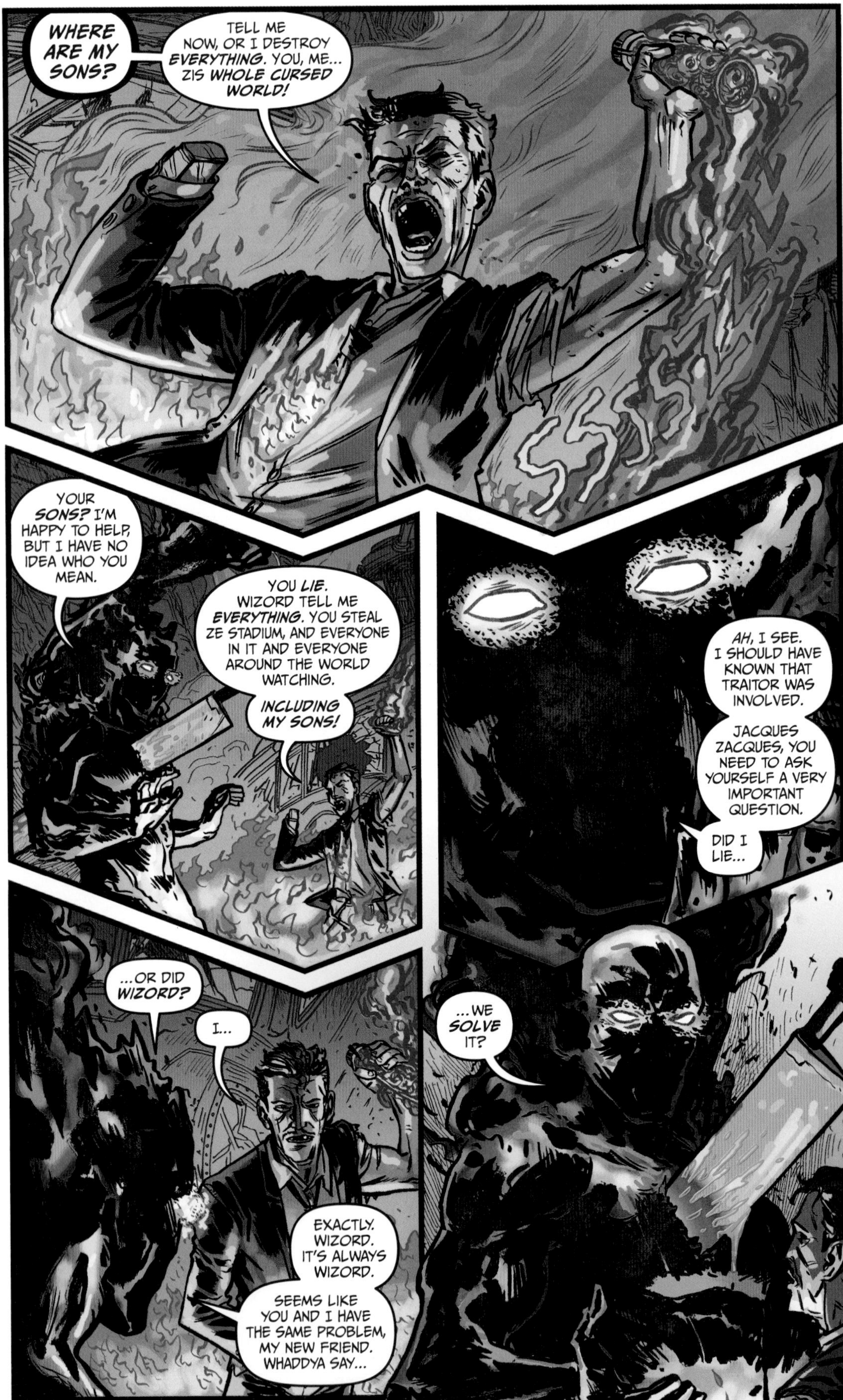
WHERE ARE MY SONS?
TELL ME NOW, OR I DESTROY EVERYTHING. YOU, ME... ZIS WHOLE CURSED WORLD!
YOUR SONS? I'M HAPPY TO HELP, BUT I HAVE NO IDEA WHO YOU MEAN.
YOU LIE. WIZORD TELL ME EVERYTHING. YOU STEAL ZE STADIUM, AND EVERYONE IN IT AND EVERYONE AROUND THE WORLD WATCHING.
INCLUDING MY SONS!
AH, I SEE. I SHOULD HAVE KNOWN THAT TRAITOR WAS INVOLVED.
JACQUES ZACQUES, YOU NEED TO ASK YOURSELF A VERY IMPORTANT QUESTION.
DID I LIE...
...OR DID WIZORD?
I...
EXACTLY. WIZORD. IT'S ALWAYS WIZORD.
SEEMS LIKE YOU AND I HAVE THE SAME PROBLEM, MY NEW FRIEND. WHADDYA SAY...
...WE SOLVE IT?

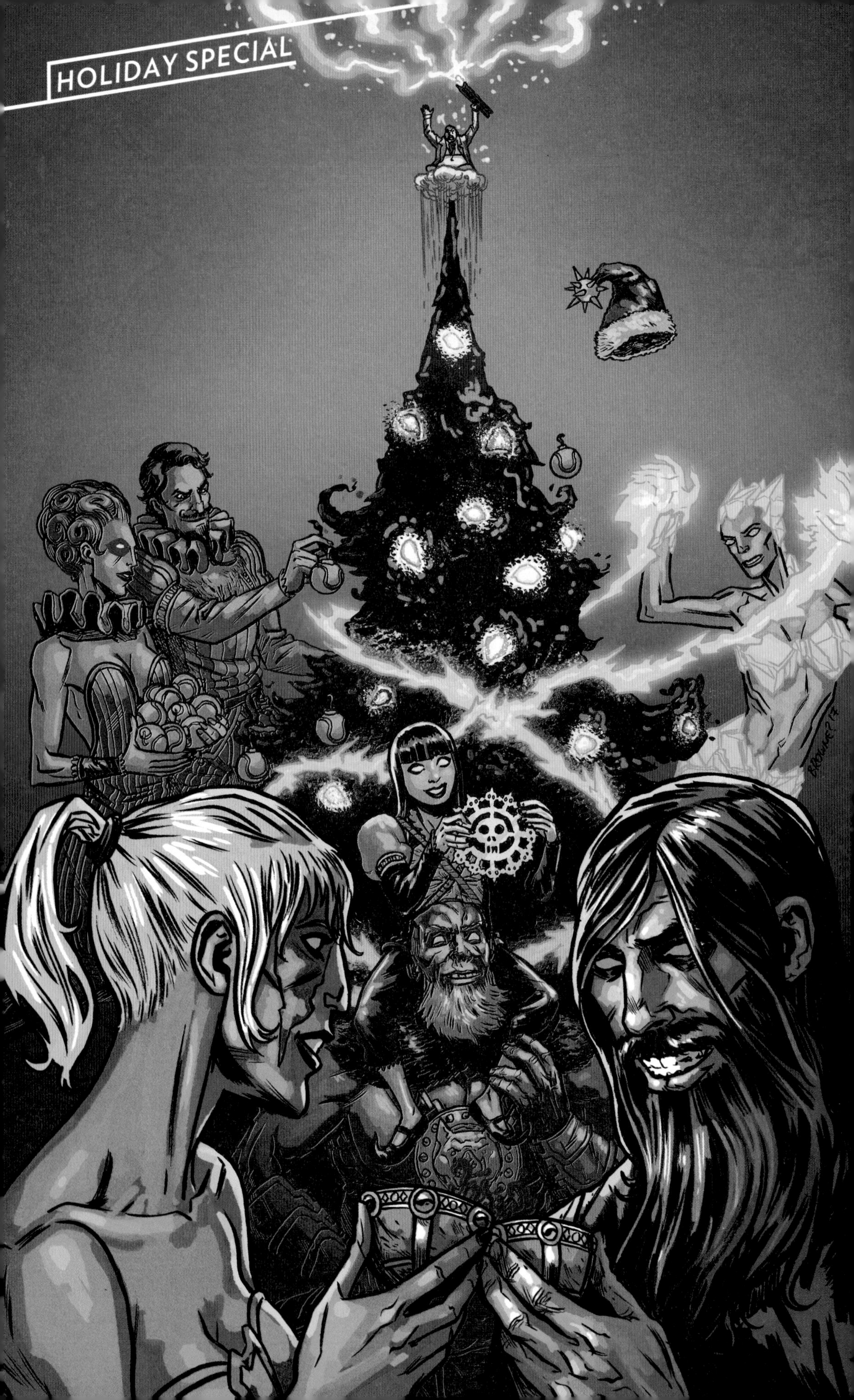

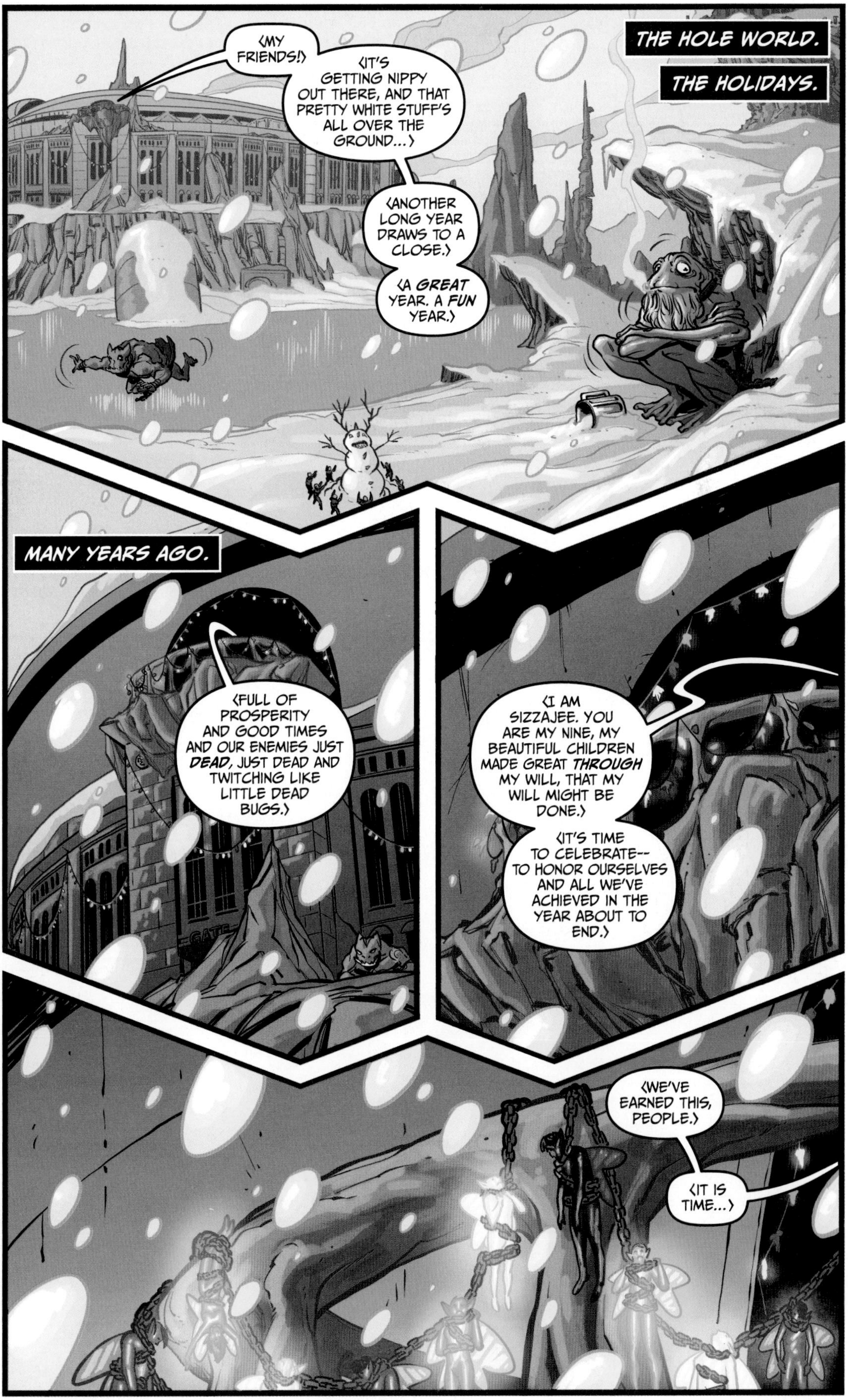
THE HOLE WORLD.
THE HOLIDAYS.
‹MY FRIENDS!›
‹IT'S GETTING NIPPY OUT THERE, AND THAT PRETTY WHITE STUFF'S ALL OVER THE GROUND...›
‹ANOTHER LONG YEAR DRAWS TO A CLOSE.›
‹A GREAT YEAR. A FUN YEAR.›
MANY YEARS AGO.
‹FULL OF PROSPERITY AND GOOD TIMES AND OUR ENEMIES JUST DEAD, JUST DEAD AND TWITCHING LIKE LITTLE DEAD BUGS.›
‹I AM SIZZAJEE. YOU ARE MY NINE, MY BEAUTIFUL CHILDREN MADE GREAT THROUGH MY WILL, THAT MY WILL MIGHT BE DONE.›
‹IT'S TIME TO CELEBRATE-- TO HONOR OURSELVES AND ALL WE'VE ACHIEVED IN THE YEAR ABOUT TO END.›
‹WE'VE EARNED THIS, PEOPLE.›
‹IT IS TIME...›

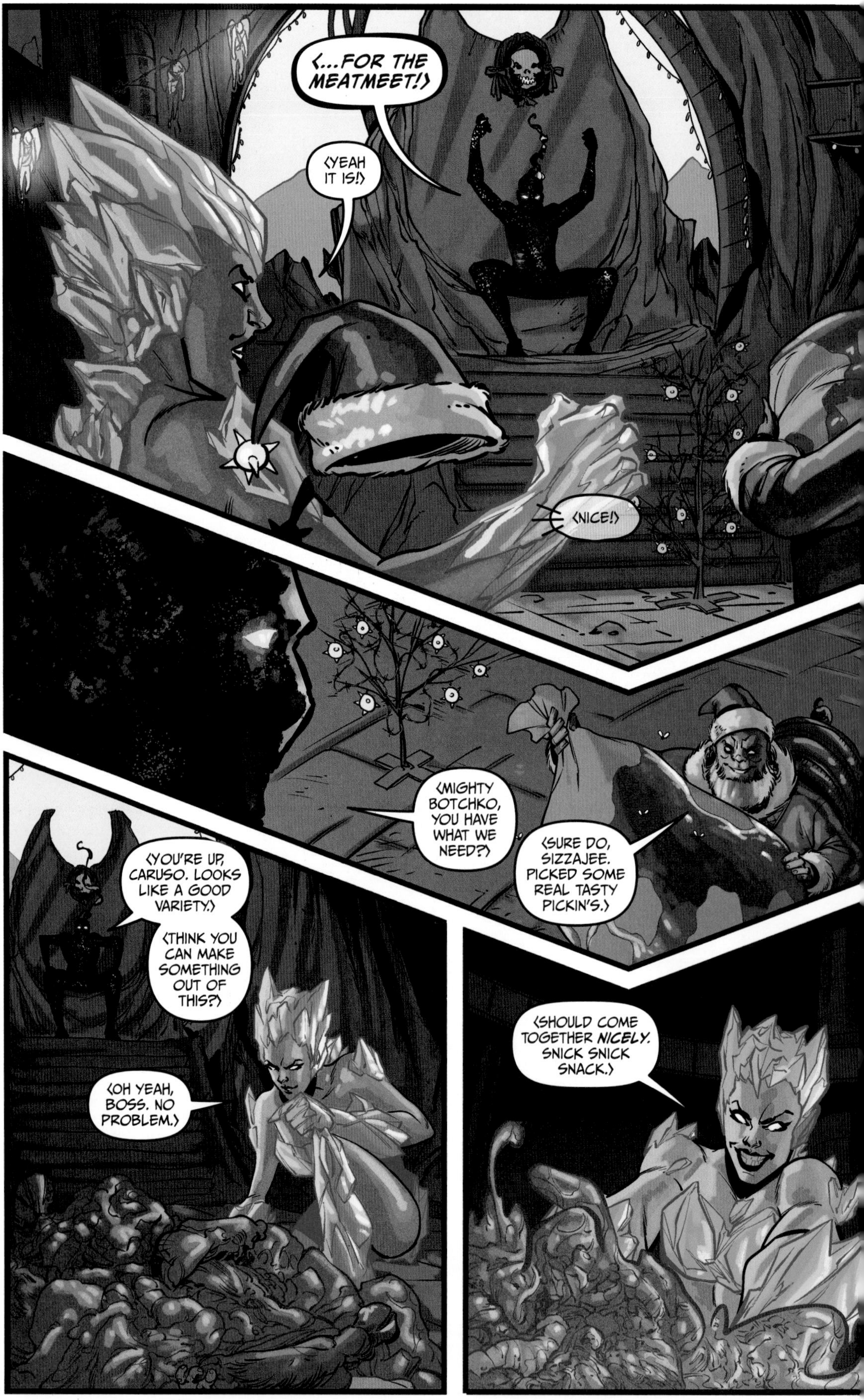
‹...FOR THE MEATMEET!›
‹YEAH IT IS!›
‹NICE!›
‹MIGHTY BOTCHKO, YOU HAVE WHAT WE NEED?›
‹SURE DO, SIZZAJEE. PICKED SOME REAL TASTY PICKIN'S.›
‹YOU'RE UP, CARUSO. LOOKS LIKE A GOOD VARIETY.›
‹THINK YOU CAN MAKE SOMETHING OUT OF THIS?›
‹OH YEAH, BOSS. NO PROBLEM.›
‹SHOULD COME TOGETHER *NICELY*. SNICK SNICK SNACK.›

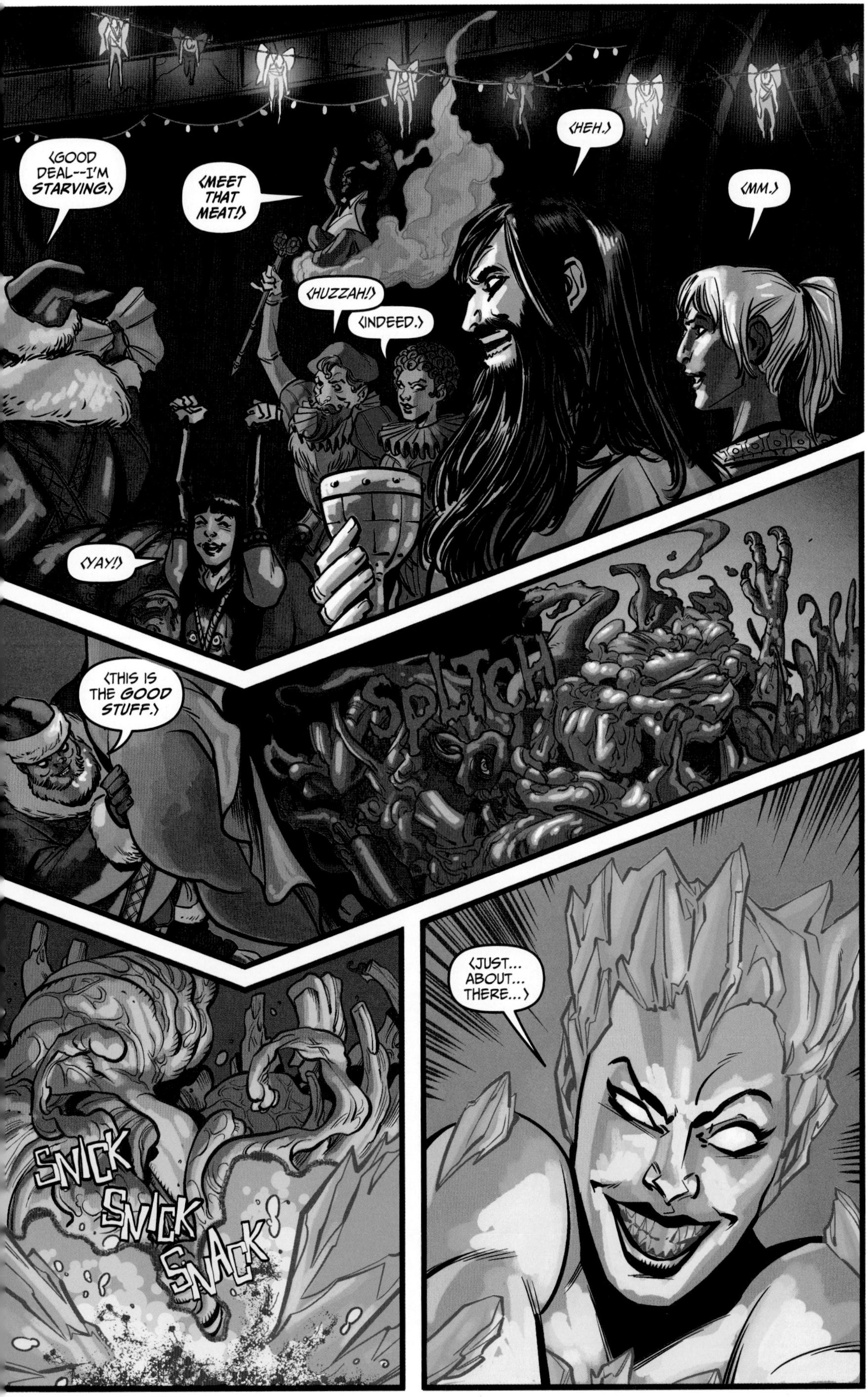
‹GOOD DEAL--I'M STARVING.›
‹MEET THAT MEAT!›
‹HEH.›
‹MM.›
‹HUZZAH!›
‹INDEED.›
‹YAY!›
‹THIS IS THE GOOD STUFF.›
SPLTCH
SNICK
SNICK
SNACK
‹JUST... ABOUT... THERE...›

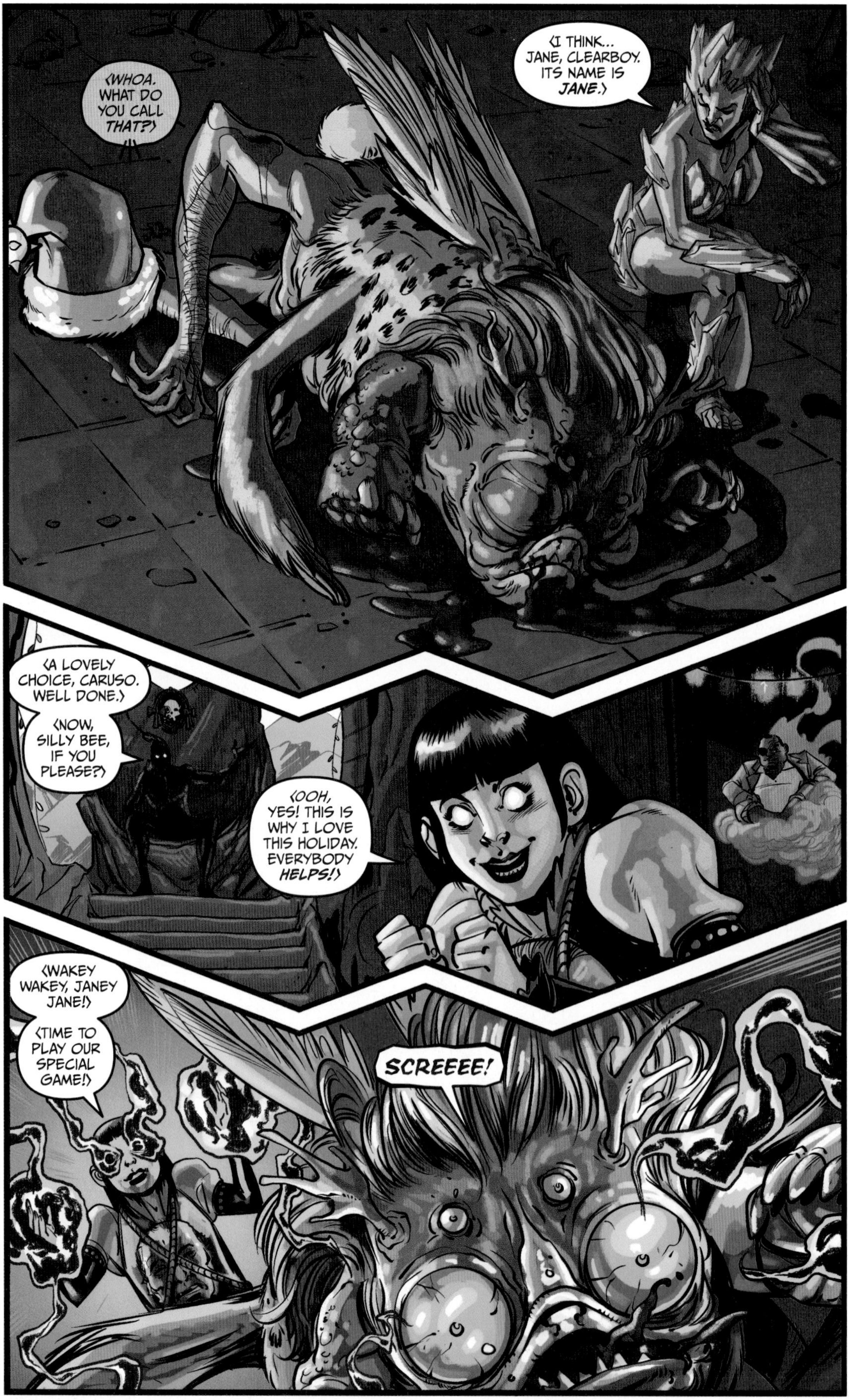

⟨WHOA. WHAT DO YOU CALL *THAT?*⟩
⟨I THINK... JANE, CLEARBOY. ITS NAME IS *JANE.*⟩
⟨A LOVELY CHOICE, CARUSO. WELL DONE.⟩
⟨NOW, SILLY BEE, IF YOU PLEASE?⟩
⟨OOH, YES! THIS IS WHY I LOVE THIS HOLIDAY. EVERYBODY *HELPS!*⟩
⟨WAKEY WAKEY, JANEY JANE!⟩
⟨TIME TO PLAY OUR SPECIAL GAME!⟩
SCREEEE!

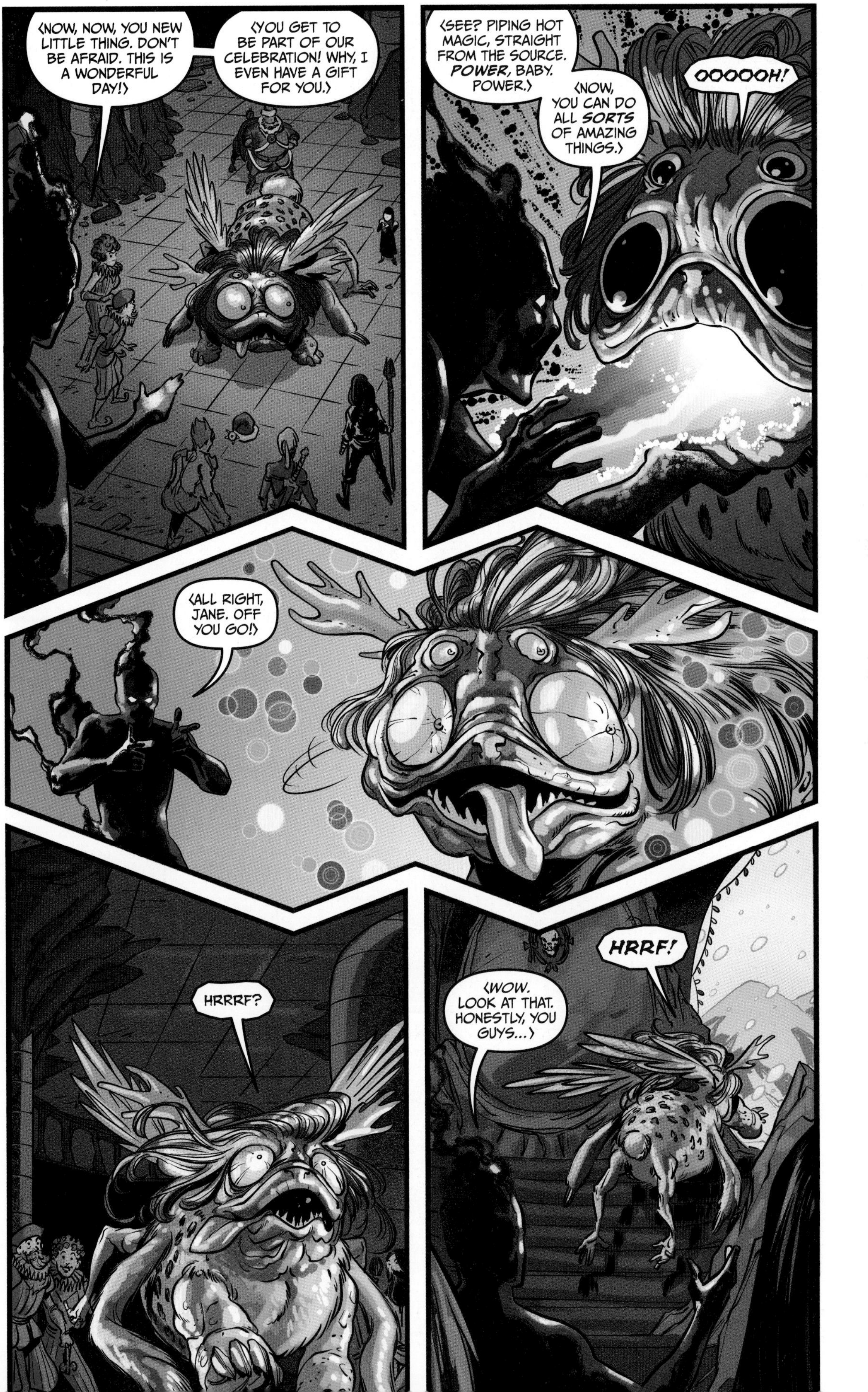

‹NOW, NOW, YOU NEW LITTLE THING. DON'T BE AFRAID. THIS IS A WONDERFUL DAY!›
‹YOU GET TO BE PART OF OUR CELEBRATION! WHY, I EVEN HAVE A GIFT FOR YOU.›
‹SEE? PIPING HOT MAGIC, STRAIGHT FROM THE SOURCE. POWER, BABY. POWER.›
‹NOW, YOU CAN DO ALL SORTS OF AMAZING THINGS.›
OOOOOH!
‹ALL RIGHT, JANE. OFF YOU GO!›
HRRRF?
HRRF!
‹WOW. LOOK AT THAT. HONESTLY, YOU GUYS...›

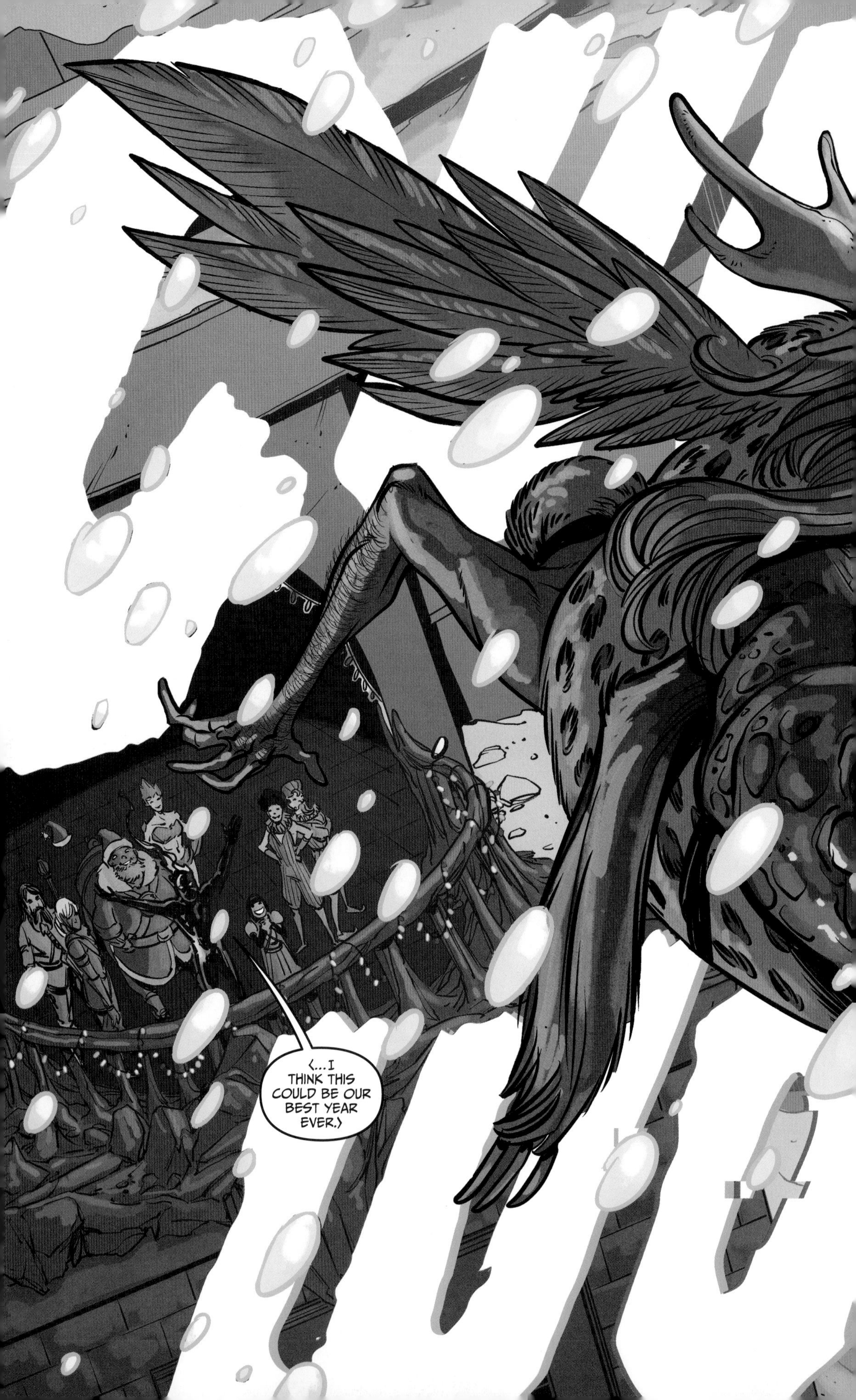
〈...I THINK THIS COULD BE OUR BEST YEAR EVER.〉

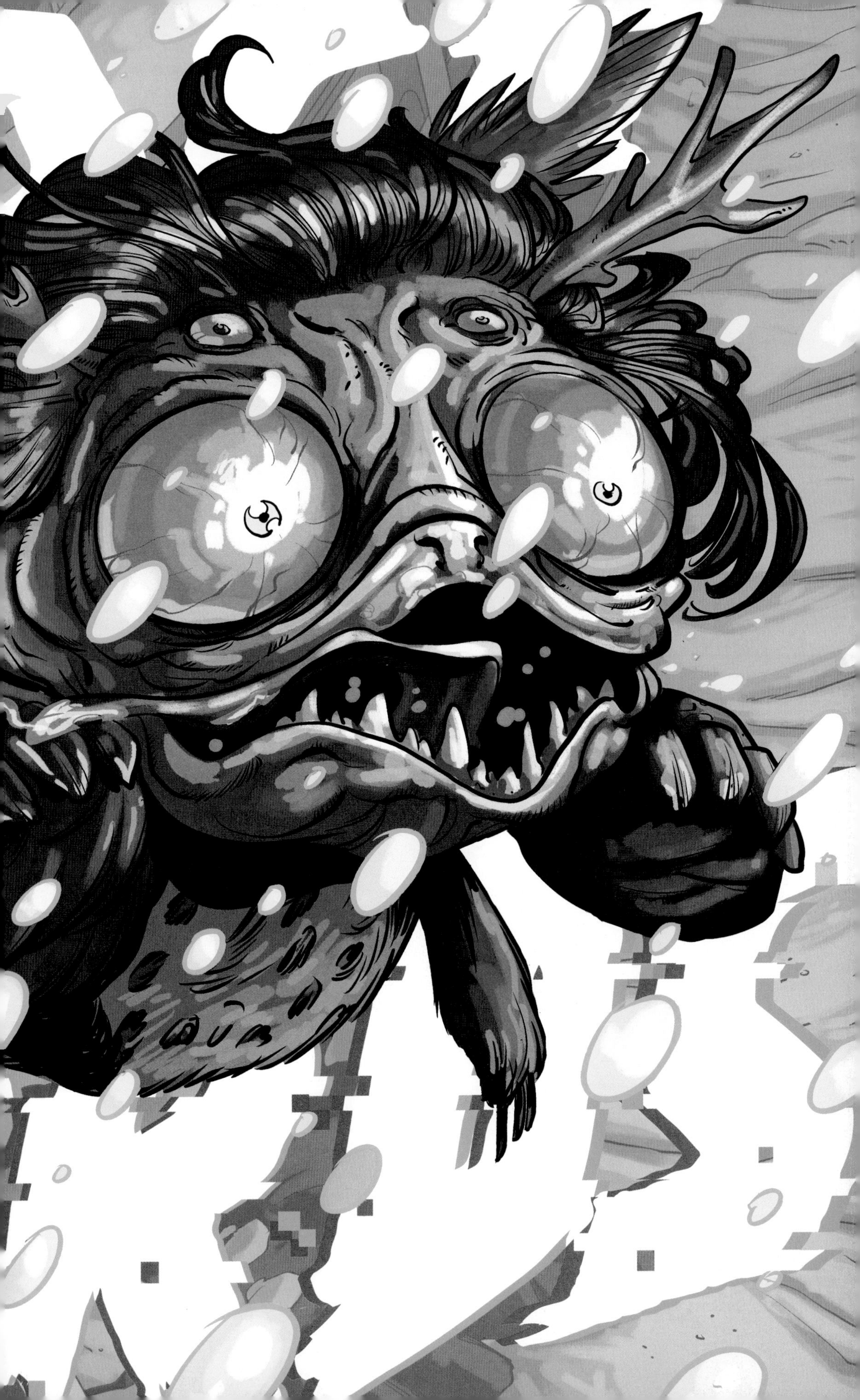

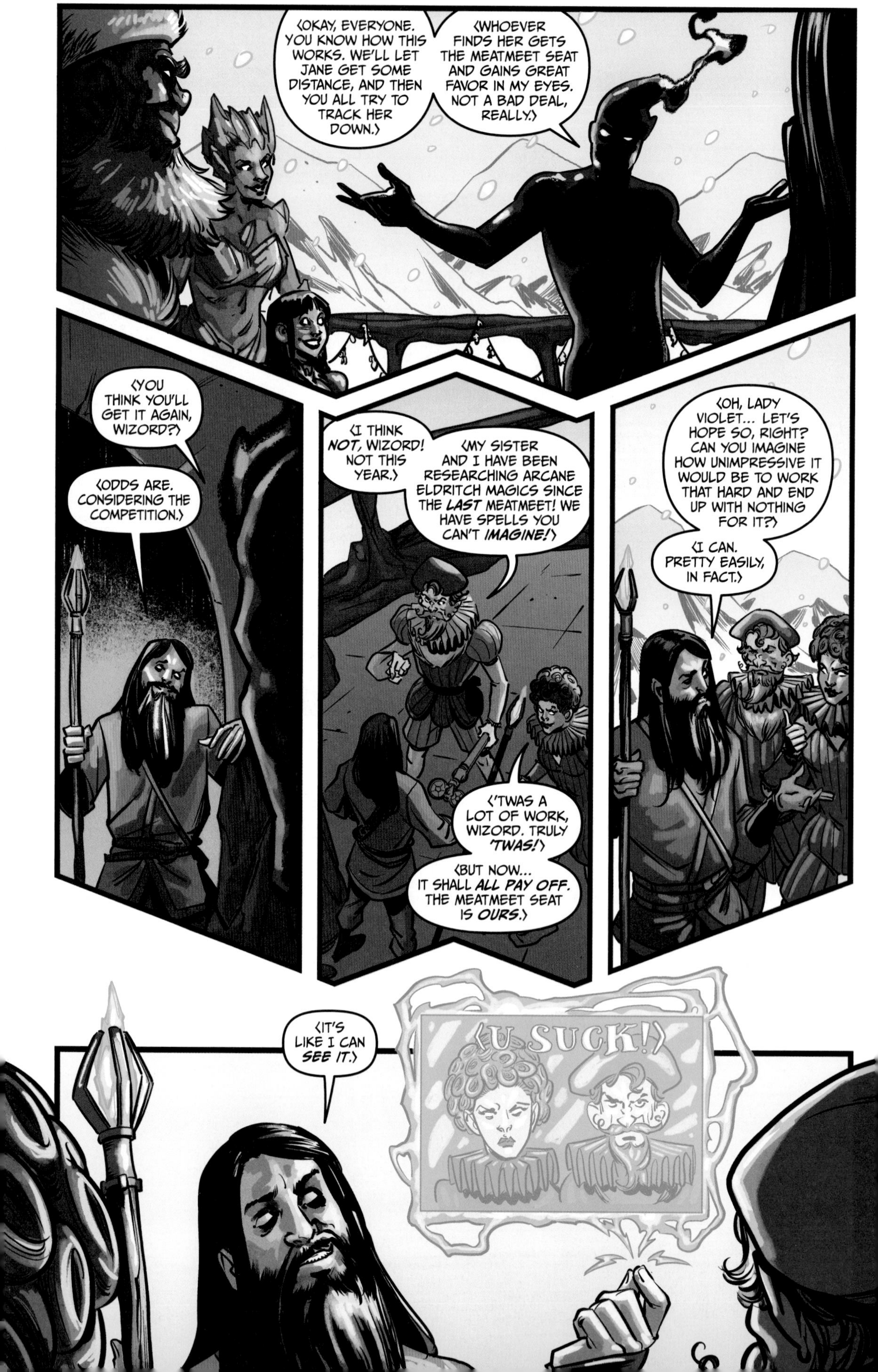
<OKAY, EVERYONE. YOU KNOW HOW THIS WORKS. WE'LL LET JANE GET SOME DISTANCE, AND THEN YOU ALL TRY TO TRACK HER DOWN.>
<WHOEVER FINDS HER GETS THE MEATMEET SEAT AND GAINS GREAT FAVOR IN MY EYES. NOT A BAD DEAL, REALLY.>
<YOU THINK YOU'LL GET IT AGAIN, WIZORD?>
<ODDS ARE. CONSIDERING THE COMPETITION.>
<I THINK *NOT*, WIZORD! NOT THIS YEAR.>
<MY SISTER AND I HAVE BEEN RESEARCHING ARCANE ELDRITCH MAGICS SINCE THE *LAST* MEATMEET! WE HAVE SPELLS YOU CAN'T *IMAGINE!*>
<'TWAS A LOT OF WORK, WIZORD. TRULY *'TWAS!*>
<BUT NOW... IT SHALL *ALL PAY OFF.* THE MEATMEET SEAT IS *OURS.*>
<OH, LADY VIOLET... LET'S HOPE SO, RIGHT? CAN YOU IMAGINE HOW UNIMPRESSIVE IT WOULD BE TO WORK THAT HARD AND END UP WITH NOTHING FOR IT?>
<I CAN. PRETTY EASILY, IN FACT.>
<IT'S LIKE I CAN *SEE* IT.>
<U SUCK!>

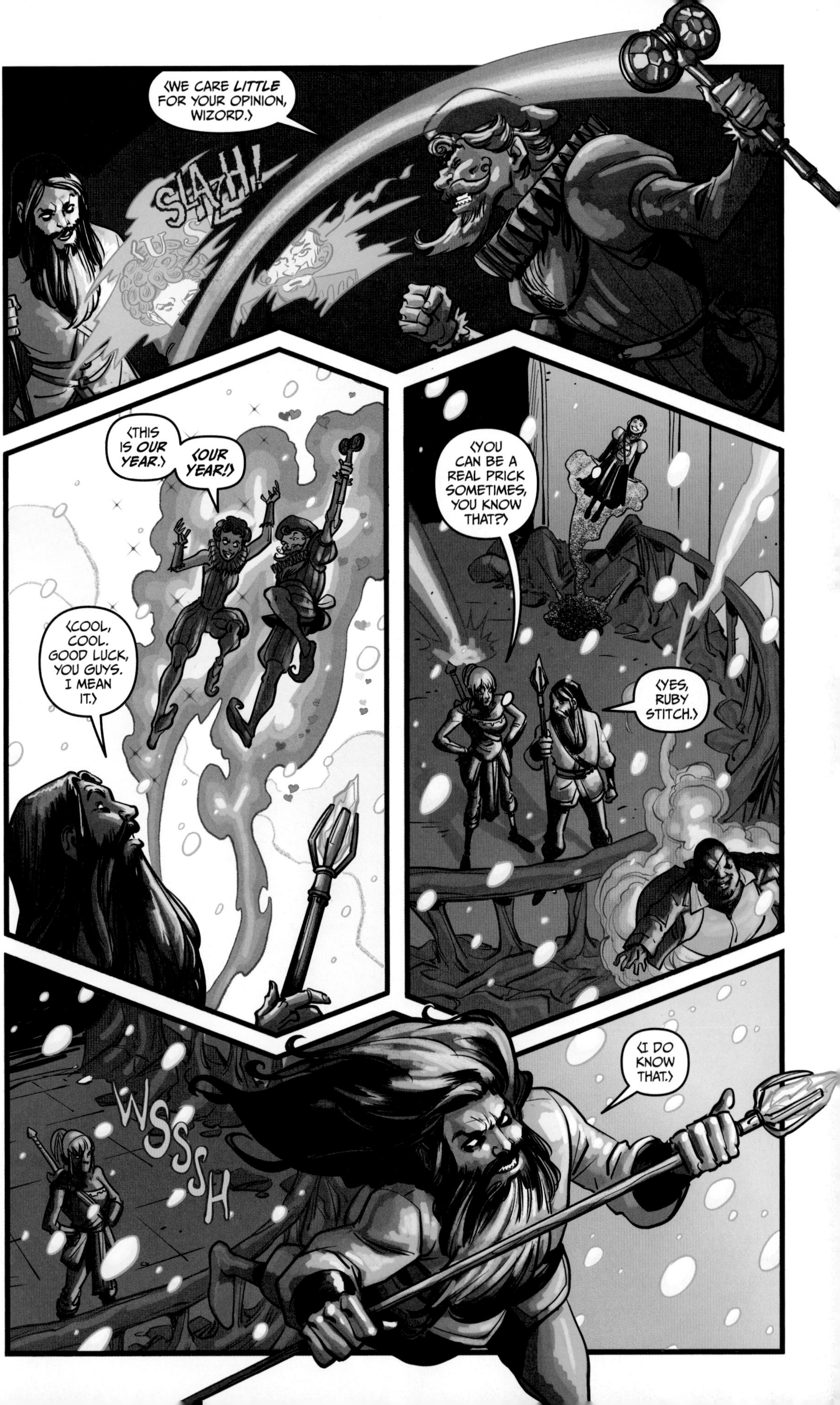

‹WE CARE LITTLE FOR YOUR OPINION, WIZORD.›
SLAZH!
‹THIS IS OUR YEAR.›
‹OUR YEAR!›
‹COOL, COOL. GOOD LUCK, YOU GUYS. I MEAN IT.›
‹YOU CAN BE A REAL PRICK SOMETIMES, YOU KNOW THAT?›
‹YES, RUBY STITCH.›
WSSSH
‹I DO KNOW THAT.›

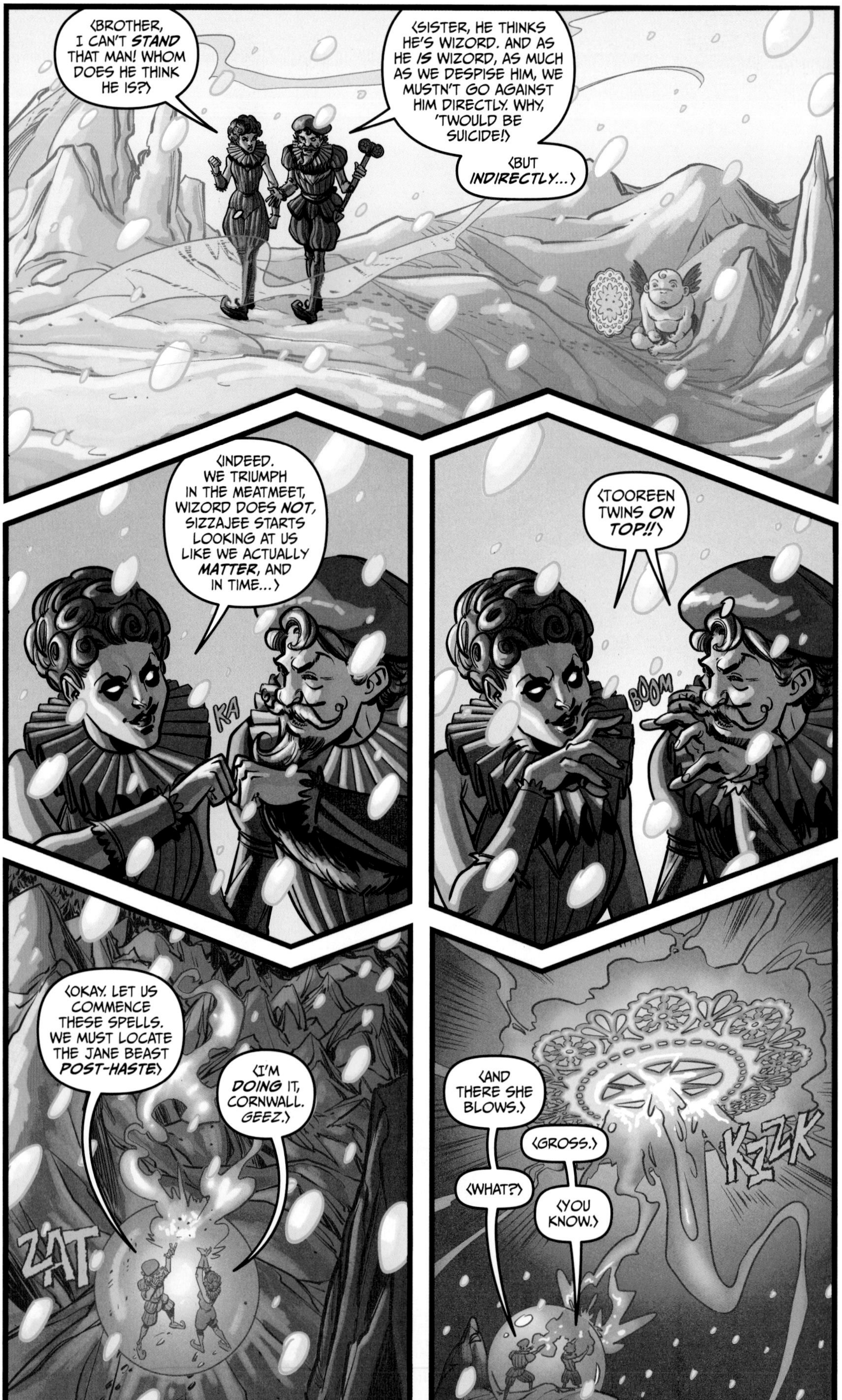
‹BROTHER, I CAN'T STAND THAT MAN! WHOM DOES HE THINK HE IS?›
‹SISTER, HE THINKS HE'S WIZORD. AND AS HE IS WIZORD, AS MUCH AS WE DESPISE HIM, WE MUSTN'T GO AGAINST HIM DIRECTLY. WHY, 'TWOULD BE SUICIDE!›
‹BUT INDIRECTLY...›
‹INDEED. WE TRIUMPH IN THE MEATMEET, WIZORD DOES NOT, SIZZAJEE STARTS LOOKING AT US LIKE WE ACTUALLY MATTER, AND IN TIME...›
KA
‹TOOREEN TWINS ON TOP!!›
BOOM
‹OKAY. LET US COMMENCE THESE SPELLS. WE MUST LOCATE THE JANE BEAST POST-HASTE›
‹I'M DOING IT, CORNWALL. GEEZ.›
ZAT
‹AND THERE SHE BLOWS.›
‹GROSS.›
‹WHAT?›
‹YOU KNOW.›
KZZK

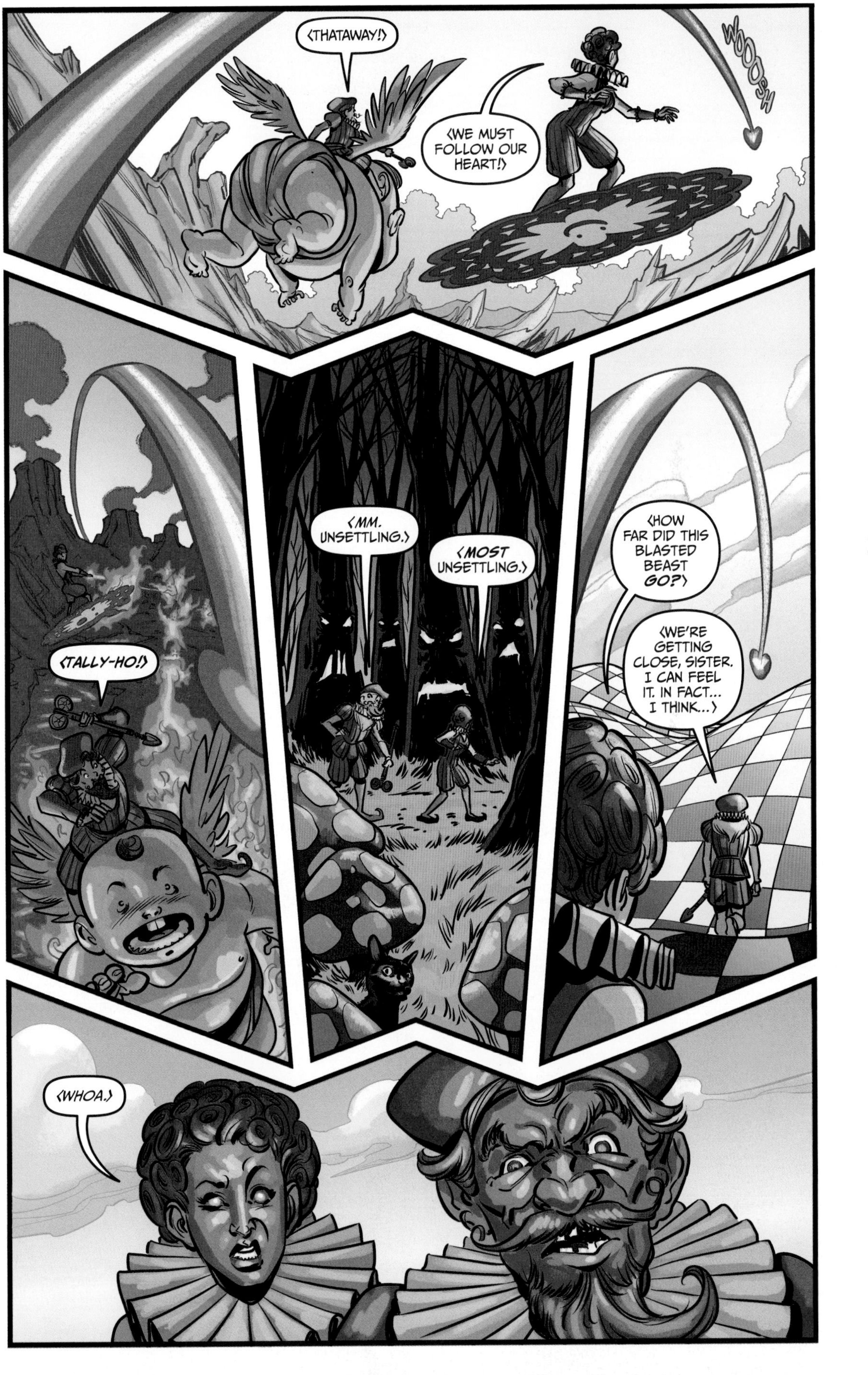

‹THATAWAY!›
‹WE MUST FOLLOW OUR HEART!›
WOOOSH
‹TALLY-HO!›
‹MM. UNSETTLING.›
‹MOST UNSETTLING.›
‹HOW FAR DID THIS BLASTED BEAST GO?›
‹WE'RE GETTING CLOSE, SISTER. I CAN FEEL IT. IN FACT... I THINK...›
‹WHOA.›

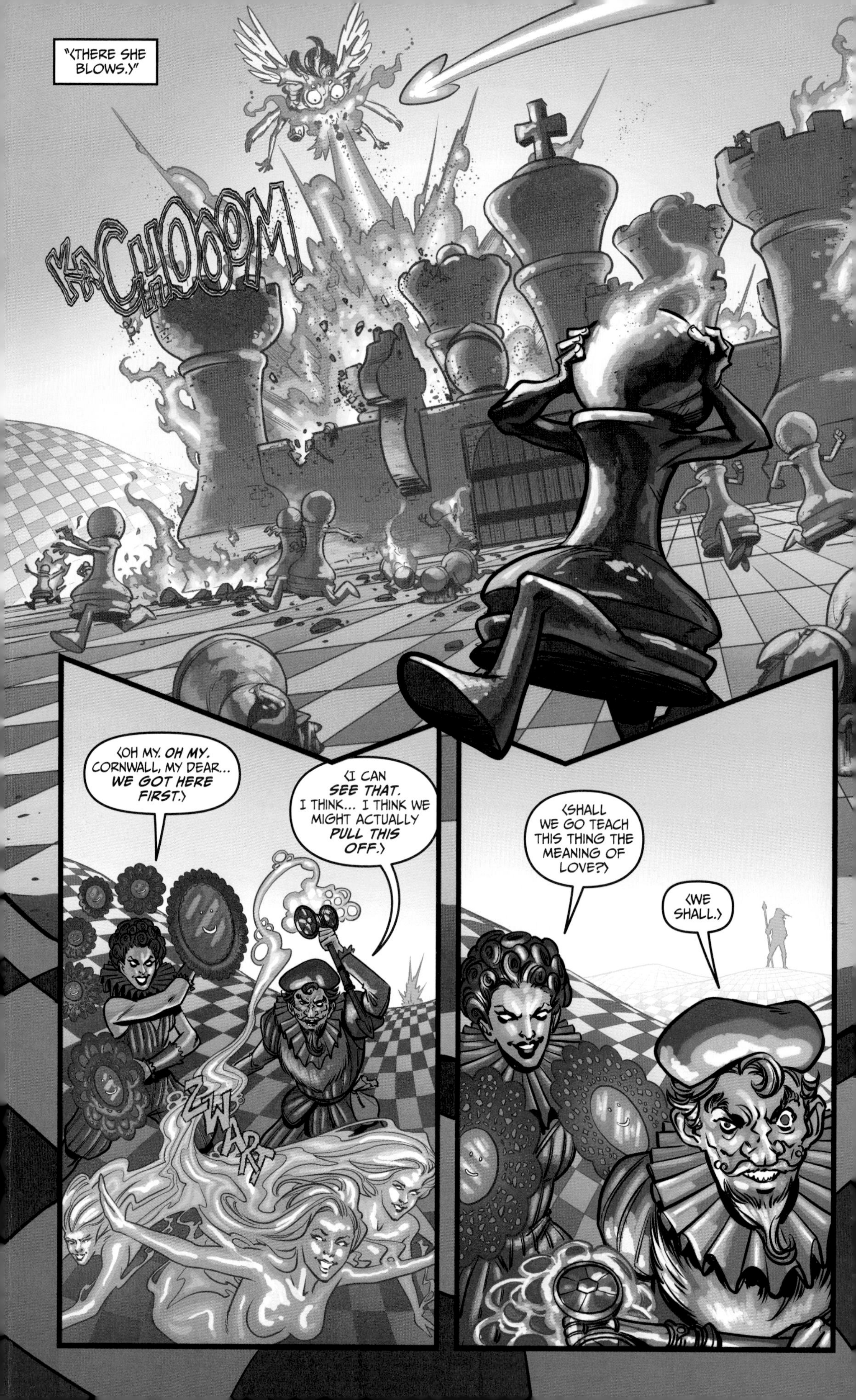
"‹THERE SHE BLOWS.›"
KACHOOOM
‹OH MY. *OH MY.* CORNWALL, MY DEAR... ***WE GOT HERE FIRST.***›
‹I CAN ***SEE THAT.*** I THINK... I THINK WE MIGHT ACTUALLY ***PULL THIS OFF.***›
ZWAPT
‹SHALL WE GO TEACH THIS THING THE MEANING OF LOVE?›
‹WE SHALL.›

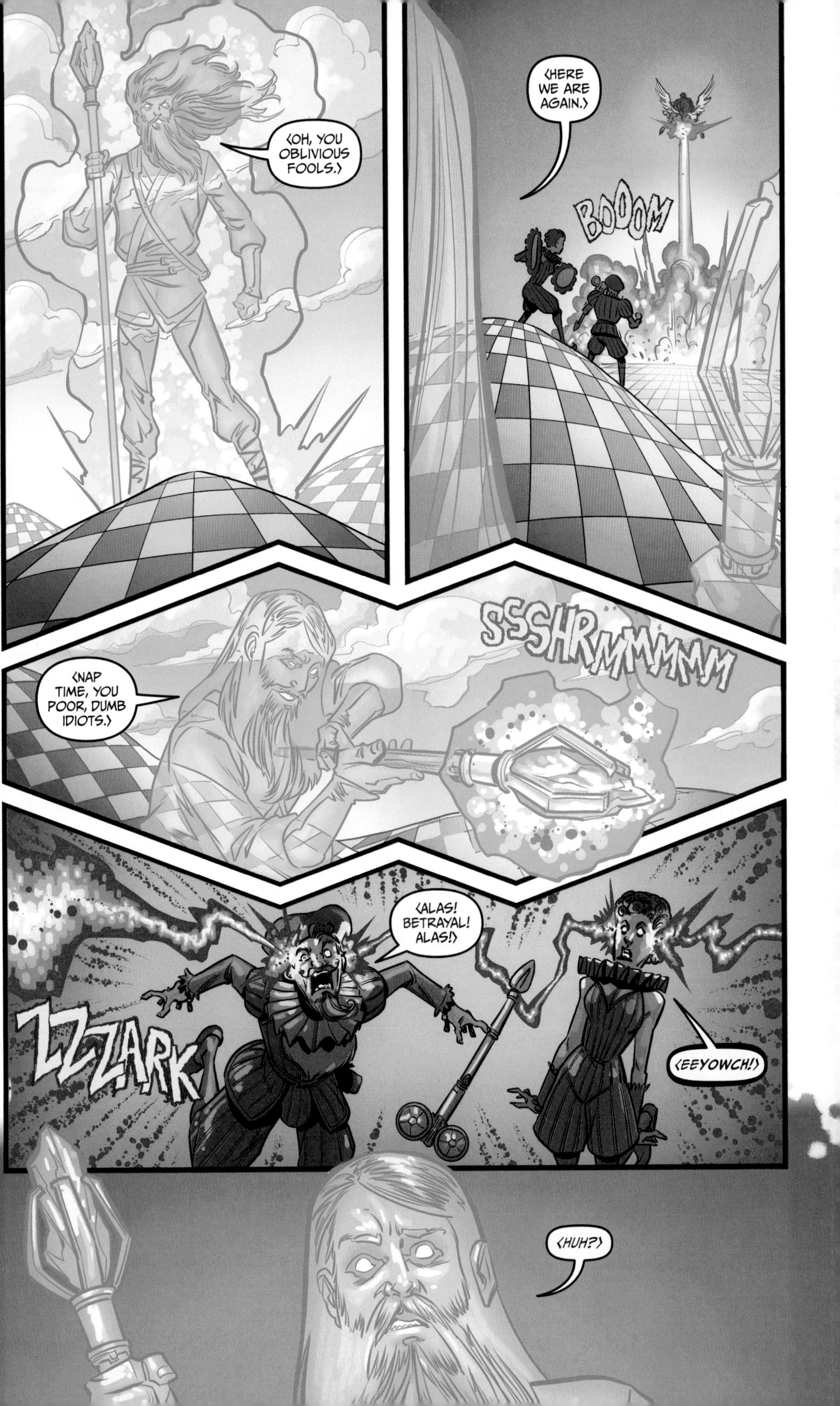
‹OH, YOU OBLIVIOUS FOOLS.›
‹HERE WE ARE AGAIN.›
BOOOM
SSSHRMMMMMM
‹NAP TIME, YOU POOR, DUMB IDIOTS.›
‹ALAS! BETRAYAL! ALAS!›
ZZZARK
‹EEYOWCH!›
‹HUH?›

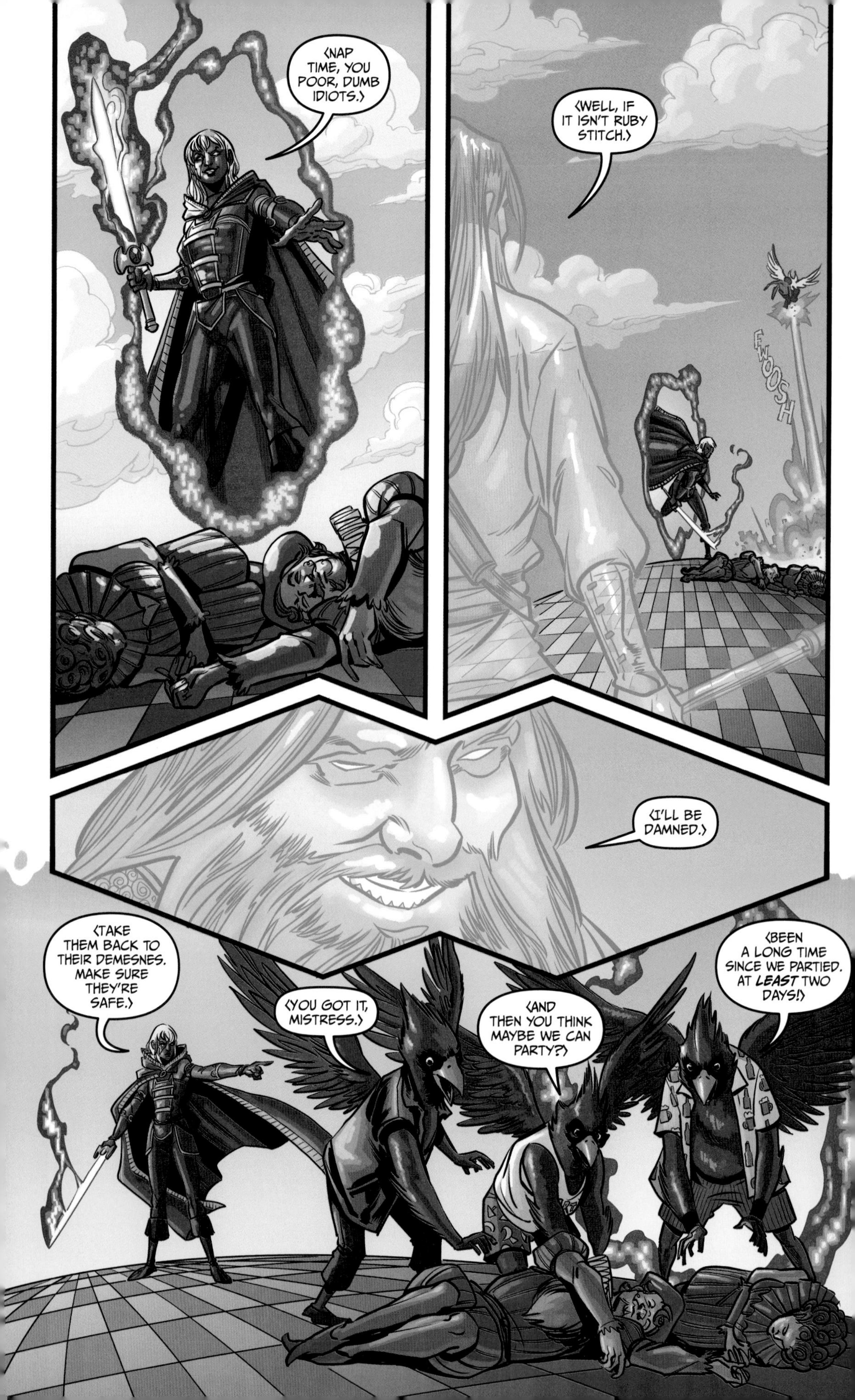
‹NAP TIME, YOU POOR, DUMB IDIOTS.›
‹WELL, IF IT ISN'T RUBY STITCH.›
FWOOSH
‹I'LL BE DAMNED.›
‹TAKE THEM BACK TO THEIR DEMESNES. MAKE SURE THEY'RE SAFE.›
‹YOU GOT IT, MISTRESS.›
‹AND THEN YOU THINK MAYBE WE CAN PARTY?›
‹BEEN A LONG TIME SINCE WE PARTIED. AT *LEAST* TWO DAYS!›

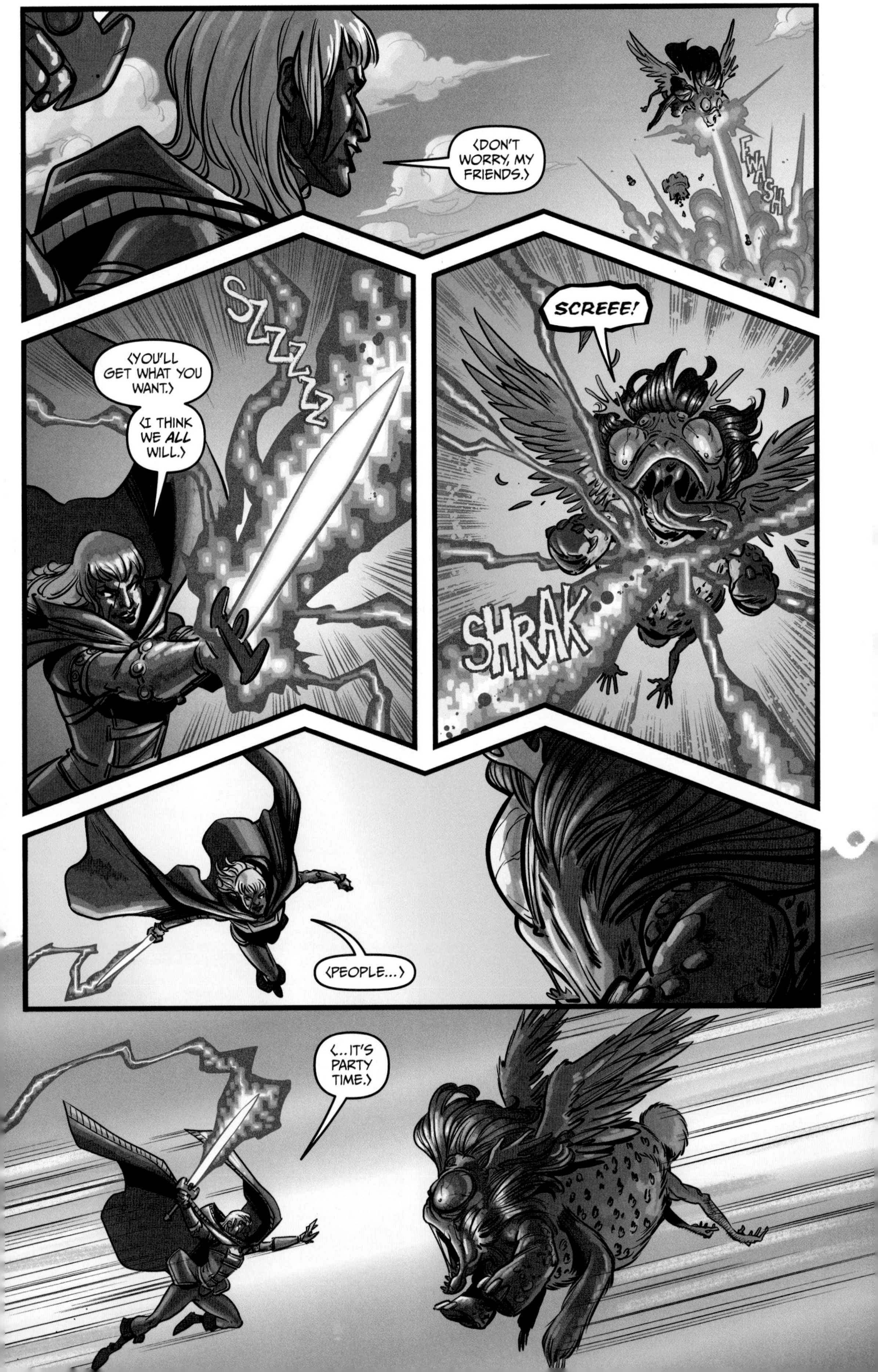
‹DON'T WORRY, MY FRIENDS.›
FWASH
SZZZZZ
‹YOU'LL GET WHAT YOU WANT.›
‹I THINK WE ALL WILL.›
SCREEE!
SHRAK
‹PEOPLE...›
‹...IT'S PARTY TIME.›

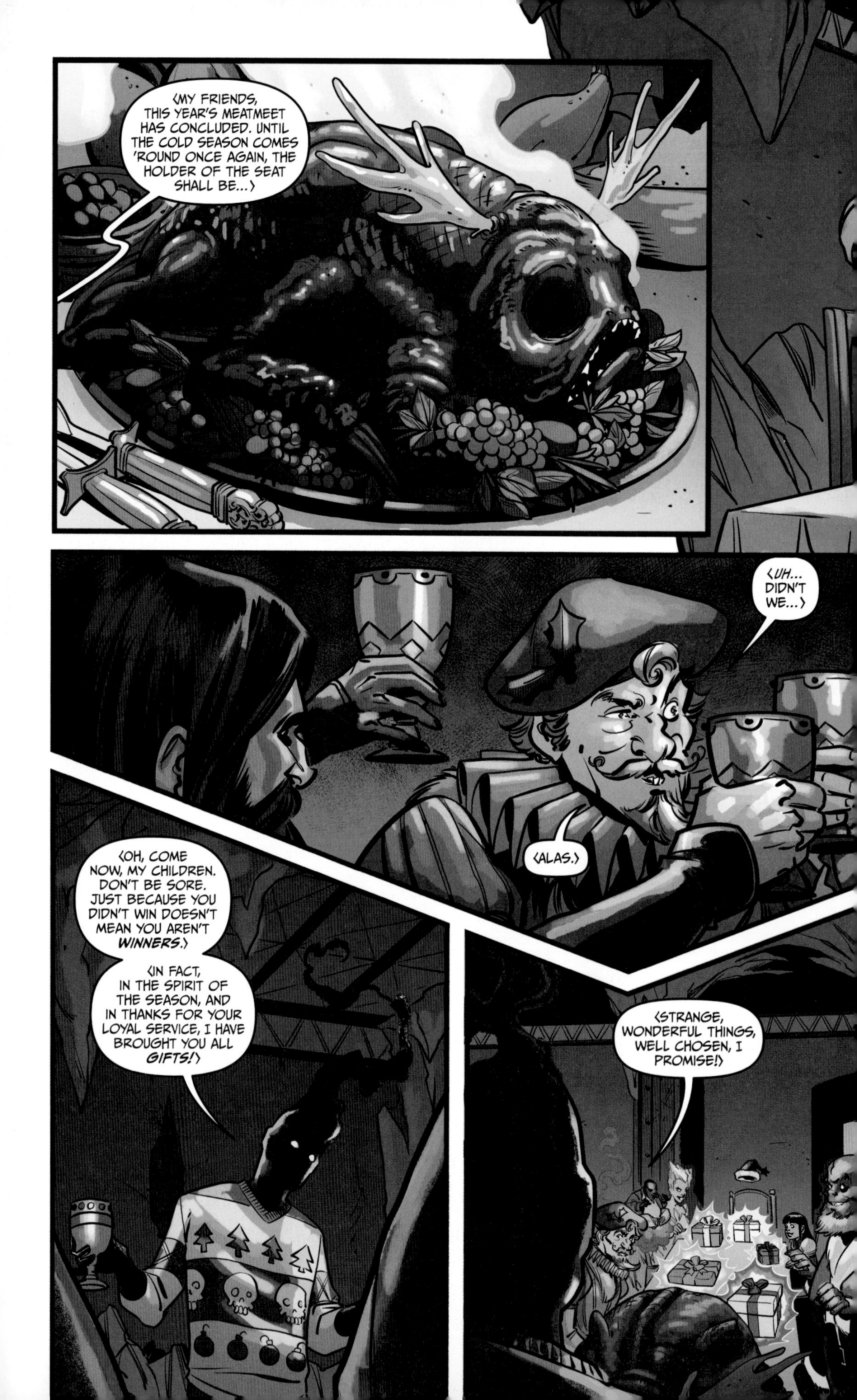

⟨MY FRIENDS, THIS YEAR'S MEATMEET HAS CONCLUDED. UNTIL THE COLD SEASON COMES 'ROUND ONCE AGAIN, THE HOLDER OF THE SEAT SHALL BE...⟩
⟨UH... DIDN'T WE...⟩
⟨ALAS.⟩
⟨OH, COME NOW, MY CHILDREN. DON'T BE SORE. JUST BECAUSE YOU DIDN'T WIN DOESN'T MEAN YOU AREN'T WINNERS.⟩
⟨IN FACT, IN THE SPIRIT OF THE SEASON, AND IN THANKS FOR YOUR LOYAL SERVICE, I HAVE BROUGHT YOU ALL GIFTS!⟩
⟨STRANGE, WONDERFUL THINGS, WELL CHOSEN, I PROMISE!⟩

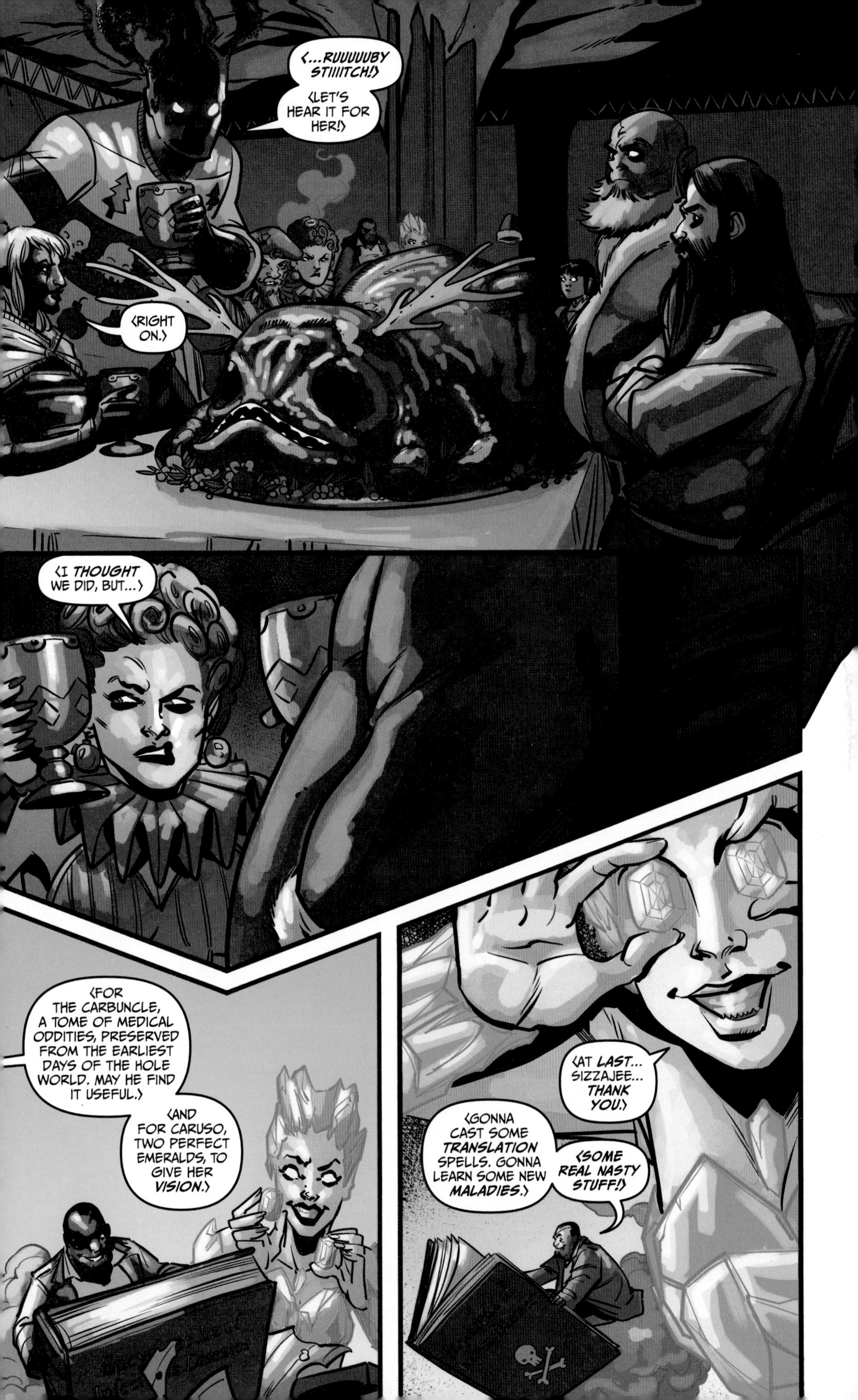

‹...RUUUUUBY STIIIITCH!›
‹LET'S HEAR IT FOR HER!›
‹RIGHT ON.›
‹I *THOUGHT* WE DID, BUT...›
‹FOR THE CARBUNCLE, A TOME OF MEDICAL ODDITIES, PRESERVED FROM THE EARLIEST DAYS OF THE HOLE WORLD. MAY HE FIND IT USEFUL.›
‹AND FOR CARUSO, TWO PERFECT EMERALDS, TO GIVE HER *VISION*.›
‹AT *LAST*... SIZZAJEE... *THANK YOU*.›
‹GONNA CAST SOME *TRANSLATION* SPELLS. GONNA LEARN SOME NEW *MALADIES*.›
‹*SOME REAL NASTY STUFF!*›

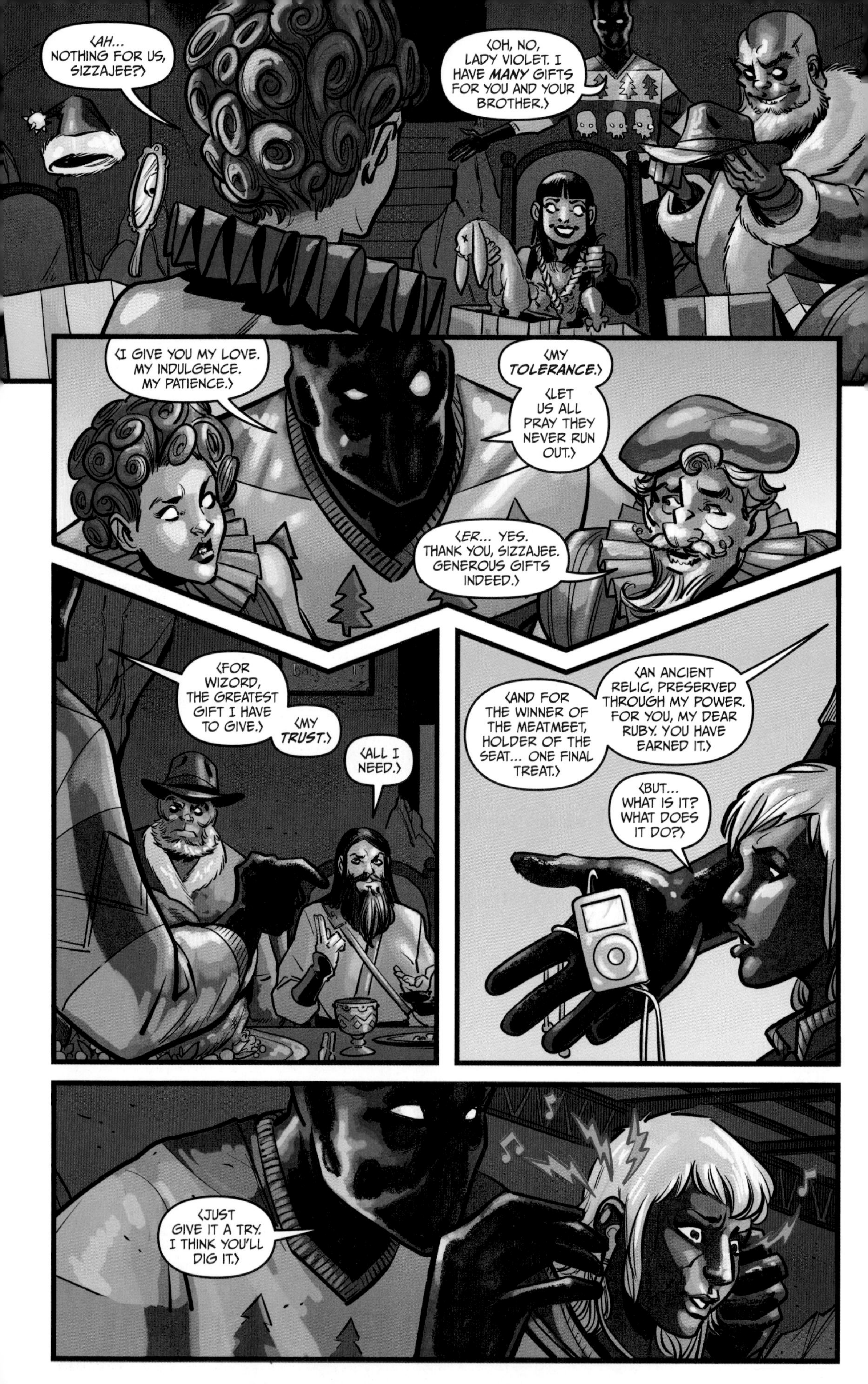
‹AH... NOTHING FOR US, SIZZAJEE?›
‹OH, NO, LADY VIOLET. I HAVE MANY GIFTS FOR YOU AND YOUR BROTHER.›
‹I GIVE YOU MY LOVE. MY INDULGENCE. MY PATIENCE.›
‹MY TOLERANCE.›
‹LET US ALL PRAY THEY NEVER RUN OUT.›
‹ER... YES. THANK YOU, SIZZAJEE. GENEROUS GIFTS INDEED.›
‹FOR WIZORD, THE GREATEST GIFT I HAVE TO GIVE.›
‹MY TRUST.›
‹ALL I NEED.›
‹AND FOR THE WINNER OF THE MEATMEET, HOLDER OF THE SEAT... ONE FINAL TREAT.›
‹AN ANCIENT RELIC, PRESERVED THROUGH MY POWER. FOR YOU, MY DEAR RUBY. YOU HAVE EARNED IT.›
‹BUT... WHAT IS IT? WHAT DOES IT DO?›
‹JUST GIVE IT A TRY. I THINK YOU'LL DIG IT.›

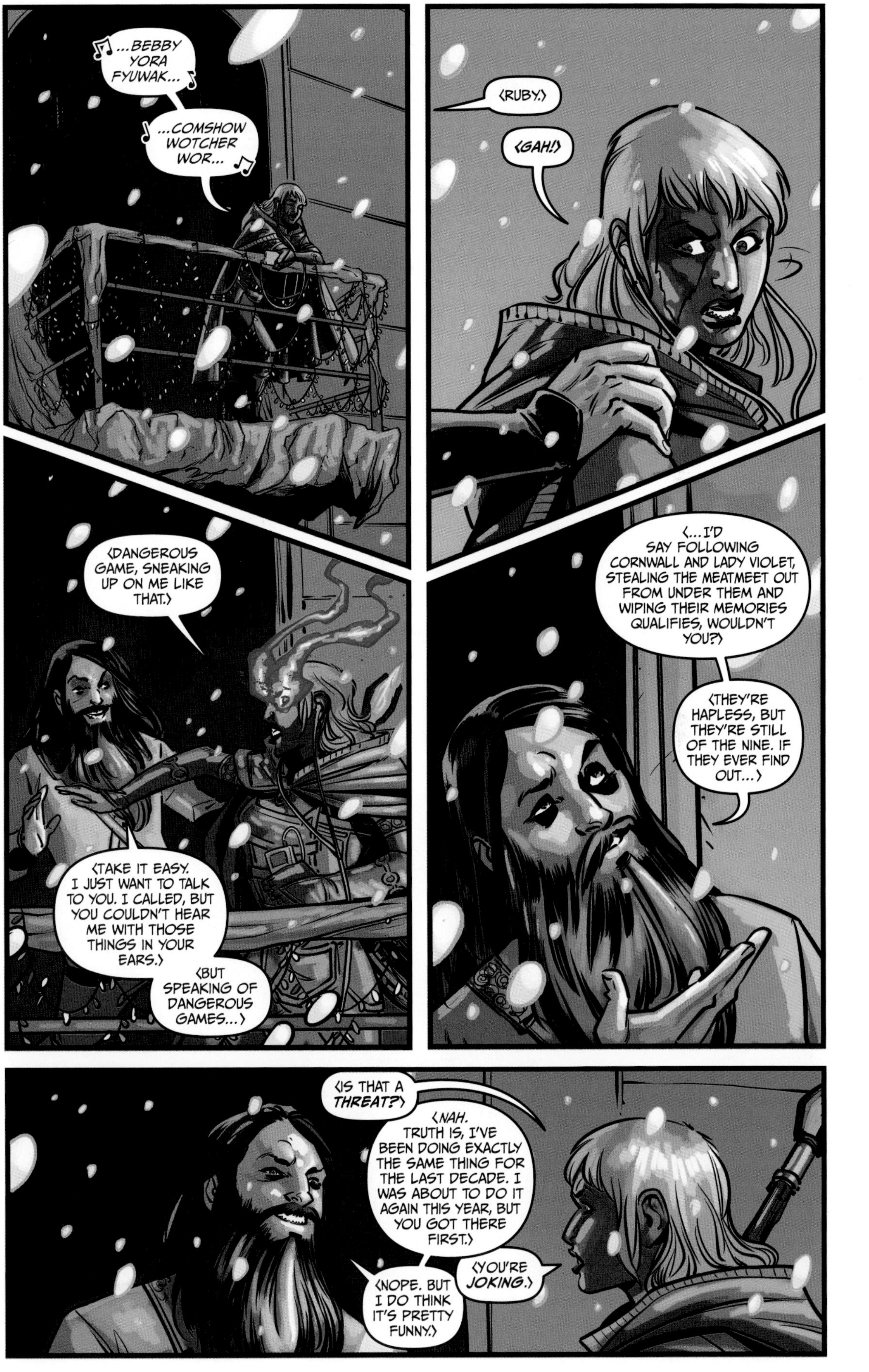
♪ ...BEBBY YORA FYUWAK... ♪
♪ ...COMSHOW WOTCHER WOR... ♪
‹RUBY.›
‹GAH!›
‹DANGEROUS GAME, SNEAKING UP ON ME LIKE THAT.›
‹TAKE IT EASY. I JUST WANT TO TALK TO YOU. I CALLED, BUT YOU COULDN'T HEAR ME WITH THOSE THINGS IN YOUR EARS.›
‹BUT SPEAKING OF DANGEROUS GAMES...›
‹...I'D SAY FOLLOWING CORNWALL AND LADY VIOLET, STEALING THE MEATMEET OUT FROM UNDER THEM AND WIPING THEIR MEMORIES QUALIFIES, WOULDN'T YOU?›
‹THEY'RE HAPLESS, BUT THEY'RE STILL OF THE NINE. IF THEY EVER FIND OUT...›
‹IS THAT A *THREAT?*›
‹*NAH.* TRUTH IS, I'VE BEEN DOING EXACTLY THE SAME THING FOR THE LAST DECADE. I WAS ABOUT TO DO IT AGAIN THIS YEAR, BUT YOU GOT THERE FIRST.›
‹YOU'RE *JOKING.*›
‹NOPE. BUT I DO THINK IT'S PRETTY FUNNY.›

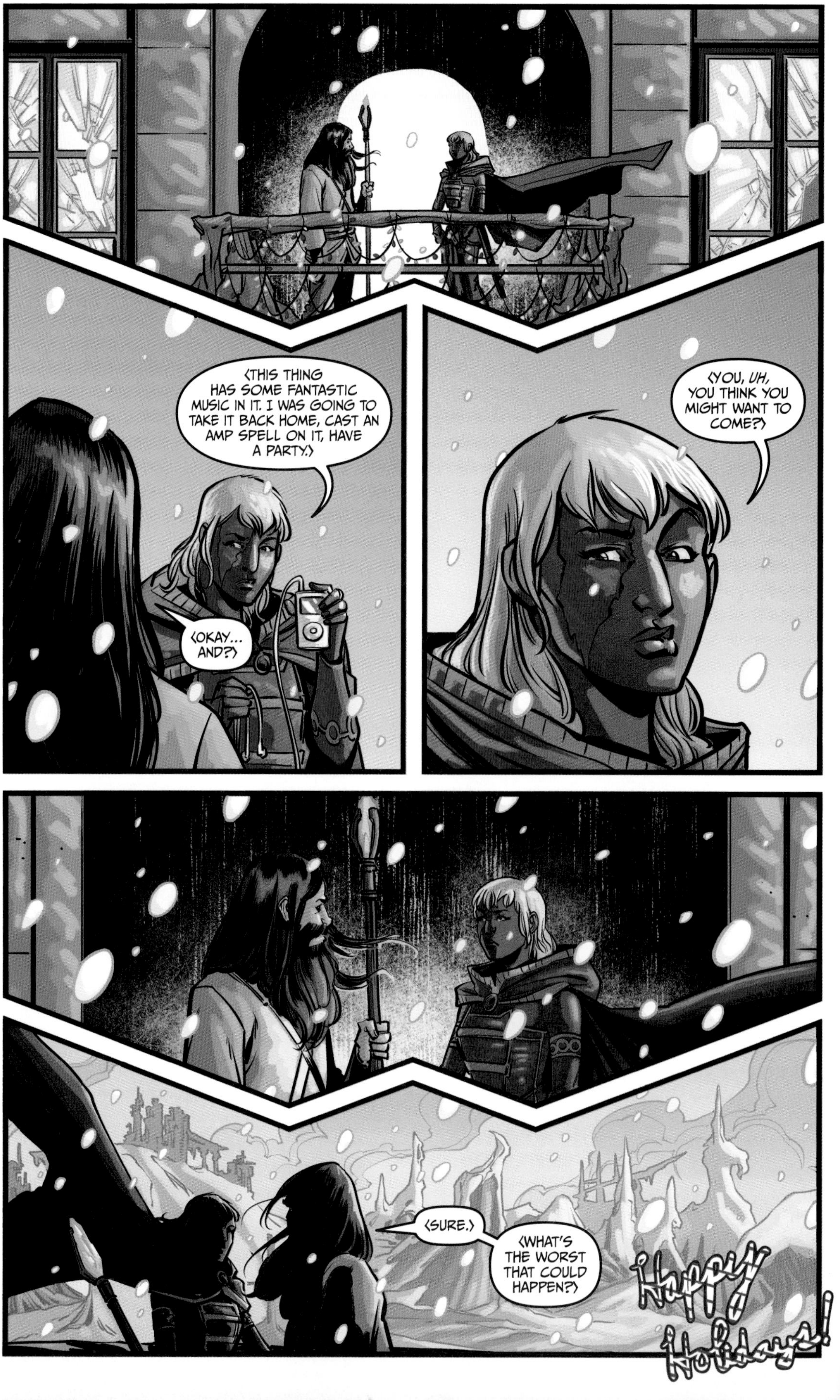

⟨THIS THING HAS SOME FANTASTIC MUSIC IN IT. I WAS GOING TO TAKE IT BACK HOME, CAST AN AMP SPELL ON IT, HAVE A PARTY.⟩
⟨OKAY... AND?⟩
⟨YOU, *UH*, YOU THINK YOU MIGHT WANT TO COME?⟩
⟨SURE.⟩
⟨WHAT'S THE WORST THAT COULD HAPPEN?⟩
Happy Holidays!

ISSUE SIX VARIANT COVER
BY **RYAN STEGMAN & RYAN BROWNE**

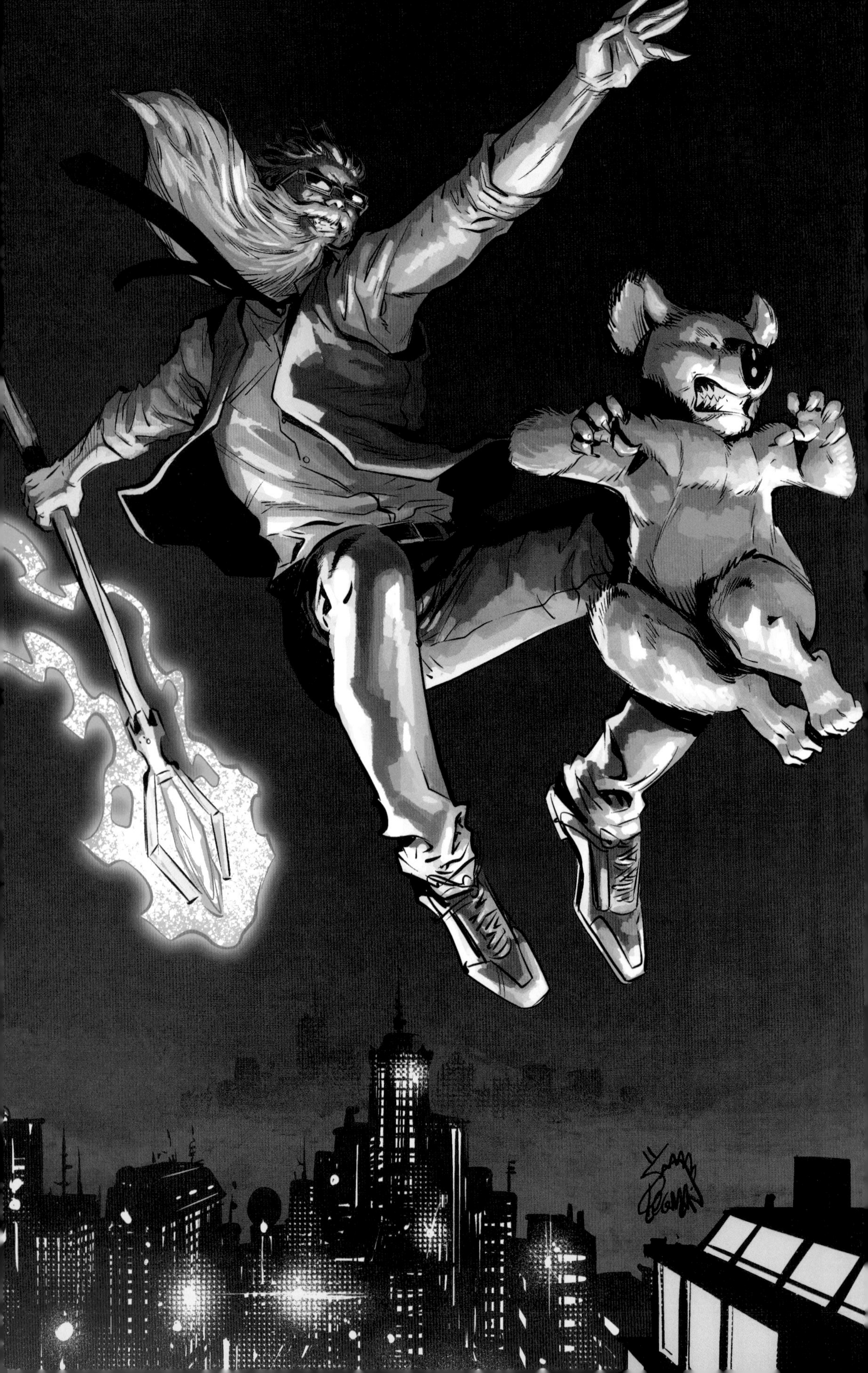

SUE SIX VARIANT COVER
RYAN BROWNE

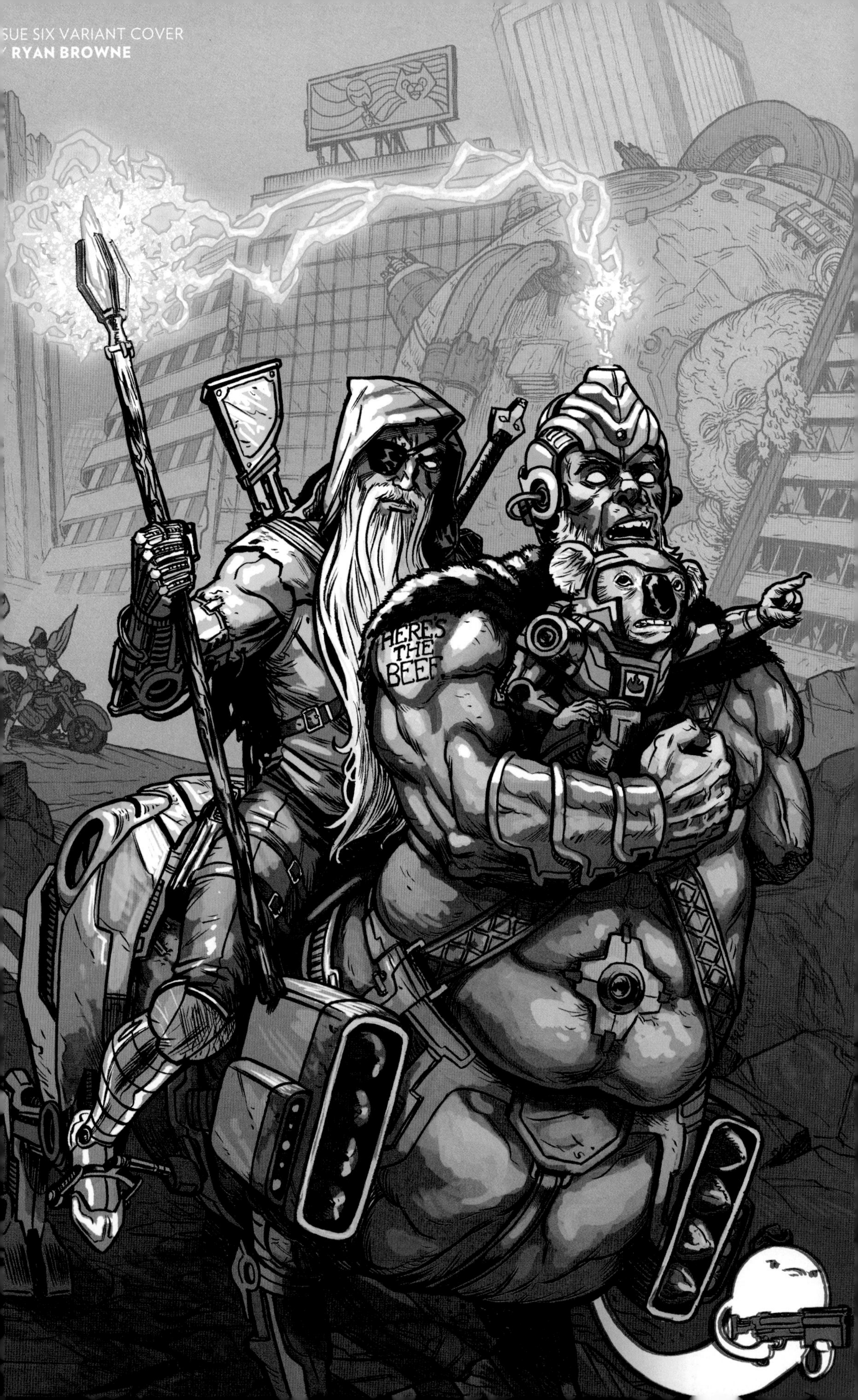
HERE'S THE BEEF

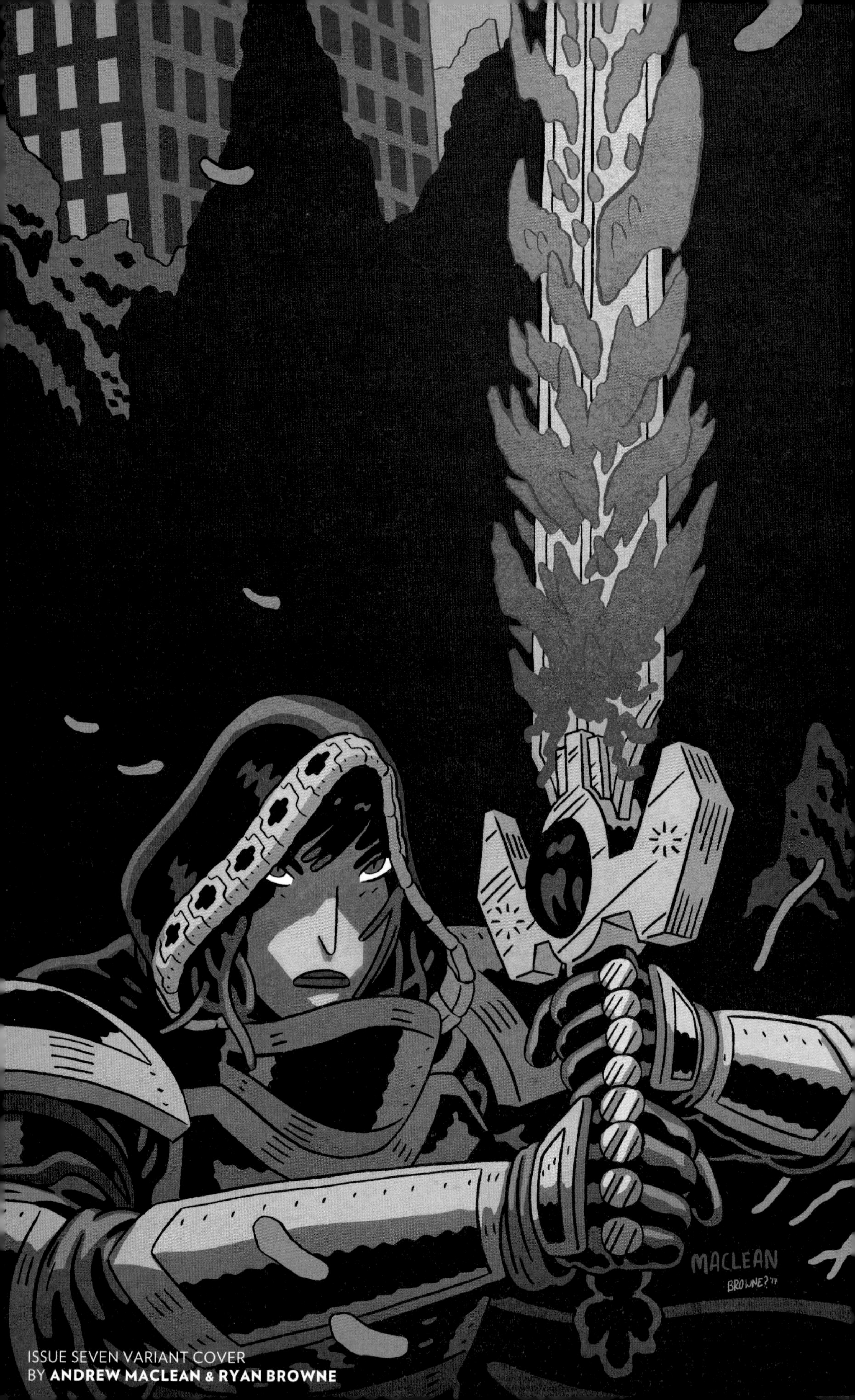
MACLEAN
BROWNE? '17

ISSUE SEVEN VARIANT COVER
BY **ANDREW MACLEAN & RYAN BROWNE**

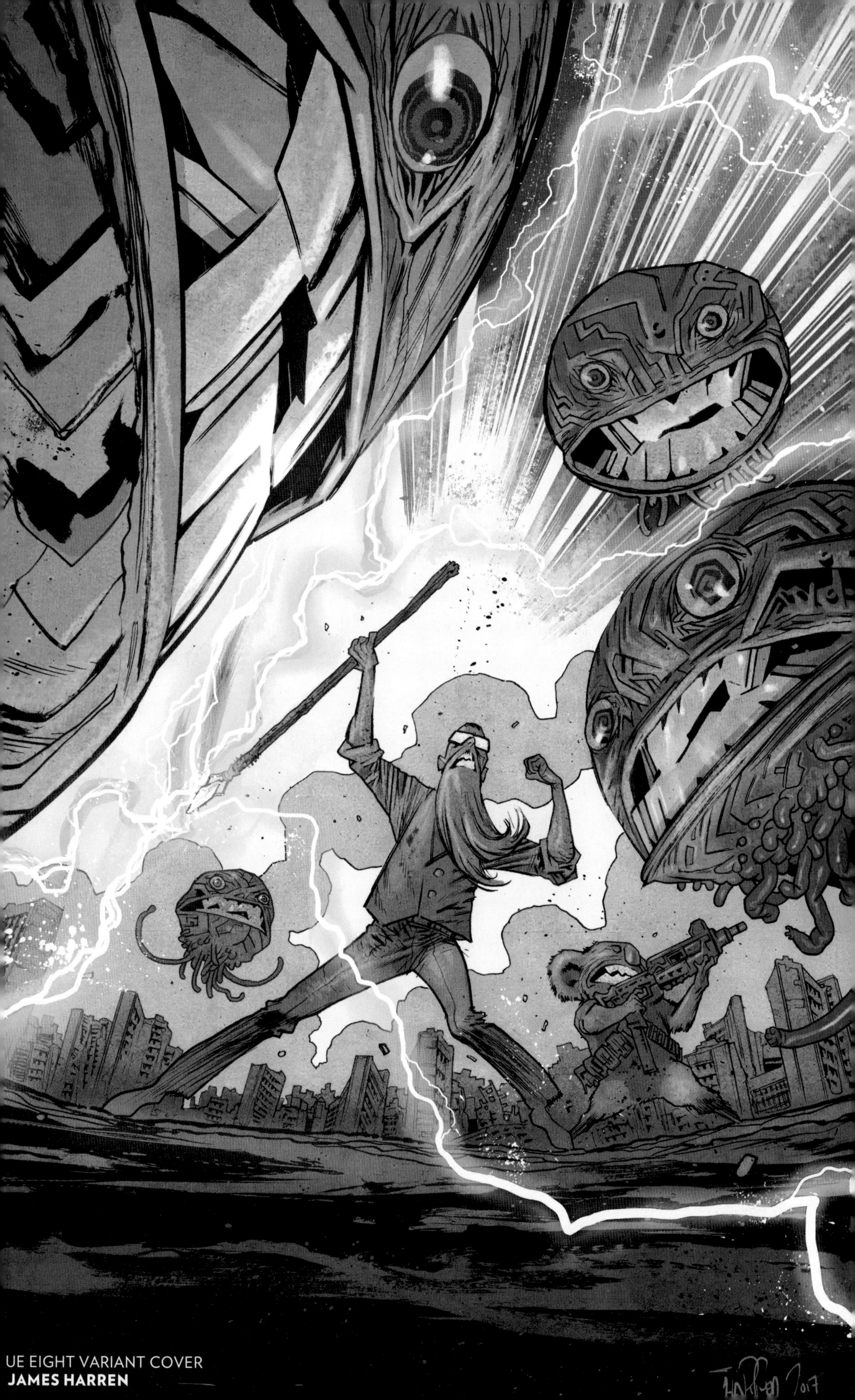

UE EIGHT VARIANT COVER
JAMES HARREN

ISSUE NINE VARIANT COVE
BY **STEVE SEELE**

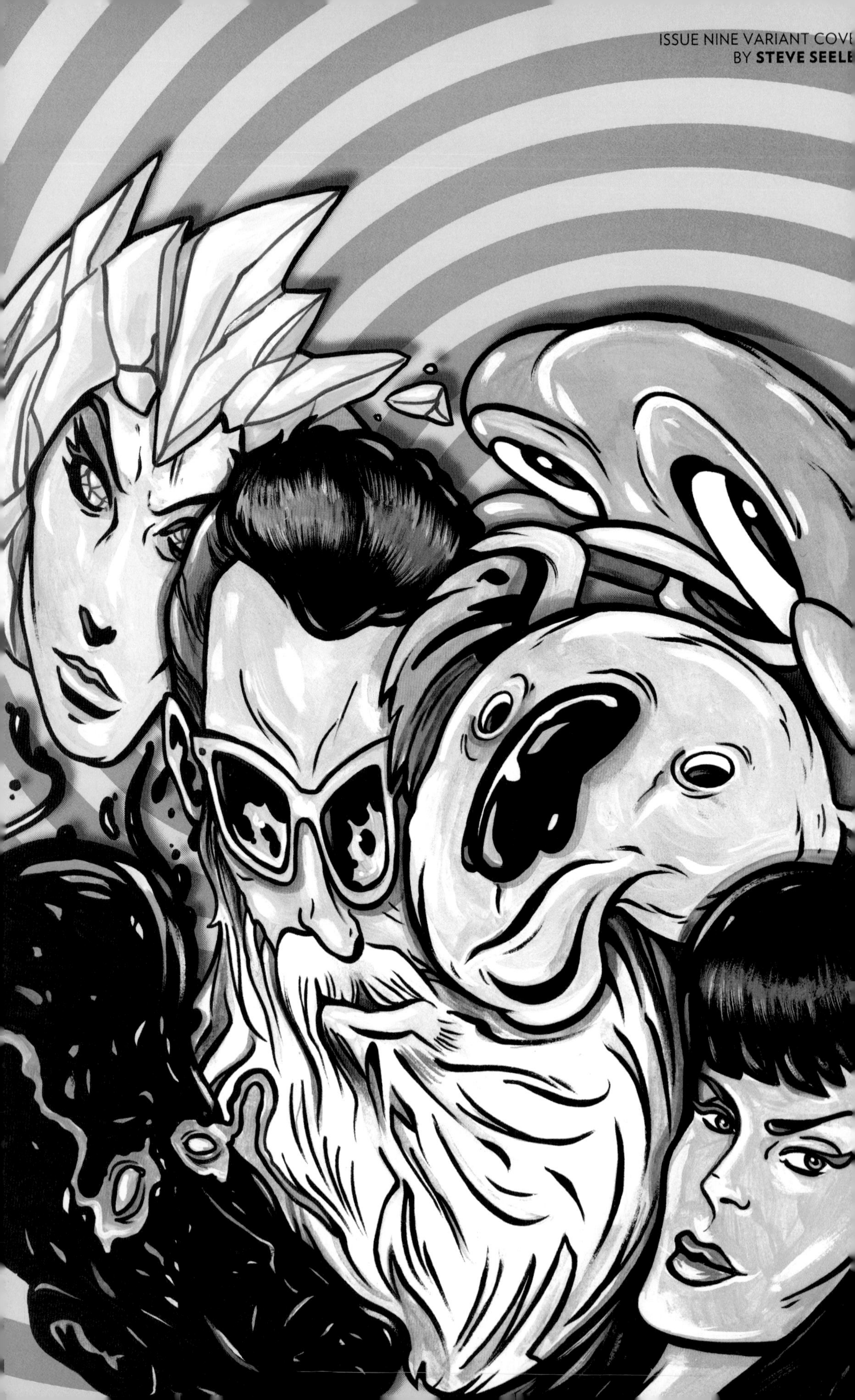

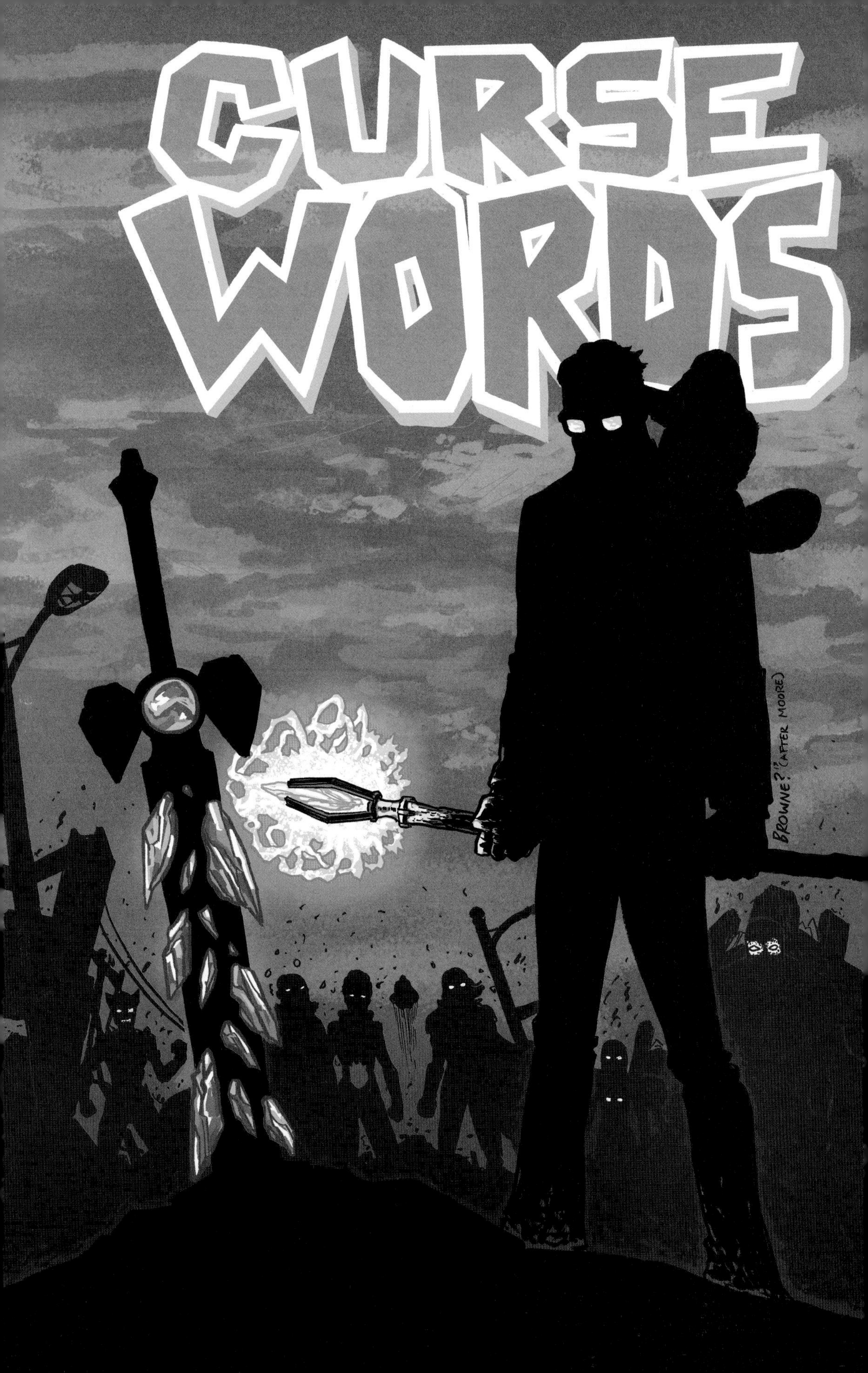
CURSE WORDS
BROWNE?! (AFTER MOORE)

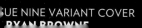

SUE NINE VARIANT COVER
RYAN BROWNE

ISSUE TEN VARIANT COVER
BY **JENNY FRISON**

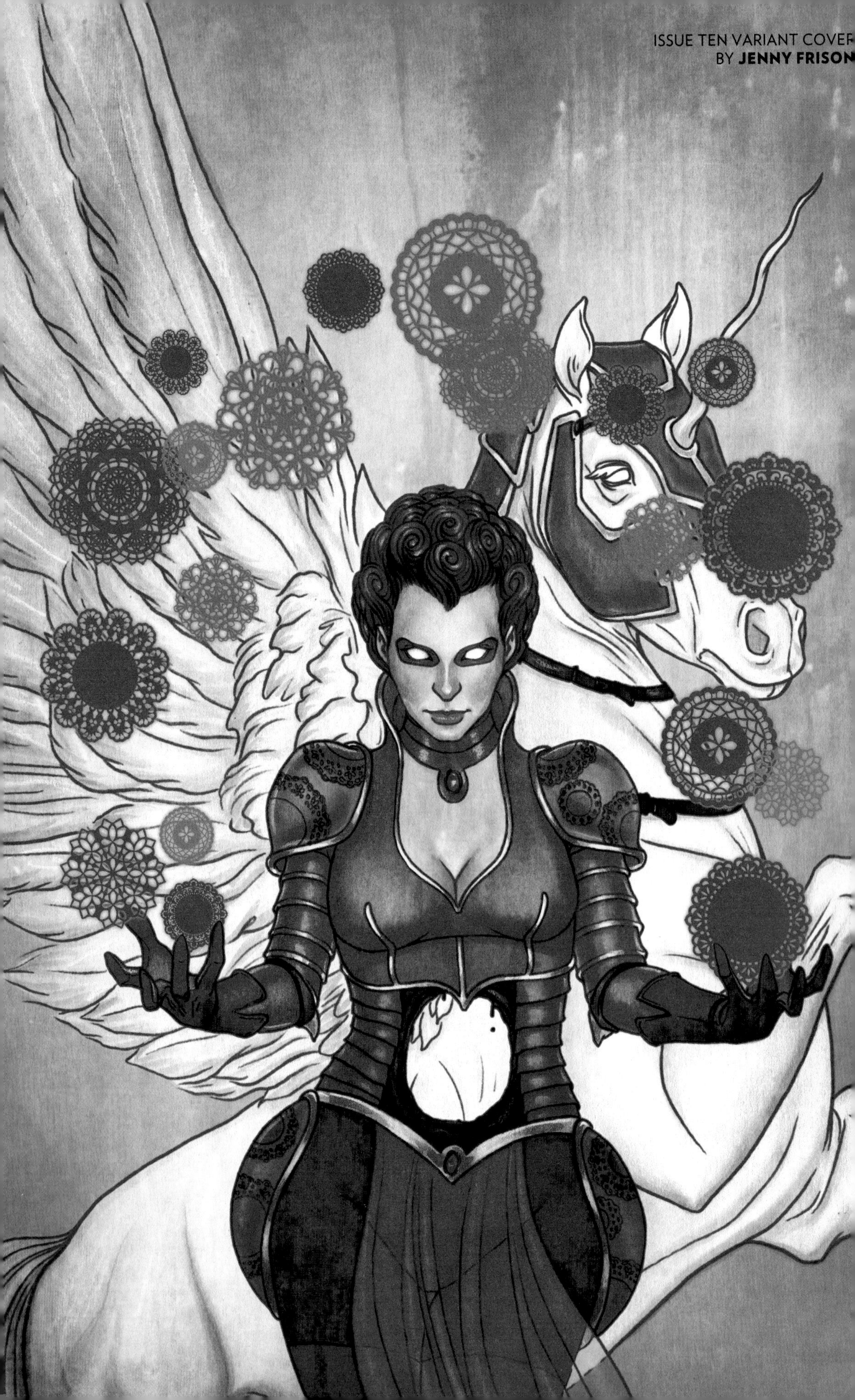

HOLIDAY SPECIAL VARIANT COVER
BY **MIKE NORTON & RYAN BROWNE**

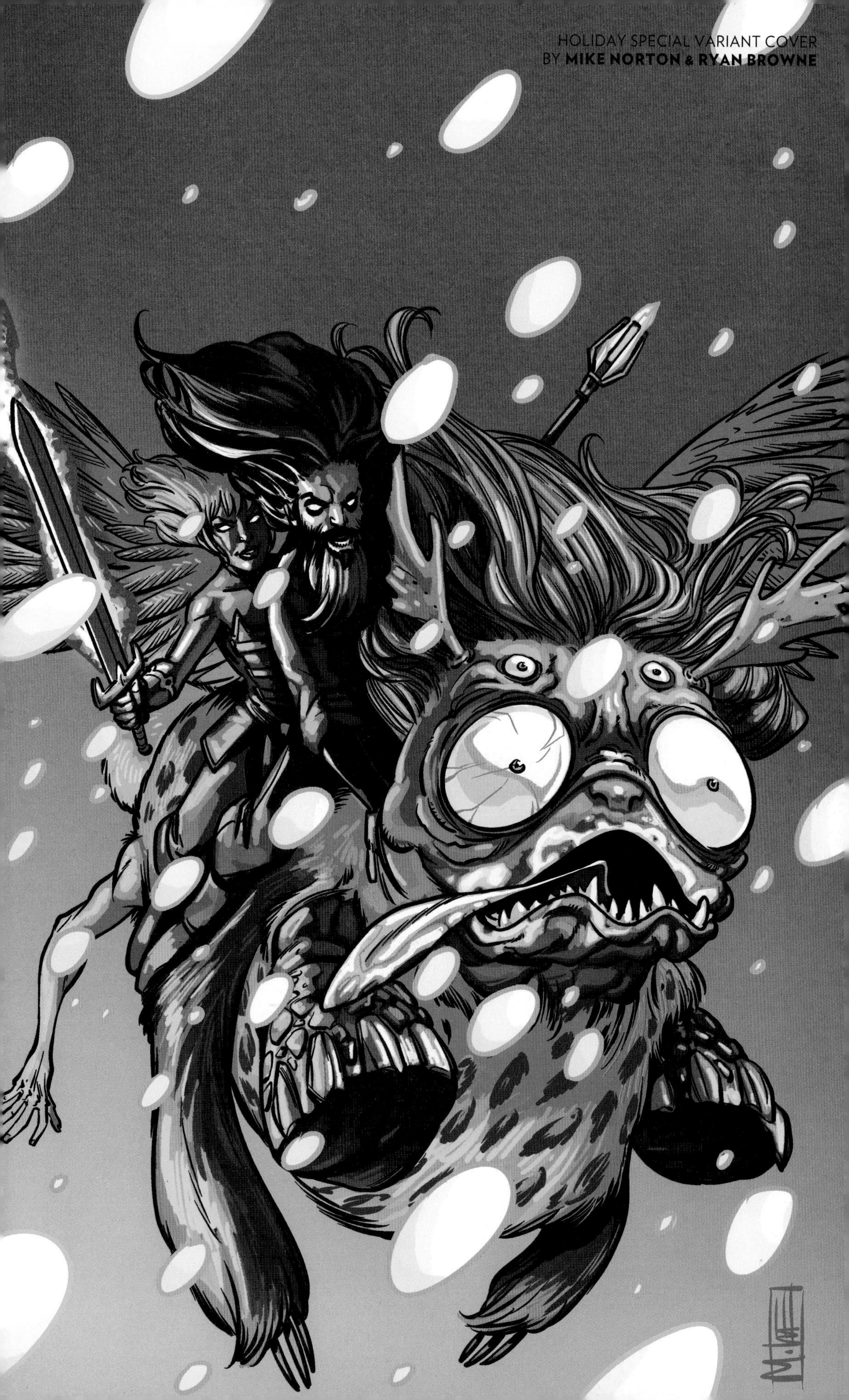

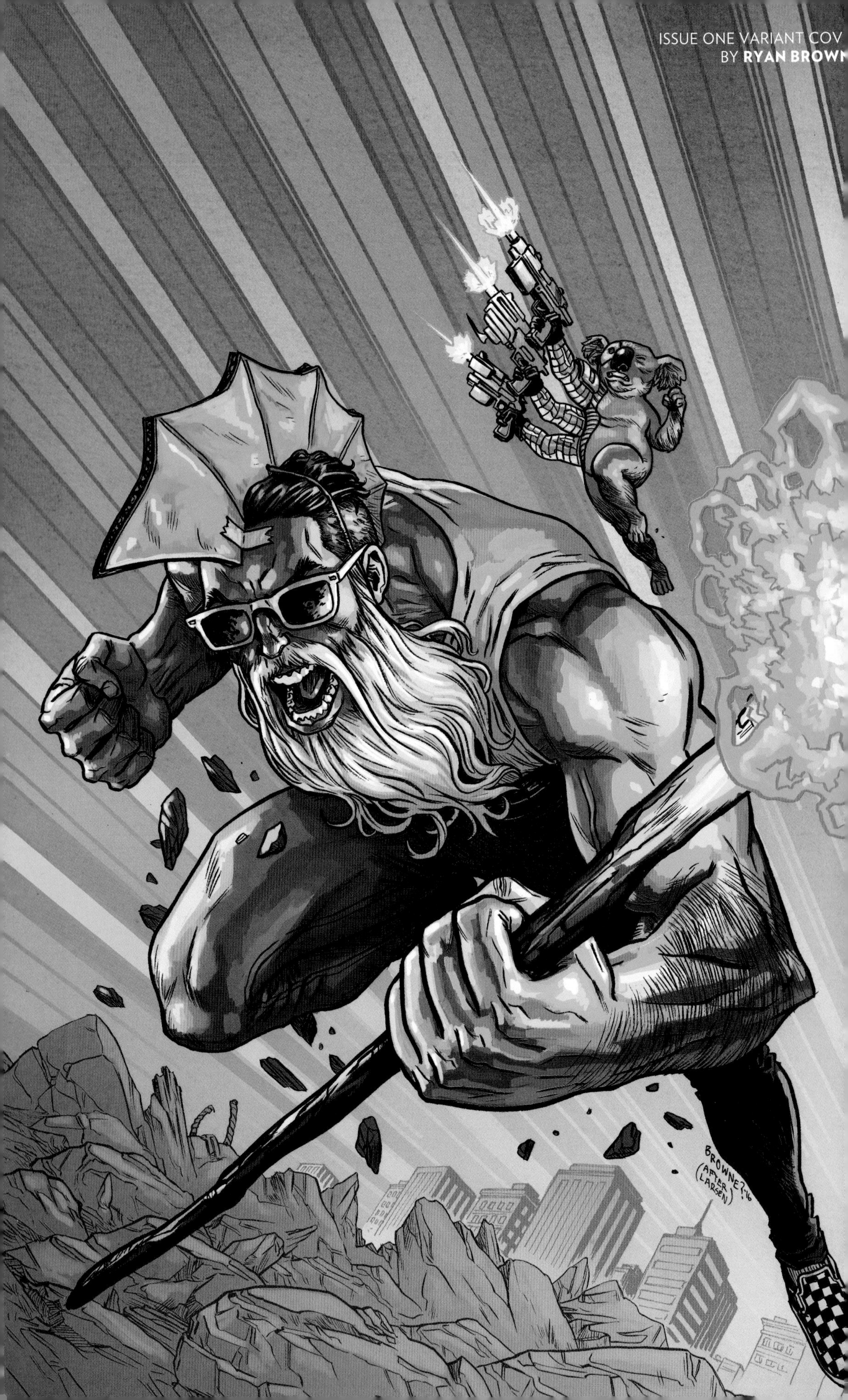
BROWNE
(AFTER LARSEN)

ISSUE ONE VARIANT COV
BY **RYAN BROWN**

SUE ONE VARIANT COVER
Y **RYAN BROWNE**

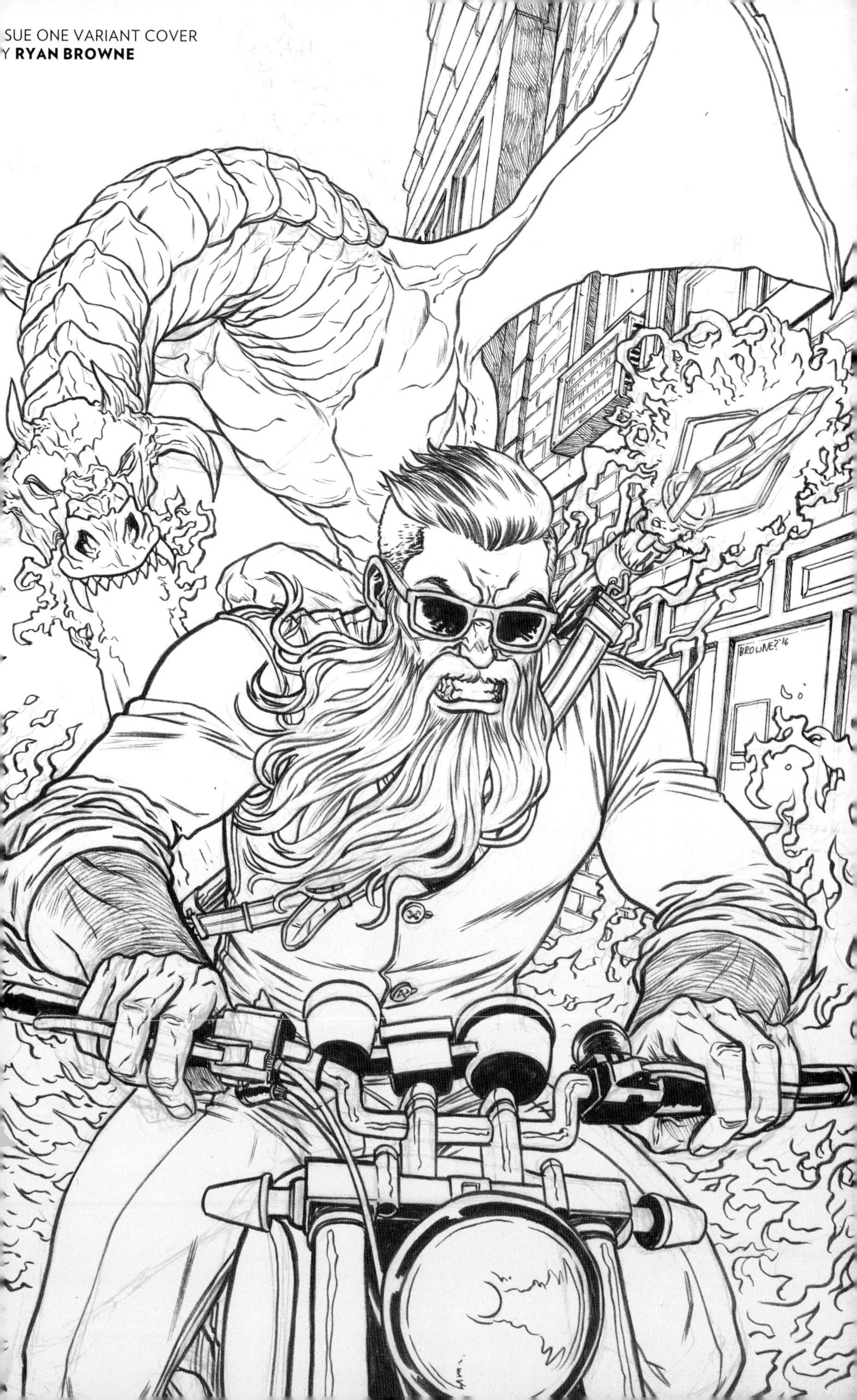
BROWNE? '16

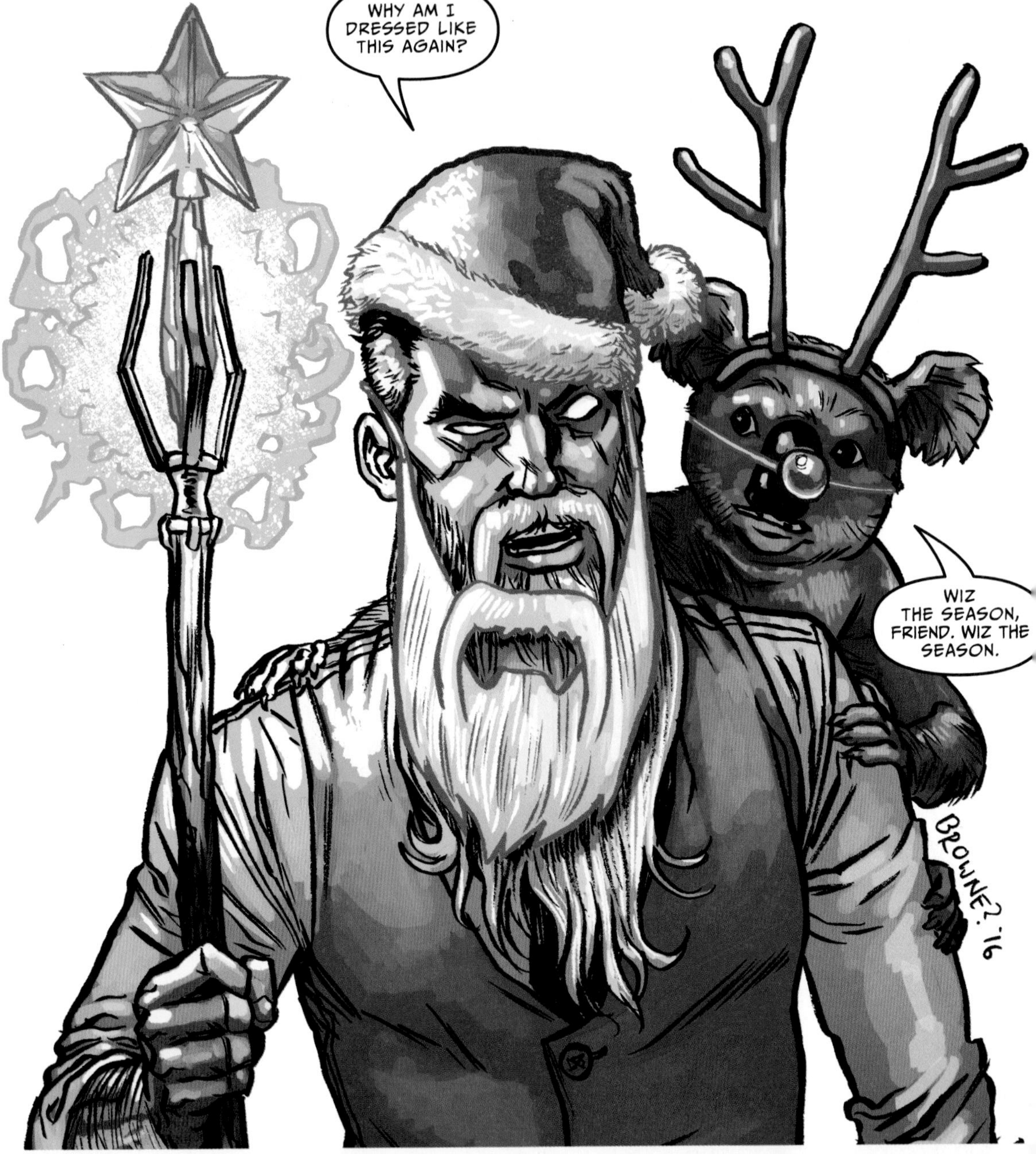
WHY AM I DRESSED LIKE THIS AGAIN?
WIZ THE SEASON, FRIEND. WIZ THE SEASON.
BROWNE?'16

ABOUT THE AUTHORS:

CHARLES SOULE has written many comics for Marvel, DC and others--*DAREDEVIL, STAR WARS, THE DEATH OF WOLVERINE, INHUMANS, SWAMP THING*... all kinds of stuff. He's also the creator of the award-winning epic sci-fi series *LETTER 44* for Oni Press, and his first (hopefully not last?) novel, *THE ORACLE YEAR*. (Don't tell any of those other projects, but *CURSE WORDS* is his favorite.) He lives in Brooklyn, where he also plays music of various kinds and practices law from time to time. Follow him on Twitter @charlessoule.

RYAN BROWNE is an American-born comicbookman who is co-responsible for *CURSE WORDS* (which you just read) and wholly responsible for *GOD HATES ASTRONAUTS* (which you should go read if you haven't). He currently lives in Chicago with his amazing wife and considerably less amazing cat. Also, he was once a guest on *The Montel Williams Show*--which is a great story and you should ask him about it. Catch him on Twitter and Instagram @RyanBrowneArt.

GOTTA QUESTION FOR THE CW LETTERS PAGE? HIT US UP AT WIZORD@WIZORD.HORSE (YES, A .HORSE URL IS A REAL THING AND WE BOUGHT ONE).